IMAGINARY

Friends

Cambria Tognaci

IMAGINARY FRIENDS

First Edition
Trade paperback edition | July 2018

ISBN-13: 978-1-7325231-1-1

Printed in the United States of America

For my sweetest Momma.

ACKNOWLEDGMENTS

First and foremost, I would like to thank my editor, Anna Davis, for her endless hard work and patience. I thank her for her constant effort and time she poured into making my very first novel the best it could be. Without her, Imaginary Friends would cease to be where it is now.

I would also hugely like to thank Krisan Adams for her creativity and imagination in creating the cover. Her patience and hard work through this journey was stupendous. The cover is more than I could wish for.

Along with Krisan, I would like to thank Kaitlyn O'Connor for designing the cover in the beginning through her generosity, talent and creativity.

I of course have to thank Caitlin Kenton and Layna Lundberg for their ideas, opinions, thoughts and encouragement through this all. They have inspired and shaped my ideas for characters, the Quest, the Villages of Remedium and every little, minuscule detail. Thank you.

Lastly, I would like to thank my family for their constant encouragement and support through this process. They never doubted my abilities and have been by my side since I started playing around with ideas back in 2013. My love and appreciation for them is everlasting.

Prologue

The clamped bedroom window revealed a silver moon hung in a rainy sky. It was not the pernicious sort of rain that shook the entire house, but rather it was an elegant sort, nice for listening. The fresh, earthiness of it cast a calm chill throughout the Carroway's home.

The youngest Carroway daughter huddled in the bedroom corner with a yellow and gray quilt on a twin-sized mattress. It was difficult to distinguish if she was shivering from the cool air, or from the fear that swelled deep inside her belly. The eldest of the Carroway children sat diagonally across from her younger sister on the opposite side of the room. She sat patiently by the door, waiting for him to get home. Where was he exactly? It was a mystery to her. But at that moment the house was hollow from his lack of presence, and she couldn't help but think that now would be the perfect time.

She could see the mirror from where she sat. It rested against the bare white wall covered with a brown stitched blanket. *This would be the perfect time*, she thought again. *This would be the safest time.* She slowly rose from the warm corner that consumed her. She guessed that it was about midnight, and that he wouldn't be home for another couple of hours, hopefully.

The glass mirror revealed her image as the burlap blanket that covered the mirror slid to the ground. Her dark hair was longer than she remembered. Her legs, farther apart than she recognized. Black crescent moons slept beneath her eyes. She was curious as to what her full body looked like, for the big black shirt she wore hid her real body, her real figure. Just a peek, that's all. To see what she really looked like. To know if any markings were visible.

No, she couldn't bring herself to do so. He told her she's beautiful. He told her she's perfect. But what if, perhaps, he was lying? No, he wouldn't. He couldn't. What a silly thing to think. But what if? *Just lift up your shirt*, her mind begged.

She impulsively grabbed the seam of the worn-out tee before she could change her mind, then stole a look at herself in the mirror—but all she was able to see were the black, terrified eyes of a little girl, a broken little girl. She tugged her arm up to her bellybutton and stretched the rest of the baggy shirt up.

Although the lighting of the clamped room was only a flickering glow, the marks were vibrant. There was a bluish-purple disfigured circle right below the left side of her ribcage. The sight exposed the white of her eyes and made her heart rate increase. *Is this beauty? Is beautiful the scars that run all over my neck and shoulders?* She turned to her side to see what else was written on her skin. Tears began to bottle up in her eyes as she discovered five green bruises branded across her torso.

"Don't cry. Don't cry," she told herself silently.

Those two short words felt like the most challenging words. She knew that it was okay and safe to cry, that at this moment he was not here and she could cry. But she couldn't allow it. She had to stay strong for Emmie, her baby sister. If she were to cry now, Emmie would realize that they are not safe—not protected—and never were. She couldn't allow Emmie to know that. Emmie couldn't grow up thinking that her older sister was weak. She *wouldn't* allow it. She was okay.

Suddenly, she heard a door slam. She immediately pulled down her shirt, slipped the cover back over the mirror, and tiptoed to the corner by her sister. She took a slight glance, only to find a pair of eyes glazed with fear. They could hear his heavy footsteps wandering in the kitchen. Their spines straightened, and their jaws clenched tightly with anticipation.

The slam of a drawer being thrown open made Ellisia jump, and she heard the clanking of supplies as his thick hands searched for what his selfish mind desired. She could feel Emmie's heavy breathing on her arm, and hear both of their anxious hearts thumping.

"Ellisia!" A horrific yell.

She stayed silent.

"ELLISIA," he wailed again.

Ellisia's arms spiked with goosebumps as her name echoed.

His deafening footsteps began to thump on the narrow hall floors to the hidden bedroom in the back of the house.

Ellisia knew, exactly at that moment, what was about to happen, and she knew that Emmie knew, too.

The bedroom door slammed into the wall where the doorknob had created a hole throughout the years. A brown boot stepped into the room and his towering body followed.

His sorrowful, drunk face made a pit in Ellisia's stomach. She could feel Emmie's hammering heart against her arm.

His eyes were bloodshot and his skin was bright scarlet. His hand held an object that Ellisia prayed she would never see.

A gun.

She stood up, shielding little Emmie's fragile body with her own. If he were to kill one of them, she would not know what to do. He had already murdered their mother and he couldn't get away with another. *Wouldn't* get away with another.

"Ella. Emily." He didn't even know his own daughters' names. What a sick man. "You two are just so beautiful." He let out a vociferous drunken laugh. "So much like your sweet mother." He spat on the word "sweet" like it was venom in his mouth. "Where is she?"

Ellisia stared at his over-worked, trembling body. "She's not here anymore," she said, carefully.

"WHAT DID YOU DO WITH HER?" he screamed, throwing a glass bottle of vodka at the wall. The bottle shattered and shards rained down on the torn-up carpet. Ellisia could hear Emmie weeping and struggling to find her breath.

"You did something with her," said Ellisia with shut eyes. He trudged over to where she stood over Emmie and began to squeeze at the sides of her arms. Ellisia could feel his fingers digging into her bones. The pain burst through her body.

The gun remained in his left hand.

Ellisia's thoughts ran as fast as her heart beat. Ellisia knew that even if she was the one to get shot and leave her baby sister behind, maybe Emmie would still have a chance to escape and find a new family.

"I did. Didn't I?" he said.

He squeezed her arms tighter.

"You two," he laughed as his words echoed off the walls. "You two are just so beautiful."

His liquored smile focused on Ellisia.

"Your mother hated you, Ellisia."

The next thing happened before she could blink.

He raised the heavy black gun to his own head and pulled the trigger.

His limp body fell to the ground.

Ellisia grabbed Emmie before she could get past her to their father.

Red and blue lights flashed in the front yard. Big heavy men in black suits grabbed Emmie away from Ellisia's arms, both of them screaming for each other. Two large men held Ellisia's arms back, as she reached for her baby sister.

Straight to her left she could see her father in his own blood bath. And that is the last sight she had of him.

Six Months Later

The day the girls arrived to their new home was the precise day spring began. As the black van with intimidating, shaded windows pulled up to the house that day—a house framed by freshly cut grass and flowerbeds boasting new pink and orange blooms—Ellisia felt claustrophobic with anxiety. Being only eleven years old she had no idea what to expect from this remote foster home in a small town in Oregon.

To the left of her sat tiny, silent Emmie, her fingers tightly in her lap, sweat gathering upon them. Her brown hair hung on the very top of her head with a green ribbon around it, and although Ellisia told her multiple times to stop playing with it, the ribbon had begun to fall out.

"What are you thinking about?" Emmie asked, looking at her sister.

"What are *you* thinking about?" Ellisia gazed out the window, even though the dark tinted windows muted the colors outside, like looking through a pair of sunglasses.

At least they got to stay together, Ellisia reminded herself. After six months in an orphanage, this foster home was to be their new beginning—a fresh start from the case that had leaked on front page headlines with titles like, "Former Chief David Carroway Sexually Abuses His Two Daughters," and "Former Chief David Carroway Murders His Wife," and "Former Chief David Carroway Found Dead."

"I'm thinking about wondering what you're thinking about." Emmie didn't take her eyes off her sister.

There was a quip of silence as the tires screeched to an abrupt stop making Ellisia fling into her congested seatbelt.

"I'm thinking this is going to be a nightmare," Ellisia said.

The man driving opened his door and came to the side to help Ellisia out, but she'd already opened the door by herself.

"Hello, hello, hello!" exclaimed a rather exuberant lady wearing a light blue sundress. "We are so excited to have you here!"

Ellisia glanced around the house as they entered. She nearly dropped her small duffle bag as she noticed a grand stairway accompanied with an even grander balcony. These people must be rich, she thought. No wonder they had a locked gate around the property.

"Everyone! They're here," called the overly-enthusiastic woman.

A couple of children popped up. Some came down—more like slid—from the staircase, and others came from various rooms from downstairs. Ellisia's heart raced as more and more kids crowded around her and Emmie.

"Is this everyone?" asked the woman, taking a mental head count. "Aw! We're missing Scott." She took a few steps away from the group. "Scott, they're here."

A tall man slowly came into view and Ellisia, out of habit, took a slow step back as he got closer.

"Sorry. I was just working in the garage. Hello there." The man smiled while wiping off his dirty hands.

"Alright, everyone," the woman said, clapping her hands. "This is Ellisia and Emmaline. They're going to be joining us for a while."

The words pierced through Ellisia's ears as she realized this was reality. After being paralyzed with fear for four years and then sitting in an orphanage for another six months, this was actually happening.

"I go by Emmie," Ellisia's sister squeaked.

"That's a wonderful nickname, *Emmie*." The lady smiled. "And you, Ellisia, do you have a nickname as well?"

Ellisia looked up from the ground as she realized she was being questioned. Everyone stared at her, waiting for a response. She took note that this might be the one and only chance she got to change her name. She'd always been "Ellisia" and nothing more. But now she could get rid of that.

"Elle."

"Elle?" asked the lady, tilting her head.

"Yes."

"Like the letter?" A small black girl giggled.

"Yes. Like the letter."

"That is lovely if you would like it," said the lady. "Now let me introduce everyone to you girls."

In all, including Elle and Emmie, there were seven kids. Elle forgot most of their names by the end.

"And I'm Lilian Everson. This is my husband, Scott Everson."

The man smiled and held out a hand for them to shake. Emmie took it hesitantly but Elle didn't take it at all. With a casual nod of the head, he stepped back in line.

Soon after, everyone went back to where they were and the day carried on—leaving Emmie hopeful with the new children, and leaving Elle apprehensive.

Chapter 1

Five Years Later

With her recently bought book in her lap, Elle sat burrowed in the overgrown grass. The sun was beginning to yawn with soft oranges and glowing lavenders as a cool breeze began to blow overhead. Elle didn't seem to mind the sweet chill of air during the Oregon evenings, in fact she rather enjoyed it.

If she wasn't reading, most days she sat up in her room with the door locked so her roommate couldn't enter. After five years of meeting various kids, she'd come to the rather bleak conclusion that there were too many unwanted babies in the world, and unfortunately she was one of them—and there was absolutely nothing to be done about it.

With this mindset Elle had swept into a darker section of her mind, the section where spiders spin cobwebs and settle into their new homes. She became frozen in depression. Although years of required group and individual therapy sessions hadn't done much to relieve Elle's worsening condition, reading outside in nature seemed to improve her mood.

Her books became her therapy. Kindly, Mr. Everson never held back from buying her new books every time he went out. But on this particular evening every time she looked back down at the paperback, a rustle of leaves disturbed her peace.

She looked up from the book to find the ordinary space filled with rich green trees, as always. Perhaps it was just her imagination.

It was just about six o'clock, Elle guessed. She should probably be getting back to the house for dinner, but instead resumed right where she left off in the book. Then she heard the same peculiar noise. Perhaps an animal of some sort? But if it weren't? Then what? The house was heavily gated so nobody could possibly enter without the access code.

The thick branches of the large oak shook. Suddenly her stomach lurched with panic. Carefully, she slowly glanced up just one more time. Again, nothing. Just the same old tree she had come to every day for the last couple of months. She took a deep breath and settled back down and tried to read again, but she could no longer focus on the small black words in front of her.

"Hello," came a voice from above.

Elle dropped her book to the ground as the voice rang through her ears. Had she imagined it? She stayed frozen in place and looked up to the low branch to her left. To her shock a boy effortlessly balanced on a thin branch. He angelically jumped down to the ground as Elle sat, speechless.

The boy looked to be around her age, but at the same time seemed timelessly older. He had mangled, dark brown hair with a couple of strands falling into his piercing blue-green eyes. His eyes looked so stunningly bright, even celestial, that the color seemed as if it were dripping down his cheeks.

"Who—" Elle attempted, caught in a state of stupefaction. "How—"

"Whoa, don't startle yourself there," the boy said. His voice didn't sound like an ordinary voice, it sounded much like deep bells ringing.

Elle was shocked with disbelief. How could someone have features of a human, but at the same degree look a million times otherworldly?

"It's alright, you see, I'm not a bad—"

"How did you get in here? Who are you? You need to leave," Elle said, her mind bursting with adrenaline.

She snatched her book, stood up, and walked toward the house to find help. Although, she kept finding it rather difficult to not look backward.

"Wait," the boy said, following her. "I can explain."

When Elle realized the strange—yet remarkably beautiful—boy continued walking her way, she clumsily tripped and fell back into the bed of grass.

"Are you okay?" The boy stifled a laugh but seemed genuinely concerned.

Elle immediately got up. Panicked that she was *still* near the boy, she began to run back to the house.

Elle consciously looked back to see if he was still there. But as soon as she glanced back again, the boy had already disappeared into the forest. Only the same old conifer and pine trees remained.

Several weeks passed with no return of the mysterious boy. Elle had come to the conclusion that perhaps she was going mad—that the boy she saw was nonexistent. There was absolutely no possible way of anyone without a passcode to enter the Everson's property. And Elle had never once seen that boy in the years of living with the Everson's. She was afraid to ask anyone if they knew of the boy from the trees. She didn't want Mrs. Everson thinking she was any more insane than she already was—that Elle now had imaginary friends roaming her mind. She did give a slight thought to the possibility that Mr. Everson would be more understanding, because he didn't seem to hover as his wife often did. Mrs. Everson was usually on high guard of Elle over the other children. She constantly asked how she was feeling, or why she didn't want to eat lunch with the other kids. After this constant questioning and invasion of space, Elle became a bigger fan of Mr. Everson, with whom she only shared a couple of words every now and then.

Elle was somewhat shocked when she came to the realization that not all men were like her father, though—she bet—a lot of them were. After days of warring with herself in her mind, she decided not to mention the strange boy to anyone.

Although, Elle's mind didn't stop bombarding her with questions. All these unanswered questions demanded answers that were not being given. Soon, Elle's mind became utterly mentally drained. She became so overwhelmed with mental exhaustion, she began to go to bed right after dinner and sleep all the way until lunch time. Even when she woke, she'd stay under the sheets. She forced her mind to believe the boy from the trees was simply her vivid imagination.

She decided on this until one exceptionally windy night when she was about to climb into bed at last. That night Elle was feeling less anxious than normal because for the first time in months she got the room to herself. Her roommate was unfortunately feeling poor and slept on the couch downstairs to be closer to Mr. and Mrs. Everson's room, in case she needed anything.

Just as Elle reached to turn off her bedside lamp an odd knock thumped on her window. Her initial thought was that it was a tree hitting the window from the wind, then soon remembered there was not a tree by her bedroom window. Instantly, Elle thought of the mysterious boy.

"He's here," Elle thought out loud.

This idea split her mind in half. On one side she was overjoyed that he was back at last, thus confirming she was not schizophrenic, after weeks of considering the possibility. And the hallucinated boy was not a hallucination at all! Now she could get some answers. But the other half of her mind was in a frenzy of terror. Anxious thoughts swelled and swelled.

Another couple of louder knocks, and Elle's heart felt like it was thumping out of her chest. The saliva in her mouth suddenly became hot. Her throat began to tighten.

Elle shifted her feet to the ground with her eyes tightly shut. Very, very slowly she turned her head to the window. And even slower, opened one eye, and then the other. As much as she'd tried to prepare for this moment, she was still startled to see the boy from the trees effortlessly crouched on the windowsill outside, balanced comfortably on his tiptoes while his knees slid up against the glass.

At this perspective, Elle got a better picture of him. He wore dark blue jeans cuffed above a pair of chunky over-worn black boots, with a dark grey V-neck on top and a black jacket. The jacket seemed a little too big for him. His same, almost-black hair was unkempt on top of his head. A few strands swept his forehead, and the rest were disheveled. Elle also took note that he had tan skin; but not like her

Filipino tone, more bronzy and sun kissed, as if he'd been outside for hours.

He waved at Elle as she helplessly stared at him like he was some kind of majestic animal in the wild. He then gestured to the window hinges. She unhooked them mindlessly as if she were under a trance.

The boy fell into Elle's room without a sound. He stood up and stared at her, waiting for her to say something. As if snapped out of a trance, Elle realized what was happening. There was a random boy in her room—what was she supposed to do? She started for the door in a heap. She was just at the nob when the boy slid in between her and the door, making them uncomfortably close to each other.

"Whoa there," the boy said, as he reached for the nob, trapping Elle inside.

Frightened, she took a step backward and began to form a name for help.

"Shhhh." He wrapped his hands around Elle's mouth before she could make a single sound.

The very second he laid a hand on her, Elle's insides melted from head to toe. Images of a man's silhouette played in her mind. Pictures of a man holding her down to the ground with his large hands, forcing her to stay still when she didn't want to. The feeling of being completely immobilized, and not having any control. The feeling of fatigue setting in from no sleep. The tingling sensation of someone whispering in her ear while grasping her face on each side.

After a troublesome few seconds of trying to free her face from the boy's grip she stopped fighting against him. Her mind felt as if it were a large wave finally crashing. Even though she was shivering with goosebumps and boiling tears streaked her face, the boy had remained patient through it all—the exact same way her father did.

"You promise you won't scream when I let go of you?" the boy asked with a serious tone.

Elle screeched a pleading yes, but kept her eyes on the door.

"Or run out of the room, or try to fight me," the boy added.

Elle nodded her head fiercely, desperate for the boy to get his hands off of her—even more desperate to punch him square in the jaw.

"Alrighty then, happy you chose the right choice."

Elle stepped back immediately as soon as he let go. She clumsily backed into her bedside table while she wiped the boy's sweat off her mouth.

"Who are you?" Elle demanded. "And answer me this time."

"Alright, alright. My name is Eryk Rylander."

"How did you get past the gate? Do you know Mrs. Everson or something?" Elle begged for answers.

"I don't know Mrs. Everson, but I'm looking for Ellisia, and I'm almost positive that's you."

"How did you—"

"Let me explain, please," the boy went on. "Just calm down, I'm not going to hurt you, I promise."

Elle hesitantly nodded her head. She knew if she were to get anything out of this Eryk guy, she had to hear him out. She sat on the edge of her bed but made him sit on her desk chair vertically across from her.

"My name is Eryk Rylander."

"You said that."

"Anyway, I'm not from here. I'm from a series of villages called Remedium."

"Where?"

"I'm getting there," Eryk went on. "In the Villages of Remedium live people called Mystics."

Elle's mind began to spin.

"I, for example, am a Mystic. So don't worry, you aren't *entirely* crazy. I'm a real life person, just not exactly. What Mystics do is we find normal people, as yourself, who have been Indwelled by Charmers. A Charmer is a type of person, more like creature, that feeds off of traumatic experiences, terrifying memories and so on and so forth. Are you following?"

Elle stared at Eryk. "So you think that I have a Charm in me?"

"*Charmer*, with an 'er.' Yes."

"What does that mean? I'm going to die?" Elle said.

Eryk chuckled, shaking his head.

"No, you're not going to die, because I'm here," Eryk said.

"But if you weren't..." Elle went on.

"Okay, let me keep explaining. When you watched your dad die—"

"How do you know my—"

"Patience, Ellisia," Eryk smirked. "When you watched your father die, you weren't quite Indwelled yet, we don't think, but we think you were being watched. And so we kept an eye on you. By *we*, I mean us Mystics. But, once you came here to this foster home, tell me, what did you develop?"

Elle slumped her shoulders, though she knew exactly what Eryk was thinking.

"Anxiety, depression, post-traumatic stress, et cetera," Eryk answered for her. "So that's when we knew a Charmer attacked you. Because whenever someone has a Charmer in them they begin to develop side effects like yours. Does that make sense?"

Elle took a deep breath and didn't answer the question. She kept her eyes on the carpet as she remembered the night of her first anxiety attack. Her first vivid flashback. Since then, her mind and actions hadn't been the same. But what about—

"Emmie," Elle whispered to the ground.

"What was that?"

"Emmie. Emmaline. My little sister! You're telling me she's got some kind of freaky parasite living in her, driving her mad, too? She's only twelve!" Elle went off in a panic. Suddenly it was hard for her to breathe again and it felt as if acid was in her stomach. Her hands were drenched in sweat in a matter of seconds as they pulled on her unwashed hair.

"Whoa, no, wait—"

"Whoa? Stop saying whoa. Whoa, whoa, whoa! Is that all you can say?" Elle couldn't keep her mouth shut as she heaved in short breaths. "If this is true, it's all my fault."

"Nothing's your fault," Eryk said. "Just let me finish, please."

Ellisia began to pace back and forth whilst biting her nails, trying to come up with a plan to slaughter the Charmer in her sister.

"Emmie doesn't have a Charmer in her," Eryk blurted.

"Wait. What?"

"I said that Emmie, your sister, she doesn't have a Charmer in her," Eryk repeated. "Mystics can look at people and see if they carry a Charmer, and no one else in this house does. Only you, that's why I'm here. I came for an Ellisia not an Emmie."

Elle took a long deep breath and sat back down. "Oh."

"Yes, you have a Charmer in you, but it's okay. It's a quick removal."

"Removal? Like, what do you mean? Some kind of exorcism?" Elle queried.

"Hmmm, basically," Eryk said casually. "But you'll be okay, I promise."

"What if I don't want the Charmer removed?"

"Then that would be dumb, because you'd end up killing yourself."

"Killing myself?"

"Yeah, killing yourself. That's what usually happens to people who are Indwelled, or who don't want to be separated from their Charmer."

"Well, why wouldn't people want their Charmer removed when you tell them that?" Elle asked.

"For the most part, some people don't believe it. I think people just get attached to their insanity. Their insanity becomes their reality and anything genuinely normal seems insane to them. I think sometimes, a lot of the time, people like the feeling of being insane."

A few moments of quiet hushed the room. The sound of the wind howled outside.

"So, what do you say?" Eryk beamed as he stood up from the desk chair.

"To what exactly?"

"You know, getting actual help. Getting that Charmer out of you and actually living again?"

Elle took a moment to think about this. Leaving this house to go get help? What would she tell Mrs. Everson and

Emmie when she got back? They would think she'd completely lost it. Elle guessed she'd have to deal with that when she returned.

"I think I wouldn't mind living again," Elle said, surprising herself with the words.

"Alright then, come along Ellisia."

"Elle."

"What was that?" Eryk asked over his shoulder, as he made his way to the window.

"Elle. You can call me Elle."

"Like the letter?"

"Yeah, like the letter."

"Alrighty *Elle*, come along then."

Chapter 2

A shiver shot up Elle's spine as she stepped into the windy night. The pale moon glowed in between the clouds, and the trees seemed more alive than usual. The sky was starless, painted the perfect shade of dark blue. The color looked endless, and if you stared at it long enough, you could almost see your thoughts reflecting back at you. It relaxed your eyes, and made your thoughts unwind.

"Where are we going?" Elle shivered. She was only wearing a t-shirt and the pair of jeans she slipped on before leaving.

"You ask too many questions," Eryk noted.

Elle remained silent as they continued towards the woods. She was surprised at herself for not being more paranoid. But her curiosity over the past few days outweighed the paranoia, and her instinct told her to trust Eryk. So she went along, but kept her defense up.

Soon enough they stumbled upon a tree with a very large trunk. Eryk stood there looking up at the massive leaves. Beyond all the shivering trees in the wind, this one remained completely still.

"Here we are." Eryk beamed. "The Tree of Remedium—well, one of them."

Elle took a step back to get a better look at the giant tree. Suddenly, she realized this was not an ordinary tree. Not only was this specific tree substantially bigger, it also had white markings of names covering it from roots to limbs to leaves. Thousands and thousands of names and initials were carved in every inch of the tree.

"What are all these names?" Elle asked in utter wonderment. Her fingers traveled across the letters as her eyes widened in fascination.

"You'll find out. Follow me."

Walking around to the opposite side, he found what he was looking for. In the center of the tree was a clear indented triangle. Eryk pressed his palm into the center, and it automatically copied the print of his hand. Elle stood there completely speechless as the triangle began to glow with the traces of his palm. The print of his hand enveloped the tree. Each line and swirl like marks on a map, paced up the bark and around the limbs. The light got brighter and brighter, when suddenly the surface of the trunk slid up, revealing a tiny wooden lit room.

"Ladies first." Eryk gestured into the brightly lit room.

Elle remained frozen with disbelief. The room looked as if it could barely fit one person in it. Eryk, out of impatience, glided into the trunk of the tree as if he had done it a billion times.

"Are you coming or not, sweetheart?" Eryk asked.

Elle stayed firm in her position. Her eyes couldn't seem to take in all the names sketched into every inch of the tree. She ran her fingers through the letters to find that it was not her imagination, they really were engraved into the massive tree itself. Suddenly, the only thing her mind wanted to talk, think, and dream about were who these people were and why their names were scribbled into this tree.

"Let's go," Eryk said, as he gripped Elle's hand and pulled her to the tight space of the trunk.

As Elle stepped in, her trance vanished and the room suddenly seemed exceptionally bigger.

Immediately Elle realized that the room grew larger as she stepped in, but it was now also only occupied by herself and a boy. A hand with bony spider-like fingers grasped her esophagus, and her brain automatically shut down. She could feel someone clenching her elbows and yelling at her, but she couldn't quite make out the words. The room began to move in an upward motion as her heart dropped to her stomach and ticked harder with every passing second. Her suddenly sweaty hands pulled at her unwashed hair, and then the door of the tree trunk room slid open once more.

"Hello—oh," said a new boy waiting by the entrance looking down at Elle's hunched figure.

Just then Elle realized she was hunched on the floor with Eryk anxiously looking down at her.

"What'd you do to her?" The boy laughed, although Elle did not find the situation funny at all.

"Nothing, I don't know what happened," Eryk said back to the boy. He turned back to Elle, who was now sitting on her knees on the ground of the elevator tree. "It's over now," Eryk said coaxingly. "It's all right."

Elle looked up from her trembling hands to see the face of two worried boys looking down at her.

"What the hell is going on?" a silvery-haired girl asked, rushing over. "Don't you boys know anything at all?"

The girl with silver hair pushed the boys behind her and crouched down to Elle's level. Her lipstick was a warm shade of mauve and her eyelids were shimmery. Her breath smelled of spearmint and stale coffee. "It's alright, you can trust me. Do you want some coffee or something, tea? Maybe some water?"

"She doesn't want tea, Alaina," the boy said. "A good night's rest is what she needs. She looks like she hasn't slept in months."

"You boys just don't know how to handle anything, do you? I knew this was a bad idea, Eryk," the girl said. "Come on, I'm so sorry they were the first people you had to meet here. Follow me." She took Elle's overly sweaty hand.

"I'm fine," Elle stated, tugging back her hand. The girl looked solicitously at Elle when she did so.

Elle got up and brushed herself off. She didn't want to look weak around these new people, for a reason she did not know.

"Okay, ignore them." The silver-haired girl gestured to the boys who were now deep in conversation about sandwiches and something called "transformer."

The girl started walking quite quickly away from the scene. Realizing she was meant to follow, Elle quickened her step to be beside the girl. The girl's hair was the exact color as the moon.

"I'm Alaina Black by the way." She smiled at Elle. The simple gesture made Elle want to trust her, give her some sort of gratitude for helping her get away from the boys. "You must be the famous Ellisia Carroway."

"It's Ell-*ee*-see-uh, not El-*lis*-ee-a," Elle clarified as she tried to keep up with Alaina. "But that's not my name."

"What do you mean that's not your name?"

"My name is Elle."

"Like the letter?"

"Yes."

"Interesting, I like it. There's not too many of those, unlike Alaina. Millions of those," the girl said. "Sorry I'm walking so fast, I normally don't, but we don't have a lot of time."

"Until what?"

They continued to walk down the same path for a while. The floors and walls were wooden like a tree. The lanterns along the walls gave off a golden hue to the halls. Elle assumed they were only hung, but as she studied them closer while they walked, it became evident that they were not attached at all, but floating in midair as if by magic. Every once in a while, they would pass hanging signs that would read things like "Heliopath Training Room," or "Meadows." These signs greatly intrigued Elle. Another set of questions added to the list.

At last, they stumbled upon a massive door with thick green leafy vines strung all around it that arrowed to a room called "Café."

Alaina opened the intricately crafted door to reveal a cozy room with hanging tree vines all around.

"Wait here," Alaina said, striding off without taking in the enthralling sight.

Elle had never seen something so enchanting before. Tree stumps were carved as different shaped tables, and chairs were sewn with colorful wildflowers. The walls were braided and entangled in tree limbs and leaves that smelled of pine and mulch. It was all very calming, yet made Elle excited at the same time. It was something she had never seen before.

"Hello," came a male voice from the corner. He glided towards Elle, carrying a single blue flower which he'd carelessly plucked from the chair. "You must be Ellisia Jade Carroway—the girl we have been dying to meet."

Elle stood stunned, now anxiously wondering where Alaina went.

"I'm Leonardo Castello. I can show you around—only if you want of course—before you're initiated," he said with a smirk, stretching his hand toward the door.

Elle's breath caught at the word "initiation"— specifically of what initiation meant in this context and why it involved herself.

Leonardo continued. "Oh, wait—are you with a girl who has strange hair? And a boy named Eryk who acts like he knows everything, by chance?"

"I'm with a silver-haired girl named Alaina."

"Right," Leonardo ran his fingers through his light hair, thinking. His voice became a low whisper. "I'm just going to let you know right now, to save you the trouble, that Alaina and Eryk and his little scrawny friend, Mason, enjoy the magic of secret-keeping until one is so-called 'initiated.' But if you have any questions, anytime, you find me." He winked, gave her a pat on the shoulder, flicked the flower out of his hand, and exited the room.

Elle was speechless. The new information stung her. Her certitude of Alaina was so profound, though she had only just met her. There was something about her that led Elle to want to trust her. But with this new information, any sort of trust vanished. Her hopeful mind sighed and now she did not know who to trust.

"I'm back." Alaina huffed, holding two paper coffee cups.

Elle couldn't help but remember that Mrs. Everson never allowed Elle to drink coffee. Although sometimes she would sneak downstairs and pour herself a cup. Oh, Mrs. Everson what was she up to now? Probably sleeping or switching out the laundry. And Emmie? What would they do when they wake up and realize Elle was not there? The idea gave Elle a queasy feeling in her stomach.

"Are you alright?" Alaina asked with sincerity, handing Elle the coffee.

"Yes," Elle lied. "What's initiation?

"Follow me."

Elle was brought into a kitchen-like room with bright lights. The floors and walls were again crafted from wood and smelled richly of the outdoors. Eryk bent over a mini refrigerator, urgently looking for something to eat. His friend—the boy from earlier—sat at a circular table eating leftover pizza while intently reading a comic book of some sort.

"Do you guys ever stop eating?" Alaina jokingly asked as she sat down by the boy, who instantly perked up as she did.

"I'm hungry," he explained.

Elle took a seat next to Alaina, wondering just how many rooms this place had.

"That's Mason," Eryk said.

"Mason Montgomery," the boy said, stretching out a pizza-greased hand towards Elle. She dismissed it and he awkwardly put it down.

Mason wore thick black rimmed glasses that sat in front of his light brown eyes. His hair matched the color of his eyes, but was very unkempt under a baseball cap.

"Elle has questions," Alaina stated.

"Of course she does," Eryk said.

"We can't tell her anything until she's initiated," Mason interjected matter-of-factly.

"We can tell her the basics," Eryk said.

"Right now?" Alaina asked.

"Have you asked Tabitha?" Mason interjected.

"No," Eryk said. "It doesn't matter, she has to know at some point."

Elle became annoyed that they were talking about her as if she wasn't there, and let out an exasperated sigh.

"Fine. We'll tell her the basics, but just the basics," Mason said as he dog-eared a page in his book.

"What's your first question?" Alaina asked.

"What's initiation?"

"Well, if Eryk did his job and told you, we are called Mystics," Alaina started. "Mystics' jobs are to find people Indwelled with Charmers. Charmers are kind of like parasites and feed off of traumatizing events that people have gone through. So we find people like you, like we were, and bring you here, to the Villages of Remedium. Here we will remove your Charmer. Initiation is when your Charmer is removed. It's called the Removal, or the Transformation."

The word "removal" did not sound well in Elle's ears. That made it sound like a horrific operation, like an exorcism or something.

"Removal?" Elle questioned.

"It's not that bad," Mason offered.

"It will be worth it," Alaina went on. "Anyways, this is the exciting part. Once you get your Charmer removed you get a Myst!"

"What's a Myst?" Elle asked.

"A power," Alaina answered. "You know like, flying, super strength, that kind of thing."

It didn't sound believable to Elle. She was never one to believe in fantasies and supernatural things like that— although, the idea was exciting.

"Prove it," Elle demanded.

Eryk side-smiled. "I'm a Heliopath, I can manipulate fire in any way I want."

He set his hand to magnificent flames and put them out again, leaving his hand completely burn-free.

Elle couldn't hold back her fascination; she nearly fell out of her chair. She had never seen anything like it before. She wondered how Emmie would have reacted. Emmie would have been completely in awe.

"And I'm a Psychokinetic," Mason said. "I can move things without physically touching them, and I can teleport, too."

She realized the pizza sitting in front of them was hovering in the air.

"That's incredible!" Elle said, amazed. The pizza drifted its way over above Eryk's head. It hung in suspense, waiting to fall any second on Eryk's dark hair.

"Do it, and I'll set your hand on fire," Eryk threatened, only half joking.

Mason and Alaina laughed as the pizza fell back on the plate instead. Elle couldn't help to smile. It was truly incredible to see. Mason seemed content at the fact that Elle was so fascinated by his ability.

"And I," Alaina said, "can change my appearance to anything, or anyone I wish."

Her hands began to grow larger, and her hair darkened. Soon enough she looked like a clone of Eryk. Same dark hair with slight curls on the end, same tan skin tone, everything. It looked as if two Eryks were sitting at the table.

Eryk chuckled. "I'm still better looking."

Elle sat in wonderment. How could this all be possible? She had an odd urge to touch the replica's hair. This couldn't be real.

"I'm Eryk Rylander and I think I know everything," Alaina mocked. She even had the same voice as him. It was astonishing.

Alaina transformed back into her usual form—her dainty, silver-haired form.

"That's incredible," Elle repeated.

Suddenly the kitchen door slammed open to reveal a woman with very curly black hair. The woman was strikingly beautiful with dark freckles that sprinkled her face. Her skin tone was a warm honey brown and her eyes were a crystalline brown color that demanded attention.

"Aw, Ellisia!" the woman exclaimed. Her eyes couldn't move from the sight of Ellisia, making Elle uncomfortable. The lady cleared her throat and continued. "Hello Ellisia, my name is Tabitha, and I—we—are so happy to have you here."

Elle was tempted to smile, but was too dumbstruck by Tabitha's otherworldly appearance.

"I'm going to be showing you to your room for the night, come along dear."

Elle did not move. She had seen too many forced smiles to not recognize Tabitha's. The wrinkles on Tabitha's forehead exposed her anxiety.

"Come along," Tabitha beckoned.

Elle glanced at Eryk, who shrugged. She glanced at Alaina, who nodded.

Elle reluctantly stood up and followed Tabitha.

Chapter 3

An incandescent moon hovered in an indigo sky. It watched Elle silently, observing. For only it and the stars could predict what tomorrow looked like. How the troubles she faced now were only foreshadowing the adventure ahead of her. It knew her secrets. It knew her past. The same moon then, as it was now. Following her journey all that time. It was an intuitive moon, as well as an empathetic moon.

Elle stared at the moon as she stood delicately on the smooth wooden balcony. Although her mind was drowned in worries, she still looked like glass—like delicate china glass.

"A full moon tonight, how ironic," came Eryk's voice from behind her.

She stayed silent, breathing deeply in the fresh clean air of Remedium.

"Magic makes an appearance where the full moon arrives, you know," Eryk said, keeping his distance from Elle.

They stayed quiet for several minutes. Elle, Eryk, and the moon. Together, but silent. Only the breath of the sky and whispers of swaying leaves.

"How did you decide?" Elle asked in no more than a whisper.

He looked at her, taken aback at the sound of her voice.

"It most definitely was not an easy choice," Eryk said. "Never is, for anyone."

She looked at him, making eye contact for the first time since her first night there. His eyes were the color of the leaves draped behind him, but more vibrant and shocking. As she looked at him, he understood her unsaid question.

"I told you the night I climbed through your window that people's insanity becomes their ordinary, and anything truly ordinary sounds insane. I suppose some people enjoy the feeling of going crazy, subconsciously, without wanting to recognize it, or control it. It fuels them. Like, knowing you're something special and not having anyone understand your madness. It's unique. Your mind is mentally unique, until you realize it's not unique. In all reality it's only killing you. Eating you alive."

It made perfect sense. Except for one detail.

"Then how do you just simply leave it? Your 'unique insanity.' How did you deicide?" Elle asked.

He didn't know what to say. Then he looked at her, then at the moon, and he spoke. "My mom had me and my older sister, Ashlee, when she was only seventeen and nineteen. Instead of being a mother she dropped off the face of the earth, never to be seen again. So Ashlee's dad took us. He was an alright guy until Ashlee started to become like our mom. She would hit me. A lot. I would try to tell her dad, but he was all about men being superior to women and told me to fight back. And I knew I was physically stronger than her, but I could never bring myself to do it. I would see her eyes as she hit me, tears."

They sat in silence for a moment, listening to the rustle of leaves in the wind.

"She didn't mean it," Eryk continued. "So I would let her. She wasn't mad at me; she was mad at the world. But one night everything changed. I came home late from work. Ashlee's dad was gone, and I heard her crying. I walked in to her bedroom to find her being raped."

He became silent. Elle's thoughts became silent. Even the wind and the leaves became silent.

"Strapped to the bed."

Elle kept her eyes down.

"He got off of her when he saw me and started to beat me. Next thing I know I was lying in a hospital bed. Mason, the guy you met the other night, was sitting right next to me. Not my mother, the dad I never met, Ashlee's dad or even Ashlee. Just Mason."

Eryk took a deep breath. "I was only fourteen."

Elle wondered if Eryk had ever met Mason prior to him being in the hospital. How did Mason know he would be there that night? At that time? In that room?

"When Mason told me about Remedium I instantly thought of Ashlee. But when I told her about it, she said she was perfectly perfect and didn't need an imaginary land to solve her problems. I kept trying to get her to come with me, just for a day, but she got frustrated and thought I was the one going insane. One day she told me she hated me and to never speak to her ever again. She didn't want to get better. And she was only keeping me from getting better, so I left. I became a Mystic without her. And there's not a day that goes by where I don't check on her. She's only getting worse, when she thinks she's getting better."

"I'm sorry," Elle said.

"It's okay." A silly thing to say, because it was obviously not okay.

"I was raped too," Elle said, not knowing why she said it.

"I'm sorry."

A tear dripped from her eye. "One day there will be a world rid of Charmers."

"Yes, but without Charmers there wouldn't be any Mystics," Eryk said.

"Does it hurt?" Elle inquired, "The Removal?"

"Yes," Eryk answered honestly.

Elle was stumped by the bluntness, but remained curious as to what all the transformation entailed.

"But not in the way you think," Eryk added. "It's different for everyone."

"What was your experience then?" Elle asked. She wanted to know as many aspects to the event ahead of her as she could. To make sure if that was what she truly wanted, to leave Emmie for that.

"It's nothing you can prepare for. But you're strong, Elle. Really strong. And we're all excited for you."

"What do you mean?"

"It's just that everyone—or almost everyone—is going to be watching and waiting for the Reveal. It's always a big deal to get a new Mystic, to find out their Myst and who their Charmer is. It's strangely exhilarating. Someday you'll understand." Eryk said as he laid his grasped hands on the balcony besides Elle's.

"But why?" Elle questioned.

"Why what?"

"Why is it such a big deal?"

Eryk looked into her eyes. "Because it means Remedium gained another Mystic. It means you won."

The words echoed in Elle's mind. She never considered herself and her mental illnesses as a game. She never believed she could conquer her anxiety, depression and PTSD for good. But now she could? It sounded surreal in her thoughts.

"Oh, there you guys are," came Alaina's voice from behind them. "We've been looking everywhere for you, Elle."

Alaina locked eyes with Eryk, an unspoken understanding.

"It starts soon, Elle, come with me," Alaina insisted.

Elle nodded her head slightly to Eryk as a small thank you and followed Alaina inside to where her destiny awaited.

Elle followed Alaina through a series of wooden steps and bridges entangled with greenery and lit by the moon's luminosity. Her silent anxiety about the Removal thumped at her stomach like a constant tick of a clock in a therapist's office.

As she followed Alaina, she realized her silver hair was now down to her waist and slightly curly. It still astounded Elle how Alaina could manipulate her appearance. All the powers she had learned about astounded her.

It had been an informative day for Elle. She became familiar with several new people during the meal times. Alaina had introduced her to a boy called Louis with a very peculiar Myst. He had the ability to manipulate people's actions and control their thought processes. This particular Myst was called an Enchanter, but Alaina said everyone calls them Compellers or "untrustworthy." All throughout the day, Elle secretly hoped to see the boy she talked to in the café. Though, for one, she'd forgotten his name, and two, he never appeared. Elle met several other Mystics and learned about their peculiar Mysts. One girl had the ability to survive any climate and run faster than lightning without becoming tired. People who possessed this Myst were called Endurers. There were also Vipriuses, who could manipulate the earth's elements, such as plants and the ocean. There were Healers who could cure sickness and broken bones, but they could also induce illness if they pleased. There were so many Mysts that Elle could not remember them all.

At last they entered a large room, although this room did not look like the rest of Remedium in the slightest. Rather than exposed tree roots and greenery, it was made completely of white and glassy walls. Shiny, clean and looked as if nobody had ever stepped foot in the room.

"Alright, here we are," Alaina said. "Tabitha is going to tell you everything that you will need to know. Don't worry, I know—we all know—exactly how you're feeling. And you're going to be great and do great things. Best of luck and wishes!" Alaina beamed.

"Awh Ellisia," said Tabitha. "We are all so excited for you."

Elle barely remembered Tabitha from the other night due to her exhaustion. She began to feel apprehension with the lack of knowledge she had on Remedium. Even though everyone was so excited and proud of her, she felt like she wasn't making the right choice. She couldn't stop thinking of Emmie.

"Trust me, I understand this journey hasn't been easy for you." Tabitha placed a hand delicately on Elle's shoulder. Her fingers were dressed in gold rings and colored gems. "But you Ellisia, have the power to do incredible things. Your experiences, your fears and your troubles have affected you. But it is also your bravery, your compassion and your intellect that has brought you this far. It's those traits—selflessness and strength—that are real. All the rest are simply imaginary. Your anxiety is not you, and you are not it. Anxiety is only imaginary. And you are overcoming it today."

Each word tattooed itself to Elle's brain. It struck her that she had never been told something so encouraging. Not from her therapist. Or the Everson's. Or even Emmie.

"This is how the events are going to work. I guarantee you will be safe the entire process—"

"Does it hurt?" Elle interrupted.

"Oh, it always hurts to leave the past behind, to let go." Tabitha looked at Elle as if she recognized her from someplace else. "But once you do, it is the most painless operation you will go through."

Tabitha paused. Her eyes looked dewy like morning grass. "Now it's almost time. In five minutes you are to walk into that room over there." She pointed. "It's pretty tight. You will take off your clothes once you enter the room, and from there the Transformation will begin. Yes, it is different for everyone, but three main stages will take place. The first stage is called the Reliving, then the Removal, and lastly the Rebirth. Afterwards, there are three more steps. The Receiving, where you will gain your Myst, and the Reveal, where we announce who your Charmer was. And lastly the Retaking, where you will Retake your life from your Charmer by executing it." Tabitha recited, as if she had done so a thousand times before.

Elle took in every word. She was appalled that she was to undress and was immediately uncomfortable at the thought. As well as executing her Charmer. She wasn't entirely sure what that entailed. Why hadn't Eryk told her?

"You will do great things." Tabitha patted Elle's shoulder with empathetic eyes and exited the room.

The room suddenly seemed much larger now that Elle was alone. She realized she had not taken a clear breath the entire time Tabitha spoke. She then recognized how dry her throat was. When was the last time she ate or drank anything? She glanced over to the room, although, it did not look like a room at all. It much more resembled a closet or a fitting room in a clothing store.

What would happen if she simply did not go in the room? Would she be able to go back to Emmie? The thought of her little sister made Elle want to cry. When would be the next time she got to see her baby sister? She knew Emmie was doing well all by herself. Emmie was kind of like a Mystic already, helping and listening to all the new foster children that came to the Everson's home. Now it was Elle's turn to do the same.

She began to walk towards the room.

Her hand clasped the cold metal knob of the door and opened it. She stepped into the Transformation room.

To say the room was tight was an understatement. Elle's elbows hit the walls on either side, and her butt skimmed the door once it closed. How was she to undress? It felt like having to squeeze into a dress four sizes too small. It felt like being buried alive. It felt like being pinned to the ground to be taken advantage of. It felt vulnerable.

Beep! Beep! Beep!

A siren went off, and the walls began to slide backwards, revealing more space. Elle began to breathe again. A mirror appeared along with a piece of paper attached to it.

Taking a deep breath, Elle tugged the piece of paper from the mirror and read.

Congratulations Ellisia Jade Carroway.

Follow the instructions below. Go in chronological order. Do not skip any.

    1. Undress.

The demand seemed very odd. And although Elle felt insecure about taking off her clothes, she began to undress.

Now completely unclothed she realized how cold it was. Goosebumps stung her skin and her urge to turn around and leave the strange world forever grew stronger.

2.   Stand still in front of the mirror and close your eyes. This will begin the Reliving. Then proceed to #3.

Elle tuned towards the mirror, seeing her bare body. The clear white room exemplified her Asian skin tone she inherited from her mother. Elle had not thought of her mother in a long time. Her naked body did not carry the bruises it once held, although there would always be everlasting scars. Her cheeks weren't as hollow, her ribs weren't as evident, and her thighs were now touching.

Indeed, her appearance had changed over the years, and now it was time for her mind to change as well.

Elle took a long breath and gently closed her eyes.

The air became lighter, and the temperature increased to that of spring afternoons as Elle found herself inside a flashback of her own life.

A four-year-old Ellisia Carroway hugging her momma's very pregnant belly.

"What shall her name be, Ellisia?" Her mother speaks.

"Emma!" the young girl exclaims.

"Caroline," a man says. He effortlessly picks up Ellisia and sets her on his shoulder. Her father.

"How about Emmaline?" the mother imposes.

"Emmie!"

The picture twists and turns and the air grows heavier.

Then there was six-year-old Ellisia Carroway skipping home from the bus stop. Her frizzy black hair swings in a ponytail, and marker ink stains her little fingers.

She rings the doorbell several times, but no one answers. She sits down on the brick porch and waits. Picking at her scabby knees, patiently waiting. But nobody shows. A police car solemnly sits by the curb.

Again, the setting transforms to reveal two young girls dressing dolls in a bedroom. Loud shouting and unspeakable words ricochet off the walls. Ellisia's eyes grow to the size of the moon and three-year-old Emmaline begins to cry. In hopes of calming her sister, Ellisia exits the room to ask her parents if they could be quieter. Shouting was a common occurrence in the Carroway home.

But that particular night was different. Ellisia stands paralyzed. Witnessing her mother bawl, unable to breathe, as she's beaten with fists repeatedly on the back. Ellisia stands unable to speak. Unable to cry. Only wide eyes like an owl's, watching her mother hopelessly. Hearing her baby sister cry in the background.

Her mother makes eye contact with her. Eyes nearly swollen shut, tears streaming onto her chest. She mouths, "I love you." She musters up the courage and turns to face her husband. He pauses for a moment, staring into her eyes. And then pushes her out of disgust.

Time slows as her mother's head smacks the end of the counter. It's hard to tell if she leaves a dent on the marble table, or if it leaves a dent in her skull. Blood waterfalls from the edge of the counter creating a dark scarlet puddle on the white tile. Her father's eyes sink. His heart falls, somersaulting into the pit of his stomach. He rushes to her side. Cradles her head. His drunkenness dissipates immediately. Now he is the one crying. Crying into her hair—her rich black hair. He screams, "I am defeated." He hollers "I AM ALONE." He wails, "YOU WON." He whispers, "You won. You won. You won," as he rocks his dead wife back and forth. "You won."

The image flutters and tangles to reveal another scene.

The girls are now a bit older, holding large trash bags bigger than themselves.

"Clean," their father orders.

The girls stare back at him, dumbfounded.

"I said clean!" he demands.

They watch him as he starts to throw books, and dolls, and necklaces in the trash bags. Emmaline begins to cry and Ellisia instantly goes to coddle her.

"Don't touch her and start cleaning," their father yells. His breath smells of thick liquor. The girls have become immune to the smell.

Ellisia begins to throw away a bear with a red bow tied around its head.

"That's Mommy's," Emmaline wails.

"Your mommy's dead," their father spits. He picks up a picture frame holding a photograph of the girl's mother. "She," he points to her face—her smiling face. "She is gone." He thrusts it into the trash.

The image contorts, only to reveal the same bedroom again. This time the air is as thick as molasses, the lighting is dim, and the room is bare except for a single mattress in the corner.

A young girl is pinned down. Forced into unspeakable things. As another cries and cries and cries. Forced kisses. Harsh whispers. Bruises. Tears, and hopelessness.

It happened every night for years.

The image slowly evolved to the Everson's home. On the day they arrived, Elle thought the house was a mansion, but looking at it now, it was just an average cottage home. Three bedrooms, three bathrooms. Crafted of wood and stone in the middle of a small forest in Oregon. Being in Remedium, the house seemed a million miles away. She watched herself draw under her favorite tree. The grass was overgrown and hid her from sight. The only thing making her visible was her black hair amongst all the shades of green and yellow. Then she spotted him. She could see Eryk carelessly sitting a couple tree limbs above her.

When Elle opened her eyes again she was back in front of the mirror. Her hands sweaty, her hair disheveled and her cheeks were drenched in tears. The flashbacks embittered Elle's mind. For the past five, almost six years at the Everson's she tried her hardest to suppress her memories of living with her father. The feeling of being back in her old house was acrimonious. She could still feel the tight finger tips wrapped around her arms like cold spider legs inching up her skin. The sensation caused tingling goosebumps to spike her skin.

As Elle tried to regain a regular heartbeat, she read the next set of instructions slowly.

3. Sit down with your knees to your chest. Do not move. This will begin the Removal.

Shakily, Elle did as the instruction said. She hoped the Removal would not be as painful as the Reliving, but something told her it would be.

Sitting on the cold floor with her knees to her chest, she waited. She tried to steady her breathing. She could feel her heartbeat throughout her entire body when suddenly, a large tube began to descend from the ceiling. It moved closer and closer to Elle, and it took everything she had not to move from the glass tube beaming towards her. Three feet away. Two. Six inches from her head. It began to enclose around her, becoming thinner and thinner. Her skin painfully stretched against the glass and her head was being forced into her chest. Her neck felt like it was about to snap. Claustrophobia rolled in Elle's chest like wheels on a fast paced train. Her head became dizzy, her screams became muffled, and her thoughts turned drowsy. Abruptly, the glass became plastic and folded into every crease of her body, suffocating her to death. It was like a vacuum sucking out every piece of air inside the plastic bag, entrapping her. Elle could no long fight against the stubborn plastic. Her tongue cried for water, and her heart thumped as if she had been running for miles. Her arms and legs became sore, and she was almost positive all her ribs were broken. She was paralyzed. Her skin transitioned into a grey-blue color, and her rich black hair softened to a lifeless grey tone. Her body became a stone.

After minutes of being fossilized, a soft light began to radiate through Elle's head. It traveled throughout her, becoming brighter and brighter. Soon a golden light encompassed her entire body. It thumped with the tick of her heart. The luminosity twisted and bounced, becoming hyper and incontrollable, like a firefly trapped in a mason jar. It shot through her head like a firework, becoming encased in the plastic around her. The plastic began to mold into the former glass tube. The gold light followed the tube's path as it rebuilt itself up to the ceiling.

A sharp gust of air inhaled itself through Elle's lungs. Her eyes beamed open and her muscles began to unstiffen. She stretched out on the cold marble floor. The tips of her fingers skimmed where the wall and the floor met. Her ribcage extended, revealing each and every unbroken bone. She could feel each vertebrae extending. As she lengthened each of her limbs, her body resembled a stretched rubber band, carrying so much kinetic energy, to be shot towards a target.

Eventually, she remembered where she was. Wiping the confusion out of her eyes, she sat up. The walls were still white, the mirror still taunted her, and it was still a chilling cold temperature. The first stage was emotional pain, the second physical pain, so the last, she guessed, must be mental pain.

When she stood up, something felt odd. Not odd. Different. Her feet felt lighter. Her hips felt as if they didn't hold as much weight. And her head, for once, felt unclouded. Though, she still felt exhausted. But no longer emotionally exhausted. Elle began to laugh. She couldn't help it. A fit of giggles jingled inside her and made their way up her throat. Was she really laughing? She was. She was laughing. And it felt so good. She couldn't—and didn't want to—control her laughter. It felt nice to be uncontrollably content.

As she regained her breath, still giggling, she read the next instruction.

4. Stand up and punch this code into the keypad to the right of you: 2676-3733

Elle looked to the right of her, and sure enough there was a keypad staring at her. She walked to it and punched in the numbers. The wall slid open to reveal a hidden room. The room was dank, and made completely of cement. As Elle walked in, the already cold temperature dropped another twenty degrees. The wall slid closed behind her with a definite clonk. She knew there was no going back now. It felt like being trapped in a freezer.

She read the next instruction.

5. Lay in the Transformation Tank and shut the door. This will begin the Rebirth.

Skeptical, Elle walked to the "Transformation Tank." To her it resembled a tanning bed, but it also resembled a coffin.

Although the lid posed to be heavy, she lifted it easily. There was not much inside. No cushions or blankets for her to lay on, just more metal.

Elle tried to slow her breathing as she climbed in. It was even colder inside the tank than outside. It was so cold she could see her breath in front of her. She anxiously closed the lid on top of her. The second it closed, sounds of a thousand locks jolted. She knew there was no going back now. Again, she was trapped. She swallowed her fear and waited for the next stage to proceed.

The tip of her nose nearly skimmed the top of the tank. Her arms and legs were spread out in front her. Suddenly, blue lights erupted from all sides. Some blinked on and off like strobe lights. The vibrancy burned and blinded her eyes. She closed them tightly, trashing around in attempt to open the stupid tank, but it did not budge. The lights were not only bright, but hot as well. The cold perished. Elle's skin felt like it was melting right off. Each follicle of hair scorched her scalp. She couldn't tell if there was an actual sharp ringing, or if it was in her head.

The lights stopped. The thrashing stopped. The ringing stopped. An image appeared in Elle's brain like a movie projector turning on.

Elle's father stood by a woman, not his wife, but another woman Elle recognized. She had dark hair and skin. Tabitha. It was a younger Tabitha.

They stood under a large tree. Much like the tree with the elevator Elle went through what felt like months ago. Though, it was only the other night. Could that be right? Only the night before last? The tree was engraved with the same glowing initials as the other one Elle saw.

"You got her pregnant?" Tabitha exclaimed in outrage. Elle's father stared at his shoes. "I told you what would happen. I repeatedly told you that if you wish to remain Indwelled, do not, by any means, have a child!"

Her father remained silent.

"Do you not know how serious this is?" Tabitha questioned. "You are putting your unborn baby's life in jeopardy. I told you David! I told you. Now that baby is bound to be born Indwelled."

Her father's expression transformed instantly. "Oh well! I'm doing fine. I'm married, I'm the Chief and now I'm going to have a kid. A family. Who cares if I'm depressed, people everywhere are depressed. You can't save everyone, Tabitha! Some people don't want to be saved. I don't *need* to be saved. I'm fine," he said.

Tabitha looked him in the eyes. Tears burned the rim of her eyelids. "I care," she said. "I have cared so much about you for so long. Come with me to Remedium, and we can wait for your daughter to join us there. I can have another Mystic on her as soon as she's born," she pleaded.

"No," David refused. "We're fine. My daughter and I are fine. Maybe *you* aren't fine. Now, get out of my sight, and never come back for me or my daughter."

Tabitha let a tear fall. She had failed. She turned around and stepped into the elevator, not looking back. And on her way up to Remedium, she decided she would never fail again.

But what did Tabitha mean, "bound to be born Indwelled with a Charmer?" Was Ellisia born with a Charmer already inside her? A Charmer never found her like all the other Mystics, she was born one. Did this mean she wasn't any more human than she was a Charmer? She wasn't Indwelled with a Charmer; she *was* a Charmer.

I'm a Charmer. The three words echoed in Elle's mind over and over. Was she a Charmer? Was she never human? Why wasn't Emmie born a Charmer like her? If it was true that Charmers inhabited people to feed off of their traumatic memories, then why was baby Emmaline never even possessed with a Charmer as Elle had been? They both experienced the same harrowing upbringing. Perhaps Elle's suffering impacted her worse than her little sister?

A new image appeared.

It was eight-year-old Ellisia looking in the mirror as she practiced braiding her hair. She looked at her appearance. Her cheek bones were more defined than normal, as she had not been fed a proper meal in a while. Her hair reached her belly button, as she had not been taken to get a haircut since her mother died. Her skinny arms struggled to maintain strength as she braided.

Suddenly the person in the mirror that stared back at Ellisia, was not in fact herself, but instead was her mother. Ellisia dropped her brush to the ground. Dumbstruck, she gazed at her mother. Her mother's skin was completely unharmed. She smiled up at Ellisia. Rapidly, her eyes flashed bright green and she dissolved back into the mirror.

Ellisia screamed and began to hit the mirror with her palms in an attempt to reach for her. Where did she go? Was that truly her mother? She cried, yelling, "Come back," until her drunken father ran into the room. He hit her across the face and scolded her for speaking without permission. He covered the mirror with a burlap blanket. He told both of his daughters that if they were ever to touch the mirror, they would be locked out of the house for good. Eight-year-old Ellisia knew she should not have spoken without permission, but she could not control her bewilderment over seeing her mother again. She instantly regretted yelling. But she did not regret seeing her mother.

This memory, she knew, was real. But as time went on, she accepted it was impossible. She only imagined that she saw her mother. It could be the only logical reason. For they did resemble each other. She just missed her mother's presence so much, she imagined it. Elle convinced herself of this.

The setting transformed to show Ellisia and Emmie sitting together at the Everson's home. It was dark outside the window and the TV was playing, although Elle wasn't truly paying attention. The girls were quiet until Elle turned to her sister.

"I'm sorry," she said.

Emmie stared at her for a long time. The girls had been there for nearly three years now.

"Why?"

"Because I haven't been a very good sister," Elle said, not making eye contact.

"Yes, you have," Emmie said. "Of course you have, why do you say that?"

Elle was quiet for a long time, trying to translate her thoughts into words. For the past couple of years, Elle felt so weak—that she had not been strong for Emmie since coming to the Everson's. She watched Emmie play with the other kids, participate in soccer games, fish with Scott and go to community home school every Tuesday and Thursday. While she, herself, had to stay home because she was too mentally distraught to be around other children. Her sister accepted her past and had let it go so much faster than Elle. Her sister participated in life and enjoyed living. Elle was proud of her little sister, but it was her *little* sister being strong. Wasn't Elle, the older sister, supposed to be the strong one, the so called role model? And she wasn't. Emmie seemed a thousand times older than Elle. She felt as if she failed as an older sister.

"Because, I never make an effort to play with you. I never—"

The words got lost in her thoughts, but somehow Emmie understood what she meant.

"I understand why you don't want to play with me and the others," Emmie said quietly.

"It's not because I think I'm too old," Elle explained. "It's just hard to participate."

Emmie nodded.

"I'm sorry I've been so weak since coming here. And not being here for you. I've failed," Elle said. It felt good to finally say. She felt like she could say so much more, but she didn't know how.

It was quiet for a long time. Just the buzz of the TV and chattering of the other kids upstairs.

"But you were strong, when we were at Dad's house. You were strong the whole time." The mention of their father's house made Elle squirm. They had never talked about that time of their lives since coming to the Everson's. At least not to each other. "I know you went through so many of the sufferings for me, so I didn't have to."

A tear fell from Elle's eye. She stayed silent, hugging her knees to her chest, not looking at Emmie, though she knew Emmie was looking directly at her.

"I don't blame you for feeling the way you do. It's natural to feel the way you do actually." Ten-year-old Emmie sounded a million years old. When did she become so mature and wise? "If one of us failed at anything, it's me."

"Why do you say that?" Elle asked, now looking at her sister.

"Because I've helped so many of the kids that come and go here. At least, I've been able to make them smile once. And I never can with you. I can't even help my own sister," Emmie explained.

"Well that's not your fault," Elle refuted. "It's mine."

"But again, I don't blame you for how you feel at all. All I want is for you to get better," Emmie paused. "Even if it takes a long time."

Her last word echoed as the picture dissolved.

The vibrant blue lights came back on. This time they were not flashing. There was no beeping, and Elle was back in control of her sight and mind. The tank lid popped open. She continued to lay there. Her thoughts for once, were silent. Her heartbeat was steady. Her spine no longer felt sore.

She sat up, letting her legs hang over the side. Her skin was sticky with sweat and her hair stuck to her neck. She looked up to notice a shower made of glass on the other side of the room. She glared at her instructions.

6. *Take a shower. Take as much time as you need.*

Elle found the instruction to be a bit peculiar, but accepted. She stepped into the shower, letting the warm water rinse away her worries. While in the tank, she had forgotten how cold it was. The water temperature was perfect, it felt so nice.

Once she stepped out, there were clothes set out for her. She assumed she was to put them on, so she did. She looked in the mirror. She wore a white long sleeved dress that reached the floor in a flowy movement. It was ethereally beautiful. She had never worn something so beautiful.

Elle took a breath and read the next instruction.

7. *You have now completed the Transformation, stand in front of the mirror for further instruction.*

She read the words with appreciation beating in her chest. She folded the list of instructions in fours and placed it on the floor. She had made it. She survived the dreaded Transformation. A sudden burst of euphoria fluttered through Elle. She wanted to dance, or sing, or jump, or run for hours. Any troubling questions or doubts dissipated, and the jubilance wrapped itself around her body and tied itself in a bow. She had never experience this emotion. This emotion of complete bliss. The exultation blossomed inside her like an iris as she made her way over to the mirror.

Looking at her reflection, she realized how small she seemed in such a big room. The white dress made her light

Asian skin tone pop. She stood in front of the mirror as a new person. She waited for something to happen. She wasn't sure what was supposed to happen exactly, but she waited. As she did so, Elle realized how quiet the Transformation room was. The silence was deafening. The only reason it seemed so loud and hectic was because of her thoughts.

At last, the mirror began to lift upwards. A roar of cheering became louder and louder as the mirror got higher. Her eyes adjusted to bright stage lights when she realized she was standing before a crowd. It was a sea of people, hooting and clapping. A sea of Mystics. The stage beneath her was made of wood, as were the walls. After being contained in a room made of solid white and glass for what seemed like hours, she felt back in Remedium at last.

Tabitha strode towards her, carrying a flower crown of white gladioluses. She smiled with tears in her eyes and placed the crown on Elle's head. The crown felt rather heavy on her head but it smelled lovely. It smelled as if the flowers had just bloomed that morning. The crowd's cheering became louder. She wondered for a moment if the boy from the café was amongst the crowd. She knew for certain Eryk would be, along with Alaina and Mason.

Tabitha wore a lavender dress that dragged on the ground behind her. She wore the same colored gems on her fingers and ears. She looked astonishing under the stage lights. She almost didn't look real.

"Ellisia, it is now time for the Receiving."

Eagerness swelled in Elle's stomach as she heard the words. She almost forgot about receiving a power. Her body and mind felt so at peace she forgot to prepare for this part. She took a breath and followed Tabitha to a glass tank.

It looked exactly like the shower, without the actual shower part. It was a glass rectangular prism with silver trim. As the door closed behind her, the sound of the cheering became a low buzz like being plunged under water at a party.

A golden light luminesced around her. The heat of it danced on her skin, the feeling made her laugh. She could feel her toes tingle, then her fingertips as well. The warm light tingled her lips and nose, and brushed her thick eyelashes. It pirouetted around her shoulders and knees. The light shimmered like glitter and spun around her, entrapping her in a golden dust storm. It whispered in her ears, and dripped down her spine. And suddenly, it flew into her mouth at once. Her white dress and the white flowers transformed into an array of gold.

"Ellisia Jade Carroway," a voiced boomed, silencing the audience. "Seventeen. Battled depression, anxiety, PTSD, and PPD. Gains the Myst of Heliopathics."

The crowd cheered so loud that it hurt Elle's eardrums. Elle couldn't exactly remember what "Heliopathics" meant. Didn't Eryk say he was one?

The cheering continued, as Tabitha came to open the tank. Elle stepped out, hearing the crowd's noise burst to full volume again, like listening to music through headphones and unplugging them. Her body felt different. She felt as light as air. She felt as if she was not only living, but existing again. She felt limitless.

"Ellisia, you are now a Mystic of Remedium, congratulations!" Holding Elle's hand, Tabitha tossed her arm up as if she won a championship title. Elle stood there trying to smile as people clapped. She was proud to be a Mystic, proud that she had gone through the Transformation, but she felt she did not deserve this sort of appreciation.

Through the buzz of excitement, a large box draped with a black curtain appeared on stage from underground.

"Now time for the most exciting part—The Reveal!"

Anxiety quenched Elle's insides. She wasn't even exactly sure what the Reveal was. She knew it was the part where you find out who your Charmer was. But what did that mean? Were there different types of Charmers? Did they have names? Where did they live before Indwelling someone? The questions tangled themselves in Elle's brain.

Tabitha directed Elle over to the box. It was tall, much taller than she was. She could feel her heart knocking on her chest. The adrenaline pumped through her bloodstream. The crowd began to count down from ten until she could pull the curtain away.

Ten... nine... eight...

Her hands were profusely sweating.

Seven... six... five...

The only words her mind could form were, "What is inside?"

Four...

What was she supposed to see? What did Charmers look like when not possessing someone's mind?

Three... two... one...

Tabitha yanked the black curtain away. It fell to the ground in slow motion. The Mystics cheered exuberantly.

The creature inside looked human. But wasn't. It huddled in the corner, unclothed. The skin was a lifeless grey color. The hair was frizzy and falling out. You could easily count each rib bone. It looked disturbed, crying into its thin, bony hands. It just looked like a heap of skin. But as Elle moved closer to it to get a better look, something changed.

It slowly turned its head where Elle could see its eyes. Black eyes. The Charmer looked familiar.

It was her mother.

Chapter 4

Puzzlement flooded Elle's senses. Her muscles suddenly cramped up as if she were in the Transformation again. Her eyes widened as she stared at her mother's lifeless body. This could not be real. This must be a dream, though she could hear continuous cheers from the crowd, indicating she was still in Remedium.

Abruptly, the sack of skin and bones lying in the cage bounced up ferociously like a jaguar. The Charmer's broken fingers gripped the bars of the cage. The knuckles were translucent white while the skin sagged from them. The skin looked as if it were melting off, like a roasted marshmallow precariously hanging from a stick over a campfire.

Suddenly Elle felt Tabitha's sweaty hands on her shoulders, anxiously pulling her away from the cage.

"Ellisia," the Charmer croaked. "My Ellisia."

Saliva dribbled down its chin onto its naked chest. Elle could count each and every vein shooting out of the Charmer's neck. Its ribs were not only utterly prominent, but broken and jagged as well. Its scalp held marred bald patches while the hair remaining was stringy and decrepit. Black and blue colored underneath its hollowed eyes. And its eyes! They were a never ending black pit. No white or former deep brown colors were evident. The deep ebony color glazed them entirely. Elle had never seen anything like it. It was haunting.

Elle stared at the Charmer in wonderment. This could not be her mother, she thought as she tried to shrug off Tabitha's desperate grip. This could not be. Her mother was not a Charmer. Let alone *her* Charmer.

As if in a trance, Elle reached towards the Charmer.

"Ellisia," the Charmer said with a weak voice. "My baby. It's me."

As soon as Elle was about to touch its crippled hand she was suddenly lifted into the air. The trance snapped and reality flooded back into her mind.

Someone was carrying her over their shoulder. Like a little kid throwing a fit, she punched their back and kicked her legs in refusal to be taken away.

"Let me down!" she begged.

The guy didn't budge and progressed down a wooden hallway. She kept flailing in an attempt to be let down. She could feel the heat in her body increasing with anger, and all of a sudden her fingers were on fire. Startled, the person carrying her dropped her to the ground.

Her fingers possessed magnificent flames. It didn't burn, but she didn't know how to make it stop. She screamed as she flapped her hands desperately in the air in attempt to make it go out. She felt sick and delusional. She was delusional. She wanted out. She wanted to run away, leave Remedium, and go back in her bed at the Everson's.

"Calm down! Calm down," the guy yelled. Elle realized the guy was Eryk.

"Make it stop!" Elle yelled. "How do you turn it off?"

Eryk laughed at her response, which only made Elle angrier, making the fire expand.

"Stop laughing!" Elle said, making the flames spill down her arms.

Eryk stifled the laughter.

"Okay, okay," he said, still chuckling. "It will stop if you relax."

"I can't. I hate this!" Tears spilled from her eyes.

"It's okay, just breathe," Eryk said.

Elle began to take deep breaths, but her arms remained on fire.

"There you go. In, and out, in, out," Eryk said.

Slowly, the fire enwrapping Elle's arm dwindled down.

"I want to go home," Elle said. "This isn't normal."

Eryk sat beside her, his back against the wall.

"You'll get used to it Elle," Eryk said. "You just have to go through training for a couple of weeks until you learn how to control it."

Elle looked up at him through her teary eyes, "I don't want to control it. I don't want it. I made the wrong decision. I need to go back to Emmie."

Eryk looked at her with the saddest eyes she'd ever seen. And she had seen a lot of sad eyes. It looked as if he was at a loss for words.

"I know what you mean," Eryk said. "I felt the same way when I left my sister behind. You just have to give it some time. Plus, Heliopathics is the coolest Myst ever. You're just like me now."

She nodded, not knowing what to say. All she could think about was leaving Remedium and pretending all of this never happened. There had to be some sort of mistake; there's no way her mother was a Charmer, let alone the

Charmer that had been possessing her and driving her mad. More tears streaked Elle's face. The thought sickened her.

"It's okay Elle, I know it seems crazy right now, but you'll get used to it. Right now, I have to take you to Tabitha's." He stood up, offering her a hand to help her up as well. Surprisingly, she took it.

They began walking through a series of wooden tunnels and bridges. Remedium was quite exquisite in its features. It reminded Elle of treehouses—which she guessed, it kind of was. Everything was natural and intricate. Some of the tunnels were massive and echoed with every movement and breath you made, while others were very thin to where you had to crawl through them on your stomach. Every convoluted detail of Remedium's appearance fascinated Elle. She had never seen a place so beautifully breathtaking. The thought that she would live here was exciting as well as frightening. She just needed to get Emmie here, too.

"We're almost there, to the bungalows I mean," Eryk said.

"Bungalows?" Elle queried.

"Yeah that's where everyone sleeps, like a bedroom you could say," Eryk explained. "You'll find out your bungalow address and roommate tonight most likely."

The thought of sleep made Elle realize how exhausted she was. The crying and the Reveal had drained her emotionally. The idea of snuggling up under cozy blankets and forgetting everything soothed Elle. But what about the Retaking? Elle couldn't remember what Tabitha had said about it.

They walked across more suspended bridges dangling between trees. At first the sight of the rickety wooden bridges made Elle nervous, but then she found she rather enjoyed the feeling of being so high up in the air.

"Welcome to Remedium," Eryk announced, as they came upon a network of floating star-like huts. The sight was overwhelmingly magical. Each tiny home appeared as an oval shaped tent made of wood, each with a unique whimsical color. There were easily over a hundred, all drifting through the sky. They resembled sailing lanterns amongst the trees.

"Tabitha's bungalow is Nineteen Ivy Birch," Eryk said, snapping Elle out of her reverie.

Elle followed behind Eryk, taking in the fanciful sight. It was extraordinary. She wondered how to get to each bungalow, as they were so high up and slightly swaying with the wind. She thought to herself that she could get used to living here. Perhaps she would enjoy waking up every morning in a hovering bungalow and walking around the aimless tree paths. She began to realize too, that these were not ordinary trees. They were massive. More massive than the trees you would come upon in a rainforest. Their leaves were taller than her and were luscious in the scent of the earth after it rained.

Eryk came to an abrupt stop, making Elle clumsily run into his back.

"Sorry," she mumbled, still staring at the wondrous sight of Remedium.

They were stopped underneath a remote tunnel with leaf curtains on either side of the entrances. It made the space even darker than outside. "*What time was it, anyways?*" Elle thought to herself, as her eyes adjusted to the darkness. Besides them was a small computer-like screen hanging on the wall.

"This is how you get to your bungalow. Are you paying attention?" Eryk asked.

"Yes," Elle said. Didn't he know the difficulty of straining your eyes away from one of the most enchanting, miraculous sights?

"Good," Eryk continued. "So, what you do is turn on this here computer." He pressed the on button. A bright white screen popped up with a virtual keyboard. The brightness of the computer in the dark room burned Elle's eyes. "And all you do is type in your address and wait."

He silently typed in Tabitha's address with one hand while the other remained tucked inside his pant pocket. Elle could hear the rustle of leaves amongst the wind, and the occasional crow of a bird.

"Now you come over here to this door and your bungalow will be here waiting for you."

There was a sudden ding like an elevator arriving to the desired floor. The address appeared on the door in wooden numbers. Eryk opened the door and sure enough the bungalow awaited, floating a step away in the air.

Eryk held the door open and Elle stepped inside. It resembled a one room apartment, except it was methodically detailed and a tad smaller in size. The room was flourished in color. Flowers embellished the walls and leaves were strung as curtains. A small living room filled half the space, while a make-shift bedroom filled the other half. Intricate woven rugs covered the floor and various lamps were placed in corners of the room. Alaina and Mason were there, along with Tabitha and a boy that looked oddly familiar. He sat on a velvet black chair, looking seemingly out of place. He glanced up when he saw Elle enter the room, and she realized it was the boy from the café. What was he doing there?

"Where have you been?" Tabitha exclaimed, jumping up from the burgundy sofa. "I told you to take her here immediately Eryk, I thought you said I could trust you!"

Any sense of calmness squandered inside Elle. The apprehension in Tabitha's tone resurfaced the worriment and confusion of the latest events. The trance Remedium had set on Elle disappeared immediately, as she remembered that her mother was there, who was somehow her Charmer as well? Her mother, the brave and compassionate woman Elle knew, was the lethal thing destroying her mind all this time—the thing making her lifeless and nonexistence, the thing tearing apart her brain like weak paper.

"We had a slight mishap." Eryk rolled his eyes.

"A slight mishap. Ha! Well we got quite a bigger mishap on our hands right now, don't you think?" Tabitha said in utter disgust of Eryk's incompetence.

"Yelling isn't going to solve anything," Eryk said.

"I am tired of you screwing around and not taking my instructions when we have missions to complete. You are on probation again Eryk, and I do not want you to be around Ellisia anymore. You are not to enter the training room for three weeks. Am I clear?" Tabitha scolded like a mother to her son.

"You can't do that," Eryk protested. "You have no authority to ban me from anything."

"We'll resolve that later. For now, our attention is on Ellisia," Tabitha said.

"Elle," Eryk murmured. It seemed to bother Eryk when people called her Ellisia, more than it bothered Elle herself.

"It seems we have encountered a problem we have never experienced before. Your Charmer, Ellisia, is indeed your mother," Tabitha said.

"But how?" Elle pressed.

"There are three ways you can become a Charmer," Tabitha continued. "One, you die accordingly from suicide while being possessed by a Charmer. Two, you are killed by someone who has a Charmer in them. Or three, your life is taken from you while a Charmer still Indwells inside you. We believe she became a Charmer because your father took her life, when he, himself was Indwelled."

The words ricocheted between Elle's ears. The word murder brought goosebumps to her arms. She never said the words to herself, "My mother was murdered by my father." And now that she heard them from someone else, it made her realize how corrupt her childhood was—how harrowing her father was. It gave the saliva in her mouth a bitter taste. How could her father do that? How could anyone? It dawned on her that she had to save everyone from men like that. And she was going to. As soon as she could.

"What do we do then?" Elle jumped.

"There is the Retaking," Tabitha said.

Elle's insides melted.

"It is part of the Transformation process for the newborn Mystic to behead their former Charmer."

The words sliced through Elle. This meant one thing—if her Charmer was her mother, then she was to kill her own mother—the mother that she just got back. Maybe in a different form, but it was still the same mother she lost back when she was a child, right?

"But I can't," Elle yelled in protest. "That's my mom! The mom I lost. I—I can't kill her. I won't, I'm not going to." Elle stumbled over her words in fear.

"It's part of initiation," Tabitha said.

"Isn't there something else we can do?" Mason spoke for the first time.

"No," Tabitha clipped.

"Someone else can't do it for her?" Mason asked, even though he already knew the answer.

"No, you all know that you have to kill your own Charmer yourself with the Remedium-Lumen Sword. It implies that you have overcome your struggle, and you are in control of your mind, strength, and destiny from now on," Tabitha said.

The words felt imaginary in Elle's ears. They felt fuzzy and blurry, like slippery soap. She should have never become a Mystic in the first place. There had to be some sort of mistake, or another way.

"I'm not going to kill my own mother like my dad did," Elle argued. "I'm not going to do that."

"Ellisia, I know this must be hard for you to take in so fast, but it's part of becoming a Mystic," Tabitha said.

"No. I won't be a Mystic then. I'll go back to the Everson's," Elle threatened. "You are not going to make me kill my mother."

Nobody answered. Elle saw everyone glance hopelessly at each other. Wrinkled foreheads and white knuckles. The boy from the café—Elle could not recollect his name—looked at his lap, picking at his fingernails.

"Think of it this way," Tabitha went on. "It's not really your mother anymore. She only knows you as memories. She doesn't see you as her daughter anymore. She isn't human, Ellisia. She's a decrepit creature that injured you."

Hot tears splashed Elle's face.

"I won't," Elle muttered.

"You don't have a choice," Tabitha said with finality.

Hopelessness settled upon the room. The silence was deafening. Nobody said a word. Wasn't the transformation supposed to solve these feelings? Elle thought she wasn't supposed to feel this way anymore—anxious, worried and confused. Being a Mystic was supposed to be exciting and fun; she thought this was how she was going to reach freedom. She'd only been a Mystic for an hour or so and it's only felt more damaging than freeing.

"I have a suggestion." The boy from the café spoke for the first time.

Eryk looked up from the floor, skeptical. "Do you really?"

The boy gave him a hostile glare and continued. "We take her to see the Dealer, see what he thinks."

A hush dawned on the room.

"No way!" Eryk refused. "You're out of your mind, Leonardo."

"What's the Dealer?" Elle asked with a slight piece of hope registering back into her.

"Forget about it," Eryk shut down.

"What's a Dealer?" Elle repeated.

"Not a what—a *who*, sweetheart," Leonardo said.

"The Dealer is a powerful Mystic," Mason explained. "He can see people's whole life and future, everything they've gone through and what they might go through—"

"Nothing ever ends well with the Dealer," Eryk spat.

"Oh Eryk, Eryk, Eryk. Don't be biased. I thought we were getting along," Leonardo said.

"You—" Eryk burst, beginning to walk towards Leonardo, who carelessly sat on a velvet chair.

Alaina stopped Eryk mid-stride. "Calm down. Nothing's final yet, anyway."

Leonardo antagonistically waved at Eryk behind Alaina's back, infuriating him. Suddenly his hands were engulfed in flames. Alaina urgently jumped away from Eryk, nearly singeing off part of her silver hair.

"Eryk, get out of this bungalow right now if you can't control your anger," Tabitha said.

"He—" Eryk protested, cutting off the flames.

"Out!" Tabitha bellowed.

Eryk trudged to the door that Mason benevolently opened with his telekinesis and closed it behind him.

"Freaking Heliopaths." Leonardo chuckled under his breath.

Elle stood frozen. What had she gotten herself into?

"What's so bad about the Dealer? What's he going to do for me?" Elle questioned.

"He can help you decide what to do," Leonardo answered. "He knows everything."

"Yeah, but Eryk had a point. Nothing ends well with him," Mason said, standing up for his friend.

"What do you mean?" Elle asked.

"He's tricky," Mason began. "The Dealer always wants something in return. Hence why he's called the 'Dealer.'"

"For example, you could ask for simple advice, but he would ask you to be his eyes and ears for a week. Something like that," Alaina further explained.

"But I'll do anything," Elle burst out. This was her chance. This was the solution. It had to be.

"Perfect, I'll take you tomorrow," Leonardo offered, though it didn't sound like an offer.

"Wait a minute," Tabitha said. "Not anyone can see, what you kids call the 'Dealer.' You can't just waltz into his room demanding answers."

"Yeah, yeah, we'll make an appointment," Leonardo clarified.

"Are you sure, Elle?" Mason asked.

"Positive," Elle answered. She didn't fully understand the whole hullabaloo, but she didn't care. This was her chance, her only hope. She might not have to kill her mother after all. She didn't care if her mother was a Charmer and some kind of twisted, battered creature, it was her mother she loved unconditionally. The mother she always grieved for.

"See you tomorrow then, sweetheart," Leonardo got up from the chair, and walked to the door. "You too, princess." He winked at Alaina and left.

Mason muttered something under his breath that Elle couldn't quite catch, but it sounded something like, "Don't call her that."

Mason and Elle's eyes touched for a moment across the room. He looked troubled in thought, almost upset at Elle for taking Leonardo's advice.

"Goodnight, Elle. Goodnight, Alaina," Mason said, opening the door from across the room.

"Is Elle finding out her bungalow address tonight?" Alaina asked, turning to Tabitha.

Tabitha seemed upset as well. Elle did not understand why. She sensed there was a piece of information about the Dealer that was not being wholly announced. She felt blind amongst that knowledge.

"Yes, her address is Fifteen Willow Rowen," Tabitha said. Dark circles underneath her eyes revealed her exhaustion.

"That's my address." Alaina beamed. "I knew that was going to happen."

The thought eased Elle—somehow Alaina's spirit calmed Elle from the chaos in her head.

"Follow me." Alaina twirled to the door.

Elle began to follow Alaina, hope spreading throughout her body.

"Wait," Tabitha spoke. "Elle, I need to talk to you."

Worry reappeared on Elle's face.

"Let's step outside," Tabitha proposed.

All three of them walked out the door, back to the wooden tunnel from which she and Eryk came.

"Alaina, will you let us alone for a moment?"

Alaina nodded her head and stepped through the leafy curtains.

Elle and Tabitha stood across from each other in the dark tunnel. The starlight casted a silver glow across Tabitha's face.

"This has never happened before," Tabitha reminded Elle.

"I know," Elle said.

"I can't have you discontinue the rules only because you have a special case," Tabitha said.

Elle didn't like the words "special case" because she and Emmie were always called that amongst the unhelpful social workers and robotic shrinks.

"That is why I'm giving you ten days to come to a solution. If you have not found a solution or way around killing your Charmer by this time, you will have no choice but to kill your Charmer. Do you understand?" Tabitha asked, looking down at Elle.

Elle gulped. Ten days.

"Yes," she agreed.

"Good," Tabitha slightly bowed her head and walked through the leafy curtains.

Alaina walked back in to find Elle frozen in place.

"What did she want?" Alaina asked, concerned.

"Ten days."

"What?"

"I only have ten days to figure this out, or I have to kill my mother."

"She can't do that!" Alaina immediately objected.

"Apparently she can," Elle said.

"No. No she can't. We don't have leaders in Remedium, we have people in charge of different departments, but they can't necessarily give you deadlines on things like this."

"Well, she just did," Elle said monotonously.

"I will talk to Tabitha about it in the morning then. Ten days is nothing, that's not even two weeks, what if you need longer? Usually the Dealers can't even get an appointment with you for *three* weeks. The waiting list is typically pretty long," Alaina said.

"Okay, let's just got to bed."

"The nerve of some people," Alaina went on. "That's so annoying. Some people just assume they have all the authority and control in situations, when they have nothing to do with it."

"We'll figure it out in the morning," Elle repeated.

Alaina punched in their address and the room arrived. Elle was too tired to take in its surroundings. Her body felt drained of emotion, like a thunderstorm dwindling to a sprinkle.

"You can sleep on the top bunk if you would like, I usually sleep on the bottom." Alaina gestured to the bunkbed.

Elle climbed to the top without saying a word.

"Do you want to borrow some pajamas? We can go get all your clothes tomorrow," Alaina asked, trying to help.

"Sure," Elle said as Alaina tossed her some silky pajama pants and a t-shirt. "Thanks."

She slipped them on without a word, then plopped on the mattress in exhaustion. She fell asleep instantly.

Chapter 5

It felt like the minute Elle's head hit the pillow, she was shaken awake again.

"Time to wake up." Eryk's voice laughed along with Mason.

Elle tossed over, covering her face with a fluffy pillow. She could feel that the room was still pitch dark, what time was it? Her eyelids would not budge, and her legs felt like statues underneath the pile of cozy quilts.

"Elle Carroway. Do not make me drag you to the training room," Eryk threatened. He hung effortlessly on the ladder attached between the beds, while Mason sat on the bars surrounding the top bunk.

Elle threw the pillow without opening her eyes and it soared through the air, completely missing both Eryk and Mason.

"Well, throwing pillows won't solve anything," Eryk said.

"Or hurt anyone," Mason added.

Elle threw another pillow with all her might, but it only landed on the other side of the bed.

Eryk laughed. "We put training clothes in the bathroom for you. Get ready—we'll give you five minutes."

They boys effortlessly hopped down from the bunkbed and landed without a sound on the floor. Alaina remained deeply asleep in her bed, covered in a mountain of thick and fluffy blankets and pillows. On their way out, Mason telekinetically moved the first pillow that was thrown to the floor back to Elle's top bunk.

"Hurry up," Eryk ordered as he closed the door behind him.

Elle grunted in annoyance. She squinted her eyes open, and as she'd guessed, the room was completely dark. She peered out the window, but only to find the same thing—darkness. She sat up, unhappy. Her eyelids felt heavy with sleep, and her chest ached in exhaustion.

Three loud knocks came from the other side of the entrance door. She was sure it was Eryk and Mason telling her to hurry up.

She grumbled again, miffed at the sleep disturbance.

She climbed out of her top bunk, the air was cool like autumn mornings in Oregon. She shivered her way into the bathroom which was right besides where they slept. The bathroom was painted a forest green color and was quaint in size. There was a tiny stand up shower, a toilet and single sink with a drawer. Elle didn't mind the size, it reminded her of the bathroom she shared with Emmie and the other girls at the Everson's.

She dressed in the clothes Eryk and Mason left for her—simple gym shorts and a long sleeve polyester shirt. Elle didn't bother to look in the mirror, knowing she probably looked ridiculous. It dawned on her that she didn't even know what "training" was. Was it just some sort of work out? In that case she better put her hair up.

"Let's go!" Eryk hollered from outside the bathroom door.

"Coming!" Elle yelled back, her voice cracking with exhaustion.

Once the ponytail was up, she stepped out of the bathroom to find Eryk and Mason waiting for her in the miniature living room.

"Good morning," Eryk said. His face held the widest smile. How did he have so much energy this early?

"What time is it?" Elle asked, wiping the sleep out of her eyes.

"It is approximately 4:03," Mason answered, looking down at his wrist watch.

"Why so early?"

They walked out the door, back to the wooden tunnel with the address screen.

"Because training starts at precisely 4:05, and we're going to be late, so let's go," Eryk said, quickening his step. He was taller than Elle, making his long strides impossible to keep up with. Mason was a few inches taller than Eryk, but very thin and gangly.

"Hold on." Elle huffed trying to keep pace. Exhaustion rung throughout her body. "What about the Dealer?"

"What about him?" Eryk imposed.

"Don't we need make an appointment with him as soon as possible?" Elle asked, desperate to see the Dealer. The memory of last night zapped her mind. Only ten days. How was she going to tell Eryk and Mason?

"You don't need to worry about that. You need to worry about training before anything else, so you don't set all of Remedium on fire," Eryk said.

Elle pursed her lips but carried on walking behind them, trying to think of ways to tell them they only had ten days to come up with a solution. The breeze was biting cold and the sky was patiently dark as the moon quietly hung there, observing. The trees looked mysterious and hypnotic in the darkness. Hovering golden lanterns were placed every few yards, the only source of light. Elle didn't think she could ever get tired of the sight as they walked along an edge of a cliff. Normally that would frighten her, but she felt safe in Remedium somehow. That if she *were* to fall off the edge, the clouds would catch her and bring her right back up again.

After walking along the capricious cliff path, Eryk and Mason came to an abrupt stop.

"This is my favorite part," Mason said.

"What's this?" Elle asked, out of breath from trying to keep up. In front of them looked like a gargantuan, erratic slide. If you looked down far enough you could see all its twists and turns for miles down.

"This is how you get to the training room," Mason answered.

"Well, the *fun* way to get to the training room," Eryk said. "Ladies first."

Elle was taken back. "What?"

"It's just a slide, come along," Eryk beckoned.

She didn't know if it was the lack of sleep, or Mason's eager expression, but excitement swelled inside her.

She sat down on the top of the slide.

"Ready?" Eryk asked.

"Ready."

They boys pushed on her back and suddenly she was gliding down the monstrous wooden slide. She accelerated downwards, the cool air blowing against her skin. She couldn't help but laugh at the rush that jingled in her stomach. Then she held her arms in the air like a kid on a rollercoaster. The exhilaration spiked her skin and she cheered as she propelled toward the ground. With the rush of the wind through her hair and the vast spiral of adrenaline bouncing in her heart, she felt closer to freedom.

She reached the bottom of the slide in no time, with Eryk and Mason right behind her.

"That was a rush," Elle exclaimed, suddenly wide awake.

Mason and Eryk nodded their heads—with disarrayed hair—in agreement. They stood in front of a vast open grassland with massive caves arranged along the sides. In the far distance, silver mountain peaks were visible, and awakening magenta skies said their good mornings.

"These are the training caves," Eryk explained. "Each one for different Mysts."

Elle glanced around. It was an astonishing sight. The grass was a bountiful light green and smelled rich with morning dew. Blooming wildflowers sung hello with the wind, while a roaring stream warbled in the background.

"It's beautiful," Elle said in not more than a whisper, though she didn't mean to enunciate her thoughts.

"You should see the Meadows then, you would love it," Eryk said.

"Yes," Elle said, too distracted with the sight. She wondered if the rest of the world looked like this, and if she'd wasted all this time staying in the safe confines of the Everson's home. *Emmie would love this*, Elle thought.

"Bye Mason, see you later," Eryk said.

"See ya." Mason waved.

"Where's he going?" Elle asked.

"Like I said, each Myst has its own training cave. He's a Psychokinetic, so he goes to the Psychokinetic cave; while us Heliopaths—the coolest Mystics—go to the Heliopath training cave," Eryk explained. "Ours is over here."

She followed him a couple of blocks down from the first two caves. Lanterns hung on each side, casting a comforting atmosphere to the space.

They stepped inside the aphotic cave. Eryk held the single wooden door open for Elle and she walked in, not knowing what to expect. Fiery torches were lit every few feet and foam mats covered the floors of the dank cave. There were no windows, which made the space stuffy and dank.

"Eryk, there's something I need to tell you—"

"You're late," a woman with a thick Russian accent interrupted as Elle stepped into the line of firelight. Her features were striking. She had slick blonde hair that grazed her waist, half of it held up in a bun. Her light green eyes were as vibrant as the trees outside, and her light skin was like porcelain. Her thick lips were puckered and pale pink. In her hands she comfortably held a massive wooden spear. Something about her stance was frightening. She looked strong, confident and fearless. She reminded Elle of fire itself.

"Well, we're here now," Eryk persisted, trying to keep the situation light.

"The girl comes with me; you can go now, Eryk," the woman said.

"But—" Eryk tried.

"Tabitha told us that we are to not let you in this room. You may leave," the woman pushed, obviously not wanting to argue.

"Oh, you know Tabitha says things like that all the time," Eryk begged. "C'mon Phoenix, let me stay."

The woman—Phoenix—was about to refute when a very large man strode in. "We're wasting time. Eryk, leave. You can come later," he said.

Eryk muttered something unintelligible under his breath and made his way to the exit—leaving Elle alone in a massive room with two complete strangers, not knowing what to expect.

"Alright!" the man's voice boomed. Elle noticed he was Russian as well. "First we need to work on building your strength before anything else. Phoenix, the punching bag, please."

Instructor Phoenix slid an intimidating punching bag towards the man and Elle. She didn't say a word, too scared she might say something wrong. She found herself wishing Eryk had stayed. Suddenly the bag was set ablaze, wafting magnificent flames.

"Now. Punch the bag," the man ordered.

"What?" Elle asked in disbelief.

"You're a Heliopath now, Ellisia. Fire doesn't burn, you do," the man insisted.

Knowing there was no way out, Elle gave the bag a right hook. Her hand was left unburned, but she winced as all five knuckles cracked open with blood. The pain rang up her hand to her shoulder. It felt like punching a boulder.

The man and woman laughed, making Elle's face turn scarlet. He grabbed her right bicep with a definite grip. Elle did not like the feeling. Although she was a Mystic now, no longer harnessing PTSD, some things would probably never leave her.

"Do not put your strength here," he said. "But here instead." He put the palm of his enormous hand on Elle's abs, except there were no abs to touch. He let go. "Try again."

Taking his advice and ignoring the pain in her hand, she punched the blazing bag again. The bag did not budge, and her fingers came away with more blood.

"Again!" the man demanded.

She grimaced and did it again to find the same result.

"Again!"

She repeated.

"Fifty more times on the right, and sixty on the left. Go," the instructor's voice roared.

The woman observed her, judging each and every move. "This is going to take a while," she spat, discouraging Elle. Elle tried to ignore her and continued.

Elle's arm began to ache. Every time her punches were unacceptable in the instructors' eyes, they would add another five to both sides. She just wanted to go home, but she wanted more to prove to them that she was strong.

"What's your name?" Elle asked, continuing her punches. Her hands now came away with flames attached to them as well, but it didn't scare her after a while.

"Is that important?" he scowled. "Five extra."

The words "five extra" became an irritation in Elle's ears. She wanted to punch him instead.

She continued, her arms crying in protest. The fire became hotter, and the room became humid and sticky with sweat.

"Now for the legs."

He demonstrated how to properly kick the bag and she mimicked him.

He shook his head in disapproval. "You are very unbalanced."

She ignored him and continued to kick the bag as best she could. She could already feel the bottom of her feet beginning to bruise and blister.

"Use your core, Ellisia!" he yelled furiously. "It's all in the core."

"I have no core muscles," Elle argued.

"Fine," he scoffed, crossing his arms. "One hundred times on both legs and then we'll do some ab workouts, how does that sound?"

The woman laughed at his side.

She continued to kick, blocking out Instructor Phoenix's judgmental laughter and the man's absurd comments.

Finally, she reached a hundred on her left leg and took a step back. She couldn't seem to catch her breath and her feet wept under her. Yep, definitely bruised, definitely blistered, definitely bloody.

Elle stood there trying to steady her breathing as the flames on her legs dwindled out. She saw the man creating some sort of obstacle in the middle of the room.

"Come here," he barked.

Elle listened and walked to where he stood. In front of them was a circular pool of water with a single balance beam across it. He held the long wooden spear that Phoenix held earlier.

"To strengthen your core, and your balance, you will walk across this beam to the other side while carrying this spear."

The instructions seemed easy enough and Elle didn't object. She hopped up to the start of the beam and he handed her the spear. It was then she realized the spear weighed more than her, and she dropped it immediately.

"Every time you drop this spear, catch it on fire, or fall in the water, you start from the beginning," the instructor added, handing her back the spear. "Go!"

Elle took a breath, holding the spear flat on her palms. She took a single step, her arms already beginning to shake.

"I can't do this," she pleaded, dropping the spear to the ground.

"You're practicing until you learn." The man gave her back the stick.

She tried again, dropping it to the side.

"Again."

This time the spear caught on fire.

"Again."

Same thing.

This continued another eleven times, each time not getting any easier. *I'd much rather do a hundred more kicks*, Elle thought.

"You're not trying," the male instructor said with disapproval.

Suddenly Eryk entered the room again, urgently.

"What are you doing here," the instructor asked.

"It's almost time for breakfast," Eryk said.

The instructor looked from Eryk, to Elle, to Phoenix, and back at Elle.

"Fine. Be back at nine o'clock and no later."

"Got it," Eryk confirmed.

Elle hopped down from the balance beam before the instructors could change their minds. She followed Eryk out the door to see the sky at dawn. The iridescence was beautiful, like a watercolor painting that unified nicely with the rich green of the trees.

"How'd it go?" Eryk asked.

"Do they treat everyone like that?" Elle huffed. She stopped abruptly, her leg muscles refusing to take another step. All of her hair was nearly out of its ponytail and sweat covered the collar and sleeves of her shirt.

"Only at first. They're actually really great people once you get to know them," Eryk said almost defensively.

"Hard to believe," she said.

"They're just determined to make you the best." Eryk began walking again, and Elle followed slowly behind.

The air was crisp as they walked in silence along the edge of the cliff.

"The showers are that way—you might want to rinse off before breakfast," Eryk suggested.

"Okay." Elle turned to where he pointed and he continued to walk straight.

It seemed to Elle that Eryk might actually like the two instructors. She had no idea how this could be. She already hated them and dreaded seeing their faces again—she didn't even know one of their names. After walking through double doors to the space Elle first arrived from the tree elevator, she realized she had no idea where she was going, nor did she want to take a shower—what was the point if she was going to be at training again soon? She walked farther along, thinking of where to go. She really had no idea how to get anywhere, as Remedium was so enormous.

She was continuing to walk when suddenly she was bumping shoulders—more like her shoulders bumping his chest—with someone she recognized.

"Excuse you." Leonardo scowled.

"Sorry." Elle shied away, continuing to walk.

"Are you lost?" he asked.

"No," she lied.

"Yes, you are. Where are you headed?"

She turned to him, thinking of what to say. It was his idea to see the Dealer, and Eryk so stubbornly dismissed the topic every time it was brought up. Perhaps Leonardo would be willing to take her right then? But then again, Eryk did not seem to like Leonardo very much at all. Would it upset him if she went with him? Well, she had to nonetheless.

"The Dealer," Elle answered.

He scoffed, raising his eyebrows. "You're going to the Dealer?"

"Yes."

"Good luck with that." Leonardo began to walk away in the opposite direction. He was notably vexing, Elle thought.

"Wait," she said impulsively.

"What is it, Carroway? Realized the Dealer is nowhere near this building?" He spun gracefully around, looking down at her. He had to be at least a whole foot taller.

Elle rolled her eyes, crossing her arms.

"Do you want to take me there, then?" Elle tempted.

He eyed her up and down, gritting his teeth. "Follow me."

Elle smiled and caught up to his side. They walked through the double doors into the trees again.

"You look like a mess," Leonardo said without looking at her.

"First training session," Elle explained.

"Ah, Heliopaths have it so hard, don't they?" he said bitterly.

Elle looked at him, but his expression was blank.

"What's your power?" Elle asked, wanting to know more about other Mystics' trainings.

"They're called Mysts, sweetheart."

Elle stayed quiet. She noted he liked nicknames—but did he call everyone that?

"I can give people memories," Leonardo finally answered.

Elle was taken back by the confession; she could feel her jaw drop.

"And my sister, she can take away people's memories," Leonardo added. He didn't sound proud.

"Oh, wow. That must get devious," Elle joked lightheartedly.

Leonardo muttered something under his breath that Elle could not quite catch.

They continued to walk through a deep forest of trees, extravagantly tall and luscious in pine scent. Birds sailed overhead crowing to their neighbors, and insects ticked and jittered all around.

"You should come here during the night time," Leonardo spoke, his breath visible in the cool morning air. The sun was still rising in between the towering trees, setting sparkling crystals of dew on the leaves.

"Why do you say that?"

"The fireflies come out at night, and it's nice to see," he explained.

"That does sound nice," Elle said. Leonardo looked relaxed amongst all the trees, unlike his usual melancholy, careless attitude.

"I'll show you sometime," he said.

They walked farther into the bushy evergreen needles. Pinecones and moist soil wafted the air. Elle's muscles became more tired with every step, but she continued along, desperate to make her appointment.

At last they stumbled upon a miniature adobe-like home. Except it didn't look like much of a home. There were no windows or visible doors, nor a single front porch. It looked almost daunting the way it mutely sat there surrounded by gigantic trees.

They walked to what Elle assumed was the front of the adobe. She wondered why the Dealer didn't live in a bungalow like the rest of the Mystics.

Leonardo tapped on the wall with his fist. Nothing happened so he knocked louder. A few seconds later a scroll of paper slid out from a mail slot that Elle had not noticed before. The scroll was jagged on the edges and yellow in color.

"It's me, Leonardo," Leonardo announced, knocking again. "I have the Carroway girl."

Elle looked from Leonardo to the wall, not knowing what to expect. Her stomach felt sour.

"Did you hear me? I have Ellisia," Leonardo said louder.

Elle did not expect him to behave this way towards a Mystic with a high title. Then she wondered why Leonardo was telling the Dealer that she was with him anyway. Did it matter? Didn't they have to make an appointment first before she could see him?

"Bring her at midnight, and Anastasia," a voice boomed from the tiny home.

"Isn't Anastasia in—" Leonardo cut himself off, as if he were about to say something that he wasn't supposed to repeat. "Okay."

Leonardo began to walk away from the adobe. Elle remained looking at the mail slot, not understanding what just happened.

"Wait," she hollered, catching up. "He wants to see me tonight? I thought—"

"Keep your voice down," Leonardo said.

"Why? How—"

Leonardo didn't answer, advancing through the thick forest.

"I thought I had to be on a waiting list to see the Dealer," Elle tried again.

"Don't call him that," Leonardo commanded, his tone aggravated.

"Then what should I call him?" Elle pressed, taken back in his quick change of attitude.

He didn't answer and didn't even look at her. She continued to ask the same questions but he ignored her, his eyebrows furrowed.

Elle gave up after multiple attempts. She didn't understand the sudden change in attitude. She folded her arms across her chest.

After walking in silence for what felt like hours, Elle and Leonardo finally reached the double doors.

"Meet me here at 11:30 p.m. The café is a couple of doors down," Leonardo instructed. He then started to walk away. "Oh, also," he said, turning back around. "Don't tell anyone about this little adventure tonight. And bring a jacket, I hear it's going to be cold." He winked and headed back into the trees.

Elle watched him walk away, not knowing what to say. She conjured up an aggravated "ugh," and walked through the double doors. How was she possibly able to see the

Dealer tonight? It was in her favor though, as she only had ten days to come to a solution to not kill her mother. The thought hurt her chest. Why had Leonardo acted that way? One minute he's smiling over the thought of fireflies, and the next he's arguing with the most powerful Mystic in all of Remedium like he was his brother or something. And what was the haggard scroll for? Elle guessed it was the waiting list, but why didn't she have to write her name down? Why did he want to see her at midnight? He didn't even know her.

"Elle. There you are." Eryk jumped up from where he sat with Alaina and Mason. "We have to go back to training in like fifteen minutes! Where were you?"

"Showering," Elle lied. Though it was a very obvious lie, as her skin was sheened with sweat and her hair was in an unruly ponytail. Floating lanterns drifted throughout the room, and leafy vines entangled the walls. Mystics everywhere sat at various booths and tables, chatting away and eating naturally made food. She bet the fruit placed on the tables were plucked right from the trees outside.

Eryk didn't press for the truth.

"Sit down Elle, have a muffin." Alaina smiled, holding out a banana nut muffin.

Elle sat down in the wooden booth besides her. Mason was urgently writing in a worn out notebook while his glasses slowly slipped to the tip of his nose.

Elle picked at her muffin as the others talked about their plans. She couldn't quite focus on the words they were speaking because her mind was too preoccupied with the thought of the Dealer.

"Why don't you guys like the Dealer?" Elle interrupted something Alaina was saying. Mason stopped writing, Eryk stopped eating and they all looked at her.

"He's manipulative, you could say," Eryk answered, when no one else did.

"How?" Elle beckoned for more information.

"Like I said last night, he always wants something in return," Mason answered. Elle noted to herself that Mason was a good person for viable information—he had a very intellectual persona.

"So?" Elle motioned for a better explanation.

"*So* why mess with a manipulator? Everyone always regrets going to him," Eryk said.

"What has he done that's so bad?" Elle asked.

"One time a girl named Gabrielle went to ask him if there was a way to make her sister, Maurine, a Mystic without her going through the Transformation," Eryk said. "He said 'of course' and to bring her to him and he would make her a Mystic. So Gabrielle convinced her sister to come to Remedium with her just once. They went to the Dealer and he gave Gabrielle's Myst to Maurine, and Maurine's Charmer to Gabrielle, making her human again. And once you're human again there's no way to gain your Myst back, as you can't go through the Transformation more than once. It's impossible, it won't work."

"He has that kind of power?" Elle asked, perplexed. "I thought he could only see your whole past, present, and future."

"There's a whole bunch of things we don't know about him," Eryk said. "We need to get to training, though. And I'm staying this time."

"Don't know why you would want to," Elle muttered under her breath.

Eryk laughed and waved goodbye to his friends.

The sky was cloudlessly blue as they walked back to the training caves. A short wooden bridge led them to a treehouse a couple blocks down from the café.

"This isn't the fun way to the training caves, but a faster way," Eryk explained.

Elle was grateful that they took the shorter route. She didn't know how much longer her already sore muscles would last; she doubted she could make it through another training session.

The treehouse they entered was narrow and stuffy inside. Along the walls were various sized doors of different colors. Eryk stopped in front of a tall red door titled "Heliopath Training Room." As they entered, the temperature made an obvious increase.

"You are late again," Instructor Phoenix said.

"By one minute," Eryk pointed out.

The woman *hmphed* and walked away to retrieve the male instructor.

"Eryk. Leave," the male instructor demanded as he strode towards Elle.

"No, I'm staying this time," Eryk said stubbornly.

"Fine, start on your warm-ups. But if you disturb, distract, speak, motion or look at Elle, you're out," the man said.

Eryk stared the instructor in the eyes and smirked. He winked at Elle and headed to the fiery punching bags. She was curious to know how much better Eryk would be than her at the punching bags—until she realized the instructor had called it a "warm-up."

"We will proceed with the balance beam," the instructor said, his voice powerful.

Elle hopped on the start of the beam without complaining or eye rolling. She told herself she would really try this time, maybe it would make training go by faster.

The instructor handed her the substantial spear; her arms shook instantly.

"Remember your core," the instructor reminded. His arms were tucked behind his back.

Elle couldn't see where Eryk or Instructor Phoenix went, but she tried to banish them from her mind. She had to concentrate.

She took a step with her left foot; her body shook uncontrollably. She stood for a moment, taking a deep breath, concentrating on moving her right foot beside her left.

"Core," he reminded sternly.

Elle picked up her right foot and immediately fell with the spear into the water. It was icy compared to the humidity swarming the air of the cave. She swam to the top, leaving the spear at the bottom of the pool. She coughed as she resurfaced, her hair drenched.

"Again. Focus on your core."

Water splashed the floor mats as Elle heaved herself out of the icy water.

The instructor handed her another spear and she tried again, concentrating on her core muscles. She wasn't even sure what that quite meant so she just pictured her abs forming from the exercise.

When she got back on the balance beam she looked around the room to find Eryk laughing with Instructor Phoenix as he effortlessly punched the fiery bag swinging back and forth. He made it look like the bag weighed as much as a feather. It was unbelievable. And Instructor Phoenix was laughing. How was that even possible?

"Focus," the instructor glowered, snapping his fingers impatiently.

Elle turned away from Eryk and took a breath. She stepped on the balance beam. She picked up her right foot, concentrating. It landed besides the left.

"Good, it's all in the core."

Elle felt proud that he finally said something nice for once.

Fixated on her core, she took another step. She wobbled, but somehow it wasn't as hard. She looked down at her feet, precariously balanced on the beam. It was then she realized she was on fire. Her feet, legs, torso, everything. Not only was she on fire, her skin beneath the flames was bright scarlet, she *was* fire.

The spear got the best of her and she fell into the frigid water. The fire instantaneously disappeared and her skin returned to normal. She paddled to the surface, inhaling the air when she reemerged.

"You have learned," the instructor declared as Elle hoisted herself out of the water. "You now see that your fire comes from your core. Your control comes from you core. Do you understand?"

Elle took in his words. Never would she have thought that someone would be telling her fire came from her core muscles. It was astounding, nonetheless.

"Yes," she choked out, amazed, suddenly eager to learn more.

"Good," he said, pleased. "Heliopathics is not just a Myst for manipulating fire. It transforms you to become a creature of flame. When you are this creature of flame, you are more agile and strong than normal. This creature of flame is called your Heliopath form, and when you are not in that form you are technically called a Pyropath—or Pyro for short."

Enthralled, Elle consumed his words. She felt proud to be a Mystic and to be in Remedium.

"Phoenix, she is ready for you," Angel called over his shoulder.

Phoenix raised her eyebrows and grinned a devious grin.

"Perfect," she said, striding away from Eryk. She moved like elegant flames. "Okay, this shouldn't be too hard. You see those three torches over there?"

The three torches were on the complete opposite side of the cave.

"You must light one on fire with your right hand, one with your left, and one with your eyes. Sound easy?"

Elle stared at the torches. Surprisingly, she felt excited to give it a try.

"Eryk, would you like to demonstrate?" Instructor Phoenix motioned to Eryk.

Eryk confidently walked over to them. He stopped, facing Elle, looking into her eyes. He held out his left hand, and without looking at the target he lit the first torch on fire. He kept his eyes on Elle's and with his other hand twisted around his back, he lit the right torch on fire. Elle raised an eyebrow, trying not to show how impressed she was. With his body still facing hers, Eryk spun his head and lit the center torch on fire with his eyes. He looked back at her and smiled.

"Good luck," he whispered, and walked back to the punching bags.

Elle took a deep breath and turned towards the three torches. The fire from Eryk had already dwindled out. She concentrated on the first torch, refusing to be discouraged. Eryk had been a Heliopath for a lot longer than she had.

She held out her right hand in front of her. The male instructor's voice echoed in here mind, *"Core. Core. Core."*

She looked at the target one more time, closed her eyes and breathed. Then she released a bolt of agile fire to the torch.

She opened her eyes to see the torch exactly the way it was before. Unlit and now mocking her.

"Try again, and keep your eyes open this time," Instructor Phoenix advised.

Elle took another deep breath and stared right at the torch—the stable, uninflamed torch. She shot out her right hand, keeping her eyes open, and shot a string of fire at the torch. It caught the flame and illuminated the space around it.

Elle smiled, proud. She looked at Instructor Phoenix for an approving countenance, but all she got was, "And the next one..."

Elle lit the next one with no problem and the center one with her eyes after the third try.

"Good, you can leave now," Instructor Phoenix said, looking somewhat satisfied.

"Really?" Elle asked, surprised. The time had gone much faster for this session.

"Be back after dinner. And do not be late," the other instructor demanded.

"We have all afternoon, what do you want to do?" Eryk asked as they walked into the cool fresh air.

"I don't know," Elle said. "What is there to do in Remedium?"

"Everything." Eryk smiled. "Anything you want."

Elle pondered the options. What she truly wanted was a simple tour of Remedium, as she had no idea where anything was. But as they walked along the cliff she remembered her aching muscles.

"Is there anything that doesn't require loads of walking?" Elle asked.

Eryk touched his finger to his chin. "Like I said this morning, you should see the Meadows."

"Okay," Elle agreed. "After lunch?"

"Of course. Lunch is in thirty minutes; you might want to shower first. Meet you in the café?"

"Yeah, I'll see you there," Elle said, starting to walk away.

"Elle?"

"Yeah?"

"The showers are this way," he pointed in the opposite direction.

Her cheeks became red, as she started to walk with Eryk again.

Soon they reached the showers and Eryk left her to go find Mason.

Remedium was much quieter when she was not around Eryk. Elle could faintly hear Mystics talking to each other in the distance. Birds soared over the bristling trees in the careful breeze. It was quite peaceful.

Elle took a quick cold shower. A bar of lavender scented soap was already there, along with towels and cloths. She rinsed off and put her sweaty clothes back on, as she had no choice. She re-did her ponytail and slid on her shoes. *I really need some clothes*, she thought. She noted to herself to find Alaina soon for help about that.

Just as Elle walked out of the shower entrances, Leonardo was walking out of the woods.

He ignored her and kept walking.

She jogged up to him, not knowing why.

"Can I help you, Carroway?" Leonardo scoffed.

She pursed her lips, "Where's the direction of the café, again?"

He stopped in his tracks and looked down at her. His messy gold hair fell into his dark brown—almost black—eyes.

"Do you need a map?" he asked, irritated.

"Kinda," she admitted.

"Three blocks down," he said.

He walked away and so did Elle.

She walked in the direction he pointed, keeping an eye out for the massive double doors. A few twists and turns later she came across a long, feeble bridge. She couldn't make out what was on the other side, except for more patches of forests and treehouses connected with ladders and bridges. She shrugged and began to walk along the wooden steps. She didn't dare to look below her, as she could feel the high altitude creeping on her skin. Right now the bridge wasn't too daunting, but it could become unsteady if the wind were to pick up or if it was too dark to know where to step, because several steps were missing every couple feet.

Surely enough she reached the other side and looked around. With her head tilted as far back as she could, she saw various sized treehouses overlapping the tall, overgrown trees. Mystics entered and exited different houses and climbed along the ladders and tunnels, all conversing and laughing with one another. The village was inexplicably beautiful. Elle never wanted to leave this place. But somehow she had to save her mother, and get Emmie there, as well. The words "ten days" echoed in her brain.

She started along a circular tunnel path made of tree limbs. Surely enough, the grand double doors made an appearance. She went inside to find her three friends sitting at a table, already eating.

She took a seat next to Alaina—except that Alaina didn't look like the Alaina Elle met a few days ago. Her hair was wavy and long to her hips. It was so dark it was almost blue—like a raven. Her eyes were vigorously blue, rather than the simple coffee brown eyes to which Elle was accustomed. She wore blue eye shadow and blue lipstick. Alaina's Myst was altogether extraordinary.

As they ate and conversed, Elle stared out the café's large glass window, taking in the scenery and fresh, clean air. She watched the Mystics walking by, each one beautiful and unique. They all looked like humans in one way, but there was something peculiarly gorgeous about them. Elle didn't realize it herself, but that's how she looked as well with her flowing black hair that draped around her shoulders, and her deep honey brown eyes that made her seem innocent but bewitching at the same time. Her mother had carried her very same eyes.

Mason told her how he came to Remedium. His story blew Elle away. He had lived with only his mother, who he was super close with. They lived in a rough part of New York and his mom was caught up in a lot of bad things. He watched her get shot when he was only ten. After that, he lived with his grandmother but struggled with insomnia and

PTSD. He passionately said that nobody has any idea what real insomnia is like. Only because you stay up until five in the morning because "you can't fall asleep" does not mean you're an insomniac. And only because you visit the school counselor because you're "stressed" does not mean you have an anxiety disorder. He said he couldn't stand those kinds of people, because insomnia was the pressure of your eyes and your heart and your body buzzing to keep you awake, the constant rhythm of your heartbeat pounding at your brain to stay awake. Insomnia was the bruising eyes and aching body. Post-traumatic stress was not hoping something doesn't happen again. Post-traumatic stress was the reliving and reliving and reliving and reliving of watching your mother cut herself, slam the door on you. It was the reliving of watching your mother walk away from you and get shot before your eyes. Post-traumatic stress was not the typical breakdowns in the middle of the night. It was the constant reminder that your mother was shot in front of you. The constant sound of the gun from someone closing a door or dropping a pencil to the floor.

Elle found a whole new respect for Mason. She couldn't fully grasp the idea that everyone in Remedium had such deep, intense stories like her and Mason.

They ate and talked for another solid hour. The boys never seemed to get full. Alaina left about halfway through, and Elle couldn't help but notice Mason frown as she walked away.

"We can go to the Meadows now, if you want," Eryk said, standing up from their table.

"Okay," Elle said. "Mason, do you want to come?"

Eryk and Mason made eye contact and seemed to communicate telepathically.

"That's okay Elle. See you later." Mason rushed out of the café, into the sunny climate.

Eryk and Elle walked out of the double doors into the trees and sun. It felt much warmer now that it was the afternoon. They began their journey to the Meadows, walking along the sea of trees. The sky was crystal clear and bluer than any sky back home. The sun was golden and watchful, while the trees were protective and lovely. But the zap of Tabitha's voice telling Elle she had only ten days to rescue her mother echoed in her mind.

"Eryk, there's something I need to tell you," Elle blurted, hindering the silence.

"Yeah?" he asked. He didn't sound nervous, only casual.

"Last night, after everyone left, Tabitha told me I only had ten days, counting today, to find a solution to rescue my mother."

Eryk bit on his lips, his eyebrows furrowing, "And what if you don't?"

"Then I have to kill her," Elle said. The words stung.

Eryk drew in a loud breath and shook his head. Elle watched as his expression transformed.

"We'll find a way, Elle. Don't worry. We're going to help you no matter the cost."

Though it was nice to hear, it didn't calm the storm in Elle's mind.

"We'll figure out a plan with Mason and Alaina," Eryk said after Elle didn't say anything. "I think you'll feel better after you see the Meadows."

Elle took a deep breath and followed Eryk into a thicker web of trees.

To get her mind off the complicated mess, Eryk asked Elle questions about Emmie and why she loved her mother so much. What her favorite book was, and what she didn't like about the Everson's. He asked her where her favorite place to be was and what her favorite memory was. He asked what she valued about others, and what she wanted to get out of life. How she liked her tea, and why she didn't enjoy thunderstorms. She told him about her mother's compassion and bravery. She told him she loved being around trees because they made her feel free. She explained how she liked people who made effort, and who were gentle with their words. She told him about how wise Emmie was and how she would probably make a better Mystic than her. She explained to him that the Everson's tried to make her happy, but it wasn't happiness she needed, she needed life. She didn't need therapy sessions and whiney kids, she needed to experience how the real world worked outside of foster care and court rooms. She told him she didn't prefer tea, and rain wasn't her favorite because that meant she was stuck inside with the Everson's all day.

"Emmie loved the rain though. She always pleaded with Mrs. Everson to let her play in the rain. I miss her. When will I be able to see her again?" Elle asked.

"Elle, there's something I need to explain to you," Eryk said.

Elle's expression dropped. "What is it?" she asked.

"When someone becomes a Mystic and joins Remedium, everyone they knew on earth changes. I mean, their memory is altered so they don't remember them," Eryk winced at the words, too afraid to look at Elle's face.

Elle didn't say anything. She stopped in her tracks, staring down at her feet.

"Their life doesn't change at all—circumstances or outcomes don't change, only their memory of you specifically," Eryk said, trying to make it better.

"Oh," was all Elle could muster up.

"But that's okay. Emmie is still safe with the Everson's," Eryk tried again. Nothing helped. "And you can always visit her, check on her, get her to come to Remedium if she becomes Indwelled."

"So if Emmie were to see me right now, she wouldn't recognize me?" Elle asked in only a whisper.

"That's right."

"Oh."

Eryk understood her silence and let her think for the rest of the walk to the Meadows.

When they finally reached the Meadows a slight breeze whistled through the timber. The sight was magical and enchanting. Eryk was right, Elle fell in love with the place the second she stepped through the gate. She tried to extinguish the thought of losing Emmie out of her mind as she walked through the soft green grass that covered their ankles and stretched for miles. Lilacs and baby breaths swept the floor and bushes. Different colored flowers sang in harmony throughout. A stream of fresh water trickled nearby and in the far distance a visible majestic waterfall dazzled in the golden sunlight. Hummingbirds cooed from their nests, while orange and blush butterflies pirouetted through the fresh air. Bees collected nectar from all the blooming flowers and hanging tree branches slept beneath the immaculate sky.

"Do you like it?" Eryk asked, in an attempt to take her mind elsewhere.

"It's beautiful," Elle said.

Eryk stifled a laugh. "I come here after training a lot."

Elle turned to face Eryk.

"Why do you like training so much?" she asked.

"I just...I don't know," Eryk said, trying to find the right words. "It's very therapeutic, you could say."

"How?" Elle asked.

"I don't know. When I came to Remedium and was Transformed, everything just seemed so unbelievable. I never had a mother or a father really, and Angel and Phoenix filled that void, I guess. They didn't give up on me, and I didn't want to give up. They were determined to help me," Eryk explained.

"Angel?" Elle said. "That's his name?"

"Yeah, Angel and Phoenix aren't their real names, though," Eryk answered.

"What are their real names?"

Eryk smiled. "You always have so many questions. The Transformation didn't change that about you." Elle shrugged her shoulders, she was only curious. "Don't worry, I love it." He smiled and looked down at the overgrown grass. "Phoenix's name is Dzana, and Angel's is Sasha. Angel was her Seeker."

"Interesting."

"It is pretty cool actually. They fell in love right when they met. Angel started calling Dzana 'Phoenix' because he said she was like a bird of fire—that she was very talented right from the start."

Elle could see how Phoenix got her name. The way she moved, the way she spoke, it was all very elegant and strong like a bird. The nickname fit her well.

"And Angel got his nickname because his students called him the Angel of Fire because he was so powerful and confident and ambitious," Eryk further explained.

"They're very, um...what's the word? Evil," Elle said, only half joking.

Eryk laughed. "They aren't *evil*. They're just determined to get you the best as you can be. I promise, they get better."

"Mmm hmm."

"They're really good people, Elle. They're very caring. They helped me a lot when I first came here," Eryk tried.

The continued to wander along the beds of grass, through wild flower patches of black-eyed-Susans and cherry trees.

Elle distracted herself from the echoing thoughts of Emmie by asking Eryk more questions about his life prior to being a Mystic. More about his sister, Ashlee, and his stepfather. What his favorite film was and where he grew up. She asked him about his morals and beliefs and his political views. About his dream destination and what he hoped for in the future. She asked him about how he met Mason and Alaina. He told her how Ashlee was insane but she was one of the most thoughtful people he'd ever known. He explained how his stepfather was about the complete opposite of him and they never agreed on anything. He told her he hated politics and ignored it at all costs. He said he would love to travel all over the world, how he didn't have a number one place he wanted to go, he wanted to go everywhere. He told her how he liked exotic and insightful people—the kind of people who could think well in any situation. He valued determination and authenticity. He explained to her how Mason found him because he was his Seeker.

"And then I Seeked Alaina and we remained friends. Then Mason told me he liked her, so we all became friends. Don't tell Mason I told you that," Eryk explained.

"As if it's not obvious?" Elle laughed. "He's clearly in love with her!"

Eryk laughed. "Yeah, he doesn't know that though."

"It's funny those two, Mason and Alaina."

"What do you mean?" Eryk asked.

"Well, they're complete opposites, aren't they? A perfect binary," Elle said.

"They are," Eryk nodded in agreement.

They walked under the warm afternoon sun. After a while, they sat in the intricate tree branches, overlooking the Meadows and part of Remedium. Elle wanted to live there, right in the Meadows.

"Eryk, I have a question," Elle said. "Why did my mother become a Charmer?"

Eryk looked taken back at the sudden change in topics, but complied. "Like Tabitha said, your dad was Indwelled when he killed her."

"No, I know that. But why would that matter?" Elle inquired.

"What do you mean?"

"I mean, my mother never did anything wrong. She was never possessed. So why would it matter if she was killed by someone who was? She never intended..." Elle's words dwindled off in the silent peace of the Meadows.

Eryk pondered the thought for a moment.

"Perhaps one person's evil can be carried to another," he said. "Sometimes people don't ask to become monsters. Perhaps evil is contagious."

Elle took in the words. Insightful words, they were.

"I'm sorry she's your Charmer, Elle. I really wish you didn't have to go through this. I couldn't imagine."

Elle looked at his stunning eyes. They were soft and thoughtful. She wondered why he was so kind and helpful to her. She wondered why he had to go through the things he went through to become the person he is now. And she wondered the same about herself.

Before she could reply, Eryk spoke again.

"I couldn't imagine how I would deal with having my mother as my Charmer. I never really knew my own mother. I'm not even sure what she looks like. I always imagined her looking like Ashlee. All I know is that her name is Marie. Even though I never had a relationship with her, I still can't imagine having to kill her because she was my Charmer. Killing my actual Charmer was hard enough. No one truly wants to do it. When you pick up that sword used to kill Charmers, and look into your Charmer's face, you see their desperate pleading expression; it says, 'Don't kill me.' And you see their soulless eyes, their deteriorated body, and know that is the creature that drove you to insanity—the creature that's been in your head this whole time, causing panic attacks from overthinking, causing post-traumatic stress and never being able to live the same. And you look at that monster before you. And you tell it 'I am in control of my mind, not you.' And you behead the demon with the sword out of anger, out of grief, out of insanity. And then—and then that monster of your mind perishes, and it lies on the floor in a heap of skin and bones, and you look at it, not being able to catch your breath."

Eryk stared at the waterfall in the background. His chest moved fast. It seemed as if Remedium was muted.

"It's a question without an answer," Elle said. "You go years asking yourself, asking the world, maybe God, 'Why me?' But that question is never answered. So you take what comes to you and handle it. You deal with it the best you can. One day at a time."

"And that is why we are here," Eryk said. "Because we took it one day at a time."

They continued to talk for hours. They climbed different trees and took off their shoes to skip in the stream. The water was cold and clear. Little fish said hello. Eryk gathered every flower he could muster and handed them each to Elle. Oranges and greens and yellows and blues. Something in Elle's chest felt different. Something felt looser, like a snap of a rubber band. She didn't know if it was the freshness of Remedium's air, but she felt like she could breathe again.

Soon the sun began to slide down the blue sky, creating shades of purple and gold, and the grass became cold beneath their feet.

"We should probably head back to the café," Eryk said.

"Okay," said Elle.

They walked through the Meadow's black iron gate and headed to the cafe. The walk no longer seemed long. Elle felt as if Remedium was timeless.

They entered the double doors yet again and luckily the café wasn't crowded yet.

"Is this the only place for food around here?" Elle asked.

Eryk chuckled. "No, it's not. We have a cafeteria and kitchens for each training room. That's where we were the first night you were here, the Heliopath's training room kitchen—and we have a market if you want to stalk your own food in your bungalow, but this is typically where Mason and I go, because it's usually not as busy as the cafeteria."

Elle nodded her head as Mason and Alaina sat down across from them.

The four Mystics ate together. Elle felt comfortable with Mason, Alaina and Eryk. They were easy to talk with and never left her out of the conversation; though she only had more questions to ask.

After dinner Eryk and Elle walked back to the training rooms.

"You are late." Instructor Phoenix scowled as soon as they walked through the door.

"No, we aren't," Eryk argued. "We're four minutes early, actually."

"Whatever. Start on your warm ups, both of you," Phoenix instructed.

Elle and Eryk began their warm ups, though Elle was nowhere near Eryk's level. Her punching bag still didn't budge, and only reopened the scabs on her hands and feet. They were to punch two hundred times on both arms, and kick three hundred times on each leg, because of Elle's "unbalanced" problem.

"Thanks, Elle," Eryk hissed, half joking.

"Don't mention it."

After their warm ups they did several kinds of drills focused on aiming, agility, stamina and core strengthening. And again, Eryk had no problem while Elle struggled behind him. But it was obvious to Angel and Phoenix that she was improving.

When they were dismissed Elle realized the time. It was 12:02 and Leonardo told her to meet him at 11:30 by the double doors.

Eryk was talking about something as they exited the cave but Elle was lost in thought. How was she supposed to get there in time?

"...and I'll take you back to your bungalow," Eryk offered.

"No, that's okay," Elle said.

"What?" Eryk asked, confused.

"I want to stay here and talk to Instructor Phoenix a bit," Elle lied.

Eryk looked at her skeptically.

"I do, I'll figure my way back to the bungalows," she insisted, her words fast.

Eryk bit the side of his cheek, one eye raised. "You hate Phoenix."

"Yes, I know. But maybe I should get to know her, so I hate her less," Elle said.

"Okay, whatever," Eryk said, walking away. "Goodnight."

"Night." Elle waited for him to get out of view and then made her way to the double doors by memory.

She walked fast, practically running. *Please still be there, please still be there.*

Elle turned another corner and at last she saw the golden double doors, and Leonardo leaning against them, his hands in his jacket pockets.

"There you are, Carroway," he said, standing up straight as he noticed her. "Ready to make a deal with the Dealer?"

Chapter 6

They headed into the woodland of trees. It was quite difficult to see anything that wasn't directly in front of them. Leaves crunched beneath their feet as they walked in silence.

"How do you know where to go?" Elle asked, her hands out in front of her so she wouldn't run into hanging tree limbs.

"I just know," Leonardo clipped.

Elle dropped the subject. It astounded her that Leonardo could make his way through the jungle of trees effortlessly during both daylight and darkness. He must've known the woods very well.

They continued through the thick leaves in darkness. The trees were so tall that the stars in the sky weren't visible anymore.

A rustle of leaves sounded behind them, sending goosebumps up Elle's arms.

"What was that?" Elle asked nervously. Stopping in her tracks, she looked around wide-eyed. Leonardo carried on in front of her, unbothered by the disturbance.

"It's just Anastasia," he called over his shoulder.

Elle caught up to Leonardo before she could lose sight of him.

"Who?" she asked.

"My sister. The 'Dealer' wanted her to come," Leonardo explained, using hand quotations when he said "dealer."

"Why?" Elle asked.

"Does it matter?" he snapped.

Anastasia jogged up to them. Only the silhouette of her face was evident in the tenebrous lighting.

"Didn't care to wait for me, Leo?" Anastasia growled. Though it was dark, it was easy to see her obvious eye roll.

"Oops, Annie. Must've forgot," Leonardo said.

The three walked without talking, Anastasia's arms folded across her chest.

"Don't even know why I had to come," Anastasia jeered, her nose in the air.

"Wasn't my idea," Leonardo said.

"Can't take care of yourself, can you, baby brother? Need your big sister to come along with you?"

Leonardo ignored her.

Elle walked awkwardly two steps behind the siblings. It interested her that Anastasia was older than Leonardo—she didn't picture Leonardo being the younger child in his family. Although, Anastasia couldn't've been that much older, because they looked practically the same age.

The wind picked up as they walked farther along. The closer they got to the center of the forest, the harder it was to see.

"Hey, Heliopath, some light would be helpful at the moment," Anastasia said.

She didn't know how Anastasia knew that she was a Heliopath, and she hadn't even thought about using her fire as a light source. All this time walking, it never even occurred to her that she possessed the ability to make light. Hopefully all the hours of training today would pay off for this one moment.

She focused on her core and snapped her fingers—like Eryk did—and surely enough, flicks of light bounced on her fingernails.

The flames were captivating. Though, Leonardo and Anastasia didn't seem nearly as fascinated, they didn't even say thank you.

The walk to the Dealer's adobe was a notably long walk. Elle didn't understand how Leonardo knew the way so clearly, as every tree looked the same in the darkness. Elle was cautious to not catch any drooping leaves or vines on fire. She wondered if that had ever happened before.

The closer they got to the center of the forest, the colder it became. The soil beneath the Mystics' feet was chilled and moist. Spiky leaves were bleak against their skin. Elle's feet and legs became sore and were beginning to feel like Jell-O as they arrived to the windowless, uninviting adobe. A shiver rang throughout Elle's body.

Leonardo knocked on the front wall of the miniature home—though it did not look like much of home.

"It's me. I have Ellisia," Leonardo hollered as he continued to knock. Anastasia stood beside him with her arms crossed; she almost looked bored.

Suddenly four black lines were being drawn across the concrete wall. They formed a rectangle together, which became three dimensional. A doorknob began to fashion into place and soon enough an entrance to the adobe was magically constructed. Leonardo twisted the knob and walked inside. Anastasia—with her arms still crossed—followed, and then Elle.

Inside the lighting was dim, but the space did not appear to match the rundown exterior by any means. The interior was elegant and luxurious. The carpets were deep blue and the walls were black; glass lamps and vases were placed all around. Magnificent intricate curtains were hung above and on the walls. Elle always associated the word "magical" with Remedium; but magical didn't quite fit this place. No, this space was much more cryptic.

"Ellisia Carroway, at last," a voice from the corner mused. "It is such a pleasure to finally meet you."

A man—the Dealer—stood up from a chair behind a grand desk. He glided over to where Elle stood. She glared up at him as he took her hand and shook it firmly in both of his. He closed his eyes and inhaled deeply as if he were taking in the moment.

"Please, sit," he said as he pulled out one of the three chairs sitting in front of the regal desk.

Elle sat down hesitantly. She had a bad feeling stirring in her stomach; *maybe this wasn't a good idea*, she thought. Leonardo and Anastasia took a seat on either side of her. They looked relaxed, almost comfortable, beside her. As the tension festered in her shoulders and throat, she realized that she felt trapped.

The Dealer sat across from her behind a cherry wood desk. He intertwined his fingers together and stared into Elle's eyes. Uncomfortable as she was, she stared back at him, her back straight. He was much older than her and the Mystics sitting on either side of her; he was probably around Tabitha's age, maybe a little older. He had deep ebony eyes. They were so dark, yet so entrancing they looked like crystals. Like obsidian. He had dark hair that reached his shoulders and blended in with his beard. He reminded Elle of a crow.

He smiled. "You are a very interesting soul, I don't believe I have ever stumbled upon someone as yourself."

Elle gulped at the words. She felt the same way about him.

He chuckled. "Ellisia, do you know what I do? Do you know why Mystics from all over Remedium come to me for advice?"

Elle couldn't find her voice while she watched his snake-like lips move as he spoke. She nodded her head.

"Do tell me," the Dealer beckoned.

Elle took a breath. "I've heard that you are powerful. That you can read people, that you can see their future, past and present."

The Dealer nodded his head slowly, a smirk caressing across his face.

"That would be correct. Not only that. When I touch or make eye contact with an individual, I know them. I know their thoughts, their character, who they truly are. I see every side, perspective and shape of them. I know their purity, morality and beliefs. I know them better than they know themselves. I know what is best for them. And I am here to help them, as I am here to help you," the Dealer explained.

"So you can help me then? Truly help me find a way around killing my mother?"

"Yes, of course. Your mother, Jadine Esmund-Carroway. A brave and generous soul, with big ambitions, more than she can handle. Trusting, too trusting. She loved you. My, she loved you more than any living creature walking the planet. You carry her name in the middle of yours. Jade. Lovely name. You resemble her much, don't you?" The

Dealer was staring into the distance as if daydreaming every syllable. "But your sister, Emmaline, resembles your father much more. She carries his green eyes. Not much Filipino runs through her exterior. You don't want to admit it, but it bothers you that she looks your father. You love her as much as your mother does of course, but you feel like you will never escape your father when you look into her eyes. Perhaps that is why you always distanced yourself from her?"

"Alright!" Elle burst out, scaring herself. She couldn't handle the flashback. She did not want to think of Emmie and how she could never see her again. How she could have been a much better sister and role model to her when she still had her. She did not want to think any of those things.

"My apologies, your reading comes on quite strong. It's impossible not to analyze every detail. You had such an extraordinary life," the Dealer said in a whisper, which was actually more of a hiss.

Elle would never have chosen the word "extraordinary" to explain her life, and she would have never dreamed of anyone knowing she didn't enjoy Emmie's eyes. She loved her baby sister with all of her heart, even if her eyes were unbearable to look at—she still would do anything in the world to protect and love her forever.

"I need your help," Elle carried on, changing the subject back to the point. She didn't know if it was polite to call him the Dealer to his face, so she decided to stay away from the word. "After my Transformation the other night, when it came to the Reveal we found out—"

"That your mother was your Charmer," the Dealer finished.

Elle nodded, Leonardo shifted in his seat, and Anastasia stared vacantly at her nails.

"How can that happen?" Leonardo asked.

"Jadine Esmund became a Charmer because David Carroway killed her when he was Hosted. And just like any Charmer, she needed to feed off of traumatic memories to stay alive. She already knew a source—her own daughter," the Dealer explained.

"I know that, but why would she choose her own daughter?" Leonardo questioned. The words hurt Elle's ears. Although, she was curious herself.

"I have yet to look at or touch Jadine, and when I do, I will have your answer," the Dealer said.

"I thought she was here?" Leonardo inquired.

Anastasia shot him a fierce look.

"They're moving her here today," the Dealer said, eyeing him.

"Wait, why? My mother will be here, with you? Why?" Elle asked.

"They keep the Charmers here with me when they need to be kept longer. Nothing to worry about, young Ellisia," the Dealer rationalized.

"Why though?" Elle beckoned.

The Dealer looked at Anastasia, then Leonardo and back at Elle.

"They just do," he said with finality.

"They just—" Elle began.

"She will be here with me and nothing will happen to her. Do you want my help or not?" the Dealer scowled. The tone of his voice was fierce, and even Anastasia tensed up slightly.

All Elle could do was nod her head again. This man wasn't a man you questioned. He wasn't the kind of man you got answers from, either.

"Darling, you will have to learn how to use your voice if you want something. I will say it again; do you want my help or not?" Each word slid off of his tongue like dripping frigid water from stalactites.

"Yes," the word shook through her teeth.

"Wonderful," the Dealer smiled maliciously. "The final way to become a citizen of the Villages of Remedium, is to kill your Charmer and sign your name on the Tree of Remedium. If you don't have a Charmer though, you won't be able to kill it. Let's say your mother isn't a Charmer anymore," the Dealer pitched.

"Can you do that?" Elle's voice filled with hope. "Make my mother human again?"

"I can. If you do something for me."

"Anything," the word left Elle's lips before she could think it.

The Dealer grinned. "I will need you to gather three ingredients in order for me to create a potion that will transform your mother back into a human. Before I tell you what they are, I need you to sign this contract." He opened a drawer in the massive desk and pulled out a scroll and pen. "This informs you that you will perform the task and finish the task for me, and that you will not go back on your word at any given time. That you are loyal to me and trust my assistance."

He placed the pen and the scroll in front of Elle. It was thinned and yellowed. Words covered it from top to bottom with a tiny line underneath for her signature. She signed it with confidence. She was going to save her mother.

"Wonderful." The Dealer smirked and took the scroll immediately from her.

Elle couldn't hold the shudder within her. She was hopeful again, but something inside her moved uneasily.

The Dealer took out another scroll and smoothed it out in front of them. He read it aloud.

"Here are the three ingredients: Number 1) I will die in the fall and be buried in December, though I will entrance you with rest of my recommenced members. Number 2) You have not listened to me. You have shattered me; you have damaged me forever. You cannot live without me. I am close to Hades sleeping with the man who took two of me and created two of me. And the third riddle you will receive when you find the second."

The words sunk into Elle's mind. These weren't ingredients, these were riddles, methodical crafted riddles.

"But those aren't—" Elle stuttered.

"That's all I will give you. Goodbye." The Dealer stood up from his chair.

Elle stood up with him, infuriated. She wasn't here to solve some meticulous riddles; she was here to save her mother. Now with only nine days left she didn't have any time to waste. She couldn't simply sit around solving riddles. She needed the ingredients single handedly. He had to know that.

"But I only have nine days to save her! I don't have time—" Elle's voice gave out as she watched the Dealer walk away from where they sat. "You never said—" she tried again. "You can't just walk away!"

The Dealer didn't stop as he turned the corner that lead to a dark hallway. The rage thundered through Elle's chest. This is what everyone had meant when they said the Dealer was "tricky." She didn't have any time, she needed to collect these ingredients before her nine days were up. She had to tell Eryk, Alaina and Mason as soon as she possibly could. They could help her, the Dealer never said anything about not having someone help her. She had to talk to them immediately.

Elle stomped to where they entered the adobe and the four black lines appeared once more. She threw herself out of the door and began walking into the forestry of darkness. Maddened with the unexpected twist of events, she ignored Leonardo calling her name from behind.

"Ellisia, calm down!" Leonardo hollered as he caught up to her.

She began to walk faster, with tongues of flames wavering her arms, making their way up her neck.

"You're going to burn down Remedium, take a breath!" Leonardo shouted.

She mumbled furiously and picked up her pace even more, until she was practically jogging.

"One, you're running the wrong direction, and two, you're catching leaves on fire," Leonardo hollered as he ran with her. "Freaking Heliopaths," he said to himself.

Elle took no notice of his words as hands of flames snatched passing branches of leaves. Her skin became glassy red again like it did in training as the fire thickened.

Leonardo ran in front of her and shielded her from going another step. She collided into him full force and fell onto the forest floor. The fire dwindled down, and Leonardo quickly patted down the few ashes that attached themselves to his shirt.

His words flooded into her mind. He was right. She needed to calm down before all of the Village was burned down.

"I have to go talk to Eryk," she said, catching her breath as the flames dissipated.

Leonardo rolled his eyes and helped her up.

"It's almost two o'clock. Talk to him in the morning," Leonardo said. They started to walk again, this time in the correct direction to the bungalows.

Elle was silent for a moment as they walked through the trees. Her adrenaline was pumping, and every so often a flicker of flames would dance on her skin.

"Tabitha told me I only had ten days to figure something out. If I don't..." Elle couldn't bring herself to say the words again. Her mind was spinning in all directions.

"It's not really your mother, you know?"

"Yes, she is," Elle snapped back. "She's my mother until those ten—now nine—days are up. Unless I figure out these stupid riddles."

"Right, well good thing I grabbed them for you," Leonardo pulled the now folded scroll of riddles out of his jacket pocket and handed it to her.

She snatched it from his hands without a thank you.

They continued to walk through the darkness. It was difficult to see, but Elle was too scared she wouldn't be able to control her Myst. She was lucky that the few leaves that caught on fire had dwindled out quickly.

"I'm not going to kill my mother."

"I wouldn't want to either," Leonardo said in only a whisper. He looked down at his black boots when he said it.

The walk from the Dealer's adobe to the bungalow seemed much shorter than the one from the café. When they stepped away from the few final trees, the sapphire sky was brilliant with gold stars and a silver crescent moon.

Elle didn't say anything as she walked away from him. She didn't expect for him to follow her; she never saw him by the bungalows.

Elle glanced behind her but he was already gone, consumed by the mountain of leaves. The silhouette of the forest against the silver radiation from the moon resembled a castle—a beautiful, magnificent castle of leaves.

Elle typed in her address and her bungalow door appeared a moment later. She turned the knob and stepped in. To her surprise the lights were brightly turned on with Eryk, Alaina and Mason sitting impatiently on the sofa.

"Where've you been?" Alaina asked as Elle entered the room.

Eryk and Mason were in the room as well. They stared at her, anticipating her response. She was stuck. She couldn't lie or dance around the truth as she'd originally planned; there was no breaking her deal with the Dealer.

"I need your help," Elle blurted out, as she plopped down on one of the sofas and slid the riddles in front of her. "I didn't listen to you guys, and I'm sorry, I should have. But it's too late to turn back now."

"Wait, what are you talking about?" Eryk nearly yelled.

"I went to the Dealer tonight and we made a deal," Elle began.

"You what?"

"Leonardo took me to see him, and we made a deal. He said he could make my mother human again if I find all the ingredients that can make the potion," Elle spoke rapidly. Eryk rolled his eyes in fury at the mention of Leonardo.

"What are the ingredients?" Mason inquired.

"I don't know! That's the problem, he only gave me these riddles to solve in order to know what they are," Elle explained, anxiety building in her chest.

"Wait, so, you don't know even know what they are, much less *where* they are?" Alaina asked.

"No, I don't know anything," Elle said. "And I only have nine more days to figure something out. I can't kill my mother. I can't do it, and this is the only answer—these riddles."

"I'll help you. Let me read them," Alaina offered.

"I'll help, too," Eryk said quietly.

Relief flooded Elle. She thought Eryk would be furious with her for going behind his back. She figured he would never help her, or even listen to her explanation. She had obviously misjudged him.

"I will die in the fall and be buried in December, though I will entrance you with the rest of my recommenced members," Alaina read aloud.

The room went quiet. Everyone's thoughts went silent as they took in the words.

Alaina read it again.

"Maybe we should sleep on it," Alaina suggested after nobody said anything. "It's two in the morning."

"Elle is supposed to be at training in a couple of hours." Eryk sighed. It didn't feel like two in the morning to Elle. The adrenaline had dissolved all the exhaustion from yesterday's activities.

"I'll go tell Angel and Phoenix what happened. Alaina and Mason, you go talk to Tabitha. And Elle, you get some rest," Eryk proposed.

"Sounds good," Mason said, while getting up from the sofa. Alaina followed him out the door with the scroll of riddles in her hands.

Eryk and Elle sat alone in the bungalow. Elle had light purple bags underneath her eyes.

"I'm sorry, but I can't just go to sleep while you guys are busy solving the problem I created," Elle said.

Eryk shook his head. She was right, there was no way to turn back on a deal with the Dealer after the scroll was signed.

"You don't have to apologize. I understand," Eryk said, not looking up at her. "We're going to figure this out."

Elle looked at him, hopeful. Did they really have a chance?

"Get some rest," he said. "I'll be back soon."

Chapter 7

A couple of hours passed but Elle laid awake in the bunkbed, her eyes peeled wide open. Her mind wouldn't shut up. Ten days. Nine days. Heliopaths. Fire. Training. Riddles. The Dealer. Her Charmer. Her Mother.

There was a desperate knock at the door taking Elle out of her repetitious thoughts.

"Elle, it's me, Eryk."

Elle half crawled, half fell, from her bed and stumbled to the door to open it.

"Did you sleep at all?" Eryk asked as he flicked on the light switch. The light was rudely invasive to her eyes.

"No," Elle said, rubbing her eyes. "Did you find out anything?"

"Yes," Eryk answered, as the bungalow door opened again.

Mason and Alaina walked through the door.

"I have a theory," Eryk said.

"What's your theory?" Mason asked as he sat on the sofa. Alaina took a seat across from him.

"I talked to Angel and Phoenix and they both agreed the riddle sounds like some sort of plant. So on my way over here, as I took in the sight of Remedium, it occurred to me that, what if it's the Tree of Remedium?" Eryk said.

"The Dealer wants the Tree of Remedium?" Alaina questioned dubiously.

"It makes sense though," Mason interjected. "'Though I will entrance you with the rest of my recommenced members.' Recommenced means restart, so 'restarted members'. We're all restarted when we go through the Transformation. Well, 'reborn' is a better word for it. And the signatures of the members on the Tree are hypnotic to humans."

"The Dealer wants the entire Tree of Remedium?" Alaina repeated. "That seems highly unlikely."

Everyone looked at each other, stumped for conclusions.

"Maybe it's only part of the Remedium Tree," Mason offered. "Trees don't die in the fall, only the leaves do," Mason further explained.

"So the Dealer wants every single leaf on the Tree of Remedium?" Alaina asked.

They were lost in thought again. None of it made sense. The second they came to a solution, the illogic outweighed it again.

"There's nowhere in this riddle that tells us how much," Eryk sighed.

"But that has to be the answer," Mason said.

"I'll talk more about it with Angel and Phoenix. Elle and I have to go to training," Eryk said.

"And what do we do?" Mason asked.

"You and Alaina can ask around, research and get as much information as you can on the Tree of Remedium. There's something we're missing," Eryk said. "Let's just figure this out, we need to know a location to go to tomorrow."

"Tomorrow?" Elle asked. "We need to leave today, right now!"

"We can't," Eryk said. "Tabitha wants you to get more training before we leave."

Elle huffed in defeat. All she could think about was the clock ticking away the seconds she had left to save her mother.

"It's okay," Alaina reassured her. "I'll start gathering as much information as I can right now."

"I'll come with you," Mason followed, although Alaina didn't say anything in return.

Elle and Eryk made their way to the second entrance to the Heliopath training room. This one was the closest to the bungalows but had the most bridges—six total. Some of them swayed above flowing rivers or streams, and others tangled in intricate tree branches.

They reached the treehouse and stepped inside the training room. The temperature increased significantly, as each torch was delicately aflame.

"We must get started," Instructor Angel declared as soon as he laid eyes on Elle. "You are leaving to go on this Quest tomorrow, am I correct?"

"Yes," Eryk confirmed.

By tomorrow they would only have eight days left, and they still had no idea what or where the ingredients were. But Elle had to stay focused.

They started on their strengthening warm ups with one hundred punches on each arm, and one hundred kicks on each leg. This time the fiery bag budged slightly, but Eryk's swayed like the tree branches in the wind. Although this made Elle angry, she liked the competition. She wanted to be as good of a Heliopath as Eryk, or better.

After the warm-up, Elle practiced transforming into her fiery form with Instructor Phoenix. She watched Eryk transform first. One minute he was Eryk, and the next he was fire. The sight was—she couldn't deny—quite terrifying. Although it was a ghastly thing to witness for the first time, it was wholly incredible. She was eager to try as soon as Eryk transformed back into a Mystic.

Elle took a breath and thought of the fire beneath her skin. She pictured flowing lava replacing her blood and thought of her skin igniting. She transformed. She became a Heliopath.

Instructor Phoenix laughed. "Ha! She's a natural!" she exclaimed. "Angel look, she's a natural!"

Elle turned to see Eryk standing with his arms crossed and mouth slightly ajar.

Instructor Angel began to clap.

"You can transform back now," Instructor Phoenix insisted.

Elle thought of her Mystic form, sucking the fire back in her skin as Instructor Phoenix told her to do. When she became Elle again, she pursed her lips, then smiled mockingly at Eryk.

"Incredible." He slowly clapped. "Simply incredible."

They continued to train all through the afternoon, stopping once to eat lunch in the training room's kitchen. During their break, Eryk told Angel and Phoenix about his theory of the Remedium Tree being the answer to the riddle. They agreed it made sense, but were confused at how they were supposed to gather every leaf off of the Tree.

"The Dealer needs only a branch of leaves, not all of them," Phoenix blurted out as if the answer had suddenly struck her. "The Tree of Remedium follows its own seasonal patterns. We're going into fall right now. Each branch of the tree restarts—or *recommences*—its leaves one at a time. The riddle wasn't talking about the actual members of Remedium being renewed, it was talking about the leaves being renewed," Phoenix explained.

"So we have to figure out which branch of the Tree is first to drop its leaves?" Eryk asked.

"That is my guess," Phoenix answered.

"Is there a way to confirm the theory before you leave tomorrow?" Angel asked.

"No." Eryk shook his head. "But I think Phoenix is right."

Once they finished lunch, they immediately began training again.

Angel and Phoenix constructed a complex obstacle course for Elle and Eryk to complete. The course wasn't easy. There were three sections. The first part she had to light moving torches on fire while dodging sinking holes of water and balls of water being thrown at her by a guest Mystic called a Hydrosensus. The second section she had to run on a moving mat—like a treadmill—and jump or duck rotating beams. Sometimes she had to shift to her Heliopath form to avoid the low beams and right back to her Pyro form to jump over the next. Her legs felt like deadweights beneath her as she moved to the final section. The last section she worked with Eryk to shift into their Heliopath forms and climb to the top of the cave on a rock wall, while dodging spirts of water from all directions, in order to light a hanging torch on fire—

all under five minutes. Even Eryk struggled. But the fourth time around they finally succeeded.

Once they finished the obstacle course, they were given a forty-five minute break to do anything they wanted. Elle suggested they visit the Meadows again, but Eryk said it would take too long to get there. Disappointed, Elle told Eryk she was going to go on a walk instead.

As she left the training cave, she realized she'd been wearing the same clothes for the last two days. She desperately needed to find Alaina. She decided to check if she was in their bungalow first, though Elle doubted she was.

The distance from the training caves to the bungalows seemed much shorter than her first day in Remedium. She typed in Fifteen Willow Rowen and stepped inside the bungalow door. It was vacant of Alaina's presence. Elle looked around the miniature house for any clues to her whereabouts. She noticed the clock read 5:39 and guessed that Alaina must be on her way to the six o'clock dinner. There were three dinners you could attend in Remedium: a five o'clock, a six o'clock, or a seven o'clock. She exited the bungalow and made her way to the café. This was a much farther walk.

Although, the second she stepped out of the door, a tall boy stood in her way.

Leonardo.

He glared down at her through his dark eyes.

"Why is it, out of everyone here, you always seem to be in my way?" Leonardo queried.

Elle was lost for words. Only a few "uh's" and "um's" escaped her mouth.

"I was just on my way to the café, is all." Elle composed herself.

Leonardo scrunched his eyes. "Whatever," he said, and walked through the new bungalow door that appeared.

It closed loudly behind him, making Elle jump.

That was weird, she thought.

She had never seen him near the bungalows, much less entering one. Then she thought of last night, and how he didn't go to one then, either. Strange.

She shook the thought away and continued to the café. Once she reached the double doors she spotted Alaina outside the café chewing a piece of spearmint gum and looking at a book. Her hair was the color of the sky and her eyes were back to their normal shade of brown.

"Alaina," Elle called.

Alaina looked up and closed the book, "Elle."

"What's that?" Elle pointed to the book.

"Just a book Mason recommended." She smiled. "What's up?"

"Well, I was thinking that I should probably have some clothes for the Quest," Elle explained.

"Oh yes, of course." Alaina perked up. "There is a bazaar a couple cliffs down, I'll take you there now."

They made their way along the paths, rickety bridges and wooden ladders. Lanterns began to glow as the sun set in the background. Elle told her about the progress of the riddle, and Alaina became excited at the news. Alaina told her how Mason has been busy Seeking, but had been thinking about the second riddle as well. It finally felt like things were coming together.

Alaina chitchatted about Mason and Eryk and other Mystics she knew in training. She also added how she was mostly excited to spend all day with them during the Quest. She said it would be fun. But Elle didn't view the trip as being "fun" per se. She was repeatedly told it would be a dangerous journey.

The bazaar took place in a large, leafy treehouse. Banners and fairy lights were hung all around, and shelves upon shelves were scattered about. Elle and Alaina looked through racks of miscellaneous objects and boxes full of random supplies. They picked up t-shirts and pants, along with packages of food for the trip. Alaina talked the entire time. Once their baskets were full, they left the bazaar.

"We don't need to pay for this stuff?" Elle questioned.

Alaina giggled. "In Remedium, there is no worry about money. We help each other. There is no 'rich' or 'poor.'"

Elle enjoyed the thought of that. If only it was like that back in the real world; foster care would be highly improved if money was never an issue. She wondered if Alaina was ever in foster care. Or how Alaina came to Remedium in the first place.

"Alaina, can I ask you something?" Elle's tone of voice changed.

"Are you going to ask how I became a Mystic?"

"How'd you know?"

"I've observed that everyone's tone of voice goes the same when they're about to ask that question. But I don't mind. I'll tell you."

Elle looked at Alaina with admiration. Alaina was so open and smart. She never met anyone like her at group therapy.

"I basically grew up in the hospital," Alaina began. "I moved to America from the UK when I was six. Soon after moving, I began to develop severe social anxiety. My parents thought I was just a shy little tot, until my teachers informed them I had abnormal behavior with other students. Now, my parents are prestigious people, so anything abnormal in their life would simply not do. I will also note that my mother had seven miscarriages before having me, so she just wanted me to be her perfect little child. My parents took me to a child specialist who announced I had Borderline Personality Disorder. I began therapy right away. Of course, it never worked. I grew up in therapy and doctor visits, testing different medications, instead of having birthday parties and playing outside. I became depressed by the time I was ten years old. I quit sports and ran away from any and all human interactions. I didn't know how to act around kids at school. I would have mental breakdowns by randomly screaming and throwing chairs. The kids thought it was funny. Every doctor visit was the same. Soon I started cutting. As I grew older, I started drinking and smoking. Then one day Eryk showed up, brought me here and voila. Here I am."

Elle didn't know what to say. There was never anything to say after someone told you that side of their life. All Elle knew was how incredible Alaina was. And how many Mystics there were in Remedium that all had deep, intense stories like her and how incredible they were, too.

"You're a strong person, Alaina."

"You are too, Elle," Alaina said. "Now, get back to training. We have a Quest to complete."

They parted ways. Alaina took the bags of clothes and food back to the bungalow, while Elle walked back to training. She found the twisting slide was the shortest route and decided to take that. She was becoming more familiar with Remedium's erratic paths.

Once she entered the training cave, they got to work right away. Phoenix practiced with Elle on target practice and control. Eryk informed Phoenix that Elle had trouble taming her Myst when she was angry. Phoenix took that to heart by trying to make Elle extra feisty during the exercise. Elle was eager to keep growing in the skill, but she couldn't deny how agitated she was getting every time Phoenix shouted the word, "Again!" Elle caught herself on fire and back to normal at least forty times until she refused to do it again. But of course that only resulted in doing it another thirty times. She made sure to get Eryk back for this.

Training continued. Exercise after exercise, with zero breaks. Elle could feel her sore muscles already. How was she supposed to go on the Quest tomorrow if she couldn't move a single limb? She told this to Phoenix, but Phoenix said to either suck it up or kill her mom. That shut her up.

In the midst of another agility drill, Elle noticed the time. It was 10:57 p.m. She was so surprised to see the hands pointed to those numbers that she had to double check.

"It's late," she pointed to the clock on the wall to Eryk. He was just as surprised but seemed content. Elle could tell he loved days like this.

"I think you are okay for today," Phoenix said. "You have improved greatly, Elle."

"Thank you for your help," Elle said.

"I wish you the best of luck on your Quest tomorrow," Phoenix said.

Elle was eager to get started. She wanted to leave right away, but she could also feel the bags under her eyes pleading her to sleep. She could feel her knuckles and feet throbbing under their bandages. And not to mention that she smelled of sweat and a campfire. It made her laugh inside a little, that she actually smelled of fire, that she almost smelled burnt in a way.

"Truly, best of luck," Angel said. He didn't smile or hug them or shake their hands. He stared at them. He stared at them like it was the last time he would see them.

"Thanks," Eryk said. Elle nodded her head in agreement.

Eryk and Elle turned on their heels and left the training cave. The moon was quietly hanging in the sky, coated by drifting clouds. It watched Elle and Eryk walk up the grassy hill and to the cliff's side.

"Would you care if I stayed back with Angel and Phoenix for a little longer?" Eryk asked after a couple of steps.

Elle looked up at his eyes. They were still vibrant blue even in the darkness. Elle was told that Mystics had enchanting eyes only to humans, but Eryk's still looked insanely bright and beautiful.

"Sure, is everything okay?"

"Yeah, yeah. I just want to clear some things up is all," he told her.

"Okay."

"You know your way to the bungalows by now, right?"

"I do."

"Cool," Eryk said, as he turned back down the hill.

The second Eryk left, the Villages of Remedium became much quieter. The sky was still. The trees were still. The only sounds were the occasional hoot of a faraway owl, and the patter of Elle's footsteps. Remedium was so mystifying in the nighttime.

As she walked along the edge of the cliff, Elle's mind wandered to tomorrow. Where would they be headed? She knew they were to go to the Tree of Remedium, but where exactly was that? As far as she knew, it was in the Everson's backyard miniature forest. That forest had seemed massive until she came to Remedium, but now it only felt like couple of trees. The Remedium Tree couldn't possibly still be there. Then where would it be? Eryk would probably know. She almost turned to ask him, but remembered he wasn't there. She'd become so used to him being on her right side the last couple of days, it felt odd when he wasn't. It felt empty. She'd come to really enjoy Eryk's company. He made her feel wanted, a feeling she'd never experienced before. She knew that if she was still Indwelled she would be terrified of him. She tried to recollect her memory of the first time she saw him, but it felt like ages ago. All she could remember was his alluring eyes. They were so completely intriguing, so captivating. She would never get tired of his eyes. Then she subconsciously thought of Emmie. All through training, walking, eating, and talking, Emmie never left her mind. How could Emmie possibly forget about her? Could a Mystic really take away her memories?

And then a thought disturbed Elle. Was it the Mystics that took away the memories, or was it the natural force of Remedium's power? She remembered Leonardo telling her that his sister's Myst was the ability to take away people's memories, while his was to plant memories. Was Leonardo's sister the one who took away her baby sister's memories? Suddenly angry at Anastasia, Elle tried to shift her thoughts elsewhere.

There was a rustle of leaves behind her as she was about to reach the bungalows. Startled, she turned around, only to find Leonardo.

"You scared me," Elle said.

"Oops," he responded passively.

They walked together in silence. Elle didn't know what to say to him, nor did she *want* to say anything to him. He tricked her into seeing the Dealer, he probably knew exactly what he was going to do, and he took her there anyway. And now she was to go on that treacherous Quest with all her new friends and risk their lives. Also, his sister was pure evil for taking away Emmie's memories. Even though she didn't know for sure if it was Anastasia or not, she told herself it was, just to cast her anger somewhere.

"I want to take you somewhere," Leonardo said.

"What?" Elle asked. Not because she didn't hear him, but because she was surprised.

"I want to take you somewhere," Leonardo repeated. "I want to show you something."

Not having any idea where or why he would want to take her somewhere, she was too curious to turn down the opportunity.

"Okay," she said.

Leonardo stifled a shy smile. He grabbed her hand and pulled her into the forest.

"Where are we going?" Elle questioned, pulling back her hand. She couldn't ignore the immediate regret. What was it about him that made her want to be with him? She couldn't decipher.

He didn't answer as he took her hand again and pulled her farther into the thick blanket of trees. The sky became invisible as they traveled farther. The air became cooler and fresh, and Elle allowed him to hold her hand, specifically so she wouldn't lose him in the dark woodland maze.

They didn't talk the entire way, but sometimes Leonardo would inform her that they were almost there or to watch her step.

Soon they stumbled upon a wide open space. Enormous trees circled the perimeter while wildflowers swept the rich green grass. The star-scattered sky was visible and hundreds of beautiful golden fireflies danced across the area. The sight was enchanting. The glow of the fireflies lit up the never ending darkness to a low mystical blue. They spiraled while they hummed the melody of the forest and moon.

"This is..." Elle was at a loss for words. There was no perfect summary for the sight.

Leonardo pulled her into the center of the circular opening. The fireflies flickered hello. The two Mystics stood in the middle of falling golden glitter.

"I love it here," Leonardo told her. "I thought you would, too."

Elle looked up wide eyed at the flying insects. This had to be her favorite part of Remedium. She looked back at Leonardo, whose eyes watched hers. She noticed him for the first time, truly took in his features clearly. His eyes seemed softer in the golden light. Warm brown, rather than deep. His dirty blonde hair was nicely messy as always, as some strands swept his forehead. His skin was olive and tan, like everyone's in Remedium. He was tall compared to Ellisia. Much taller, actually. He wore a simple white shirt with three brown buttons on the chest, the top one unbuttoned. There in that that moment, he didn't look as old as he usually did. She wondered how old he actually was.

"You would be right," she whispered.

They found themselves laying on the bed of grass under an immense conifer tree, watching the fireflies perform.

"When did you discover this?" Elle asked.

"Anastasia and I would come here when we were younger. She refuses to come now," Leonardo answered.

They conversed in low voices so as not to disturb the peace.

"How long have you been in Remedium?" Elle asked, not knowing if it was a personal question or not. She actually wondered *how* he became a member of Remedium.

"We came when we were eleven," Leonardo told her. "My sister and I."

Elle nodded her head. "Is she older than you?" Elle asked.

"Only by a minute."

"Oh," she said, surprised. Twins. Anastasia just seemed so much more in charge, Elle assumed she was older.

They laid in silence, watching the fireflies glow. It was pure magic. Emmie would have loved—

Elle stopped herself from thinking of her little sister. Emmie didn't know who Elle was anymore, and she just had to accept it. But she didn't want to. She wanted Emmie to be brought here.

"Your sister, she likes the Dealer?" Elle asked, distracting herself from the thought of Emmie.

"It's complicated."

"Tell me," Elle said as she turned on her side to face him.

His expression was blank.

"She looks up to him," he said.

"Why though?" Elle asked. "He just sent me and my friends off on a dangerous journey that we may or may not survive."

"I don't know."

Elle didn't pry. She was beginning to conclude that Leonardo was a complicated person—intricate and complicated. She just wanted a better understanding of him because she couldn't read him, so she stayed quiet.

"When's your birthday?" Leonardo asked randomly, rupturing the silence.

"September first," she replied. "When's yours?"

"October twenty-seventh."

They observed the flickering, dancing fireflies. They never got bored of the sight.

"Do you come here a lot?" Elle asked.

"Every night," Leonardo told her. "But it's always better with somebody else."

Elle laughed. "You bring girls here a lot then?" She was joking of course, because she figured that of course he did.

"Only you," he declared.

She sat up. "You're lying."

"Am not."

"I don't believe you," Elle said as she crossed her arms and laid back down.

After talking and laughing on and off for an hour, Elle slipped into a dreamless sleep. Her muscles relaxed, her face relaxed and her eyelids laid delicately closed. Her mind was at ease from all the crazy events of the day.

As the fireflies floated away one by one and soft pink hues smeared the sky, Elle could feel Leonardo slip his arms beneath her body and carry her through the evergreen trees back to the bungalows. She pretended to stay asleep, but couldn't help the small smile that played on her lips.

Chapter 8

When Alaina tried to wake her, Elle woke up disoriented, expecting to be laying in her bed at the Everson's. Distraught, she sat up and looked around the bungalow.

The events of last night flooded back into her mind like a gust of wind. Training. Eryk. Leonardo. Fireflies. Whispers. Leonardo.

Leonardo.

Last night he wasn't his usual emotionless, arrogant character. He was somewhat pleasant to be around. The thought made Elle dizzy.

"W-what time is it?" Elle asked, her eyes heavy and body sore.

"It's about six," Alaina said.

Six in the morning already? What time did she fall asleep? Then she remembered she'd fallen asleep in the forest and Leonardo carrying her to her bungalow. How did he know her address? Did Alaina hear them? Her stomach sank.

"We need to get going. Eryk and Mason are ready. We have to talk to Tabitha before we leave," Alaina said.

Elle grunted. She threw off the fluffy blanket and slowly dismounted the bunkbed. Her legs cried in protest, her arms ached. Her head spun with the lack of sleep.

"Get ready and meet us in the café," Alaina said. She walked out of the bungalow, leaving Elle alone in the dark room.

Elle thought about how easy it would be to climb back in bed and close her eyes again. The idea was tempting, but she knew she couldn't.

"Ugh!" she said, penetrating the silence of the room. Birds chirped outside the window, and the sound became irritating.

She made her way to the bathroom and turned on the shower before she could change her mind. She stripped off her sweaty, stinky clothes and jumped under the cold running water. The soap smelled of almond and honey.

After the shower, she brushed her teeth and put on some clothes that Alaina left her. When she looked in the mirror she didn't recognize herself. She never saw herself as a Mystic until this moment. Although her eyes were brown, now they were bright and sparkly. Her skin looked clear and fresh, and her hair was thick and resilient. She didn't look sick or depressed. She looked healthy and alive.

She combed through her wet hair and took one last look around the stunning bungalow. She didn't know when she would be back, let alone if she would *ever* be back.

Making her way to the café as Alaina told her, Elle thought of last night. Her mind was stumped at the fact that it was Leonardo in her memory. Though he didn't bring up anything personal, he'd opened his mind to Elle. The memories of the forest and fireflies made her stomach flop. She didn't know what this feeling was, and she didn't know why he made her feel this way. But then she thought of Eryk, and how mad it would probably make him if he knew where she was last night. *Why did they not like each other?* Elle thought. She made a mental note to ask Eryk, when the time was right.

She turned the cliff's corner and pulled one of the double doors open. She walked down the hallway and found the café door, which was covered in leafy vines that were beginning to welt.

At first Elle didn't see Alaina waving to her, because she looked much different than the last couple days. It was when she saw Eryk and Mason, that she assumed it was Alaina. Her hair was shoulder length and pale blonde and her eyes were bright and hazel.

"Tabitha should be here in—"

Eryk stopped midsentence as he noticed Leonardo and Anastasia enter the café. He looked back at Elle, and his face contorted.

Elle's stomach somersaulted at the sight of Leonardo. He didn't return the glance.

Eryk slammed his fist on the table, causing the few Mystics around them to look in their direction.

"I just realized something," Eryk said.

Eryk stood up, fury flaming in his eyes, and walked over to Leonardo.

"How many times do I have to tell you to stay out of my head?" Eryk shouted, fire dancing on his fists.

"Don't know what you're talking about," Leonardo sneered. Anastasia grinned behind him.

"You know exactly what—"

Then Tabitha entered the café, and Eryk instantly put the flames out and stepped back.

"Is there another problem here?" Tabitha asked.

"Not that I know of," Leonardo said.

"Very well, come and sit, we have things to discuss." Tabitha ignored the obvious tension fuming around the room.

Eryk stared at Leonardo, gritted his teeth and turned around. Leonardo chuckled behind him and Eryk pressed his lips together to hold back the rage growing inside him.

"What happened?" Mason whispered to Eryk as he sat back down.

"I'll tell you later," Eryk whispered through his teeth.

Alaina and Elle looked at each other, their foreheads wrinkled.

"You all will be attending the Quest, is that correct?" Tabitha asked, taking a seat at the head of the wooden table.

The four Mystics replied yes.

"Very well. And you all understand how this will be a dangerous journey throughout?" Tabitha asked.

"Yes," the Mystics said in unison.

"Okay. I am aware you are searching for the Tree of Remedium, is that correct as well?"

They all four said yes again.

"Great. Ellisia, if you do not know, Remedium views the earth in four quarters." Tabitha pulled out a map and spread it in front of them. "There is Venusira, Sepiototumn, Belltheria and Gemmasus. The Tree of Remedium is currently stationed in Southern Belltheria." She circled the continent of Asia with her finger.

Taking in the foreign language of Remedium, Elle looked down at the colorful map. She wondered if she had followed the traditional steps it took to become a Mystic, if she would have learned the history and customs of

Remedium in a classroom setting. At least that was how she pictured it.

"I wish you four the best of luck," Tabitha said, rolling up the map. "Oh, and remember, eight more days."

Nobody said thank you.

Tabitha nodded and exited the café.

As soon as the door closed behind her, the Mystics turned back to each other.

"So what was that whole thing about, before Mrs. Helpful came in?" Alaina asked Eryk.

Eryk looked at Elle, but she had the same expression as Alaina. The curiosity was agitating.

"He placed a thought in my head last night," Eryk growled.

"He what?" Alaina shouted.

"When?" Mason added.

"What?" Elle was still confused.

"After training, I was planning on taking Elle to her bungalow and then going to mine, but instead Leonardo made me think I had to talk to Angel about something, so he could be with Elle," Eryk explained.

The words floated in Elle's mind like feathers. Then her stomach plummeted. Leonardo manipulated Eryk's mind to get her alone? She knew there was something not right about last night. This had to be it. Eryk wouldn't have left her randomly like that. He would have walked her to the address cave, and then walked back to Angel and Phoenix.

"I wonder how many times he's done that," Mason thought aloud.

"Never mind that, where did he take you?" Eryk asked Elle, his eyes becoming big.

Elle sat in disbelief. But why would Leonardo not just ask her? He didn't have to get inside Eryk's head. And then she realized, it was Leonardo. The Leonardo last night—the talking, laughing, laid back one—was not the real Leonardo.

"Nowhere, he—" Elle couldn't think of the words. How would they react? Did Mason hate him as much as Eryk did? She knew Alaina wasn't fond of him…

"What did he do?" Eryk pressed.

"Nothing. He, um, he walked me to the address cave," Elle lied.

"That's it?"

"Yeah, that's all," Elle answered, a little too quickly.

Eryk, Mason and Alaina traded glances.

"He didn't take you anywhere? Do anything?" Eryk asked, skeptical.

"No. We need to get going," Elle changed the subject, standing up.

"Right," Alaina said incredulously as she stood up, too. She handed Elle a little silver backpack. "I made everyone a bag. It has food, water, clothes, bandages and other stuff like that."

The two boys stood up, and they all stared as Mason quickly stuffed more muffins and fruit into his bag.

"So what do we do first?" Elle asked.

"First, we need to find out when the next train to Belltheria leaves," Eryk answered.

"I'll go look for that," Elle offered.

"No, I will," Mason intervened. "I'll be quicker." Elle pursed her lips. It still annoyed her how she didn't know her way around Remedium yet.

Mason was gone in the blink of an eye.

"What will we do when we get there, to Beltherian?" Elle asked.

"Belltheria," Alaina corrected. "And Elle, if you haven't noticed, we're more of a figure-it-out-when-we-get-there type of people."

Elle felt stumped, because she was definitely not that type of person, she needed plans and lists.

In that same minute, Mason popped back.

"The first train out of Remedium to Belltheria leaves at eight a.m.," Mason informed.

"But that's not for another hour and a half," Eryk moaned.

"I know. Is there anything we can do in the meantime?" Mason asked.

Mason and Eryk continued talking, but Elle's mind wondered off. They only had eight more days to finish the Quest and return to Remedium. The minute she was brought to this beautiful magical place, she was forced to leave. She didn't even get to know her way around—never even got to train with other Heliopaths. But she knew she had a job to get done. She was going to save her mother.

Her mother—a decrepit, lifeless creature. She had only seen her briefly during the Reveal. And now she was leaving on a dangerous, life threatening journey to save her. She had to see her one last time. Even though she was in the form that destroyed her life and mind, she had to look at her, see her, hear her, talk to her without anybody interfering or pulling her away.

"I want to see my mother," Elle spoke, interrupting Eryk and Mason conversing. "Just one last time."

"Do you know where she is?" Eryk asked.

"Yes, they're keeping her with the Dealer," Elle answered.

Eryk's face dropped.

"Do you know how to get there?" Eryk asked, despite the tension on his face.

"No, but I know someone who does," Elle said.

"Okay, fine. You go see your mom. Mason and I will start on the next riddle at the train station, and Alaina, you can find a map of Belltheria," Eryk said. "Everyone meet back here at 7:30."

The Mystics turned from each other, heading different directions. Elle went inside the double doors and into the café again to hopefully find Leonardo still there. She circled around the place twice and there was no sign of him. More and more Mystics began filling in the space. She wondered why everyone woke up so early in Remedium.

"Looking for something, Carroway?" Leonardo said from behind.

"Yeah, you," she said. "I need to see my mother before I leave."

"And you need me?" Leonardo asked tersely.

"Yes, I don't know how to get to the Dealer's without you." Elle became frustrated, he was acting like last night didn't happen.

"Find a Compass, I'm busy," Leonardo said, walking away.

"A compass?" Elle shouted as the café door swung closed behind him.

"Ugh!" Elle slumped down at an empty table. "What good is a stupid compass going to do?"

Why did he have to act like this? She wanted to see her mother, and Leonardo was the only person who could take her. He was so confusing. One minute he was talkative and insightful and the next he was completely blank like a piece of printer paper.

Someone tapped on Elle's shoulder so lightly she barely felt it.

"Did you say you needed a Compass?" a little voice spoke. The owner of the voice was a very small girl, probably around the age of five. She had mousy brown hair and a heart shaped face. She looked like a little doll.

"No, that's okay," Elle said. She couldn't help to think of Emmie when looking at the girl. She didn't want to turn back around, she wanted to stay with her and talk to her until she had to leave.

"I'm a Compass, I can help you," the little girl said in a high soprano voice.

Elle turned completely around, staring into the girl's curious eyes. If she had green eyes rather than blue, she would have resembled Emmie much more closely.

"Wait, what did you say?" Elle asked.

"I can help you, I'm a Compass," the girl repeated.

A compass? Maybe...

"Yes, yes I need help finding somewhere," Elle gleamed with hope.

"Oh yay!" the girl jumped up and down.

A Compass must be some sort of Myst. Leonardo didn't mean an actual, physical compass, he meant a Mystic.

"What is it exactly you do?" Elle asked the girl. Even though Elle was sitting down, she was still taller than the child.

"I know where everything is!" she beamed.

Elle muttered the word "perfect" under her breath and stood up from the table.

"Can you show me where the Dealer's adobe is?" Elle asked, bending to her level.

The girl nodded her head, took Elle's hand, and guided her to the forest.

They began twisting and turning through the never ending mountain of trees. The girl didn't let go of Elle's hand the entire time.

"What is your name?" Elle asked.

"I don't know," the girl said. "But everyone here calls me Tula."

Elle was surprised. "Why Tula?"

"Because Momma found me by the tulips. She said even though I'm a Compass, she's still going to teach me to be a Heliopath." Tula looked especially proud.

"Wait, is your mom Phoenix?" Elle was shocked.

"Yeah! Are *you* a Heliopath?" Tula was in awe.

Elle nodded her head.

"That is the most awesome-est thing ever!" Tula squealed.

They continued deeper into the forest. It felt like it was taking longer than normal, because Tula had very short strides. Tula talked the entire way, and never ran out of things to say. She told Elle about her about friends in training and how they weren't very nice to her because she was so tiny. But she said she'd be done with training when she turned seven, which was still a year and a half away, but she seemed happy at the fact nonetheless. She also told Elle how she knew all of Remedium and knew how to get anywhere she wanted.

"What's your name?" Tula asked.

"Elle," she replied.

"That's a funny name," Tula giggled.

"I've heard." Elle laughed with her.

They continued to walk deeper in the forest. It felt like they had been walking forever.

"Are you sure you know where you're going?" Elle asked.

"Yes," Tula snapped. "We are almost to the Dealer."

Elle kept quiet, since Tula did not like being doubted, obviously.

"Momma tells me not to go by the Dealer," Tula said.

"Why not?" Elle knew the answer but wanted to know what Tula would say.

"He tricks everyone, and tricking is not nice."

Elle smiled at her innocence, but Tula wasn't wrong. She hoped Phoenix would never find out about this little excursion. If Phoenix told Tula not to go by the Dealer's, and Elle was making her go anyway, Elle's training would make the last couple of sessions look like a simple warm up.

"I told you! I told you I knew where the Dealer was!" Tula laughed.

"Thanks Tula," Elle said. "Do you think you could wait right here, while I go inside?"

Tula placed a finger on her chin and looked up at the sky. "I think so."

"Great. Don't go anywhere, wait right here. I won't take long," Elle said slowly.

Elle knocked on the adobe wall. It hit her then what she was about to do. She was back at the Dealer's—the man who tricked her into a dangerous journey. She wanted to throw all her frustrations at him, every word, and every thought.

The black lines outlined and created the door. Elle turned the knob and stepped in. The air was cold; the room was silent.

"Ellisia," the Dealer hissed. "What brings you here today?"

Elle gulped. His presence was like a snake. But at the same time a snake didn't fit him well enough. He was cleverer than a snake.

"I wanted to visit my mother before I left," Elle answered through her teeth.

"How sweet of you." He grinned. "She is in the back room to the right."

Elle took off down the short hallway and found the last door. She stood in front of it, her hand on the cold knob. Her mother—the mother she thought was dead her whole life—was behind this door.

The door screeched open and inside was a barred cage.

Elle could faintly hear the Dealer speaking to someone in the other room.

"I need Annie," he whispered. Anastasia? Elle wondered.

But she became too distracted to eavesdrop as she saw a puddle of skin and bones on the floor of the cage. It looked worse than the first time.

Elle tiptoed slowly to the cage. Up close she could make out the shape of her Charmer. She laid on her stomach, the few strands of hair she had left covered her face. Her thin-as-a-tree-limb arms stretched over her head. Her legs were a deadweight, and the skin wrinkled to the bone. There wasn't any muscle.

The skin flopped over onto its back. The sight made Elle nauseous. This wasn't a human. This wasn't any sort of creature. This wasn't even a skeleton.

"Is that you my daughter?" a voice croaked in not more than a whisper. The sound was almost inaudible but it echoed off the walls.

"Yes," Elle said. She stepped closer to the cage. If she reached out her arm she would have been able to touch the bars. She sat down, crisscrossing her legs.

Her mother turned her head to see Elle. Elle tried not to look sickened at the dilapidated face. Its skin was drooping from its prominent cheekbones, and its nose appeared to be broken. Its lips weren't visible and its eyes were wholly black. There were no whites to its eyes, no deep brown color as Ellisia's. Just never ending, sullen black.

Elle couldn't help the images that played in her mind. She knew people killed their Charmers with a sword by beheading them. And she couldn't help but picture what that would be like, to pick up some magnificent sword and slice her Charmer's head off. But this Charmer was her mother. It didn't even need to be kept in a cage, because it couldn't move, could barely talk, or pick up its hand. Could barely breathe. Why did she have to kill it?

"I'm going to save you," Elle told the creature. "I'm leaving today to find ingredients to a potion that will help you."

Its eyes were hard to look at. They were beady, rodent eyes, and Elle couldn't tell where they were looking exactly.

The Charmer tried to sit up but only fell back down.

"You want to help me?" it croaked.

"Yes," Elle said instantly. "You saved me once, from Dad, and I'm going to save you."

Elle couldn't tell for sure, but it looked like it smiled.

"You are good," was all the Charmer could say. Shortly after, a fit of blood dribbled from its mouth and down its neck.

Elle couldn't stand the sight any longer. She turned to walk out the door but the Dealer stood in the doorframe, his arms crossed.

"Jadine Esmund-Carroway. Grew up in a small town in California. She was a dreamer—a writer—with a big imagination. She never fit in well with the others at her school her whole life. Her parents were divorced and she lived with her father. Her mother cheated on him a countless number of times, and then was put in prison for involuntary manslaughter."

"Stop," Elle said, trying to get through the door, but the Dealer didn't move.

"Her father was an alcoholic. Beat her and her brother occasionally. Her brother ran away when he was fourteen, and she still has no idea where he is. When she graduated high school she moved to Oregon and that is where she met your father, isn't?" The Dealer grinned.

"Okay, stop," Elle said. Fear ringed inside her, she wanted out of this little room at the end of the hallway.

"Very well," the Dealer said, and stepped out of her way. Elle walked—practically jogged—to the door of the adobe.

"Your mother followed the only path she ever knew, was ever exposed to," the Dealer shouted as Elle was about to go out the door.

Elle turned around, "My mother is a great person," she yelled. "And I'm going to save her!"

She walked out the door and slammed it behind her before the Dealer could say anything else.

Infuriated with the Dealer and creeped out by the sight of her Charmer mother, Elle hollered Tula's name when she wasn't anywhere to be found by the adobe.

Panic flooded Elle's chest.

She couldn't lose Tula.

Phoenix. What would Phoenix do if she found out Elle lost her child?

And Angel.

"TULA!" Elle hollered continually, the name ricocheting off the towering trees.

"Up here!" Tula giggled.

Elle looked up, but all she saw was the tremendous trees and wilting leaves.

"I don't see you," Elle yelled back, still looking.

"Behind you," Tula giggled more.

Elle turned around, and there was Tula, precariously sitting on a thin tree branch about twenty feet into the air.

"Tula, get down here. I need you to take me to the train station. Do you think you can take me there?" Elle asked.

"Of course," Tula said. She easily climbed down the hovering tree like a squirrel.

"Great," Elle said.

They started walking through the forest once again. The second time through the woods with Tula seemed to go by faster, but Elle still had no idea how to navigate alone through the trees. She didn't understand how Leonardo did it without being or having a Compass. She wondered then how much of his time was spent in the forest, and why exactly.

Elle and Tula reached the opening to the cliff at last. Out of the blanket of trees, the sky was finally visible.

"Why do you have to go on a train?" Tula asked as they started down a wooden path that Elle had never explored before.

Elle thought of the question. What would be the best way to tell a five-year-old what she had to do?

"I have to visit Belltheria."

"Why?"

"Because I have to visit the Tree of Remedium," Elle explained.

"Why?"

"Because."

"Because why?"

Annoyed, Elle didn't answer. She was glad Emmie was never one to ask questions, she waited for answers to come to her.

Darn it, she was thinking about Emmie again. It was so natural to her mind to think of her baby sister. She distracted herself from the thought and focused on Eryk instead.

Eryk had surprised her the past few days. Times that she thought he would be angry, he wasn't. Times she thought he would be frustrated, he wasn't. When she thought of Eryk the words "determined" and "patient" came attached with him. In training he was strong willed to finish the drill, but he was also patient to get the drills done efficiently. Elle admired that about him. She liked to do drills quickly to get them over with—which only made them feel longer. She was eager to start the Quest. But Eryk seemed ready to take as long as they needed.

Tula skipped in front of her as they entered a narrow wooden tunnel which resembled a massive hollow log. Tula's tiny voice echoed off the walls and she laughed as they did.

"We are almost there. I can feel it!" Tula exclaimed as they exited the log tunnel.

They walked along several wooden bridges, some hung above roaring streams. Tula wasn't bothered by the height or the water below. Elle guessed she'd been doing that since she could crawl.

Soon a large train station came into view. The stretched out dome shape, made out of thousands of glass windows, was entangled in vines and tree roots. The sun beams danced on the glass, making the station glitter amongst the greenery.

"Elle," Eryk said from behind her.

She turned around, revealing Tula.

"Tula?" Eryk questioned. "Oh, you helped Elle come here didn't you?"

Tula smiled and nodded her head, her cheeks turning pink.

"Hey," Elle said, bending to Tula's level. "Do you think you could keep this little adventure between you and me?"

Tula locked her lips with a pretend key and tossed it over her shoulder. Her wide blue eyes stared up at Elle and Eryk.

"Thanks Tula, you can go back now," Elle said, turning back to Eryk.

Before Tula left, she lightly tapped on Elle's back again with her little finger.

"Yes?" Elle asked.

Tula pressed her lips together and waved Elle down to her level.

"What is it?" Elle asked, bending down again.

Tula cupped her mouth with her hands and whispered in Elle's ear, "Is he your boyfriend?" she asked.

Elle laughed and stifled her blush. "No, is he yours?"

Tula laughed out loud and shook her head. She turned on her heels and started skipping away from the train station, her dark brown hair bouncing behind her.

"What did she say?" Eryk asked, smiling.

Elle shook her head. "Nothing."

Eryk chuckled. "Ready to begin the Quest?"

"Let's do it."

Chapter 9

The train to Belltheria boarded at precisely 7:42 a.m. and it wasn't a typical crafted train. It was constructed completely of wood from trees, and had little circle cutouts for windows. Thick vines and luscious leaves twisted throughout the interior. The benches and seats were made of wood, and even the wheels were wooden.

Elle, Eryk and Mason climbed aboard when the doors opened. Nobody else was on the train other than the two conductors. The three friends took a seat in a middle compartment and waited for Alaina to arrive.

Eryk told Elle how they'd made no progress on the second riddle and how they decided to focus on finishing the first mission. Mason, obviously annoyed, folded his arms and looked out the open window.

A few more Mystics entered the train, taking seats away from where Eryk, Elle and Mason sat. It was quite a spacious train for so few passengers.

Suddenly Alaina was running through the aisle of the train, almost missing her friends.

"Sorry I'm late," Alaina said, out of breath.

"Everything alright?" Mason asked. He sat on the edge of the bench, leaving an extra space by the window.

"Just making sure I packed absolutely everything we need. Can you scoot over?"

"I saved you the window seat," Mason explained. "I know you like the window seat."

Alaina smiled and sat down by the window.

"The train doors to Belltheria are now closing," a loud voice boomed over the intercom. "Ladies and gentlemen, please remain seated at all times. We will arrive to Belltheria at approximately 10:25. Thank you for your patience and we do advise you this journey will be bumpy."

The moving train started to pick up speed, becoming quite noisy. Elle held on to the sides of her seat to keep herself steady, but it didn't help much.

"So how did things go with your mom?" Alaina asked.

"What?" Elle shouted.

"How did things go with your mom?" Alaina repeated louder.

"She's..." Elle stopped. How *did* things go with her mom? She wouldn't classify that experience as "good" or pleasant. But she wouldn't say it was bad either. Her mother just needed help, a lot of it. The image of her mother's ruined body came back into her mind and Elle shuddered.

"I'm going to help her," Elle yelled to Alaina.

Alaina nodded in reply.

Everyone jiggled and bounced awkwardly in their seats as the train continued. It was far too loud to talk, so they looked out the window trying not to make eye contact. Every once in a while someone would sigh, and Elle could have sworn she heard Mason humming to break the silence, but it just made things more awkward.

Elle sat by Eryk who sat by the window. The benches were small and their arms and legs touched. It bothered Elle at first, but she got used to it.

Mason attempted to talk to Alaina, but she was too lost in thought to hear his words. Every few minutes he'd try again, but she took no notice. Eryk would chuckle at his failed attempts and Mason would roll his eyes. Elle felt kind of bad for Mason. If only Alaina would recognize how much he cared for her. Sitting side by side they looked like complete opposites. Alaina, with her attractive blonde hairdo with purple underneath and her huge round hazel eyes; and then Mason, with his thick glasses that sat crookedly on his freckled nose. His light amber eyes with fuzzy eyelashes that swept against his glasses when he blinked, and his unruly curly brown hair that was impossible to maintain.

Mason and Eryk started talking loudly about videogames and movies. The hum of Eryk's voice after a while made her eyelids heavy and she was swept into sleep before she could reject it. Without meaning to, her head fell onto Eryk's shoulder. She could feel his body tense beneath her, but then relax. Then she fell into a dreamless sleep without thought.

Elle jerked awake to the quick screech of the train. Her eyes flew open and when she realized she was practically laying on top of Eryk, she sat up immediately.

"Sorry," she muttered, now wide awake.

"Welcome to Belltheria, home of some of the most extravagant jungles on earth!" the intercom blared, hurting everyone's ears. "Please grab any belongings and make your way to the exit."

"I slept the whole way?" Elle scrambled for her backpack.

"Oh yeah, you were out in the first five minutes," Eryk said.

Standing up, the Mystics grabbed their backpacks and headed towards the exit.

Elle stepped down from the train steps, and as soon as her feet hit the ground a wave of energy zapped her body. She was no longer in Remedium. She was back on Earth. The train had stopped in a bodacious rainforest. The climate felt heavier and warmer and the trees looked much smaller, but were still massive compared to the trees in Remedium.

As Eryk, Alaina and Mason stepped down from the train, they took in their surroundings.

"You know, I've never been to Belltheria before," Alaina said.

"You'll love it," Mason told her.

The train zipped off behind them, leaving a cloud of dirt behind it. The four Mystics watched the bulky train disappear. Then they were alone, and there was no going home.

"Time to find the Tree," Eryk said.

"The Tree is most likely in the closest rainforest to the train station," Mason said.

"But then how come when Eryk found me, the Tree was in the backyard of the Everson's?" Elle asked.

"The Tree is a magical plant. It's everywhere at once when it needs to be. But the Tree also has a centralized location, and right now it's in Belltheria," Mason explained.

Elle nodded and looked around. In Remedium the forests smelled lively with plants and moist soil, but here it smelled like rainwater and mosquitos. It wasn't an awful smell, just different. There were a lot more bugs and animals already. Elle wondered why they didn't bring a Mystic like Tula with them to tell them where to go. Wouldn't that have been a lot easier?

"Do you have that map of Belltheria?" Mason asked Alaina.

"Yes," Alaina said, swinging her backpack around and taking out a long map.

"We should have brought Tula," Elle said.

"Tula's crazy," Eryk replied. "She comes into Heliopaths training a lot and messes with all the equipment and tries to distract me."

"She's got a pretty big crush on you." Elle laughed.

"Everyone does." Eryk winked.

Elle rolled her eyes. "But really, why didn't we bring a Compass?"

"Well for one, they're all super annoying," Alaina interjected, turning around to face them.

"That, and none of them were willing to come. Mason and I tried because it would obviously be helpful, but they all turned down the offer, said it was 'too dangerous' and 'impossible,'" Eryk scoffed.

Elle pondered the explanation. Was it really that dangerous of a journey? So far the scariest thing that had happened was seeing a spider spin a web a few trees down.

"Why do they think that, though?" Elle asked.

Eryk laughed. "You aren't scared of anything, are you?"

"They think because the Dealer set this upon you, it's bound to be life threatening," Alaina said.

Elle pursed her lips. She didn't enjoy the Dealer's presence, but she also didn't not trust him. At first, she was angry with him for giving her stupid riddles, causing them precious time, but without his deal she wouldn't have a chance to save her mom. He at least gave her a chance.

They walked several miles into the rainforest. The trees were droopier here than in Remedium, and there were various creatures all around. Bugs flew all around them, and colorful frogs hopped from leaf to leaf, lizards scurried the forest floor and little monkey eyes stared at the newcomers suspiciously.

Elle had never seen monkeys or frogs. She was never taken to a zoo but remembered Emmie talking about one. She wished she could have taken Emmie to the zoo when she still had her. Emmie would love—

She shook the thought away. The air was moist and humid, and water dripped from high above trees. The sky was barely visible and disappeared completely from view at times. They took turns holding the map and leading. When it was Elle's turn, she was confused on what to do. She had never held or owned a map before. One time Emmie drew her a map of—

She stopped herself, listening to Eryk's instructions.

"Zoom in on that map," he was saying.

"What?" Elle asked.

"Look," Eryk took his pointer finger and thumb and slid them apart and back on the map. The map's appearance changed and shifted, the colors blurring, until it focused on a bird's eye view of an extravagant rainforest.

"It's like an iPad, but actual paper," Alaina said from behind them.

"Cool," Elle said, taking in the map. She had never owned an iPad, or an iPhone for that matter, Mrs. Everson wouldn't allow it.

"The Tree isn't actually pinpointed on here," Eryk explained. "This is just to show us where exactly we are and what ground we've already covered. So right now we're east, heading north, we want to keep heading north. Make sense?"

"Think so," Elle answered.

As Eryk, Mason and Alaina followed Elle, she kept her eyes on the large map to keep them in the right direction. Multiple times she tripped over growing tree roots or burrowed holes, sometimes falling to the dirt.

After tripping a third time, Eryk intervened.

"Okay, maybe that's enough," he laughed. "I'll make sure to remind Angel to work on your balance."

Annoyed, she shoved the map in his hands and walked behind Mason.

Eryk whistled as he led the group. They walked through thick underbrush and hopped over fallen tree trunks. It rained off and on, but the rain was warm and didn't cool the humidity.

Eryk kept his place as leader and soon they started a little game. Eryk titled it the "Thinking Game." They had to choose a category and each person (in order of the line) had to say an object in the category on the top of their head. If you took too long or repeated an answer, you were out.

"Hamburgers." Eryk started off the next category, which was food—as they were getting closer to lunch time.

"Sandwiches," Alaina said.

"You can't say that," Mason refuted.

"Yes, I can," Alaina said.

"'Sandwiches' is too broad, you have to be more specific," Mason argued.

"Ugh! Fine, *ham and cheese* sandwiches *with lettuce and tomato*," Alaina said.

"Okay, I'm actually getting hungry," Eryk interrupted.

"Me too," everybody said.

"Let's stop?" Eryk suggested.

"Yes," everyone agreed.

They looked for a semi-open spot, and without any luck they sat down where they were, exhausted.

Mason and Eryk immediately dumped out the contents of their bags— granola bars, apples, packed sandwiches, drinks and clothing items fell out.

The Mystics ate in an oblong circle, refueling their energy. They only had eight days left. Eight days to find the Tree of Remedium, eight days to gather all the leaves, eight days to solve the riddle, eight days to find the ingredient, eight days to figure out the other riddle. It sounded impossible in Elle's thoughts. Why couldn't the Dealer be more specific? When she thought of the Dealer, she couldn't help but think of Leonardo, and wasn't too sure why. After all, he knew his way to the adobe like the back of his hand, insisted that they didn't call him "the Dealer," and somehow convinced him to see Elle without being on the waiting list.

Leonardo. He hadn't been very pleasant the last time they spoke. What if that was *the* last time they spoke? She needed help, and he was only bitterly distant. That couldn't've been Leonardo in the forest with her last night. It was probably some trick. That thought made Elle choke on her water—luckily nobody noticed. What if Leonardo hadn't put a thought into Eryk's mind, but her's instead? What if the whole firefly adventure was a false, implanted memory? But for what? The only reason would be to get to know her better. But why? Something wasn't adding up with Leonardo and the Dealer. It made her food taste bad.

"Why do you hate Leonardo?" Elle asked, interrupting the conversation.

Alaina stifled a laugh and Eryk's face contorted.

"Who actually likes him, for one?" Eryk said.

"But why do you specifically not?"

Mason, Alaina and Eryk exchanged glances.

"I'm sure he'd be happy to tell you himself," Eryk mumbled.

Elle knew that was the end of the discussion and didn't try again. She didn't want Leonardo to tell her, because she had a feeling he would twist his words and she wouldn't get the entire truth. She wanted to hear the words from Eryk, firsthand.

They packed up the rest of their food and wrappers and started walking again. Elle's muscles ached from yesterday's training, but she ignored the pain as best she could with each step.

Alaina insisted on leading for the next hour and nobody objected. Alaina seemed to be the only one with energy. Elle couldn't tell if Mason was tired like her, as he didn't talk much. His eyes were focused on the path in front of him, and his mind seemed deep in thought.

Continuing to hike the rainforest, they carried on the Thinking Game again—this time the category was animals. At first, Mason suggested countries in Southern Belltheria, but everybody rejected that idea.

Alaina was out first again, and Elle got knocked out when she repeated, "Snake." It was down to Eryk and Mason.

"Flamingo," Eryk said.

"Rhinoceros," Mason said.

"Jaguar."

"Boni Giant Sengi."

"Okay, what the hell is that?" Eryk exclaimed.

Alaina and Elle laughed.

"Formerly known as the Elephant Shrew?" Mason tried.

Everybody looked at him questioningly.

"Lives in the Boni-Dodori forest in Kenya?" Mason further attempted.

"I think you made that up," Eryk said.

Everybody laughed, except Mason. He was just too smart for the rest of them, and had won every game thus far.

Mason and Eryk conversed with each other as they searched for the Remedium Tree. Alaina was becoming tired, and Elle's body cried in protest. She had done more physical activity in Remedium in the last couple of days than she ever had her whole human life.

The air became denser as they reached three o'clock. Vibrant colored birds flew overhead, some swooping down to scoop up a bug or two. Elle was fascinated at the sight of the yellow beaked birds. She wondered that if she had had a normal life and went to elementary school she would know what that bird was called. But she didn't have a typical childhood, and that was why she was there now, as a Heliopath, in an attempt to save her Charmer mother.

At five o'clock, Mason traded Eryk for leader, so Eryk walked with Elle at the back of the line.

"How are you?" Eryk asked, their steps becoming synchronized.

"Fine," Elle said. "My muscles are sore."

"We'll stop soon for the night."

"No. We need to keep going, we only have eight days," Elle insisted.

Eryk smiled.

They walked. And walked. And walked. Mason led them, swerving in and out of trees, up and down the erratic jungle ground, and around growing rain puddles. Butterflies flew about, anteaters wandered around and families of sloths lazily hung from elongated tree branches.

"Okay, I feel like we are accomplishing nothing." Alaina huffed, putting her hands on her knees.

Everybody stopped and looked at her, then at each other. They were all glazed with sweat and carried puffy eyes. Their clothes hung and stuck awkwardly on their bodies, and their shoes were caked with dirt and rainwater. Mason's glasses were fogged up and he had to take them off to wipe them with his shirt.

"Do you have another suggestion?" Eryk asked irritably.

"No. I just don't think walking around in hopes to see the Tree is doing us any good," Alaina said.

Elle pursed her lips to the side, thinking. She agreed with Alaina. They had been traveling all day, the sun was beginning to set, and soon there wouldn't be any light. The rainforest was much too enormous to scout for a specific tree in less than eight days. They had to change their tactics. Elle looked around her, tuning out the sound of Eryk and Alaina arguing. Flying bugs circled around them, a yellow lizard scampered up a tree, and she could hear spider monkeys examining fruit from the canopy. If only they could see what the monkeys could see, they had a great view of the forest.

"How tall is the Remedium Tree?" Elle asked.

"As tall as these trees, probably taller," Mason answered. "Why?"

"I was just thinking, if we could get a higher view of the forest, it might be easier to find the Tree," Elle explained.

"That's brilliant," Eryk said.

"We can't climb—that would be impossible," Alaina refuted.

"Not if you're trained in agility and climbing," Mason said, eyeing Eryk and Elle.

"We could burn down the entire forest," Elle objected.

"We can shift to our Heliopath form without being on fire," Eryk said.

Elle imagined herself as a little red monster clambering enormous trees, minus the flames.

"Well, I've never practiced that," Elle said.

"I have a little," Eryk said.

"It's worth a shot," Mason said.

"I'll do it, but back up just in case," Eryk ordered.

Elle, Mason and Alaina took multiple steps back immediately.

Elle watched Eryk in anticipation. Angel and Phoenix had never even mentioned to Elle shifting without fire. And if they didn't find it important, that must mean they found it too problematic.

Eryk's eyebrows furrowed together, almost touching. His face squinted as his eyes focused on his inner Heliopath. His eyes became glassy and blazed red. His skin blushed, then turned scarlet, then deep burgundy. A few flames sparked off his transforming fingers, but he remained glassy red and fireless.

Alaina, Mason and Elle watched Eryk begin to climb the closest tree. Insects and amphibians darted out of the way as Eryk mounted the trunk. He climbed like the spider monkeys they saw during lunch. He was quick and efficient. A few times he couldn't control the natural ashes that flickered off him, but they weren't strong enough to burn anything. Elle held her breath as she watched him disappear into the burly greenery.

Soon, he was out of sight, but the three remaining Mystics kept their heads tilted up. Elle didn't know if she had the ability to climb that high. She had only practiced climbing in the training cave—which was not too exceptionally tall. All she could think was, *please be okay, please don't fall.*

They could hear leaves rustling and birds soaring out of the way and screeching in acrimony.

Everything went silent. The trees went still, the birds and monkeys hushed, the creatures stopped dead in their tracks. The three Mystics looked around, alarmed. The forest was silent, even the talkative cicadas.

Flooomp. Eryk, now engulfed in flames, slid down the massive trunk of the tree, catching it on fire as he descended. He plopped on the ground, startling his friends. Then he frantically transformed back into his regular Mystic form.

"Run!" he shouted.

The Mystics grabbed their bags and darted in the direction Eryk pointed. Elle didn't know what was happening, but she ran faster than she ever did, keeping her eyes on Eryk's back.

"Hurry!" Eryk yelled over his shoulder.

Elle didn't dare look behind her, she could feel the heat of the flames on her heals. She quickened her step, catching up to Alaina.

Alaina darted through trees left and right, Elle right behind her. They lost sight of the boys but quickly found them again. Elle ignored the fierce pain in her muscles that felt like she'd tore through each ligament.

They took a sharp turn, and Elle slid on her side in the slippery mud. It was then she saw the roaring wall of fire chasing them as it consumed the forest. Eradicating anything living in its path. Mutilating the rich colors and creatures' homes.

Alaina pulled her up just in time before the flames could swallow her body.

"There's a river over here," Eryk said, his words turning into coughs.

"Hurry!" Mason shouted.

With his Myst, Mason knocked down enormous trees behind Elle to block the monstrous flames. It bought them a few seconds, but didn't last long. The fire devoured the wood rapidly.

The sound of the gargantuan trees falling behind her, made Elle jump in horror and run faster.

They reached the edge of a cliff, the water not too far below.

A ravenous monster of fire bellowed behind them.

"We have to jump," Mason said.

"Are you sure?" Alaina asked, looking down.

"There's no time," Eryk answered. "Go!"

Alaina looked at Mason and he nodded his head. They took three steps back, the fire slithering closer and closer. They sprinted and jumped off the impending cliff.

"No!" Elle screamed as they dropped from the cliff and out of sight.

The fire roared at their backs.

"They're okay, let's go," Eryk said, taking Elle's hand.

They counted down from three, Elle closed her eyes as they plummeted to the water.

They tumbled through the air and slammed into the murky water like falling onto hot cement.

Plunging into the depths of the mysterious river, pain rung throughout Elle's body. The water was warm and felt acidic on bare skin. She couldn't tell if her eyes were closed or if the river was too dark to see. All she saw was black—the caliginous of the rocking river.

Regaining consciousness, she kicked herself to the surface. Alaina and Mason struggled to paddle in place. They clung to each other, their eyes wide, and Mason glasses-less. Relief flooded Elle when she saw them, and then stopped. She spun around, twice. And then again.

There was no sign of Eryk.

Chapter 10

"Where's Eryk?" Elle cried.

Worry deteriorated the relief in Alaina and Mason's eyes.

"He was with you," Alaina said.

"Eryk!" Elle called again, trying to remember when she let go of his hand, whether it was before or after they hit the water.

Alaina and Mason joined in, screaming his name. It echoed off the sides of the cliff and bounced off the rippling water like a skipping stone.

Elle plunged back under the surface, but it was too somber to see anything.

"Eryk," she cried, louder. Tears fell from her cheeks into the water.

"We need to get out of here, this isn't going to help us find him," Mason said.

"There's a strip of land right over there, I can see it," Alaina said. "We can't stay here."

"But—"

"We'll see him better on land," Mason said.

"Fine, but let's hurry." Elle choked back a sob.

They swam with the current to the strip of land and heaved themselves up and out of the atrocious water.

Elle's legs dragged beneath her; her head spun as she breathed in the dense air.

"Eryk!" Alaina and Mason shouted again.

The three Mystics regained their breaths and stopped to listen for any reply.

"Please, Eryk. Answer," Elle screamed, her throat aching. "Answer me, Eryk Rylander!"

Elle plopped back on the rocky land in exhaustion as they became quiet again.

The river roared. The birds cawed. The monkeys hopped from branch to branch. Then they heard a faraway voice.

Not knowing if she imagined it or not, Elle sat straight up. "Eryk, we're here," she shouted.

"I hear him," Mason said.

Alaina popped up too, Mason by her side.

"Do you see him?" Alaina asked, squinting her eyes to the distance.

"I lost my glasses," Mason said, "I can only see what's right in front of me."

"Eryk," Elle yelled again.

"I'm here!" a voice shouted from the distance.

Their eyes scaled the river, desperately searching for their best friend.

"I see him," Elle screamed.

"Where?" Alaina jumped.

"Right there. He's holding onto a log or something." Elle pointed to the left.

"He's moving fast," Alaina said. "Mason, you can pull him in with your telekinesis. Hurry."

"Okay," Mason said. "But I can't see!"

Alaina shifted Mason's body in Eryk's direction, when she heard him yelling for help.

"Hurry Mason," Alaina said.

Mason focused. All he saw was a mass of blurry blue. He imagined Eryk clinging to a piece of driftwood and imagined pulling him in.

"I'm trying," Mason stammered. "Is he coming closer?"

"Yes, yes, you're doing good, keep going," Alaina encouraged, desperate.

Eryk and the tiny piece of driftwood, focused into view. Elle could have sworn she heard him cheering as he rode along the deep navy river.

"A couple more feet, come on," Alaina told Mason, as he stared in the distance.

Eryk came closer and closer and Elle stood on her tiptoes at the edge of the land. Her heartbeat hammered throughout her shivering body.

"I'm okay," Eryk announced as he reached the strip of land.

Alaina and Elle pulled him in and the driftwood floated away after him. They fell on their backs, sandwiching Eryk.

"Good job Mason, good job," Eryk said.

Mason sighed and plopped on the ground next to his friends.

Relief flooded Elle and she closed her eyes, squeezing Eryk's hand beside her.

They were soaking wet and didn't care. They laid there in exhaustion and relief together, not wanting to get up.

Then, they all started to laugh, because they were deliriously tired and relieved and excited and overjoyed to be together again. All their emotions tangled up in one.

"Please tell me you at least saw the Tree," Mason huffed.

"I did, man, I did." Eryk smiled.

"We need to keep going," Elle said, sitting back up but still holding onto Eryk's hand.

"Whoa, let's just catch our breath for a second," Alaina said.

Elle laid back down. The sun sat precariously at the edge of the sky, creating a blur of colors. From gold, to blush, to deep indigo. It looked like an abstract painting. And Elle, even though she was desperate to finish the first task, wanted to lay there with her friends and watch the sun and colors fade while the moon, stars and beautiful darkness took its place. As she laid there, intertwined hands with Eryk, the thought of Leonardo reappeared back into her mind. She wondered what he was doing at that exact moment—what he'd been up to while she scavenged a massive rainforest, running from threatening flames and swimming in a barbaric river that tried to steal her best friend.

Wait. Was Eryk her best friend? She supposed so. He was the first friend she'd ever had other than Emmie. But of course, Elle tried not to think of her, as Emmie would probably never think of Elle again. She changed the thought. Eryk wasn't only the first friend she'd ever had, but he was the first person to treat her like she was a human and not a mutilated child with mental disorders. He never looked at her like she was incapable like all the therapists, doctors, courtroom figures, and Mrs. Everson did. Especially Mrs. Everson. Mrs. Everson treated Elle like she was an irreparable, lifeless body that she had to keep in her house for money. Though Mrs. Everson was never abusive like so many other foster care parents, she was never a motherly figure either. Elle was told by the other children that the parents didn't like getting attached to them because they knew they'd have to let them go too soon. Elle thought she understood that, until now. The foster kids—the abused and depressed, forever damaged children—*need* someone to be attached to them. And now that Elle was receiving that love and attachment from her friends, she realized this feeling—this passionate and growing desirous feeling—is what foster children needed. They needed to know they were loved and that someone would risk their life for them, because they never got that before. She imagined that was what real parents felt for their kids. That feeling was how she felt for Emmie. And that was what she was starting to feel for Eryk. She squeezed his hand tighter, making sure he was still there with her after losing him. She knew it was silly, because she only lost him for several minutes, but she never wanted to lose him any longer than that. She had lost so much of her life already, and she wasn't going to lose anymore.

Emmie panged into her mind again. If there was a way to turn her mother back into a human, there had to be a way to give Emmie her memories back.

"Sorry for my inability to control my fire," Eryk said, penetrating the silence.

"I'll make sure to remind Angel to work on your controllability." Elle mocked him for saying the same thing about her balance.

Eryk laughed. "Fantastic."

"Hopefully the entire jungle isn't burned down by now," Alaina said.

"Nah, I could feel it. It wasn't *that* out of control," Eryk replied. "It probably burnt out with the rain and moisture."

Elle thought of the boisterous flames that chased them through jungle. If Eryk professed that those flames were not fully out of his control, then Elle didn't want to experience the ones that were.

They were quiet again, listening to the flowing river and the sounds of the forest.

"We need to start on the second riddle," Eryk said.

Elle sat up, let go of Eryk's hand and took the scroll of riddles from her bag—somehow it was completely dry. Everyone sat up with her and she read aloud.

"You have not listened to me. You have shattered me; you have damaged me forever. You cannot live without me. I am close to Hades, sleeping with the man who took two of me and created two of me."

There was silence. Elle passed the scroll along and everyone quietly read it to themselves.

"Let's start off with what we know," Mason said. "What do we know about Hades?"

"Hades is the Greek God of the underworld," Alaina said.

"Yes," Mason said.

"So, the next ingredient is close to the underworld?" Alaina asked.

"Well the underworld is where the dead are," Elle offered. She didn't know much about the Greek mythology, but it had always fascinated her anyway.

"Yes," Mason said. "So the ingredient is close to death, or is dead maybe."

Everyone reread the riddle again, slower this time.

"The ingredient is sleeping with someone?" Alaina was too confused.

"Maybe it's buried?" Elle theorized.

"That could make sense." Mason looked impressed.

"Maybe it's not dead, but broken? It says it's shattered, it could mean literally," Eryk said.

"So, it's broken and buried," Alaina put together.

"Maybe," Mason said. "It's a good start."

Elle was stumped. If it was broken then it had to be an object, but it said that you didn't listen to it as if it were a person. She couldn't untangle the jumbled words in her head.

"Let's just finish the first task," Alaina said.

"Oh yeah, you saw the Tree of Remedium?" Mason asked Eryk.

"Not too far from here actually, a few miles north," Eryk said. "We should go."

"I need my glasses." Mason motioned to his eyes with a wry smile.

They all laughed. It felt good to laugh after the intense events of the evening.

"Do you think you can use your Myst?" Alaina suggested as she sat back up.

"I don't know where they are though, somewhere in there," Mason pointed to the deep flowing river.

"You might as well as try," Alaina said.

Mason shrugged his shoulders. His curly hair was sopping wet as he walked to the edge and put his fingers to his temples. Elle watched him focus as he thought of his thick black glasses sitting at the bottom of the river.

Then, from the left of the river, a pair of glasses emerged from the water and hung in the air. Water dripped from the spectacles and they flew to Mason too fast, hitting his forehead before falling back into the water.

Elle picked them up out of the water before they could get too far.

Mason sighed with relief. "Thank you."

"Is this a bad time to mention that I lost my bag?" Eryk said.

"Why doesn't Mason just use his telekinesis again?" Elle said.

"I'm not familiar with it," Mason said. "I won't be able to get in touch with it."

"We can worry about that later," Eryk responded. "Let's get going."

The Mystics grabbed their belongings—the ones that still had belongings, anyway—and Alaina took out a climbing rope from her backpack. This section of the cliff was about half the height as the one they jumped from but was still tall and steep.

Everyone agreed that Eryk was probably the best climber and should be the one to climb without a rope and carry it up instead. Alaina handed Eryk the soggy climbing rope from her bag. He took it and started to make his way up the steep, rocky cliff. Elle watched nervously from the ground, but trusted he wouldn't fall.

He was a quick climber as he ascended up the side of the cliff. He heaved himself up onto the ground of the forest and tied the rope to the closest tree. He gave them a thumbs up and swung the rest of it down to his friends. The rope was long, but was still a couple of feet away from touching the rocky ground.

"It's not too bad," Eryk informed them. "If you slip, Mason can catch you in the air. He should go last."

Elle watched Alaina grab onto the end of the rope and use her upper body strength to heave herself upward. Elle's arms ached just from watching. Alaina swung her body into the jungle's floor and stood up, proud.

"You're turn, Elle," Alaina said.

Apprehensive, Elle grabbed onto the end of the daunting rope. It was heavy and swung back and forth with the simple touch. Using her upper body strength, Elle pulled herself up the rope like Alaina did. She tried not to think of the pain shooting up her arms as she swung her feet onto the rocky side of the cliff. She tried concentrating all her weight on her feet so her arms wouldn't ache as much. It helped a little, but not much. She mimicked Alaina's movements as she clambered up the rope.

Once she reached the top, Elle flopped onto the muddy grass and breathed. She looked at her burning hands and they were bright red. Too exhausted, she closed her eyes. She wondered when she would be just as good as the other Mystics. It was apparent that she had less training than her friends, but she wanted to be at their level eventually. She wondered how many training sessions with Angel and Phoenix that would take.

Mason simply teleported up the cliff. Eryk untied the rope from the tree and Alaina shoved it back into her backpack.

Elle sat back up. The sky was turning navy. Drenched with river water, they all looked totally wrecked.

"Let's at least get to the Tree tonight," Eryk said.

Eryk just never gave up. Even after sprinting away from outrageous flames and almost drowning in a pernicious river, he still wanted to keep going.

"Come on guys, we don't have to gather the leaves tonight, let's at least get there," Eryk insisted.

"You're right," Elle said. The words "eight more days" rung in her head.

"It's not far," Eryk said.

The four exhausted and determined Mystics stood up and started to walk back through the jungle once again.

They trudged through the trees. Nobody talked, nobody complained, nobody started the Thinking Game. Elle enjoyed the silence and listened to the whispers of the jungle—the chirp of the restless crickets, the mother birds saying goodnight to their young ones, the monkeys swinging back home and the toads hopping through the ponds.

Some trees were burnt from Eryk's fire, but the damage wasn't bad. Elle thought Angel and Phoenix would be proud of Eryk's performance today. Maybe not his lack of control, but his persistence. She was proud of him at least. All she could feel was her sore muscles and lack of rest, but Eryk exuberated determination and liveliness.

"You have not listened to me. You have shattered me, you have damaged me forever...sleeping with the man who took two of me and created two of me." Mason murmured under his breath. "Took two of me, created two of me."

"Figured out anything yet?" Alaina called over her shoulder.

"No," Mason grumbled. "You cannot live without me..."

They walked farther and farther, becoming closer to the Tree. Darkness consumed the jungle. The only sounds were the sleepless insects and the four Mystics stepping noisily through the leafy, muddy ground. A few miles north was beginning to feel like a thousand worlds away.

They had been walking so long, Elle could no longer feel her legs move. They did it on their own. Each and every step.

"I know I said this an hour ago, but this time we really are almost there because look," Eryk pointed.

Simultaneously, Elle, Alaina and Mason pulled their heads up from the ground. And there it was. The beautiful, magical tree they had been searching for all day. Right in front of them, in all its glory. It was huge and otherworldly compared to the other trees. The Tree made the others look hideous and overgrown. Silvery blue lights of signatures were sketched all over the trunk and limbs. The light glowed brightly in the darkness, almost hurting Elle's eyes. The Tree of Remedium was pure hypnotic magic.

Though the Tree's mesmeric powers could not affect Elle now as a Mystic, she was still drawn to it. All the weight of their recent treacherous events lifted from her shoulders. They made it. They survived the first task. The erratic emotions of the day wore off as Elle stared at the wondrous tree. The word "tree" almost didn't fit the appearance. It was in fact a tree, but it felt like so much more. This magical tree saved her life. It was the tree that brought her refuge and joy. It was her remedy. Perhaps that was how it got its name.

As Elle looked at the Tree of Remedium she thought of where she would be now, if she hadn't stepped inside it with Eryk. She felt like a completely different person then—that if she were to see a photograph of herself taken a month ago she wouldn't even recognize it. She wondered if Emmie was still doing well at the Everson's. Even though Emmie experienced similar things to Elle, she never let it ruin her. She never attracted a Charmer for some reason. Maybe Elle wouldn't've either if her Charmer hadn't been her mother. So why did her mother choose to destroy her, and not Emmie? She was glad Emmie wasn't chosen, though.

"I'm starving," Mason said, taking Elle out of her reverie.

Everyone slumped down by the Tree and started taking food out of their backpacks. Elle hadn't realized how hungry she was until Mason mentioned it. All the contents of her backpack were still wet, but she didn't care as she devoured a premade peanut butter sandwich.

"I'm going to start a fire," Eryk said.

"Why? It's humid," Alaina said.

"Because I'm soaking wet." Eryk walked off to gather sticks, taking Mason with him—who fit a whole sandwich in his mouth.

"My feet are so sore, what about yours?" Alaina said.

"Yes," Elle answered, not really paying attention to the question.

They sat quietly for a moment. They could hear Eryk and Mason's voices from the distance.

"Can I ask you something?" Alaina said.

"Yeah."

"Do you like Eryk?" she asked.

"Yeah, he's great," Elle replied.

"No. I mean, do you actually like him, more than a friend?"

The question made Elle stop chewing. She swallowed hard and looked at Alaina, whose eyes were wide with curiosity.

"Why do you ask this?" Elle asked, mostly because she did not know the answer herself. She'd only just met him.

"I just thought..." Alaina's voice trailed off.

They were quiet again.

"I just thought...because I see how you look at each other," Alaina stuttered. "You know, he wasn't supposed to be your Seeker, but maybe he was."

"What do you mean?" The remark took Elle off guard.

"I guess you don't know how Seeking works. You basically are assigned to someone based on your compatibly with that person. Your instructors assign you, taking into consideration what personality would fit with the person needing to be rescued. Angel and Phoenix assigned Eryk to Seek someone else, and when Eryk found out he didn't get you on Assignment Day, he was really upset. I'd never seen him so upset before. So, he figured something out and took your Seeker's place," Alaina explained.

Elle was shocked. Angel and Phoenix didn't think her and Eryk were compatible enough?

"Well it worked out, anyway," Elle said.

"I should let Eryk tell you the rest of the story," Alaina replied.

Elle wondered what Alaina meant by the rest of the story. Eryk stole her Seeker's place, brought her to Remedium and now she's a Mystic. What else mattered? She pondered what Alaina told her. She said Eryk "figured something out." What was that something? Then the question hit her—who was supposed to be her Seeker?

"Who's my real Seeker?" Elle blurted out just as Eryk and Mason came back.

Eryk dropped the pile of sticks in his hands.

"You told her?" Eryk fumed.

"No. I didn't say anything about Leonardo," Alaina defended, covering her mouth as soon as the words slipped out.

"What about Leonardo?" Elle exclaimed.

Eryk gritted his teeth, took a deep breath and looked at Elle's eyes. "Leonardo was your Seeker."

Chapter 11

"What does that mean?" Elle asked, her face grave.

Mason crafted the pile of sticks to hold the flames proficiently. He avoided eye contact with Elle and Eryk, as did Alaina.

"It doesn't change anything," Eryk said as he lit the wood on fire with a single finger. "It just means that the instructors of Remedium thought Leonardo would be better to Seek you."

"So they were wrong, what's the big deal?" Elle inquired.

"The big deal is that Eryk broke the number rule in Remedium and the number two and third rule to Seek you," Alaina fussed.

"I wouldn't say it was the number one rule," Eryk said.

"One of them," Alaina said.

"Well, what happened?" Elle couldn't wait any longer. She figured this was probably why Eryk hated Leonardo and why Leonardo hated him. She was too curious to keep waiting for the answer. The answer of why the two boys she was most drawn to couldn't stand to be near each other—let alone hear each other's names.

Eryk inhaled deeply. He looked at Alaina and Mason and they understood. They got up to go for a walk, leaving them alone.

"I'll start from the beginning," Eryk spoke once Alaina and Mason were out of view. "I had been a Mystic for three years—training, learning, the whole thing. It was finally the season for Heliopaths and other Mystics—including Anitari's, the Castello twins' Myst—to Seek again. I had sought three times and it was unsuccessful. The five days leading up to Assignment Day they showed the Mystics a panel of the people with Charmers that had been found last Seeking season. And there you were."

Eryk looked at Elle's wide brown eyes. She sat in silence, as she listened.

"A picture of you was at the very bottom left of the screen. In the picture you were reading your book under an oak tree. For each person, under each picture was the mental disorders they possess. And if you tap on the picture it will tell you their story. I had read a couple, but I remember thinking they all sounded the same after a while. Then I saw yours. And I wondered what you were about. What your name was and why you were reading alone outside. They don't even say the names on the panel, which I think is ridiculous, because they're all about 'you are not your disorder' but then they put the disorder and not the name? Anyways, I read your summary and remember pronouncing your name Elle-*iss*-ee-uh, and that your story stood out. Not only because it was terribly sad, but because how could a girl go through all these things—abuse, rape, incest—and just be reading under an oak tree? So many girls and boys, who experience those things are usually chopping off their hair, running away, and cutting their skin. But no, not with you—

you were just sitting there, reading, like a normal day, a normal girl.

"So the next day Alaina helped me sneak into Tabitha's office to steal your records. I looked up your address and I skipped training, then I left Remedium on a train to Sepiototumn, to go find you. I wasn't assigned to you, not yet anyway, but I didn't care. Then I took a plane and then a bus and then a cab and I finally found you."

"Was that the day you scared me when I was reading?" Elle said.

Eryk laughed. "No, not yet. I didn't want to scare you by the way, that was my last intention, but I guess I forgot I don't look normal to human eyes. But I just wanted to talk to you. In person you were so tiny—not as fragile as I imagined, as everyone said you were. And then I tried to talk to you, but you were frightened. I didn't want that. I thought I would have a chance to explain, but you ran away. I was really mad at myself because that was exactly what I didn't want. So I went back to Remedium.

"Of course I heard the wrath of Angel and Phoenix when I got back—and Tabitha, but I don't care about her. She told me someone had to be specifically assigned to you because you were a 'special case.'"

The words made Elle flinch, she hated those two words more than anything.

Eryk went on. "Tabitha said that you were afraid of males and that you would never come to Remedium if a boy Seeked you. She said that she had been watching you your whole life and that you were her main priority, and that I ruined it."

Elle's mind flashbacked to the Rebirth. The memory was fuzzy but she remembered Tabitha talking—nearly yelling—at her dad. Saying that his child will be born Indwelled. She remembered being confused if that meant she was a Charmer or if it just meant she hosted one. It was made clear then, since her father was Indwelled when he conceived her, she was born *with* a Charmer, not *a* Charmer. But she thought her Charmer was her mother? And then why wasn't Emmie Indwelled as well? All the questions hurt her head.

"She said that when you became Indwelled, she wasn't surprised. She thought you had been Indwelled from the start, but you weren't, Emmie was."

"Emmie? But I thought—"

"She outgrew it the older she got. That happens sometimes. You saved her from so many beatings, she was strong enough to fight off her Charmer.

"But anyways, Tabitha was furious at me for going to see you. She banned me from the Seeking season and training, but I knew Tabitha was wrong about you. Even though I saw you for a short few minutes, I knew that I couldn't give up on you. I had to be your Seeker. If someone else otherworldly like me came into your life, you would be too freaked out. At least you would have recognized me if I went back. I could just imagine some other Mystic trying to talk to you, frightening you more than I did, and then you running inside to tell your foster parents, and them accusing you of having 'imaginary friends' or something ridiculous. And then it was time for Assignment Day and Phoenix had told me all week that she was working things out for me. I was pretty confident that I would get you, and then as you know, Leonardo Castello was crowned your Seeker. I never liked him. And so when I found out Leonardo was your Seeker and not me, I can't tell you how furious I was. Because for one, he's not a girl—the main reason Tabitha was mad at me for going to see you. And two, he's probably the most unpleasant, cold hearted Mystic to ever walk Remedium, besides the Dealer. And three, in no way is he compatible to you. I could not, and still can't, imagine in what way Leonardo's personality matches yours.

"As upset as I was, I wasn't planning on doing anything about it. There was nothing I could do. Until Leonardo approached me, and then I had no choice. He and his sister were trying to mess with mind and take away my memory of you. Too bad they didn't know I was sitting by a Bouncer—a Mystic who can deflect powers. And of course the Bouncer told me, so I set Anastasia's bungalow on fire and Leonardo's on accident. I swear I didn't do it intentionally. But then a Hydrosensus got in my way and Leonardo tried to make me think I resented you. It didn't work because he was too distracted by the fire. Anyways, Leonardo and Anastasia were in 'critical condition' once Seeking started. Nobody was assigned to you anymore, and I thought that was dumb, so I visited you again, and that was the day I 'scared' you. And now here you are, and here I am."

Elle didn't know what to say. The whole explanation sounded like chaos.

"Why didn't they want you to remember me?" Elle asked in no more than a whisper.

"I assume so I wouldn't get in the way," Eryk tried.

They were quiet, staring at the flames in front of them.

"And you didn't get a punishment or anything?" she asked.

Eryk bit the inside of his cheek. "No, not really. I got banned from training until the end of the Seeking Season, which ended when you got initiated. Angel and Phoenix didn't agree with that punishment, so they only trained me every other day instead. The thing about Remedium is that it's not ran on laws and punishments. It's free and runs on peace. But every civilization has to have some sort of order, and I disturbed that."

Elle nodded her head, not really listening to the words anymore. She couldn't get her mind off Leonardo now. How could Leonardo want to take away Eryk's memory of her? How was it possible to wish that on a person? Without Eryk, she had no idea where she would be. Leonardo couldn't've done what Eryk did for her. Could he? Leonardo, a distant mysterious boy, could never have convinced her to go to some magical land with him. As beautiful as he was, he was also daunting—like an intriguing nightmare. And that is not what Elle needed. The instructors were wrong, they had to be.

"What are you thinking?" Eryk asked.

"How did Leonardo ever get assigned to me in the first place?" Elle replied.

Alaina and Mason returned. They didn't ask any questions and Eryk didn't try to read Elle's thoughts.

Everyone pulled out their tightly wrapped sleeping bags from their backpacks and laid beneath the magical tree. Eryk slept in the branches of the Remedium Tree since he'd lost his bag. The four Mystics cozied into their spots and succumbed to their exhaustion.

When Elle eventually fell asleep, the sound of Mason moaning woke her up again. She laid flatly on the ground, staring up at the Remedium Tree's hanging leaves. Mason wailed sounds of pain, waking up the critters of the jungle.

"Mason, are you alright?" Alaina whispered, unzipping her sleeping bag.

Alaina tiptoed over to Mason who sat hunched up with his head between his knees. There was sounds of puking and agony.

"Oh no, oh no," Alaina said as she sat by Mason.

Elle could hear Alaina rummage through a backpack. She pulled out a water bottle and made Mason drink.

"Let's get you out of the sleeping bag, come on," Alaina said.

Mason was a deadweight under Alaina's arms. She transformed her arms to be stronger with muscle and she heaved her sickly friend from the puke covered blanket. Mason moaned as she did.

"Mason, you're burning hot," Alaina said. "We need to change your clothes."

Just as she said that Mason threw up again, staining his shirt with brown and green liquid. The pungent scent made Alaina gag. Mason groaned loudly in torment.

"Okay, it's okay," Alaina soothed. She slipped his puke drenched t-shirt from his body and off his arms. His chest and thin stomach were blazing like Eryk in his Heliopath form.

"What's wrong?" Eryk muttered, waking up.

"It's Mason," Alaina wailed. "He's sick, really sick."

She took a shirt from her own backpack and poured water on it. She patted Mason's forehead that sat in her lap and his burning shoulders and chest.

"That's not good," Eryk said, hopping soundlessly from the Tree.

He stared down at his friend. Mason's eyes were closed in exhaustion, and his mouth hung open. His skin was bright pink and his face was a distasteful green color.

"He threw up twice," Alaina told Eryk as she patted Mason with her shirt.

"Do you think he just ate something bad? Or is it worse?" Eryk asked, concerned.

"I don't know. Maybe he swallowed too much river water? Hopefully it's just a bug," Alaina stammered.

Mason rolled on his side and threw up again. Alaina held him up so he wouldn't choke. She continued to hold the wet shirt on his forehead, though it was only making the shirt warm and sweaty instead.

"Let's sit you up against the tree," Alaina said.

Her and Eryk took each of his arms and dragged him to the Tree. It was cooler in the shade, but not much. They placed his back against the trunk but his head lolled to his shoulder. Alaina made him gurgle with water as best as she could.

"Is he okay?" Elle asked.

Eryk looked up at her instantly. They all had the same expression on their face. Complete and utter worry.

"We should get him back to Remedium," Eryk said.

"Get him a clean shirt from his bag," Alaina ordered. She pushed him to drink more water.

Mason groaned. "I can't leave."

"You have to, you're sick. We'll be okay," Alaina said.

Eryk returned with a brown shirt in his hand and gave it to Alaina. She put it over his hand and through his arms.

"Maybe someone should go with him to tell Tabitha, and get him to a hospital," Elle suggested.

"I'll go," Eryk volunteered.

"No," Alaina objected instantly. "I'll go. You should stay with Elle."

Eryk didn't argue.

"I'll sign Mason into the Remedium clinic and then tell Tabitha. Maybe she'll let me come back," Alaina said.

Mason moaned loudly. He held his stomach in one of his hands and his eyes were scrunched tightly together.

Alaina found the indented triangle of the Tree and pushed her hand in. Just like it did with Eryk's the night he brought Elle to Remedium, it traced the pattern of her hand and twisted the image around the bark. The names and initials glowed and the print swirled up the tree. At the bottom of the trunk a camouflaged door slid open and the tiny elevator awaited inside.

"Wait," Mason said. The single word took so much effort for him to say. "The riddle."

Alaina, Elle, and Eryk looked at each other and then back at Mason.

"What about the riddle?" Eryk asked.

"It's..." he dozed in and out of consciousness.

The three Mystics stared at him eagerly.

"A heart," Mason forced out, and then fell into unconsciousness again.

"A heart?" Elle uttered.

Alaina pulled Mason into the elevator and it started to close.

"Good luck," Alaina said. "I'll see you—"

The door shut and they were gone. Elle and Eryk looked at each other.

"The answer is a heart?" Eryk asked.

"Who's?" Elle added.

"I have no idea." Eryk shook his head.

It was obvious neither of them had gotten much sleep. They didn't know what time it was, but it was still dark.

"Guess it's just me and you now," Eryk said.

"Guess so."

Elle couldn't get the sight of suffering Mason out of her head. He looked so frail, so weak. The smart, smiley Mason had dissipated into a feverish, diseased boy. She hoped with all her heart he was okay. She'd known the Quest would be dangerous, but watching Mason struggle reminded her again of the reality of that danger.

Chapter 12

Sunbeams leaked between the thousands of leaves and onto the Tree of Remedium. The Tree shimmered amongst all the mundane trees. If there were to be any hikers throughout the forest they would be drawn to the Tree of Remedium—its magical properties mesmerized average eyes.

The gold lighting danced on Elle's eyelids. She woke up feeling refreshed from the pure exhaustion of yesterday's events. Sleeping next to the Tree of Remedium rejuvenated her mind and body. She was ready for the day's events.

Above her, laid Eryk. His mouth hung wide open and his eyes laid closed. His hair looked nearly black in the shade of the Tree. Elle didn't want to disturb his slumber.

With pursed lips, she turned away from her sleeping friend. She would let him sleep for just another half hour and in the meantime, she would practice her Myst.

Elle then sat crisscross by the burned-out campfire from last night. The wood was covered with embers but was still durable enough to be lit again. She took a breath and held up her right hand. Spreading her fingers out, she concentrated on her core. She was really sick of the word "core" as Angel and Phoenix had said it at least ten thousand times during training. The tips of her fingers sparked a few times and then bright orange flames caressed her skin. The sight still amazed her. She touched the tips of her fingers together. The flames traveled from one set of fingers to the other. Now all ten fingers were possessed the beautiful orange glow. Elle loved her Myst.

Alternating hands, Elle practiced setting the wood on fire and sucking the fire back into her fingers. After doing this several times, the sun glowed radiantly and it was now time to wake up Eryk. The forest didn't feel threatening in the slightest. Elle guessed being near the Tree of Remedium made the place feel secure. It was nice to have a steady heart beat again, but then she remembered what happened during the night. Mason. There was still a form of apprehension pinching her stomach. The safety was only an illusion, they were still on the Quest and the Quest was dangerous. She wondered how Mason was doing.

Eryk laid in the same position. One of his arms flopped over the side of the branch and his feet touched the trunk. His eyelids fluttered open as Elle spoke his name in a low voice from below. In a sleepy daze, he clumsily fell from the branch and hit the ground hard. Elle laughed as he got up, wiping the dirt from his shirt.

"Why didn't you wake me earlier? What time is it?" Eryk said, startled. His dark hair was in disarray but his eyes were alert.

"It's not late, no worries," Elle said as she reached for her backpack. Eryk smiled at her placid tone.

They sat down on the long light green grass and munched on some breakfast bars. It was so quiet in the forest that it didn't feel right. It wasn't that the birds weren't cawing or the monkeys weren't scouring the trees. It wasn't that the tigers were resting or the amphibians were taking a break from the ponds. It was that two bodies were absent, and everything felt still.

"Do you think Mason is okay?" Elle said in whisper because it was too silent to use anything more.

"I really don't know." Eryk shrugged his shoulders. They were thinking the same thing. The Quest felt a million miles away and far too daunting to run into it head on. Now that they were two people short, they had to be more precise and count every second.

"Last night I couldn't sleep," Eryk said. "So I inspected the Tree, trying to figure out which leaves we need to take. It took a while, but I think I've narrowed it down to two branches that could be the correct set of leaves. I thought I'd wait for you to decide; it was beginning to all look the same to me."

Elle nodded and scoffed down the rest of the stale breakfast bar. The heat was spoiling their food supplies and making the water too hot. They needed to get out of the jungle.

They walked over to the two branches Eryk had tagged last night. They were both on the bottom row and looked nearly identical.

"You figured this out all last night?" Elle asked.

Eryk nodded his head slowly.

"I couldn't decide between these two," Eryk pointed again. "I wanted your opinion."

Elle studied the two branches of leaves. Both light green with the occasional brown spot. Both curled tipped. Both weak veins. They were the same. Elle remembered her own tiny forest back at the Everson's. She loved when the leaves began to change various colors. It was all so calming to be surrounded by the reds and soft yellows. It was her refuge.

And as she stared at the leaves of the Remedium Tree, she almost felt a pang of longing for her old refuge.

"They look just alike," Elle said after several moments of uselessly eyeballing each leaf.

"Exactly," Eryk said. "Did you think we missed something in the Riddle? Maybe it's two branches."

Elle pondered the idea. She was certain they had solved the riddle correctly. It had to be one of the two branches Eryk chose. Mason would have been able to figure it out.

"No, it's got to be one of these. Not both," Elle said. She reached out a hand and touched the leaves. Perhaps the textures would reveal the correct set. The first set was rough from the protruding veins and jagged on the sides, they smelled luscious of morning dew and freshly mown grass. She continued though with the second set. These leaves didn't feel so rough on the surface but were lighter in color.

"So? What do you think?" Eryk asked as Elle stepped back.

She bit the side of her lip in thought. The rougher yet greener leaves? Or the smoother but less green leaves?

"Hmmm," Elle thought. "That one." She pointed to the first set of leaves that possessed a rougher texture.

"You're four hundred percent positive?" Eryk asked.

"Positive."

"Alright, that one it is," Eryk said.

He began plucking the delicate leaves one by one. She placed the backpack on the ground and started to help pluck the leaves.

They worked quietly alongside each other, tearing the leaves from their home in order to revive Elle's mother back to a human. The silence was peaceful. That was one of the nice things about Eryk. Elle didn't feel forced to start a conversation to avoid awkwardness. She was naturally comfortable around him, as he was around her. She never felt the need to explain her words or actions. He just knew and understood. It was a nice feeling to have. And that was one of the best things about Eryk.

As they went along, Elle realized just how ginormous the Tree of Remedium really was. A single branch held up to hundreds of leaves, making the task not seem so simple anymore. Each time she plucked a leaf and read the signature of the member on it, it hurt just a little.

"What happens to the signatures?" Elle asked.

"The leaves grow back with them on," Eryk answered. "I forget how much you don't know about Remedium."

It frustrated Elle that she hadn't learned everything about Remedium. She wanted to so badly know everything about the magic of Remedium and all that it acquired.

"Then tell me. Tell me the history," Elle said.

"I can't, I'm not allowed," Eryk said.

"Well, why not? I want to know." Elle scrunched her eyebrows together.

"I said 'I can't' not that I won't."

Elle smiled and plucked another leaf from its limb.

"The Villages of Remedium have existed forever. When the earth was created, so was Remedium. They say the first Mystic to live in Remedium was an angel named Protector. Protector possessed every Myst imaginable. She was very powerful and intelligent. When she arrived to Remedium, it didn't have a name and it was very small. She was also the only one alive in Remedium and she wanted companions. So, she decided to build a village out of the trees for all the people she would bring. She valued naturalism and truth. She was a very hard worker and got quite carried away when she built the village. When she finished, it looked like a kingdom of treehouses and she couldn't've been more satisfied with her work. She wanted to build a bridge to heaven to gather the other angels to live with her. She began to build the bridge but she ran out of stone and wood because heaven was too far away. Upset that she would never see the other angels again, she decided she would have to bring humans to her village instead. She hadn't heard nice things about earth and was hesitant on bringing the creatures that destroyed their earth to her own land. She did not want her land to be destroyed as well.

"After weeks of indecisiveness she built a magical train to take her to earth and found the land at last. It was worse than she thought. As she roamed the world looking for the correct person to bring back with her she was exposed to terrible things. She saw children crying, teenagers running away, adults screaming. She witnessed sickness, robbers, cheaters and murderers. It terrified her. She wanted to only bring back those who were being hurt—the ones who were stolen from, cheated on, kidnapped. She wanted to save them from dangers and nightmares, and bring them to the security and peace of her land. One night she found a lost boy who rummaged through the trash bins for food. He had cuts on his face and rugged clothing. Protector held her hand out to the boy and he took it instantly. Protector dug a tunnel— the tree elevator—and they climbed up to the inviolable village. It was then Protector saw a harrowing creature dwelling the little boy. She removed it with her power and out came a disgusting mutilated body. The Charmer's name was Post-Traumatic Stress. She killed the creature, but when she turned around the boy was on the floor, unconscious. Not knowing what to do, Protector gave the boy a portion of her power. She gave him the power of strength and endurance. The boy woke up as the power replaced the hole Post-Traumatic Stress had created. He was made brand new. He was safe. He was no longer living in the trapped world. Protector named him Freedom. So next time Protector went back to earth she brought Freedom with her. They both found two people to bring back to the village. All four humans possessed the same horrifying creature as Freedom had. Protector removed the creatures and replaced them with powers. The names of the creatures were Anxiety, Depression, Paranoia, and Bipolar. When one of the humans gained the power Protector gave her, she beamed of jubilance. She said, 'this power is my remedy to my mental illness. Thank you for curing me when no one else could.' It was thus Protector decided to name her village Remedium, as it would be humans' remedy for their traumatic experiences on earth. Every human that was brought to the Villages of Remedium would have their illness—their Charmer—removed and be gifted a power—a Myst. They began calling themselves Mystics when they realized humans thought they looked mystifying from their power inside them. And Charmers got their name when Anxiety told them they charmed people to allow them to feed off their tragic emotions and memories. And that is the creation of Remedium and Mystics and Charmers."

Eryk took a deep breath as he finished the last few words. He loved the story about the creation of Remedium.

"I like that story," Elle finally said after the words settled into the air. She plucked more leaves and dropped them in the bag. "Where is Protector now? And Freedom? And the others?"

"Mystics don't live forever, Ellisia." It was the first time Eryk had ever called her Ellisia but she smiled when he said it. It sounded nice through his strong lips.

"You called me Ellisia," Elle said.

"Oh, uh, sorry," Eryk stumbled over his words, not knowing what to say.

"No, it's okay, really," Elle insisted. "I don't mind. I like both names."

"It doesn't bother you?" Eryk asked.

Elle was quiet for a moment. She had been pondering this thought for a long time. It was like a jumbled knot of string she was trying to untie in her head. Every time she thought of this stubborn knot, little tears would swell her eyes and made her even more frustrated.

"Not that much anymore. It hurt when I heard it after I was taken from him. Because all I could remember was him screaming that name over and over or whispering it in my ear—"

She shook her head. Even though she was a Mystic now, and even though she didn't have any mental disorders, memories still hurt.

"And I didn't want to hear his voice when someone else would say my name, if that makes sense. But when I went through the Transformation and saw my mother, and then saw her as a Charmer and saw her go from a beautiful strong woman to a decrepit body, I realized my name was not only from my dad, but from my mother as well. She named me Ellisia. And maybe the name isn't so bad after all. But the memory of my dad will never go away. Only because my illnesses are gone, he will always be a part of me," Elle said in one breath.

Eryk didn't say anything, and a thoughtful expression remained on his face. Elle knew how he felt. After hearing so many of the foster kids' stories there were no right words to piece together to make them feel okay.

"I understand. I admire your strength." Those were the only sentences Eryk could muster.

She smiled at the ground as a few tears swelled in her eyes. Never had she ever heard someone tell her those words. Never had she ever even told them to herself, because her attachment to her father—her attachment to her abuser—was greater than herself in her mind.

"Attachment is very hard," Elle said, still looking at the ground.

"Tell me," Eryk beckoned. He didn't say it in a demanding tone, he said as if he wanted to hear her words and her thoughts directly from her mind. He wanted to know what she was thinking and why. He wanted to understand.

Elle thought of the words in her mind and the best way to say them.

"It's just that even though I'm a part of Remedium and a Mystic and am far away from him as I possibly can be, I will always be bound to him somehow. No matter the distance and no matter if I never see him again I will always be tied to him. The thing about attachment is that it never leaves you, even when you believe you are unattached. Even when you truly forgive and let go, you can still be attached. And even though he terrified me beyond words, I still love him. I still love him because he is my dad. Yes, I love him. But I don't want to love him, and I want to cut the fragile and decrepit string between us, but I can't find the scissors to do it."

Tears fell with each of Elle's words. Those were the exact words that had been burrowing themselves in the depths of her stomach, creating a lump that could not be ignored. And now that she finally released the words, the lump collapsed and her throat cleared.

Eryk looked at her as she cried, as she dropped the leaves she was holding and cried. He took a step towards her and held her in his arms. He didn't say anything; he didn't hush her.

After holding in all her thoughts, her troubles, her insecurity; after folding her memories like clothes into drawers and locking them away for so long, she finally found the key once more. She let Eryk's arms wrap around her and didn't let the memories tell her to push him away. She wanted him and she wanted to be free. So she hugged him back as the last few tears dripped down her face. She was grateful for him.

It was beginning to rain once again as the second bag started to overflow from the abundance of leaves. The rain was cool and refreshing as Elle and Eryk picked off the last remaining leaves. They didn't talk much after the last few tears left Elle's eyes. Now she just felt groggy and sleepy. But she also felt better.

"And that would be the last one." Eryk beamed as he placed the final withering leaf into the backpack.

Elle smiled at their accomplishment. Although the task took all afternoon, it had been therapeutic. But now since they were finished, it was time for the second task—the second task for which they still had not solved the riddle. Even with Mason's hint, the riddle was not clear enough.

"Time to send them to Remedium," Eryk said as he zipped up the second bag with difficulty.

Elle grinned at his satisfaction and pressed her palm into the indented triangle like Eryk and Alaina had. It traced the pattern and print of her skin and copied it onto the Tree. The lines danced and swirled up the tree trunk and seeped to the branches. This time it glowed bright purple, which was lovely against the rich brown. The elevator door opened to reveal the yellow lit room. Eryk tossed in the backpacks and the door closed after them.

"How do we know the Dealer retrieved them?" Elle asked as the elevator and hand prints dissipated.

"Before we left, Mason told Tabitha that we would be sending leaves up the elevator soon. She said she would keep them safe in her office," Eryk explained.

"Okay, good. Now we need to figure out the second task. We only have seven days left to complete two more tasks," Elle said. She began to roll up her sleeping bag and stuff it in her backpack, along with water bottles and food wrappers.

"Good point," Eryk said as he rummaged through his pocket for the scroll of riddles. "The riddle is: You have not listened to me, you have shattered me, you have damaged me forever. You cannot live without me. I am close to Hades sleeping with the man who took two of me and created two of me."

Elle intently listened to the words, keeping in mind Mason's clue—a heart.

"So we know it's a heart," Elle said after he finished. The thought made her shudder.

"So we just need to figure out *whose* heart."

Eryk read the last line of the riddle again. "Sleeping with the man who took two of me and created two of me."

Elle shook her in frustration. "That doesn't make sense. Nobody *creates* hearts for a living."

Eryk laughed at the smart remark, and Elle began to laugh, too.

Suddenly their fit of laughter was cut off.
A vociferous ringing noise surrounded them.

Chapter 13

They both covered their ears instantly; the sound was agonizing.

"What is that?" Elle yelled over the blaring noise. Her ears and head burst with terrible pain.

Although Eryk didn't hear what she said, he replied, "It sounds like it's coming from over there." He pointed and regretted it immediately. The loud beeping shocked his eardrum.

"What?" Elle shouted.

Because it was too loud to hear each other, Eryk walked over to where he thought the intense beeping was coming from. He aimlessly blasted fire at the noise. It was a high ringing noise and made them want to rip their ears off.

"Eryk? Ellisia?" The high-pitched ringing shut off altogether and a booming voice replaced it. "Eryk? Ellisia? Are you there?"

In relief, Elle dropped her hands from her ears.

"What?" Eryk shouted. "Who are you?"

"Eryk. It's Tabitha. I'm contacting you through the map," the voice echoed through the jungle.

"Can you turn the mic volume down or something?" Eryk shouted in frustration. "You burst our ear drums."

"The map you hold has a twin. Twin maps are capable of finding each other and contacting each other. The Compasses created them when they were first introduced to Remedium," Tabitha explained.

Elle rummaged through the various backpacks, trying to find their own map. It was at the bottom of Eryk's, amongst all the food and soggy clothing. Elle spread it out on the wet jungle ground in front of them, and instead of the original print of the map it was a live video of Tabitha's face.

"Aw! There you are." Tabitha smiled as the image of Elle and Eryk popped up on her map.

"So why are you contacting us? Is there a problem?" Eryk asked.

"No, absolutely not. I retrieved the bags of leaves and they're locked away in a vault in my office," Tabitha answered.

"Then what do you need?" Eryk fumed.

"I hope you don't talk to Ms. Ellisia with that attitude," Tabitha snapped. Eryk rolled his eyes. "I contacted you to inform you that your reinforcements will be there shortly—"

"Reinforcements? What do you mean reinforcements?" Eryk demanded.

"To take Alaina and Mason's place, of course. They were the first to volunteer," Tabitha said.

"Who?" Elle asked before she could hold in the question.

"They will meet you at the train station. You are not to leave Belltheria until they arrive," Tabitha said, ignoring Elle's question.

"We don't need any reinforce—" Eryk started.

"Good luck." Tabitha smiled and then faded from the map.

Eryk and Elle looked at each other as Tabitha's voice dwindled away.

"I see why you don't like her." Elle frowned.

Eryk shook his head from his utter disapproval of Tabitha. "She's quite obnoxious, isn't she?"

"Unhelpful," Elle agreed. "Does this mean Mason isn't okay?"

"I don't know. I really hope he is," Eryk said. "I'm sure he's okay. Let's get going to the train station."

"Lead the way," she said.

They started to make their way through the depths of the tremendous trees. The weather was warming up again, it felt humid like it did the first day of hiking through the jungle. Elle's muscles were sore from yesterday's walking and running and jumping and swimming. Her ears began to throb from the blaring noise of the map. She had never done so much physical activity in her life. It was thrilling in a way. She liked the rash decisions and sprinting through the trees for her life with her friends. She didn't know why she enjoyed it so much, because she was typically an efficient person with lists and plans to achieve. Perhaps running for her life didn't seem so dangerous when she was with Eryk.

Without the map it would be impossible to navigate through the thick jungle. After several minutes in, the trees were already beginning to blend together. It was like walking through a fun house with strange mirrors that distorted your image. Without a magical map from Remedium, anyone would surely die in the jungle. Were they supposed to die in this jungle? Was that the Dealer's plan all along? Elle couldn't see what the Dealer would gain out of their deaths, but now the farther away they got from the Tree of Remedium, the more dangerous the circumstance seemed.

"When will we be able to contact Mason and Alaina do you think?" Elle asked, even though she knew the answer.

"Probably not until we get back from the Quest," Eryk said.

It was frustrating, because Elle desperately wanted to talk to them. She wanted to know if they were okay.

"They'll be fine. Angel and Phoenix told me before we left, that they would help us as much as they could from Remedium. They're probably making sure Mason and Alaina are okay," Eryk said.

Knowing Angel and Phoenix were taking care of her friends, gave some relief to Elle. She trusted her instructors. Even though they were tough, they knew what they were doing.

"You're very close to Angel?" Elle asked as they moved between trees.

"Yes. Angel and Phoenix practically adopted me when I came to Remedium," Eryk answered.

"How so?" Elle beckoned.

"When I came to Remedium, I didn't want to be a Mystic. I felt guilty for leaving Ashlee—my sister—behind without a trace of memory of me. Training got my mind off of it. And over time I started showing up to training a lot more frequently than everyone else. They let me eat with them sometimes, and we just got to know each other. Sometimes I would even fall asleep there. The training cave feels like home," Eryk explained. He spoke with certainty and purpose.

"Are Phoenix and Angel together?" Elle asked, not knowing why she never wondered that before.

Eryk chuckled. "Yes, they're married. They adopted Tula together."

"Yeah, what's the story behind that?"

"It's a long one," Eryk said.

"Tell me."

Eryk drew in a long breath. "Angel was born and raised in Russia. He was born Indwelled, making him a psychopath. Most psychopathic children, including Angel, try to fill that void—that longing for emotions—by killing small animals. He had six other siblings, his father was dead, and his mother couldn't afford to take care of the family. Then one day, he killed his brother. He won't tell me the circumstances around the event. Finally, a Mystic found him and brought him to Remedium. Angel said that after he went through the Transformation, it was the oddest feeling he had ever experienced, because he could feel every emotion he had never experienced before. Happiness. Sadness. Joy. Grief. Guilt. Before he was Transformed, living without emotions was like living blind.

"It was on his sixth Seeking Mission that he was assigned to Phoenix. Phoenix's mother died giving birth to her, and her father was poor. When she was out one day, she was kidnapped. She was sixteen, and so were the other four girls that were kidnapped by the same man. She lived with them for three years, being tortured daily. One day when their captor was gone, Phoenix and one of the other girls escaped. They ran as far as they could and tried to look for help. The two girls stopped for the night under a tree. When Phoenix awoke the next morning, she found her friend dead. Hanging from the tree."

"The girl killed herself?" Elle asked.

"Yes. She killed herself. Phoenix was crying beside her when Angel found her. Phoenix followed Angel into the Tree without a thought. She visits her friend's grave every year.

Then five years ago, when she was visiting, a baby was crying in a nearby tulip patch. The baby was naked and malnourished. Phoenix took her back to Remedium with her. The baby went through the Transformation like everyone else. Angel agreed that they would keep the baby and call her Tulip. Phoenix started singing 'Tula-Tula-Tulip' over and over as the toddler ran around the training cave. Since Angel and Phoenix were taking care of a child they called their daughter, they decided to get married. Weddings in Remedium are simple and intimate events. Tula was their flower girl, and instead of throwing rose petals down the aisle she tossed tulips instead. I was there too; I was one of the groomsmen."

Elle laughed. For some reason she could not picture Eryk as a groomsman. She could not picture him in a tux and smiling seriously for pictures with brushed hair.

"They're really good people. It just takes time to get used to how they work," Eryk said.

"I don't doubt they're good people," Elle replied.

It was obvious now to Elle how much Angel and Phoenix meant to Eryk. It was almost as if they were the parent figures he never had in his life.

Eryk and Elle moved deeper into the forest. She truly had no idea where they were anymore, or how far they had traveled. Her toes were beginning to go sore, so they must have been walking for a while. Sometimes Eryk would hum besides her and Elle liked it. It was a simple tune in a low hum. It made her sleepy.

They traveled and trudged through the jungle grounds. The air was thick with bugs swarming all around. It smelled of the sewer and diseased fish—they must have been close to a swamp. The humidity made it harder to walk and breath.

Eryk and Elle stopped once for a lunch break. They ate some sandwiches that were going stale, but their water was too warm to quench their thirst.

The determined, yet tired Mystics continued through the thick underbrush and muddy slopes. Every so often Eryk would tell Elle the distance they had left, or how much more time they had until they reached the train station. But to her it felt a million miles away, an impossible destination.

"Okay. So, a heart," Elle blurted out, rupturing the eerie stillness of the jungle.

"Right. A heart," Eryk repeated.

"Sleeping with the man who took two of me and created two of me," Elle memorized the last stanza as it was the only words circling her mind.

"Maybe it means a literal man," Eryk suggested.

Elle nodded her head, trying to add that into the puzzle. "So which man?"

"The man who took hearts and created two hearts."

Elle ignored his unhelpful comment. How can someone take hearts? How does someone create hearts?

"How is a heart created?" Elle asked, trying to hear her thought processes out loud. She remembered that this technique had worked for Emmie when she did her homework.

"Hmmm, maybe a drawing? Maybe this man is an artist?" Eryk tried.

Elle accepted the idea, but it didn't feel right. Why would the Dealer need an artist's heart in order to transform her mother into a Mystic?

"It has to be an important aspect of my mother's life," Elle said.

"You mean you think the heart is from someone your mom knew?" Eryk questioned.

"Has to be."

Eryk pressed his lips together in a thin line. "Okay, do you know anyone that died that was important to your mother?"

As he asked the question, the answer became blatantly obvious.

"My father."

Chapter 14

As soon as Elle said the words it was as if the jungle came alive. Birds rustled in the leaves. Monkeys violently swung nearby. Frogs leaped back into the water.

Her mind flooded with images of her father—the man who killed her mother. The man who hit her repeatedly. The man who did unspeakable things. The psychopath. If it wasn't for her father, she wouldn't be a Mystic. She would never have met Eryk. She would never have been brought to Remedium. She wouldn't be fighting her way through a life threatening jungle to save her mother that he killed and turned into a Charmer.

And now she needed his heart.

That was the piece they were missing to the puzzle.

"I think you're right," Eryk spoke.

"I think so, too," Elle said emotionlessly.

The air felt even thicker as each word hit Elle's heart.

It made sense. Her father took two hearts and created two. He took two hearts by killing himself and his wife. He created two hearts by having Ellisia and Emmaline. He transformed Jadine Esmund into a Charmer when he involuntarily murdered her. He wasn't only a piece to the puzzle, he was the *most* important piece.

She didn't even know where her father was buried. She didn't attend his funeral and didn't even know if he had one or not. Who would want to attend a psychopath's funeral? What speeches would've been made there? He wasn't honorable. He was a drunk. An abuser. He had nobody that ever cared for him. He didn't deserve to be well dressed in a casket. He deserved to rot in the dirt.

Elle and Eryk started to walk again. The closer they got to the train station, the more Elle wished for good replacements. They needed someone else's mind to help them assess the situation. With only seven days left, they needed to figure things out. And quickly.

After walking for another hour and a half in the sweltering heat, Elle opted for a break and Eryk didn't decline. They sat down with a *huff*. All Elle wanted to do was take a freezing cold shower and go to bed. She knew what it was like to live in an uncomfortable environment, but this level of exposure was abhorrent. And now that she knew what the next task was, it didn't make her any more eager to get out of the cloying jungle.

"We're almost there, just a little over a mile more," Eryk informed.

Elle sucked up her emotions and jumped back up on her feet. No matter how morbid the circumstances felt, she agreed to do the Quest. And she was going to do it proudly and efficiently. She had to save the mother that was taken so early from her.

"Let's do this," she said defiantly, mustering up the last bit of strength she had for the day.

Elle didn't miss the obvious smile that Eryk tried to stifle.

Elle kept her eyes on Eryk as he walked in front of her. The ends of his dark hair clung to his sweaty neck and his eyes looked even more vibrant than usual amongst the dank and dark greenery of the jungle. His shirt was drenched in sweat and outlined every muscle in his body. He had dark circles under his eyes. Sometimes Elle didn't believe Eryk ever got tired—he had so much stamina and ambition. She wondered how he felt about the next task. Elle was beginning to learn that Eryk was quite unpredictable with his expression at times. Most the time he was open and honest, but other times he became closed off in conversation or stirred them a different way to avoid answering questions.

The Mystics walked along, desperate to get to the train station. They needed fresh water. They needed fresh food. Their legs were beginning to go wobbly and their ears thumped with each step they took. The jungle was extraordinarily giant and Elle was ready to leave it behind.

As time continued, the trees were becoming thinner and the sky started to make an appearance. Elle was surprised when she saw that the sky was a warm shade of blue. They had been walking all day long with only two short breaks in between.

The end of the jungle came into view and butterflies flew through Elle's stomach. They had completed the first task. They had solved the first riddle, they had hiked the dangerous jungle, they had plucked every single leaf and they'd survived! It felt like a huge accomplishment to Elle. When she had signed the contract with the Dealer, she had no idea what she was in for. People doubted her. People feared for her safety. But here she was, skipping out of one of the most dangerous jungles in the world as if it was an amusement park. She *was* going to save her mother. And she was ready for the next task.

When Eryk and Elle stepped ahead of the last tree at last, they couldn't help but to yell out a cheer of contentment. They were finally rid of the disgusting muggy jungle and were now closer to finishing the Quest. It felt infinitely refreshing to see the entire sky. The train station was only a block away and then they could relax until the next task.

As Eryk and Elle started their way to the train station, somehow the topic of Leonardo popped up.

"So, are you, uh, friends with Leonardo?" Eryk asked, stammering on each word.

Elle furrowed her eyebrows instantly. She had not thought of that question herself, and she had not thought of Leonardo all day. Leonardo was definitely an intriguing person, but Elle couldn't forget that he was also unpredictable and controlling.

"Ummm." Elle thought. "I really don't think so." It bothered her knowing that Leonardo attempted to manipulate Eryk's mind into thinking he resented her. It hurt Elle's stomach to even think that Leonardo would try to do such a thing. "Why do you ask?"

Eryk was quiet for a moment, thinking.

"I guess I just don't want him to hurt you in any way. I don't want him to bother you," Eryk said the words slowly.

"I can handle getting my feelings hurt," she said quietly. She didn't want Eryk to protect her. If she wanted to be in Leonardo's life, she would. But right now, it didn't matter anyway. They were on a Quest, a dangerous Quest, and she knew she might never see Leonardo again. She didn't know if that made her sad or not. When she thought of Leonardo, a mass of conflicting emotions swarmed in her head.

"I don't deny that you can," Eryk said. "I just want you to be okay."

"I'm fine," Elle snapped back. The topic of Leonardo with Eryk was very frustrating. She supposed it was because she couldn't figure out her emotions towards Leonardo, making it difficult to talk about him.

Eryk didn't say anything but his eyebrows remained furrowed. Elle could feel the tension between them, but let it go. She knew Eryk wasn't one to hold grudges or hang on to his anger. It was a trait about him that she liked because she knew she was the opposite.

They walked the rest of the way to the trains without speaking. Elle was at war with her mind. She had just got the thought and image of Leonardo out of her head. Now he was back and wouldn't leave. All the conflicting emotions rushed back in as if they'd never left. She had no idea how she felt about Leonardo. She didn't know if she wanted to be friends with him knowing how selfish and tricky he could be. But then there was that night—the fireflies, the quiet chats, the peace. It was natural and comforting, yet exciting as an adrenaline rush. She didn't know who Leonardo was. She had no idea. He was just a giant unsolvable mystery. It frustrated her that she couldn't figure him out.

When they finally entered the train station, Elle was trying to shove Leonardo out of her mind. She had to focus on the upcoming task. Eryk bought them some waters and food and they sat down at a small table to eat.

"I apologize if I upset you," Eryk said, looking Elle in the eyes.

"It's okay," Elle said as she self-consciously looked down. His bright eyes and dark eyelashes were hypnotic. She felt that they made her light brown eyes look drab and boring. She hated him for his eyes. Because if it weren't for his eyes it would be so much easier to stay mad at him, even though she knew she was truly just mad at herself.

Eryk laughed through a side smile and shook his head.

"What?" Elle looked up.

"You're funny," Eryk said.

"Why do you say that?" Elle beckoned.

"You're just..."

"Just what?"

"Interesting."

Elle folded her arms.

Eryk continued laughing but Elle didn't say anything. They ate their food and talked about the Quest. They wondered what the third task would be, as they did not have the riddle for it yet. The Dealer told Elle they would receive the next riddle when they completed the second task. But she wanted to know now. They only had seven more days.

"I wonder how Mason is doing," Eryk said.

"We should figure out a way to contact Alaina."

"We should. If we're needing replacements though, then I'm assuming that means Mason is still not better."

Elle didn't know what to say back. The thought of Mason still in pain made her sick to her stomach. It was her fault he was on the Quest in the first place. She so wholly wished he was getting proper care, and she so wholly wished they could find a way to contact Alaina soon.

The clock continued to tick by.

"When is the train supposed to arrive?" Elle asked as her heart thumped with anticipation.

"Any time now, actually."

They both watched in apprehension as the train screeched to a halt.

Maybe the replacements would be more Heliopaths. Maybe it was someone Elle would recognize. They had to be smart. They had to be quick. They had to be determined to complete the Quest as much Elle and Eryk were.

Through the windows, people began to stand up.

The train doors slid open.

And out stepped Anastasia and Leonardo Castello.

Chapter 15

Eryk's eyes flew back to Elle's, but hers remained on Leonardo. Eryk searched her face for any clue to how she was feeling but she looked as white as a ghost. The twins were in a deep conversation together. Anastasia's eyebrows were set in a v-shaped figure as Leonardo spoke rapidly to her.

The Castello twins were the replacements? Why would they volunteer to take part in the Quest? Did Leonardo actually plan to help Elle? Elle's head spun.

Leonardo and Anastasia walked over to Elle and Eryk. They were oddly in sync together with how they walked and how they moved—it was almost cat-like. Their facial expressions were the same. Their body languages were the same. In that moment Elle wondered how she didn't suspect them to be twins in the first place, and she couldn't put together what on earth they were doing in the Belltheria train station.

"Good evening Ellisia, Eryk." Leonardo curtly nodded his head to each of them. His golden hair was swept to the side and his dark eyes were unreadable. His civil manners were anything but comforting.

"You two actually volunteered?" Eryk asked, his eyebrows raised.

"We did, and we're here to help," Anastasia said. She swung her body next to Eryk, who scooted away instantly. "I'm not here to scare you, Rylander. Calm down." She crossed her legs and ran her hand through her thick dark hair.

"Then what are you here for?" Eryk shot back.

"To help you, of course," Leonardo spoke as he took a seat next to Elle. She moved over a bit without taking her eyes off Leonardo. She was at a loss for words.

"We all know that's not the case. Just tell us, why are you here?" Eryk demanded. He glanced at Elle who looked as emotionless as a rock. If it wasn't for her wide eyes, he would've thought she was asleep.

"We're here because we want to be, and nobody else was up for the job," Leonardo replied with honest eyes. Eryk stared at them, searching for any sign of untruthfulness. Something wasn't right.

"Yeah, sorry about your friends." Anastasia's voice was like a fragile knife that shook Elle out of her reverie. "Alaina and Mason were their names?"

"Yes," Elle said, a little too fast. Everyone looked at her and she sunk down in her seat.

"Do you know anything about them? Have you heard anything?" Eryk asked.

"I'm sure they're fine," Anastasia said as she studied her fingers. "Last I heard they were in the clinic."

"Alaina too?" Elle asked before Eryk could.

"Mmhmm," Anastasia said with too high pitched of a sound.

Elle and Eryk looked at each other. Both their eyes were wide. Did this mean Alaina was sick too? Could Anastasia be wrong? Spinning thoughts chased each other like warm and cold air on the brink of a tornado. She shouldn't've brought them on the Quest. The Quest wasn't safe for anyone.

"I should finish the Quest alone," Elle said, her eyes blank.

"No, you shouldn't," Leonardo said without hesitation.

"Yes, I should. I don't want to risk anyone else getting hurt—"

"We knew the risk when we agreed to come," Eryk said. "It was our choice, not yours. It's not your fault Mason got sick."

Anastasia chuckled to herself and Leonardo shot her a fierce look.

Elle looked at Leonardo, who sat a little too comfortably in his chair. His breathing was normal; his body was relaxed. She didn't know how he could feel so at ease knowing how dangerous the Quest was, but his calmness was contagious. She believed his words. She knew that she truly did need help to complete the Quest. Without the help of Eryk, she would still be on the first task.

"Fine. You can stay," Elle said. "But nobody gets hurt."

"Or what? You'll hurt us?" Anastasia snickered and flicked her hair off of her shoulder.

Elle ignored the comment and looked at Eryk. He looked frigid next Anastasia. She had never seen him so anxious before. They should have constructed a plan before meeting up with the replacements. They only had seven days left and time was starting to tick faster.

"So what's the plan?" Leonardo asked nonchalantly. Elle could not figure out his mood.

"We need Elle's dead father's heart," Eryk answered.

Leonardo looked a bit surprised. "And where is that?" he asked curtly.

"That, we are not sure of," Eryk said.

"So you're saying you don't have a plan?"

Eryk looked Leonardo straight in the eyes. Elle could feel the tension fuming around them, it made her want to slip off the chair and run a million miles away from the train station. They had to get the second task started tonight and she couldn't have her two friends trying to kill each other the entire time. She didn't even know if she would classify Leonardo as her friend, but if he wasn't her friend, then what was he, exactly?

"No, we don't have a plan yet," Elle said, breaking the tautness. "But we need to make one now, we need to get started tonight. So please, just get along for now."

"I'm not the one with the problem, sweetheart," Leonardo said.

"Don't call her that," Eryk mumbled under his breath.

"Okay stop," Elle nearly shouted. Anastasia chuckled to herself, which made Elle's frustration rise. "Stop. We need to start the second task and we're wasting time. Even if you hate each other, get over it. If you don't want to be helpful and get things started again, please leave right now and go back to Remedium. I can do this myself."

Everybody went quiet. Even the Mystics walking by stopped for a moment. Eryk took a deep breath.

Anastasia slowly started clapping her hands. Eryk and Elle looked at her while Leonardo pretended he didn't notice.

"Thank you for that Ellisia, truly," Anastasia said. "What do you suggest we do to get your daddy's heart?"

Elle ignored the shudder crawling up her spine and through her chest. She tried to tell herself that it wasn't her dad's heart. She told herself that it was just a terrible dead man's heart that would cure her weak mother—as if that was any better.

"We need to find where he's buried," Elle answered.

"You never visited his grave?" Anastasia asked, her nose wrinkled up as if she smelled something bad.

"No," Elle answered. "But I have a few places in mind. I figured there has to be at least one or two graveyards in the town I lived in, in Oregon."

"We have to travel to Sepiototumn then?" Leonardo asked, his voice quiet this time.

"Yes."

"That's a long train ride from here," Leonardo said.

"I'll go see when the next train leaves," Eryk volunteered. Anastasia sat up from the booth chair and Eryk slid out after her. She took her seat once he left.

Elle felt instantly less comfortable being alone with Leonardo and Anastasia. The twins looked at each other and back at Elle. As Elle sat by them she looked very out of place. The twins were both tall and striking with thick, voluminous hair and daunting yet interesting black eyes, and sharp angles of collarbones and jawlines. Elle was shorter and thinner, with less prominent defining features. She was more birdlike than catlike.

"Why didn't you visit your dad's grave?" Anastasia bluntly asked. Leonardo shot her a fierce look, but she ignored it and stared at Elle for the answer.

You don't want to tell Anastasia," Leonardo placed in Elle's thoughts.

"I don't want to tell you," Elle said and crossed her arms. She truly didn't feel the need to tell Anastasia about her personal life. But then that got her thinking, how *did* Leonardo and Anastasia end up in Remedium?

Anastasia eyed Leonardo and he stared at her back. Elle didn't know what was going on, but she felt awkward as she watched the siblings intently stare at each other—it was like they were communicating through their minds.

"Well, do you know how he died at least?" Anastasia tried again.

Elle didn't answer. She looked out the window even though it was pitch black outside. It was the same color as the twins' eyes.

"Do you know what I do, Ellisia?" Anastasia asked.

"You can take away people's memories," Elle replied, not taking her eyes away from the window.

"And do you know what my brother can do?" Anastasia went on.

"Give people memories," Elle said. Her patience was becoming shorter by the second. What was taking Eryk so long?

"Right," Anastasia said.

"So?" Elle beckoned with a hint of sass.

"So," Anastasia mocked Elle's tone. "I would keep that in mind."

It was then Elle looked from the window and saw the devious smirk contorting Anastasia's face. It set off a lingering anger within Elle. She didn't know if it was the tiredness she was feeling or the sudden changing emotions from the last thirty minutes, but all she wanted to do was blast fire at the girl sitting across from her. Elle had never felt such a deep, frustrated anger in her life. The way Anastasia grinned made the hairs on the back of Elle's neck prickle. She wanted to melt away the satisfied smirk and never see it again. She wanted Anastasia to leave the table immediately and never come back.

"Will you excuse us for a second," Leonardo said calmly to Elle, yanking Anastasia away from the booth.

Leonardo dragged his sister by her bicep to the opposite side of the train station.

Elle was too exhausted to even attempt to eavesdrop on their conversation. She caught a couple words though. "Trust." "Care." "Rivals." Leonardo looked unbothered, but Anastasia looked as if she was having a panic attack. She looked at her brother in the most disgusted, agitated way.

The twins walked back to Elle. She kept a careful eye on Anastasia as she sat down.

Leonardo leaned over and whispered to his sister. Anastasia shot him a glance and he nodded his head fiercely.

"My apologies," Anastasia said with an eased voice. Elle raised an eyebrow at her. "We're here—I'm here—to help you. We won't use our Myst on you. Or your friend."

"I don't trust you," Elle shot back.

"But I trust you, so..." Anastasia gave back.

Elle stayed quiet. She truly did not know what the best option for her and Eryk was at this point. Leonardo and Anastasia coming on the Quest threw everything off balance. She trusted Leonardo more than Anastasia, but even then, she knew how tricky Leonardo could be. She saw his dark side as everyone else did, but she was also exposed to his other side. She needed to be alone to think it all through, she needed time to rejuvenate her mind.

Eryk walked back in a hurry, his expression anxious. He looked from Elle to the twins wondering what happened while he was gone. Elle shook her head to tell him to ignore them.

"A train to Sepiototumn leaves in thirty minutes. I got us all tickets and you're very lucky I did." Eryk gestured at

Leonardo and Anastasia. "But for now, we need to store up on food."

Eryk and Elle purchased bags of food and sandwiches at the small concession stand in the train station, while Leonardo and Anastasia waited for the train to arrive. The food filled their backpacks full and would last them several days.

Elle was most desperate to get to Sepiototumn, so when the train finally arrived after a dreadful half hour of listening to Anastasia complain about random things, she was the first to jump out of her seat and walk to the train's entrance.

Eryk followed quickly behind her and whispered in her ear, "What are you thinking?"

She took the wooden train steps two at a time and paced down the hallway of the skinny train to the last compartment on the left. "I really don't know what to do anymore," Elle said rapidly under her breath.

"That's okay," Eryk said. "You can stay in here alone. Get some sleep, it's a long ride."

Elle didn't know if she wanted him to stay with her or not. She knew she needed some time alone to rethink everything that had happened and what the future held on the other side of the train.

"Thank you," Elle whispered as Eryk slid the wooden door closed with a screech.

In Elle's compartment it smelled of old wood and dirt after it rained. The glass window in the compartment was crooked and the seats were bare, dented wood. This must've been one of the older trains. She didn't care. She was too tired to care.

"Ladies and Gentlemen, Mystics of Remedium, please take your seats, the train doors are now closing. We will be traveling to Sepiototumn today, the second quarter of the world. We will arrive at precisely 5:07 p.m. on October thirteenth. This will be a long and bumpy ride so please remain in your seats at all times." The conductor's voice droned on about snacks and where the bathrooms were located.

Across the train, Elle laid wide awake. Her eyes focused on the chipped white wooden ceiling as the world became a blur out her window. Even when she tried to sort out a different thought, Leonardo kept reoccurring in her mind. She wished she had a journal to write down everything she was feeling, so she could organize her thoughts and predict what to do accordingly. Leonardo, Leonardo, Leonardo. What was she to do? Before he had arrived, she had just gotten him out of her head. He was like a repetitious melody. She never would've predicted that he would be Mason's replacement, but now here he was. Prior to Leonardo coming, she never knew what she thought of him. When Eryk told her that he manipulated his mind, all she felt was utter disgust and disbelief towards Leonardo. But she could never forget being alone with him in the middle of Remedium's forest, surrounded by fireflies. But then a terrible thought surfaced—what if that was a false memory? The thought made her stomach sick. She didn't know if she could trust him or not. No Mystic in all of Remedium believed the Dealer was good, especially not the ones who thought he wasn't even a Mystic like the rest of them. If nobody trusted the Dealer, then why did the twins? It was easier for Elle to understand why a person like Anastasia would trust the Dealer, but not Leonardo. But then again, Elle could not deny Leonardo was rude. Just the way he acted. Arrogant. Sly. Manipulative.

Leonardo was not a good person. But then, something inside told her otherwise.

Just then there was a knock on the compartment door. Elle could not make out the figure through the distorted glass frame.

"Yes?" Elle said. The train was noisy as it jostled from side to side, so she wasn't sure if the person on the other side of the door heard her. She sat up just as the door slid open.

Though the lights were very dim, Elle knew who it was right away and her throat automatically tightened.

He shut the door behind him with a piercing screech and sat across from Elle. She stared at him as if he was a stranger from another world.

"Carroway," Leonardo said with a curt nod. He leaned over, his arms perched on his legs with his fingers interlocked. His eyes were wide and his lips fit perfectly together. He smelled of old dusty paperbacks.

"Castello," Elle played back. He smiled at his hands when she did. "Why are you here?" The words came out before she could lock them up.

"I want to talk to you," he answered, his voice rough.

"No, I mean, why are you on the Quest?" Elle was surprised she was able to ask the question so confidently. She hoped the darkness covered her faint blush. Why was she blushing?

He chuckled. "Isn't it obvious? I'm here to help you retrieve the ingredients for the potion, of course," Leonardo said.

Elle looked at him suspiciously but all she saw was his dark, never ending eyes. She mimicked his movement and sat back against the hard wood.

"Is that true?" Elle asked, crossing her arms.

"You think I would lie?" Leonardo retorted.

She uncrossed her arms. "I don't want to play any games. I just need to transform my mother back into a human, so she's not a Charmer anymore."

"You think I would play games with you, Ellisia?" the rhythm of his voice made the hair on Elle's arms stand. It felt invasive.

Uncomfortable, Elle stood up and leaned against the window instead. She told herself to breathe and keep her mind open.

"Did you really volunteer to come here?" Elle asked.

"Do you not trust me, Carroway?" Leonardo asked, as if he was insulted.

Elle stared at the passing trees. She did not dare look at Leonardo. She had to remember this was the same person that took her to a magical place in Remedium. Though, it felt like this was someone completely different, like a stranger with a bad reputation.

Leonardo stood up to stand across from her. He looked out the window too. The moon was invisible amongst the silvery clouds. His light hair glowed in the dark room, while a shadow covered half of his face. He looked as mysterious as the invisible moon.

"Ask me," Leonardo said, after several minutes of silence.

"What?" Elle said, finally looking up at him. She felt tiny next to him—but not because he was physically taller.

"Ask me the questions on your mind," he beckoned.

At first Elle didn't know what to say in return. But then the questions flowed out of her like the jungle's rapid river.

"Do you not remember the night before I left? With the forest and the fireflies and talking? Was that even you? Or was that some false, implanted memory you forced me to have to make me trust you for whatever reason?" The words sounded ridiculous to her as she said them, but she didn't care. She needed to know.

For once, Leonardo actually looked shocked. Not just shocked, but almost hurt.

"You think I planted those memories in your head?" Leonardo asked.

"Well, did you?" Elle beckoned.

"No, I never messed with your head about anything. I would never do something like that," Leonardo nearly shouted, making Elle jump.

They became quiet again and Leonardo sat down. All they heard was the rustle and bustle of the old train tracks and the occasional opening and closing of a compartment door.

"You have before," Elle said quietly, scared for what he would say.

"What are you talking about?" he snapped.

"You've implanted Eryk with a thought before," Elle said.

"That's different," he snapped again.

"How is that different?"

"Different time, different circumstance, you wouldn't understand."

"Then explain to me—"

"No."

Elle sat back against the hard seat, discouraged. She blew out a sigh, making the stray hairs hanging on her face fly in front of her.

"I came in here to reinforce that I'm here to help you—truly help you get those ingredients. I'm not lying about that," Leonardo said.

"And Anastasia?" Elle asked.

"I brought you to that part of the forest in Remedium to show you the fireflies because I thought you would like it," Leonardo went on. "Nothing more, nothing less. It calms me down when I'm upset, and I thought it would do the same for you." The words settled in the air like the first drops of snow sticking to a blade of grass. He looked at her with his deep eyes through his long eyelashes. She looked up from her lap and her heart beat faster.

"I will never use my Myst on you, and I'll make sure Anastasia won't either. Or Eryk," Leonardo said.

"And I will never use my Myst on you," Elle agreed.

Leonardo smiled and shook his head from side to side. "Freaking Heliopaths."

Elle laughed as Leonardo stood up.

"Get some sleep." He walked out the door and slid it closed behind him. The space felt immediately darker. Unknown.

Elle laid back into her original position and closed her eyes. She dozed off into a light slumber with the wooden wheels clipping beneath, her mind more conflicted than ever.

Chapter 16

Elle awoke by being tossed onto the floor when the train jostled over a bump. At first not knowing where she was, she stood up and looked around. Outside, the sky was a warm shade of gray. Clouds hovered high in the sky like a wall of mist—it was about to rain.

Elle's shoulder ached from the fall. She didn't remember dreaming at all, she just remembered being immersed in sleep. Yesterday had been emotionally and physically draining. Then the memory stung her. Leonardo was on the very exact train she was on now.

She stood, the wood cold beneath her sneakers. She slowly slid open the fragile compartment door, poked her head out and glanced down the hallway of the train. Most of the compartment doors were closed, and several of the glass frames were cracked and replaced with cobwebs. The lighting was very dim and the white paint was chipping. The red carpet that ran throughout the train's aisle was stained and ripped. The two words that came to Elle's mind was "old" and "eerie." It was quiet other than expeditious wheels that roared underneath the train. A lady wearing a faded peach-colored dress began to wheel a noisy copper-stained cart down the aisle. Elle watched as she knocked on the first compartment to her left. *Must be the snack lady*, Elle guessed.

With the floorboards creaking beneath her feet, Elle stepped across to Eryk's room. She slid the door open—which wasn't as loud as hers—and stepped inside.

"Elle," Eryk said, sitting up.

"We need to get started on a plan," Elle said emphatically with wide eyes.

"Yes, let's do it. Did you get some time to think?"

Elle took a seat and set her squished backpack—that she'd used as a pillow—beside her. "No, I fell asleep."

Eryk nodded his head.

"So, what do we do once we get back to Oregon?" Elle asked. Saying the words out loud felt like pretend dialogue. It truly hit her then that she was going back to the place that started it all. The hitting. Yelling. The alcohol spilt on the floors and walls. The crying, desperation and hopelessness. Emmie. Emmie was in Oregon. Emmie was in Oregon.

"Elle? Are you okay?" Eryk asked, as Elle's expression went blank after she finished the sentence. The pink of her cheeks dissipated.

"Emmie is there," was all Elle could say. She felt guilty for not thinking of her baby sister the moment she knew she was going back to Oregon. "It's fine." Elle swallowed the painful thought. *Emmie doesn't remember you*, she told herself. "We need to search for graveyards in and around Portland."

"You didn't live in Portland, though?"

"I don't know where he was buried, Eryk. He could be anywhere. He worked for the police station in Oregon, maybe they buried him," Elle explained, her voice wavering.

"Okay, maybe we'll have Leonardo and Anastasia look there, and we'll look around the town you lived in," Eryk suggested.

"You want Anastasia and me to look where?" Leonardo interrupted, as his sister pulled the door open.

The tang of his words filled the room, making Elle's stomach flop. Eryk gritted his teeth and looked away.

"When we get to Oregon, we will need to split up to find my dad's grave. Eryk and I will look in the town I lived in, and you and Anastasia will look in Portland," Elle explained.

Leonardo pursed his lips and then they settled into his usual smirk. With his arms still crossed, he took a seat next to the window just as it began to rain. Light raindrops like delicate petals of flowers dripped onto the glass window and slid to the sill. They became thicker and thicker and fogged up the window, making the browns and greens of the earth a blur.

"What? Does that not work for you guys?" Eryk asked, reading Leonardo's expression.

"Oh no, that works splendidly—doesn't it, Anastasia?" Leonardo said.

"Just splendid," Anastasia said in a sing-song voice, taking a seat across from her brother.

Elle looked at Leonardo, trying to read him, but he was looking vacantly out the window. Last night after he left, she felt as if she could trust him. She really believed him. Then he acted detached and mysterious, and Anastasia wasn't helping. Eryk looked pissed off, but always did when Leonardo was around.

"Could you guys maybe, I don't know, leave?" Eryk said.

"Ellisia, your friend is very rude." Anastasia sneered.

"We're here to help you, Eryk," Leonardo said.

"I still don't believe you," Eryk said.

"Well, learn to," Leonardo fired off, with his threatening undertone that swam beneath the sea level. It was like listening to a depressing song with a joyful beat.

"I'm not going to," Eryk argued, a fury of madness rolling in his throat. Unlike Leonardo, it was obvious when Eryk was becoming angry. "Give me one good reason why I should ever trust you."

"Because we want to be here." Anastasia stood up with fury.

Just as Eryk was about to dispute, Anastasia ran out of the room, the door slamming and breaking the hinges behind her.

Elle, Eryk and Leonardo looked from one to another. There was something else behind Anastasia's anger. Almost sadness? Elle couldn't place it.

"Excuse me," Leonardo said after several seconds of silence. His heavy boots thudded against the wooden ground as he left the room after his sister.

As soon as the sound of his footsteps vanished, Elle looked at Eryk with frustration.

"Eryk, you have to try to get along."

"I don't trust him! They're not here for us," Eryk shouted.

"Then what are they here for? Nobody wanted to help us, nobody wanted to take Alaina and Mason's position, and they did! Why can't you just let it go?" Elle said.

"Why can't you see that they're not here to take Alaina and Mason's spot? Mason and Alaina came to help you, like I did. But that's not what Leonardo and Anastasia are here for."

"Then what do you suggest they're here for?"

"I don't know. I'll figure it out."

Elle was quiet for a moment.

"Until you do, I trust Leonardo. I may not like them, and I may know something might be going on with them, but right now I'm going to take all the help I can get. And if you can't get over your judgement of them, then you can go back to Remedium with your friends," Elle said. She got up and walked out.

She went back into her original room feeling like she took twenty steps back from where she started. With only six days of the Quest remaining, she never felt so far behind. She plopped down on the cold bench and began to cry into her arms.

It was just a tangled mess. A lengthy, stringy, rotten, tangled mess. The Quest was never ending, and she was never going to find the ingredients for the potion in time to save her mother. And the Dealer knew that. Without Eryk, the ingredients would be impossible to find. Maybe he was right. Leonardo and Anastasia weren't people she could trust. But she had to. They were here, right? Leonardo had not personally given Elle a reason to not trust him. But Eryk was her friend. And she knew Eryk better than Leonardo. Yes, Leonardo was connected to the Dealer in some sort of way, but did that make him someone to avoid? She didn't know. Maybe she was only naïve. She was a new Mystic, and new to Remedium. Eryk was much more experienced than she was. At this moment she wished she could talk to her baby sister. Emmie would know exactly what to do.

The door to her compartment opened, startling her. She jumped at the sight of Leonardo walking into her room. She quickly wiped the hot tears away and sat up straight, hoping her nose wasn't red.

"Why are you crying?" Leonardo asked immediately, closing the door and locking it behind him.

"Unlock the door," Elle demanded through gritted teeth.

Leonardo crossed his arms in front of his large chest. Elle felt tiny. She was tired of feeling this way.

"I said, unlock the door, Leonardo."

Leonardo turned slowly and unlocked the door, then took a seat across from Elle with a placid expression.

"Why are you crying?" Leonardo repeated.

Elle could imagine how much of a hot mess she looked like at the moment. She felt sweat collect beneath her arms and across her hairline. She didn't want to talk to him, but oddly at the same time she wanted to shout everything about herself to him. Every emotion. Thought. Feeling. Experience. She wanted to scream every word at the top of her lungs. She wanted to run through a wide and vast field of grass and scream at the sky.

But she didn't. She didn't say a word.

"Why are you crying?" Leonardo repeated once again.

"Why are you here?" Elle asked in no more of a whisper. She could feel the insecurity in her voice as she asked the question.

"Why are you asking?" Leonardo played back.

Elle remained quiet. She listened to the rain and train wheels fill the silence. A crack of thunder struck over the train.

"Ellisia," Leonardo began. "I just want to hear what you have to say. I know that I haven't given you a reason to trust or distrust me, but I want to listen to your words. Just talk."

Elle looked out the raindrop covered window. She didn't know where to begin or what words to even make out of her mind. There were just too many things to think at one moment. Too much that had happened in the last week. Too much that had changed.

"I'll wait," Leonardo said.

But Elle stayed stubbornly silent. It was rather dark in the compartment. A single low glow of a dying lantern hung above the window. Outside the window were colors of dark gray and cold black. Their quiet bodies jostled from side to side as the seemingly ancient train rolled over the hills of the earth.

There was a soft thud on the door as a high pitched voice yelled, "Snacks!" Neither Elle nor Leonardo moved a muscle.

Then Leonardo cracked his knuckles together and sat back on his seat.

Several more minutes of quiet passed. The rhythmic rain was becoming hypnotic with occasional strikes of golden lightning.

Finally, after several more minutes of agonizing silence, Leonardo sat back up.

"If you won't talk, then allow me. Just listen. I know you Ellisia. I know you're scared, confused and uncomfortable. You have no justifiable reason to talk to me, but I want to hear you. I want to hear the thoughts of your mind. I know you're scared to come down from that tower you built so long ago to protect yourself from anyone that comes into your life, but just talk. I was meant to Seek you; you know that—don't you?"

Elle nodded, but kept her eyes on the window, even though they were not focused on the outside in the slightest. She hated his stupid words. She hated his stupid face.

"Yes, it's true," he continued. "I understand what you're feeling. I know that being a Mystic only rids your illness, but not your mind. Not your brain. You have a powerful brain. And as your Seeker, I want to know you, Ellisia. I want to help you. I'm here to help you. I promise. I am." Leonardo spoke, his words fast. It was the first time Elle ever heard any form of desperation in his voice. He was telling the truth. But she wondered if he had ever said these same words to someone else.

"I believe you," Elle said after a moment of silence.

"So then, what's confusing you? What's blocking your brain? Be honest," Leonardo asked.

Elle half smiled at his eagerness, but it quickly faded. There was so much she had been dying to say. And as she looked up to his wide dark eyes, she couldn't believe it was Leonardo Castello staring back at her and not Eryk.

"We're going back to where it all started," Elle began. "I thought once I left that terrible, terrible town, I would never go back. I've tried for the past five years to suppress all those memories. And five years later, I'm already going back? It just doesn't seem correct. Like all of this has been some sort of illusion. Remedium can't be real. Mystics aren't real. People with powers? That doesn't happen in this world. But it has and I'm here with you, traveling in this pretend magical world to avenge my mother's death? That's not real. It seems as if this is all a trick of my mind. And what if it is? What if I'm just some crazy, delusional schizophrenic? Because I know that going back to Oregon to unbury my dead father for his heart, is something a psychopath would do. Isn't it?" Elle paused for a moment. "Maybe I'm truly mad. Completely insane. Maybe you're all just imaginary friends in my head."

"Crazy people don't know or admit they're crazy," Leonardo said.

Elle thought of that for a moment.

"But I want to talk to Emmie."

"Emmie?"

"Emmaline. My sister. My little sister that I left behind at that horrid foster home so I could come here and be forgotten forever. Emmie."

"I thought that foster home was safe? That the parents weren't abusive?" Leonardo questioned.

"Just because it's not abusive doesn't mean it's safe," Elle said fiercely. "Yes, I believe it was as good as a foster care home could get, but the Everson's were as poor as dirt and didn't know how to handle mental health any better than a seven-year-old does."

Leonardo nodded. "Well if you want to talk to Emmie, just know she's not going to recognize you. What would you say to her?"

"I know she won't recognize me," Elle rolled her eyes, she was tired of thinking about it. "Besides, she might know where Dad was buried. It could help us."

"So, what are you going to do? Walk up to the Everson's door, ask for Emmie and ask her where her abusive father was buried five years ago? Then you'll sound and look like a lunatic for sure," Leonardo said.

As rude as it sounded, it was realistic. And Elle, not wanting to admit it, knew it.

"Fine, then. You do it," Elle said defensively.

"Me?" Leonardo's face twisted.

"Yes. You can say you're writing an article for the newspaper or something," Elle begged.

"How would I doing it be any different than you? We're strangers to her, Ellisia. You might as well be the one."

"Ugh. Fine. I'll do it and look stupid," Elle said.

"Fantastic," Leonardo agreed. "I'll come with you."

Elle could feel her face drop and by Leonardo's expression she could tell he noticed her change in thought, too.

"What?" Leonardo asked.

"Eryk's coming with me to where I grew up. You and Anastasia are going to Portland," Elle said as an image of Eryk flashed back into her mind. How could Leonardo make her so easily forget everything and everybody else in the world when she was with him?

"Oh yes," Leonardo remembered. "Portland, Oregon. Very, very important business to do there."

"Yes." Elle nodded.

"Guess we should start getting prepared now. We should be there tomorrow," Leonardo said.

The words made her throat fall into her stomach. She felt like she was going to gag. Leonardo stood up and stepped over to the broken door and opened it.

"See you later." He stepped out the door, leaving Elle in the darkness with only the gnawing apprehension in her stomach.

Chapter 17

The train's wheels to Sepiototumn whirled and clicked over the wooden tracks. Nearly a day had passed of traveling and the Mystics were nothing but eager to get off the train. It was decided that Elle and Eryk would confront Emmie to see if she knew where her father was buried, while the twins gathered information at his old police station in Portland. It took Elle a lot of begging, but Eryk finally agreed. He did not think it was a good idea for Elle to see her sister again, but she was so adamant on seeing her that he couldn't say no.

The warm sun was beginning to peek over the horizon as if it was spying on the quiet world of sleepy people and brewing coffee. Elle awoke to the sunbeams streaming right into her eyes. With her eyes and brain still fuzzy, she sat up. Her muscles immediately ached, and her back felt worse from sleeping on the bench. Her mouth tasted hot and sour, her hair felt greasy and tangled beyond repair. She needed a shower, but knew that a shower was a luxury they couldn't afford. There were just five days left. She couldn't believe all of yesterday was spent traveling. *What a waste of time*, she thought. If only they had Mason's Myst of teleportation.

The earth outside was full of dull colors, which meant they must have arrived in Oregon. The thought sent tiny spiders of apprehension down Elle's back. Today, they were going to get things done. There was no time to waste.

Elle jumped up and slid her tennis shoes back on her feet—she must have kicked them off in her sleep. She tied the laces a little too tight with eagerness and left her compartment. Knocking on Eryk's door, her stomach spun in circles. There was no time to hold a grudge against Eryk or Leonardo or Anastasia. They all needed to put the past behind them, including what happened the other night. Elle needed to retrieve the last two ingredients in time. She had to save her mother, to give her back the life she deserved.

The wobbly door slid open to reveal a disheveled Eryk. His dark hair poked up and curled in random places, the bags under his eyes were substantial and his posture was weak. He looked exhausted.

"Morning," he mumbled.

"Morning," Elle said back, with more pep than she felt. "What's the plan?"

"You tell me," Eryk said as he searched for a granola bar from his backpack.

Ignoring his lack of enthusiasm, Elle took a seat across from him. He threw her a granola bar, which she didn't catch, and devoured his own.

"Well, we need to get going. I feel like we wasted all of yesterday traveling," Elle said urgently. "You and I can go to the Everson's, talk to Emmie about where Dad was buried, and Leonardo and Anastasia can go—"

"You think it's a good idea to let them go off on their own?" Eryk interrupted.

"You have to trust them Eryk!" Elle unintentionally shouted. She couldn't help letting the frustration ooze out of her. She no longer cared if Leonardo was her Seeker. All that mattered was finding the ingredients in time for the Dealer.

Eryk stayed quiet.

Elle let out a frustrated cry. "Listen Eryk. I truly don't care what happened between you and Leonardo. I mean, I do, but it's irrelevant right now, okay? You got me to trust you in a matter of days, a highly impossible task, but you did. So can you trust me now? You don't have to trust Leonardo and Anastasia, just trust me."

His searing blue-green eyes looked into her's. His expression was unreadable. Furrowed eyebrows, hard lips, but soft eyes. She didn't break eye contact.

"Fine," he said, taking an aggressive bite of his granola bar.

A ball of frustration released from Elle's chest.

"I'm trusting you, and only you. Not Leonardo. Not Anastasia. Only you," Eryk elucidated.

"Got it. That's all we need," Elle said.

They stood up at the same time and walked to Leonardo and Anastasia's compartment. It was difficult to walk down the hall of the train, as it was very jerky and unstable. Broken glass shards and food wrappers sprinkled the ground, along with a thick coat of dust. Elle wondered just how old the train really was.

Eryk tapped on the twins' door with a single knuckle.

Leonardo singularly sat inside. A written letter sat on his crossed legs, which he immediately tucked into his pocket when he saw Eryk and Elle.

"Where's Anastasia?" Elle asked.

Leonardo pointed to the compartment across from his without breaking eye contact with Elle. She inferred that something went wrong between them last night.

Eryk tapped on her door and there was no answer. Just as he began to tap again, Anastasia poked her head out.

"What do you want?" she said fiercely.

"We need to go over the plan again," Elle explained.

"It's, like, eight in the morning," Anastasia argued.

"Anastasia, come on." Leonardo's voice was groggy.

She mumbled something unintelligible under her breath and stepped into the hallway. Elle and Eryk took a seat across from Leonardo, and Anastasia remained standing in the doorway. She resembled a black crow perched in a window sill.

"When we arrive, Elle and I are going to the Everson's house to speak with Emmaline, hopefully to get some information on where Elle's father is buried," Eryk began. "And you two," he pointed to Anastasia and Leonardo, "are going to David Carroway's old police station. Look around for information, ask old colleagues, that sort of thing. We'll meet back up at this train station and go from there."

"So we're for sure splitting up?" Anastasia asked.

"Is that a problem?" Eryk asked.

Anastasia and Leonardo glanced at each other.

"Not at all," Anastasia grinned.

As soon as the train came to a screeching halt that evening, the four Mystics jumped out in a hurry. It smelled of dewy grass and rain clouds, and it was all so familiar. A rush of memories and emotions ran through Elle, and she couldn't decide if it was a feeling she liked, or wanted to suppress.

As the Mystics waited for the train doors to open, Eryk turned to Elle and asked, "Are you sure you want to meet with Emmie?"

"Yes," Elle said firmly. There was a huge chance Emmie knew where their dad's body was buried.

"Just making sure," Eryk said.

Elle curtly shook her head, blowing off his worry. She understood why Eryk was concerned. She was concerned too. But she had to stomach the apprehension for now and do what they had to do to get the next ingredient. She tried not to think about it anymore. She was never one to be an impulsive person, but in this situation she knew she had to be.

When the four Mystics stepped into civilization off the Remedium train, pedestrians and bicyclists gave them the strangest looks. One man on a blue colored bicycle almost ran into a large metal pole. The four Mystics looked like exotic animals straight from the jungle. Hypnotic eyes, astounding features, covered head to toe in dried mud. They were frightening, strange and yet beautiful. Elle had never experienced a sensation like this one. When she would go into therapy or the doctors, everyone would just look at her in a sad hopeless way; but the way people were looking at her now contained amazement.

Eryk pulled the map from his backpack and unrolled it for everyone to see. Elle, Leonardo and Anastasia circled around.

"We're here," Eryk pointed to the section of Oregon titled Portland, "and Elle and I need to be here," he pointed slightly south of Portland.

"Anastasia and I will stay here and find the police station Elle's father worked for," Leonardo said.

"Do you know the name of it, at least?" Anastasia asked.

"Portland Police Station?" Elle answered with the same sour tone as Anastasia's. Eryk chuckled.

"Do you know anything about your father?" Anastasia said shortly.

Leonardo budged her. "Let's go."

Anastasia rolled her eyes and followed her brother down the street, away from Elle and Eryk.

Anastasia was right about one thing. Elle did not know anything about her father. She lived with him for eleven years and she only knew he was David Carroway, the chief of police in Portland and an alcoholic who abused his children and killed her mother. She did not know anything else about him. She had never considered it before. She never saw him as a human with a life, she just saw him as someone terrifying who hurt her.

"Come on Elle, ignore her, we need to get started," Eryk said. Elle knew that Eryk understood what she was feeling. He understood her before she understood herself. But he was right, this task needed to be finished today.

"Let's get it over with," Elle said, feeling defeated. If task three was any more difficult than this, she didn't want to know what it was. She didn't want to think about what she was going to have to do next, much less what she had to do right now.

"Do you know the way to the Everson's foster home from here?" Eryk asked gently.

Elle shook her head.

"I think I might remember. I did visit you several times, remember?" Eryk smiled lightheartedly.

Elle pressed a small smile onto her face. It was just a week ago that Eryk was Seeking her. And he knew that he was trying to make her feel better. "Lead the way, Eryk Rylander."

"Come along then, Elle Carroway." Eryk beamed, taking her hand and calling down a taxi.

This made Elle truly smile.

They arrived at the Everson's less than an hour later.

"We'll be right back," Eryk told the taxi driver.

Both Elle and Eryk jumped out of the taxi cab and walked toward the house.

"You're positive you want to do this?" Eryk asked again.

"We need to find out where he's buried," Elle said through clenched teeth. But she actually just needed to see Emmie again. One more time.

When Elle looked up at her old house, she gulped. She remembered first arriving to the home when she was only twelve. She remembered thinking the white wooden house was huge. Ginormous. A mansion. But looking at it now, it looked like an ordinary home. An average size, on a huge lot. Six acres, if Elle was remembering correctly.

A wave of déjà vu crashed on Elle. Group therapy. Doctors. Therapists. Mr. Scott bringing home books for her to read. Hiding in the closet in her bedroom. New kids every month. Every week. The little forest in the backyard. Tiptoeing down the stairs. Avoidance. Pressed lips. Hands tightened in fists. Kids running around and screaming. There wasn't a word to describe how she felt. And she wasn't sure why she felt this intensity of emotions.

Eryk stood beside her. He grabbed her hand and squeezed it to reassure her she could do it, even though he wasn't sure she was ready. But Emmie might definitely know where their father was buried, she paid much more attention to the last five years than Elle did.

"I can't do this, Eryk," Elle said, the words shaky. This is why he questioned her. Now she understood.

"You can," Eryk said. "You want to save your mother, right? Knowing where your father is buried can help us save your mother."

"But..."

"It's okay. Just knock on the door, don't think about it. I'll be right beside you. We are no longer Eryk and Elle. We are pesky reporters from Portland who want the inside scoop on David Carroway. Okay?'

"Pesky reporters," Elle repeated.

"Yes, pesky, invasive reporters. Let's go."

They walked up the cobblestone path to the front door.

Without thinking, Elle impulsively knocked on the yellow door before she could take it back. Her stomach dropped. Her chest felt like a million pounds. She felt fossilized as she did in the Transformation.

The door opened.

Chapter 18

She stood there.

Mouth slightly ajar, eyelashes reaching her confused fuzzy eyebrows.

She stared.

She was tall and lengthy. Her eyes were light green like her father's eyes. The lightest of freckles covered the bridge of her nose and soft cheeks like grains of sand carried from the beach to the road. Her thin dark brown hair nearly reached the end of her ribcage—Mrs. Everson must've been behind on monthly haircuts, again.

Elle was not expecting for Emmie to be the one to answer the door. She imagined uptight Mrs. Everson answering and she would tell her they were friends from school. Then Emmie would come down. But here she was, opening the door like she ran the house. Elle felt as if she had not seen her baby sister in years. It had only been about a week, though. Her memory must be tricking her.

"Is there something you need?" Emmie spoke, her words pungent and clear with confusion.

Elle looked for the words she had been rehearsing, but tears spiked her eyes. Words disappeared. Vanished.

"I'm sorry?" Emmie said to the lack of response. "Do I know you?"

Elle's heart skipped a beat. No, several beats. Her throat felt tight. Eryk was right, she couldn't do this, she wasn't ready for this—she should've listened. What was she thinking?

Eryk placed his hand on the small of her back to steady her. "No, you don't," Eryk answered. "We're reporters from the Portland area—"

"I'm sorry, I'm not answering any questions," Emmie interrupted and began to close the door.

"No! Wait!" Elle said, startling everyone, including herself. "I mean..."

"We just have one question, I promise," Eryk said, looking into the young girl's eyes.

Emmie opened the door wider, staring at the peculiar looking people. Her eyes searched Elle and Eryk's body but not a single light of recognition swam in her eyes.

"What is that question?" she asked. Her sweet voice was what Elle imagined rain would sound like if it could talk.

"We want to know where your father, David Carroway is buried. You think you could answer that for us?" Eryk said gently with a sympathetic smile.

"Why do you want to know?" Emmie questioned.

Eryk and Elle looked at each other, both asking each other the same thing.

"For an article, that's all," Eryk said. Elle gave a reassuring nod.

Emmie tilted her head slightly.

"Some random graveyard outside of Portland called Artemisia, but you didn't hear it from me," Emmie said under her breath. And with that she shut the door and the sound of a lock clicked into place.

Elle stood there, stupefied.

Her sister was gone from her again. The insides of her stomach felt as if they were slowly twisting up and collapsing.

Eryk put his arm around Elle's waist as if she were a crippled person and steered her away from the house.

"Let's just go," Elle said, slipping out of Eryk's arms. She opened the door to the cab and slid in. Arms crossed, she didn't look at Eryk. She didn't look at the driver. She didn't look at anybody. She said nothing. She had nothing to say because all she felt was rising anger. This was so unfair. What did she do to deserve such an off-balanced life? And she never allowed herself to feel remote anger. Or fear. Or sadness. Complete utter sadness. She sucked it up and kept going and that was the only option she had now. Again. She had to keep going. And keep going for what? No. She knew for what. And she couldn't deny it. She knew she had to help her mother. Her mother was her only hope now. Her new hope. And now she knew where the second ingredient was, and she wouldn't think about what it was. She would just do it.

The car ride back to the train station was painfully silent, punctuated only by the sound of the car wheels and the occasional honk of the horn. Eryk didn't press Elle to speak this time. Her minds spun in all directions. Circling Emmie. Circling her mother. Circling being a Mystic. She couldn't help but think that if her mother was going to be human then her mother could retrieve Emmie. She couldn't help but think that what if she were to be human again, too? To be with her mother and baby sister. To live with them, the three of them in one house. The idea was intriguing. She wouldn't let herself jump to hopefulness, though. She was a Mystic. And there was nothing that could be done. Was there?

As they were about to reach the station Elle finally spoke.

"I'm okay. We're going to get the ingredients and we're going to go back to Remedium and turn my mother into a Mystic and it will all be okay and I'll be fine."

Eryk looked hopeful. "Okay then," he responded. "I know it's hard to think about Emmie."

"It's okay," Elle interrupted. "Let's just stay focused."

At last, the cab came to a stop, and Eryk paid the driver the remaining amount of money he carried. The driver didn't look happy, but didn't ask for more and drove off.

Elle and Eryk walked to one of the benches in the train station and sat down. They both looked around for Leonardo and Anastasia, but the station was vacant.

Elle glanced up at the clock above the snack counter and noticed it read 6:40. Another day slipping right through their fingers again. Where were Leonardo and Anastasia?

"Okay, it's nearly seven o'clock," Elle said. "How did we beat them back here?"

Eryk pursed his lips. "A very good point."

"They didn't even leave Portland like we did, they just went to the police station," Elle said further.

"A very good point," Eryk repeated. "This is what I meant by 'I don't trust them.'"

Elle took a deep breath. "Maybe they're right behind us, maybe traffic got bad?"

"I'm giving them twenty minutes. And if they aren't here by then, we're going to the graveyard by ourselves," Eryk said with finality.

"Fine," Elle said tersely.

The clock ticked and ticked. Five days left.

Tick.

Tock.

Several Mystics walked by here and there, but none were the Castello twins.

Elle wanted to trust Leonardo so badly. She knew he just put up a façade for everybody else. But she saw right through it. She didn't know what the other side of him was like exactly—it was a mystery, but it was a solvable mystery. He wasn't arrogant for the fun of it. Well, maybe a little bit. But there was a reason why he acted arrogant. She just needed to reach far enough down to figure it out—like diving deep enough in the ocean to see all the sea creatures, whether they were sharks or starfish. She wanted to know, because she knew it was there. And she couldn't stop wondering how Leonardo and Anastasia were brought to Remedium in the first place. What was their Charmer feeding off of? And why were they close to the Dealer?

"The twenty minutes are up," Eryk announced.

"But, where are they?"

"I have no clue," Eryk said. "But clearly they are not here for us, Elle. We need to go to the Artemisia graveyard right now, we're wasting time waiting for them."

Elle couldn't believe Eryk's tone, but she knew he was right. Five days left. And they didn't even know where the third ingredient was, much less *what* it was.

"Fine," Elle grunted. "Let's go."

Eryk asked a nearby Mystic for twenty dollars to pay for a taxi ride, and the kind Mystic gladly gave it to them. They hopped into another taxi and left the train station behind.

Chapter 19

A sickly red sky hung above them, like the cherry red medicine children are forced to swallow. It made the excitement of being sick and staying home from school—or in Elle's case, therapy—suddenly perish, because the thought of that icky cherry red medicine on the taste buds was the cure to any illness.

After Eryk paid the driver, him and Elle stepped out of the car and walked toward the second ingredient. Elle secretly hoped that Leonardo and Anastasia might be there, but the lot was vacant of their presence.

"Eryk, we can't do this by ourselves," Elle said as a gust of wind swung by.

Eryk looked at the graveyard and back to Elle.

The graveyard was spread out on massive lot of hilly land. The trees sprouted all about were different shades of orange and red. Colored leaves scattered the cold ground, some laid on the grey headstones. It sent a shiver up Elle. She had never been here before. She had never visited her father's grave, never had the chance to, and never even gave it a thought.

"We're running out of time," Eryk said. He didn't want to upset Elle, but it was the truth. They had to do this tonight. The second task needed to be finished two days ago.

Elle knew he was right. Another blustering gust of wind spun around them. Elle folded her arms across herself. The wind was biting cold. Typical Oregon weather during the fall. It was indeed true they were quickly running out of time, but she could not imagine digging up her father's body and tearing out his—

"Eh, what are you folk doing around here? Don't ye' know we're closed due to construction?" a hunched man bellowed through yellow crooked teeth, spit flying from his mouth with every word. He also had a big fat brown mole right on his nose.

Elle and Eryk looked at each other and back to the old man. He looked as if he'd be buried in the graveyard himself any day now.

"I'm sorry," Eryk said. "We're here to visit our father, David Carroway."

The old man spat at the name. "David Carroway your father sir? I don't think so, I know that old man's story. No son." He gave another cackling cough.

"I'm his nephew," Eryk tried.

The old man sputtered a laugh, and more spit flew. "Ha! Caught in a lie you are now. Go on, you two. This graveyard is closed. Shoo." He flapped his wrinkled hands at Elle and Eryk as if they were a couple of pesky flies.

"Wait," Elle said.

The hunched back man turned back around slowly. "Ye' darling?"

"What do you know about David Carroway?" Elle asked.

The old man gave yet another cackling cough. "Not familiar with his story now are ye'? Guess you'll have to read his headstone. Oh wait! You can't get in!" The old man loudly laughed at himself, which quickly turned into a harrowing cough. He coughed and coughed and coughed. Elle thought he was going to collapse right there.

The old man walked away, his knees shaking beneath him.

"Forget him," Eryk said. He walked up to the rusted metal fence placed around the perimeter of the graveyard and began to climb it. He looked behind him, halfway there. "You coming?"

Elle grinned and began to climb up the frosty metal gate. They jumped over and landed on their feet. A sudden eerie feeling crept over Elle. It was as if she could feel her father's ghost entangle itself around her, along with every other ghost that lived in the graveyard. She shook.

Another outburst of wind cried. The trees shook violently.

"Okay, now we just have to find—" Eryk began.

"Didn't I tell ye kids to get out of me graveyard!" the old man screeched right behind them.

How did he show up so quickly after the two Mystics? Both Elle and Eryk had no idea.

"Get on with ye' selves, I'll call the cops! Ye' know!" the old man clamored with another sputtering cough.

"We have some important business to take care of, sir," Eryk tried, but he only sounded ill-tempered.

"Please sir, this graveyard is very important to us, just give us an hour," Elle pled.

The old man cackled another sickly, saliva-filled cough, followed by a snotty sneeze.

"No can do, missy, now get!" The old man cackled. "Go on!"

Elle looked at Eryk, who shrugged his shoulders. There was no use arguing with the old man. They crawled back over the gate and slumped on the ground to figure out what to do when suddenly the obnoxious ring of the map went off again, indicating that Tabitha was trying to contact them. Luckily this time the volume was at a tolerable level and did not give the Mystics a vicious headache.

Eryk pulled the crumbled map from his bag and spread it out in front of him so Elle could see. But the person staring back at them was not Tabitha. It was Alaina.

"ALAINA!" Eryk exclaimed.

Alaina looked as if she hadn't slept since being back in Remedium. Purple circles colored the underneath of her eyes. Her hair hung low in a messy bun with strands sticking up in various places. Her skin was pale and broken out. It was obvious the past few days for Alaina hadn't been easy.

"I broke into Tabitha's office and stole the map connected to yours! I have news guys, and not good news, unfortunately," Alaina said all in one breath.

"What? What is it," Elle asked.

"Do you want the terrible news or the super terrible news first?" Alaina asked, biting the corner of her bottom lip.

"Just tell us. Go!" Eryk exclaimed. Elle could feel his heart beat fast beside her. "Mason. Start with Mason"

A tear escaped Alaina's eye. "He's not doing any better, guys."

Eryk froze. Elle froze.

"The doctors, they're trying everything. They are. But he slipped into a coma right when we got here. He's only surviving on life support and there's nothing I can do and there's nothing the doctors can do, and I contemplated telling you all this because you need to stay focused, but I thought since you and Mason are so close Eryk, I..."

Her words trailed off and Eryk remained frozen.

"We'll figure something out," Elle said. But the words felt like feathers. Grains of sand and dust. Dust that covered the wooden floors of a house that hadn't been lived in for years.

Eryk didn't look up at the map. He looked at his lap, his hands intertwined, back hunched over.

Alaina continued. "Two more things. Something is going on, you guys."

Elle stared desperately at the map with her neck out stretched. The hairs on her arms stood straight up.

"I've been hearing rumors. Tons of them. You guys, the Quest, the Dealer—it's all anyone is talking about. No matter where I go, I hear your names. Everybody is predicting that the third task will be the most dangerous, the most impossible."

"Why is that?" Elle begged for more information.

"For one, the Tree of Remedium's leaves are sacred. They aren't meant to be tampered with. And two, the second task makes the first task look like fun. Elle—you must know— listen to me, you don't have to be the one to retrieve your father's heart. Let Eryk and the Castello's do it. Don't put yourself through that, please, please, please."

Alaina had a point. And it was not something Elle considered. But if Leonardo and Anastasia weren't there, she couldn't let Eryk do it alone.

"Leonardo and Anastasia aren't here," Elle explained.

"I'm not surprised." Alaina scoffed. "This is what I was getting to earlier. Something is not right. Something is going on with the Castello twins and you need to stay cautious around them. I've heard the nurses gossiping. They don't believe Leonardo and Anastasia are there to help you, they're there for something of their own."

At this, Eryk sat up. "Clearly!" he shouted. And put his head into the palms of his hands and hunched back down, his elbows resting on his legs.

Elle and Alaina took a deep breath at the same time.

"Whatever it is, you need to stay cautious. They're playing you, and you need to play them right back."

"Find out as much as you can about them and the Dealer," Elle commanded. She thought it was smart, like something Eryk would have said to do.

"Wait, how do you have Tabitha's map?" Eryk asked.

Alaina bit her bottom lip. "I transformed into her and snuck into her office. There's something important I needed to inform you—too important to wait. And it hurts my stomach to say it."

"Just say it." Eryk growled into his hand.

"Tabitha's pushing up the due date, you guys. I'm so sorry," Alaina said and instantly covered her mouth.

Eryk began to curse loudly.

"Hold on!" Elle stopped him. "How much time do we have?"

Alaina kept her mouth covered. Her eyebrows squeezed together.

"How much time do we have?" Elle repeated. Her throat and chest clenched together.

Alaina held up two fingers. "Two days," she said. "Tabitha was going to contact you tomorrow but I knew you needed to be aware right away."

Eryk cursed again, cursed Tabitha.

"Eryk, you know damn well that that wasn't her doing," Alaina said.

"What do you mean?'" Elle inquired.

"Ellisia, honey. Accept it. The Dealer is operating all of this. Leonardo and Anastasia used their Myst on Tabitha to shorten the time. They volunteered for their own sake. Not yours."

"But why? You're forgetting to ask why!"

Eryk answered. "Because they're working together, they have other plans. I told you this was all a trick. We all told you that the Dealer's 'deals' are to manipulate you into doing his dirty work. Why are you just not seeing this?" Eryk's voice rose with every syllable and Elle's heart shriveled.

"It doesn't matter at this point," Alaina said. She paused and lowered her voice. "Don't feel bad, Elle. This isn't your fault. If anything, it's ours for letting this happen in the first place. It is what it is, and we have to handle it, okay? You guys are going to get the stupid heart with or without the twins and get the last ingredient, and I'm going to figure out what the Dealer's true plan is. Okay?"

"Figure everything you can about the Dealer and call us back when you know anything of importance," Elle said.

"Will do, my love." And with that, Alaina signed off, leaving Elle and Eryk on their own, with a little over forty-eight hours left.

Chapter 20

The sky was now pitch black and the moon was nearly invisible amongst the fog. Elle and Eryk sat in dismay as they talked with each other about how to get into the graveyard without the old man calling the police. The air suddenly felt warmer as Elle watched Eryk's back become straighter and his eyes wider. She felt unusually less stressed out of nowhere as she watched Leonardo and Anastasia walk their way.

"We got the supplies," Anastasia said as she skipped over to Elle and Eryk.

"Shovels? Gloves? Scalpels? Knives?" Eryk checked.

"Check, check, check, and check," Anastasia said.

Leonardo remained quiet—but not his usual quiet, bored state. He looked melancholy as he stared into oblivion, purposely avoiding eye contact with Elle.

Under the inconspicuous moon the cemetery felt daunting. With ease, Leonardo convinced the repulsive old man to let them in. The four Mystics wandered the graveyard and searched for David Carroway's grave.

It felt as if a knot plugged Elle's throat. The graveyard was massive. Hundreds of headstones popped up in every inch, all with various dates and names. As Elle searched for her dead father's name, she remembered Alaina's words echoing in her head. *Be cautious around the twins.* She froze in her tracks and looked behind her. Eryk was on the other side of the hill and Anastasia was not too far away. When she turned back around, Leonardo was directly in front of her.

"Boo," he said.

Elle shook at his sight. He laughed.

"Cemeteries scare you, Carroway?" Leonardo smiled.

"It's a graveyard, technically," Elle spoke. Her breath penetrated the frosty autumn air like the steam of coffee lingering from a warm mug.

"Are you doing okay?" Leonardo asked.

Elle looked at him and back down at the headstone in front of her. She didn't know what to say to Leonardo. She trusted Eryk and Alaina more than Leonardo because she knew them better. Leonardo made her mad more than anything. Avoiding eye contact with her one second, then joking with her the next. It was annoying.

"Why are you asking me that?" Elle finally said, starting to walk away. She continued to read more headstones, expecting the name David Carroway to pop out at any moment.

"Why aren't you answering?" Leonardo volleyed.

Elle paused and finally looked straight into his eyes. They were as dark as the sky.

"I want to know why everyone is telling me not to trust you. I want to know why you are here. I want to know why you are close with the Dealer and how you came to Remedium." The questions poured out of her like a kettle going off. A flock of ravens fled the tree beside her.

"I can tell you all of those things. But look," Leonardo pointed to headstone to the left of him.

A simple square headstone.

Grey, plain, rock.

"David Carroway 1977-2005."

No other words. No designs. No pictures. No flowers. No plants or cards or anything.

Leonardo signaled Anastasia and Eryk over.

They hovered over Elle and looked at the bare stone.

"Let's get started," Eryk said.

Anastasia gave them each a massive shovel and they began to dig immediately. Eryk reminded Elle that she didn't have to do it, but she said she could at least help them dig up the casket to save precious time.

Elle felt sick. So sick. She wanted to lay down on the ground and never move again. She wanted to feel the dirt on her skin and the grass grow on top of her. She wanted to feel the bugs in the earth nestle in her body and squirm against her arms. She wanted to feel raven claws rest on her legs and pick at her hair. She wanted to feel the grief of the visitors of the graveyard as they said hello to their dead relatives and friends. She wanted to feel the tingle of spirits go through her and whisper their life stories in her ear. She wanted to watch someone etch her name into a headstone and place it right above her head. She wouldn't move. She wouldn't speak. Her lips would remain still. She wouldn't close her eyes. She would keep them open as she watched life continue in front her. Because the thought, the mere thought of seeing her father again would paralyze her. Cut her throat. Damage her skull. Because seeing your abuser is like seeing yourself as a ghost. Because you know that there cannot be a God out there when you and your abuser are walking the same grounds, both with a soul. Did Mystics have souls? Or was she herself only a ghost?

But she dug. Dark, wet dirt. White knuckles and tears mistaken for rain drops as rain began to fall. Rapid heartbeats. Ticking like the quickening clock. The quickening tongue of time. It never stopped speaking. She never stopped biting her lip. Eyebrows so furrowed together they hurt. Arms so sore, back giving out. Drenched in a minute. The ghosts and spirits shouted at her. Everybody shouted at her. Shouts and whispers. Screams and terrors. And then.

Clonk.

Chapter 21

Elle's eyes flooded. Her heart burst like a hurricane erupting. As Leonardo opened the casket, Eryk pulled her away before she got a decent glance. He pulled at her swinging arms and kicking legs. Mud covered them, their clothes. The rain was relentless.

Elle screamed at the sky. But the moon didn't listen.

She screamed at the stars. But they didn't make an appearance.

She screamed at the Dealer. And she screamed at Leonardo. She screamed at Anastasia. And she screamed at Eryk. She screamed for Emmaline. And she screamed for a mother—a mother that was taken away, ripped from her precious little arms because of the man in the casket who couldn't control his anger. His addiction. His fists.

She screamed.

The familiar sound of the train's wheels whirled and clicked. Elle could feel someone breathing slow deep breaths next to her. She opened her eyes to warm light. She was laying down on the train's compartment bench. Her head was in Eryk's lap and his head laid against the window. His eyes were closed, his mouth slightly ajar.

It was then she realized the graveyard no longer surrounded her. No more headstones and vicious rain. No more words to scream.

Elle sat up. It was then she also realized how stiff she felt. Her clothes clung to her body and creased themselves into her skin. She smelled rotten. Her stomach grumbled. Her head ached.

Did they get the heart? How did they get the heart? Who at this very second had possession of the heart? Elle wanted to vomit at the thought. Maybe she wasn't hungry, maybe she was going to be sick.

But then something caught her eye.

Sitting across from her, precariously folded on the bench directly across from her. A single white sheet of parchment paper, folded in half and sitting up.

Elle snatched it from the bench.

To: E
From: D

The simple words were embedded on the front in red lettering. Elle opened it instantly, her heart racing.

It read:

I have no legs, yet I constantly run.
I have no mouth, yet I roar.
Deep within the kingdom of the Hostiums.

Elle's hand covered her mouth as she read the words. The last riddle. The last ingredient. This was it. The last ingredient on their list to keep her from killing her mother. The last ingredient that was going to transform her mother into a human.

"Eryk, Eryk—wake up!" Elle shook Eryk, her voice was croaky. "You need to see this."

Eryk woke up, startled.

"What? What is it?" He rubbed the sleep out of his eyes. "Elle," he exclaimed as he realized she was awake. He embraced her. Strong arms fully enwrapped around her. "You're awake!"

"Huh? What do you mean? What time is it?" Elle looked anxiously around for a clock.

Eryk was out of breath from shock. "At the graveyard, you saw a tiny glimpse of your father and you went insane. Lashing out, screaming. You screamed for hours, it felt like. But then suddenly you stopped and then you passed out. I didn't know what happened. We carried you back to the train station. You wouldn't wake up. Anastasia wanted to take you back to Remedium."

"Wait. What?" Elle croaked. Her throat was definitely sore. "What do you mean 'we?' You said 'we' carried you back to the train station."

"Well, *I* carried you," Eryk clarified. "But after we got the heart, Leonardo, Anastasia and I all went back to the train station to figure out what to do next. We don't have the third riddle."

Elle beamed at the words, remembering why she woke him. "It's here," she exclaimed. "I woke up and it was sitting right here."

Eryk looked down at the paper and read it. His lips pursed and he read it again.

"I think I know what it is," Eryk exclaimed.

"What? What is it?"

"I don't know if I'm right, though," Eryk said. "But you wouldn't know, because you haven't learned."

"What is it?" Elle's body shook.

"So, you know how Mystics live in Remedium?" Eryk asked.

"Yes," Elle said.

"Well, Charmers live in a kingdom called Hostium. And within that kingdom there's the Obsidian Palace, where the Glass Queen rules. And within that Palace is a massive waterfall, said to cure any sickness—mental, physical, or emotional. Some say it's a myth or just a theory. But others believe it's true," Eryk explained.

"How do we know if it is?" Elle asked.

"We don't. But it matches the riddle," Eryk went on. "Waterfalls run. Waterfalls are loud. And there's a waterfall in Hostium with magical properties that could help cure your mother."

Elle sat, perplexed. "But then why does he need the other ingredients as well? Like the leaves and the heart? What are their importance if this water can cure anything?" Elle questioned.

Eryk shook his head as he sought for an answer. "I don't know, Elle. I don't know why the Dealer does what he does."

"I better get an explanation," Elle said.

"You will," Leonardo said from the door frame.

Both Elle and Eryk jumped at his voice.

"You read the riddle?" Eryk asked.

"Of course. I was the one who put it there." Leonardo smirked.

"How? Why?" The words jumped out of Elle's mouth before her mind could think them.

"Someone gave me the slip of paper. I read it, and was going to hand it to you, but you were asleep, so I left it there," Leonardo said it without a single fluctuation in his voice.

Elle wanted to believe what he was saying, but his tone and apathetic eyes told her otherwise.

"And something tells me you know how to get to Hostium," Eryk said.

"I, actually, do not. But Annie, well—you'll have to have a chat with her," Leonardo said lastly, and walked away.

Elle turned back to Eryk. His face was contorted in thought.

"You don't know how to get to Hostium?" Elle asked.

"I've only heard Mason's theories..." Eryk's voice trailed off but his expression suddenly lifted. "Elle!"

"What?" Her back shot straight up.

"This is it." Eryk beamed.

"What? What's it?"

"This is the thing that can cure Mason as well. The water from the waterfall, it can cure Mason! Mason's going to be okay."

Elle let out a weird and excited scream and clapped her hands together.

Mason was going to be okay.

And so was her mother.

They just needed to get to Hostium.

Chapter 22

"Now the hard part," Eryk said.

"Figuring out how to get into Hostium," Elle finished.

They became silent and the train's wheels on the track became louder. This was a different train from before, and Elle realized she didn't know exactly where this train was going. But the train's wood was crisper and a deeper brown than the last one. It didn't smell of mold, and all the glass windows were intact. It didn't awkwardly jostle the Mystics from side to side like the last couple of trains did.

Elle and Eryk found an unexplainable surge of encouragement to keep going. After Elle saw her sister, she thought she was going to crumble into the ground forever. And, she didn't want to admit it, but when she saw her sister's expression of prosopagnosia, Elle loathed being a Mystic more than anything in the world. She wanted to rip her Mystic soul from her body with her bare hands. But when she woke up after passing out, and realized the second task was over with, she felt hope again. Like it was a tangible thing.

"We'll have to try Anastasia," Elle said.

Elle and Eryk got up immediately and went to the next compartment over. Anastasia sat alone, looking at the plants passing by.

"Leonardo said you know how to get to Hostium," Eryk said once they were inside.

Anastasia didn't move a muscle. She didn't blink. Her breathing stayed even.

"Anastasia," Elle said when she didn't say anything.

Anastasia turned slowly around. Her eyes were strikingly dark, but underneath her right eye was a deep indigo bruise. Not from fatigue. Not from a lack of sleep.

"Remedium is in the heavens. If Hostium is its opposite, where do you think it lies?" Anastasia said through clenched teeth. Her lips were red and purple.

Elle and Eryk just stared at her. Her cheeks were sallow. Her skin, pale. What had happened to her?

Elle knew what it felt like to wear skin that looked like hers. She knew how much it ached physically, and how damaging it felt emotionally. She knew what it was like to look to in the mirror and start crying. Tears from how skeletal and crippled you look. Nothing could bandage those type of wounds.

"Anastasia, what happened?" Elle sat beside her.

Although Anastasia was always something fierce, someone intimidating and untrustworthy and manipulated people without care, she was still a Mystic and someone who had helped Elle on the Quest. Even if it might have been for another reason, she did it nonetheless.

"Hostium is near hell. The nearest thing to it. The entrance is through any of the seven seas. Remedium has the tree elevator, right? Well, Hostium also has a tree elevator, except theirs goes downwards. It's made of obsidian. When you see it, you'll know," Anastasia explained.

Elle glanced back at Eryk who said nothing. He just stared at Anastasia.

"It's invisible to Mystics and people who aren't Charmed. And I'm telling you both now: do not get caught," Anastasia enunciated.

"What exactly will happen?" Eryk asked.

Anastasia shook her head and looked outside. "You'll rot in hell."

Right then Leonardo stepped in and the compartment became instantly smaller.

"My sister and I are leaving when the train reaches its destination. This train is heading to the nearest coast. When you get off, find the Obsidian Tree and begin immediately. There's no time to waste," Leonardo informed, his tone flat.

"Why are you leaving?" Elle asked.

"Our mission to help you retrieve the heart is finished, so it's time for us to head back to Remedium," Leonardo said.

"But the Quest isn't over," Elle argued. "We still have the last ingredient to retrieve and we need your Myst."

"As much as I hate you, Elle is right. Your Myst could be very beneficial to us in Hostium," Eryk agreed.

Leonardo made eye contact with Anastasia, but she looked away.

"We have to go back to Remedium," Leonardo said with finality, and walked out of the compartment.

The door slid shut loudly behind him.

Elle looked back at Anastasia. She never thought Anastasia could look and feel that way. Something was changing, something was going on. Alaina had been absolutely right, and now it was obvious.

"Anastasia," Elle said but no other words followed. Eryk left the compartment then, and Elle wasn't quite sure why. It felt odd sitting with only Anastasia. It felt like sitting in a circus cage with a tame tiger that was rumored to be atrocious. "I know how you feel," Elle began.

"No, you don't," Anastasia spat, cutting Elle off. "You have no idea how I feel."

And right then something snapped in Elle's mind. Two very distant memories—memories that had been placed in a box with bubble wrap and securely taped up to sit in a storage unit with a complicated passcode. Memories that had been buried so deep into the ocean floor that not even the sea creatures could come close to it.

"You don't understand, Ellisia!" her father howled into her ears. The words echoing off the walls. His fist made contact with her ribs. His fist made contact with her shoulders. His fist made contact with her face and her eyes and her nose. His fist made contact with her face. "You have no idea, not a slightest clue what I have been through." He covered her mouth with his massive sweaty palms. "Stupid girl," he whispered.

The image twisted.

The room smelled plain. The walls were beige. Dust. Books. Children's paintings hung on the wall. The room was especially quiet.

"Hello Ms. Ellisia, I'm Dr. Carol, and I am so happy to meet you. How about we start with a game? Does that sound like fun?"

Ellisia nodded her head but didn't look up.

"I'm going to draw my family and tell you about them and then you're going to draw your family and tell me

about them," Dr. Carol explained. Ellisia had already done this boring game with other shrinks.

Dr. Carol showed Ellisia her husband and two kids, Kevin and Emily. Dr. Carol's family sounded a lot like the other shrinks' families.

"This is my mother," Ellisia pointed to stick figure woman with x's for eyes that was drawn in the left corner. "This is Dad," Ellisia pointed a stick figure man in the right corner that was drawn in a red crayon and also had x's for eyes. "And this is Emmie," Ellisia pointed to the stick figure girl that took up most the paper. Her eyes were drawn huge with green crayon.

"That is so lovely," the shrink gave a promising smile. "Can I ask why mommy and daddy have x's for eyes?"

"They're dead."

"Oh, Ellisia, sweetheart, I understand how hard that can be—"

Ellisia stood up from the chair and began to shout, "NO YOU DON'T! YOU HAVE NO IDEA HOW I FEEL! YOU DON'T KNOW ANYTHING, YOU'RE JUST A STUPID SHRINK WITH TWO VERY NORMAL CHILDREN AND A VERY NORMAL LIFE, YOU DON'T KNOW WHAT I'VE BEEN THROUGH YOU DON'T KNOW ME. YOU DON'T UNDERSTAND."

She slapped papers and pencil holders off the desk. Picture frames and the stupid clipboard from Dr. Shrink's hands. She ripped the stupid family portrait up and the pieces fell to the tidy, unspotted floor.

"You have no idea," Anastasia repeated, taking Elle out of her flashback.

"You're right," Elle said. "I don't. But I can thank you for helping me get the second ingredient. And I can thank you for helping me while you're in whatever mess you're in at the moment. And I owe you."

"You have no idea," Anastasia said again.

"I don't," Elle said. "But you can try to tell me."

Anastasia laughed out loud which made the hairs on Elle's arm stick straight up. "I can't. Not until the Quest is over."

Chapter 23

"Why not? Please, just tell me," Elle begged. She wasn't even sure what she was begging for.

"I won't," Anastasia said.

"But there is something, then?" Elle asked.

"There's always something," Leonardo said from behind her. "Elle, come with me."

"But..." Elle started, but stopped because she knew it was pointless. She got up and followed Leonardo out of the compartment.

The lights in the train were dim as sunset was about to fall. Elle followed Leonardo to the back of the train to a large glass compartment that was unoccupied. The Mystics slipped inside.

The golden sun casted a warm glow on the dark cherry wood. It was exceptionally beautiful and comforting.

"This sunset is amazing," Elle said.

Leonardo chuckled. "This isn't a sunset. It's a sunrise."

"Sunrise? How long did I sleep for?"

"Several hours, not long," Leonardo answered. "None of us did."

Elle didn't say anything. That meant they still had two full days of the Quest left, which was still not very much time.

Elle looked out of the vast glass window. The world escaped before their eyes. They were at the very end of the train, away from all other Mystics. Away from all other ears.

The sunrise was immaculate. A warm orange sun spilled across the sky, and space soaked the color up like a sponge.

"I wanted to apologize for something," Leonardo said, taking Elle off guard.

"For what?" Elle asked, her heartbeat quickening.

He didn't say anything back. He looked across the sky, searching for the words. Elle tried to read his body language again, but he looked neutral, as if nothing in the world was bothering him at the moment. As if nothing at all was blocking his mind. It was so frustrating for Elle.

"Well if you're not going to say anything, I'll just go about my—" Elle said as she stepped to the door, but Leonardo caught her hand and spun her back towards him.

His hand felt strange and unknown and desperate.

His face read insecure and hopeless and aimless.

It was confusion. It was desolation. It was grief. It was looking for an answer. He looked like he wanted to kiss her.

Elle pulled her hand away.

His face showed something else too. Sketched in the space between his eyes and above his nose, it showed despair. Even anguish?

It asked, "help me."

And for an unexplainable reason it did not frighten Elle. It did not scare her or make her want to run far away.

"What's wrong, Leonardo? I know there's been something wrong for a long time. Since the second I met you, and you can tell me," Elle said with gentle, slow words. It felt like the sentence took minutes to say.

Leonardo didn't look at her.

"I'm so, so sorry, Ellisia," Leonardo said. And the apology made Elle shudder. She had heard it too many times after things like this happened. Apologies were not apologies if they were only said with words.

His dark eyes looked up at hers. They were glassy, and it was such an odd sight to see.

"Sorry for what?" Elle asked.

"Everything that I've done," he said, still making direct eye contact. It almost physically hurt Elle's irises.

"But what have you done that you are so sorry for?" Elle was desperate for the answer. It had to be the same answer Anastasia was locking up as well. It was obvious then how different the Castello twins were, how they expressed themselves and needed different things. Eryk had been right about them keeping something from them, but Elle had also been right about Leonardo being different.

"Why are you here?" Elle pushed. "Why did you and Anastasia come on this Quest and why are you friends with the Dealer? Why are you even in Remedium in the first place? Why are you so upset? And why is Anastasia covered in bruises?"

Leonardo shook his head.

"Answer me," Elle begged.

Leonardo turned from her. His back now faced her and he looked out the window at the world passing by.

"In the graveyard," Leonardo began, "you were screaming at the very top of your lungs. You screamed so loud that you frightened the crows away. I'm sure you awoke some of the ghosts." The words sounded dramatic in Elle's ears. But then he said, "You screamed for Emmaline mostly. But you screamed some other words that I will never forget. You repeated over and over, 'I still love you.' You repeated it so much it became a rhythm in my head. It echoed in between the headstones and it made me want to rip my ears off my body. You repeated 'after everything' over and over as well. And I can never ever forget those words from my head, and do you want to know why? Because they were the last words my father spoke to my dying mother. They were the last words he spoke to my sister and I before he hung himself to death. And I ask you now, why you would ever love a man that did so much harm, so much damage to you and your sister? How you can even love a man that has done that to anyone? Stockholm syndrome? I don't know. But I have never and could never find those words to say back to my dead father and my dead mother. My dead family. Those words are foreign to me."

Elle was frozen. She didn't feel the need to cry, which was odd. She didn't feel the need to explain herself or give Leonardo an answer.

"And when I was crowned your Seeker, crowned the Seeker of a girl whose father killed himself in front of her, I wanted the job more than anything. And that, Ellisia, is why we are connected."

Elle said nothing. Because there was nothing to say.

Right then the train came to a screeching halt. And the conductor announced they had arrived.

"Good luck, Ellisia, on this last task. I'll be in Remedium."

Elle looked straight into his dark eyes one last time. Could this be the last time she ever saw him? She thought that once, when she left for the daring Quest, but there he was again. So no, this could not be the last night she saw him.

She turned away and left him in the compartment.

It was time for the third task.

Chapter 24

"Elle, I've been looking everywhere for you, where were you?" Eryk said as he caught sight of Elle. He grabbed her hand and pulled her to the exit.

Elle didn't answer and followed Eryk off the train. The air outside was chilling and the trees were bare. The sky was a crippling gray as the wind grew heavier. Elle didn't know if she should tell Eryk what Leonardo said. But why shouldn't she? What was Eryk going to do about it? She needed to stop questioning Eryk so much. Eryk was someone she could trust.

"We aren't far from the coast," Eryk said. His determination emanated off his body and gave Elle a sense of direction. Leonardo made her so lost and confused, but Eryk showed Elle why she was there in the first place.

"So, what are we supposed to do? Find some cryptic tree made of obsidian?" Elle asked. Questions like these always made the Quest sound so ridiculous.

"According to Anastasia, yes," Eryk answered.

The smell of the salty sea filled their lungs as they walked towards the barbaric waves. The beach was deserted, and the wind was freezing. It was hard to hear each other over the vicious wind and crashing waves against amorphous rocks.

"What do you think happened to her?" Elle asked as they searched aimlessly across the sand for anything out of the ordinary.

Eryk took a deep breath. "I'm not sure, but something tells me it has to do with the Dealer. What did she say to you when I left?"

"She didn't say anything more. All she said is that I have no clue what she's going through, and that she can't say anything until the Quest is over," Elle replied.

"So there is definitely something going on then," Eryk clarified.

"There's always something." Elle smirked to herself as she copied Leonardo's words.

"Hate to say it, but, I knew it," Eryk said.

"I didn't one hundred percent doubt you, ya know," Elle said. "It just didn't matter at the time. We needed to find the heart, and we did, and that's all that matters."

Eryk looked up at her. "You don't understand. If Leonardo and Anastasia are working with the Dealer and they're here for another reason than to help us, then the Dealer has another plan. He's using us for something else."

The words soaked into Elle's brain. It was obvious that Eryk was right, even if she didn't want to admit it. But how could they know for sure that Leonardo and Anastasia were working for the Dealer in the first place? Only because they hung around him in Remedium didn't mean they were helping him with some secret plan. She said this to Eryk and he shook his head at every word she spoke.

"He's not called the Dealer for nothing, Elle. Mason didn't randomly get sick and Leonardo and Anastasia didn't randomly become their replacements."

"You think the Dealer made Mason get sick?" Elle queried. She was surprised she hadn't thought of it before.

"Elle, come on, it's obvious. The Dealer wants something else. Just admit it. He probably got scared we finished the first task too soon," Eryk said.

Elle let out a long breath. "Fine. You're right. I know you're right. The Dealer wants something else. Anastasia and Leonardo are helping him get it. But what's *it*."

"That, I don't know," Eryk answered. "But whatever it is, it's not good. And he's using us in some way to help him get it."

"But what about my mother?" Elle nearly shouted. "Is he not helping my mother at all then?"

Eryk pressed his lips together. Elle could feel his blood pressure rise. "I don't freaking know. Let's just get this stupid last ingredient and get the hell back to Remedium to find out."

Elle didn't answer this time. Leonardo and Anastasia had actually been helpful to them. If they hadn't been there for the second task, they wouldn't have the heart already. If they had gone through all of this with nothing in return, then it wasn't a deal. A deal is two-sided.

"It's going to be hard for the tree to make an appearance if this beach is deserted." Elle changed the subject. "Anastasia said only Charmed people can see it, remember?"

"Yeah, I remember. Look out for people, I'm going to try to contact Alaina really quick, maybe she found out more information on the Dealer," Eryk said. He sat in the sand and began to dig through his backpack for the map.

A great thing about Eryk was that he didn't hold grudges. Even after arguments or tense conversations, he went back to acting casual afterwards. This was something Elle really admired about him, except he had held a grudge on Leonardo and Anastasia for a while, but it was for a logical reason.

"It says we have seven missed calls," Eryk said.

"Odd."

Eryk tapped on Tabitha's name and the map read the word "connecting." Thunder shook the sky and the map blinked to black then dissipated to a normal map.

"Bad connection," Eryk said.

"Let's keep looking, we're running out of time," Elle said.

As Eryk and Elle searched up and down the coast, the waves became tremendous and vociferous as they crashed against the protruding rocks from the water's surface. No rain fell, but thunder echoed through the clouds.

Eryk seemed deep in thought, so Elle didn't speak to him. When he was in this mood—an aggravated, on edge, type of mood—Elle knew to just let him be. She learned this in training with Angel and Phoenix. Whenever Eryk could not figure something out and got overwhelmed it became hard for him to express himself. Elle found that letting him "walk it off" (as Phoenix called it) was the best way to get out his anger. So, Elle stayed silent and looked for people anywhere on the beach.

After several silent moments of looking, a group of people walked onto the beach. There was about five or six of them, all dressed in wetsuits and carrying surf boards. Elle heard one of them say, "The waves are crazy today!"

"Do you think one of the surfers could be Indwelled?" Elle asked.

"There's more people Indwelled than you think," Eryk answered. "You haven't been taught this yet, but since you're a Mystic you now have the 'sight.'"

"I'm guessing that's when you look at a person and see their Charmer inside," Elle expounded.

"Exactly. Just look straight at that group of people. Think of your Myst, and think of their Charmer, think of them coming to Remedium."

Elle did as Eryk instructed, and it was so easy to do. Instantaneously, she saw a Charmer in two of the surfers' heads. It was weird, because she always pictured her Charmer in the center of her body but that wouldn't make much sense since Charmers control your mind, not your body.

One Charmer was inside a girl's mind. She had warm brown hair and was very skinny. She was pretty, Elle thought. The girl talked to the person beside her, who contained the second Charmer. He was large. Tall and wide. His Charmer looked fatter, as well. Seeing the Charmers inside the people's heads was almost like seeing a fetus through an ultrasound. Except the Charmers were pure bone with giant heads. They had a blue hue to them and the only word that came to Elle's mind was "broken." They looked so weak and decrepit, as they do when they are out of the body as well.

"This will become natural to you soon," Eryk said. "When you look at someone, you will automatically see their Charmer without trying."

The thought was so strange. She was a Mystic now, no longer a human that contained a Charmer like the people in front of her.

"Should we bring them to Remedium?" Elle asked.

Eryk nodded his head. "Look over there."

She looked where he pointed, and there it was. The Tree of Remedium. Sitting solemnly and beautifully as it waited patiently for its new members. It made her smile.

"Go get them," Eryk urged. "Let them show us the Tree of Hostium, and then you can show them the Tree of Remedium."

Elle smiled and nodded her head.

She walked through the cold sand to the group of surfers waxing their boards. They looked up at the strangely beautiful girl before them. Long black hair and honey skin. Peculiar, deep brown eyes that somehow shined against the gray bare sky. Everything about her was unusual yet astonishing, like some new species that walked the earth, as if she was an unknown creature from the deep sea that now walked along the shore.

"Hello," the eccentric creature spoke. "My name is Elle Carroway." She stuck out her hand for the girl that contained the Charmer to shake.

The girl's mouth lay slightly ajar. She hesitantly took Elle's hand as everyone watched in awe.

"I'm Catherine." The girl held out a trembling hand. Her skin felt like ice as Elle shook it.

"Levi," the boy with the Charmer said.

"I'm going to borrow your friends for just a second," Elle said to the other four people.

They all shook their heads quickly, mesmerized at Elle's beauty. It almost made her blush.

Catherine and Levi followed Elle away from their friends.

"I need you to show me something, and then I'm going to show you something," Elle explained. The Indwelled people nodded in agreement. "I need you to look around for a tree made of obsidian."

"Why?" Catherine asked, still staring at the alluring creature.

"It's very important to my friend and me." Elle pointed toward Eryk.

"It's right there." Levi pointed behind Elle. Elle glanced over, but saw nothing. "Obsidian is black, right?"

"Yes," Elle replied. "Can you show me to it?"

Levi nodded and walked to the tree. "It's massive, and beautiful. You don't see it?"

"Oh, I see it now," Elle lied. "You stay here; I'll be right back."

Elle walked over to Catherine. Catherine remained where they were before, staring at Eryk. Eryk sat in the sand, playing with the map.

"Catherine, can you follow me? I have another tree to show you," Elle said, taking her hand.

Catherine listened to Elle and followed her to the Tree of Remedium as if in a trance.

The Charmed human looked up at the magnificent tree in wonder. Her eyes were wide and mouth fully opened.

"It's called the Tree of Remedium, and it's going to help you," Elle explained.

"How?" Catherine questioned. She began to walk around the giant tree.

"It will heal you, it'll take away your anxieties and fears and all of it," Elle said.

"This is crazy," Catherine said. "This isn't real. Where's Levi?"

"No, wait," Elle said. "Let me show you one more thing." She looked around for the triangular indention as Eryk did when he brought her to Remedium.

She placed her hand on the triangle and it began to trace the print of her palm and fingers. The print scribbled across the trunk and the branches. It poured onto the leaves and limbs. It glowed indigo, then gold, then bright blue. Catherine watched, dumbstruck.

Soon enough the elevator's door popped open to reveal the yellow lit room.

"If you want to be cured from your mental sickness, step inside, and everything will be explained to you," Elle said.

"What do you mean?" Catherine asked. Her Charmer pumped inside her head as if it was trying to get away from the tree.

"Your mental illness, anxiety, depression, OCD, whatever it is, can be taken away if you step into this elevator. You can be better, better than you could ever imagine," Elle explained.

"Why?" Catherine questioned, "How? Why would I want to go in there? I don't have OCD, I'm bulimic."

Elle remembered asking Eryk similar questions when he was trying to convince her to go to Remedium.

"You don't want to stay like this, with whatever you're going through. You don't want to stay like this, even if you think you do. This Tree will make you better. I know what you're feeling, I was just like you not long ago, and I can assure you that stepping inside this tree will be the best decision you've ever made."

Catherine looked at her skeptically. "How do I know you're not lying?"

"Because I did it. I went into this tree several weeks ago. And now I'm here and I'm better," Elle replied. Her answer felt right.

"But what about Levi?" Catherine asked. "What about my friends?"

"Levi will you join you in a moment, I promise," Elle answered.

Catherine didn't say anything, but she stepped inside the elevator. The door closed and Elle fell to her knees.

This was the most incredible feeling she had ever experienced.

Chapter 25

Once the elevator reached the Villages of Remedium and Elle's handprints dissipated from the magical tree, she got back up and ran to Eryk. She spun and jumped in the air out of pure joy. She hugged Eryk as tight as her arms would let her. He embraced her back with a smile and swung her around.

"I see why being a Mystic is so great." Elle finally understood. The pain of losing her sister and everything that had happened in Remedium had not been the greatest thus far, but watching a broken person step into the Tree for a better life, pumped meaning and joy into Elle's lungs. She appreciated Mystics so much more. She wanted to save more people like Catherine.

"You were great." Eryk smiled. "You did great."

"Who's going to explain to her everything?" Elle asked.

"Whoever finds her first, so most likely Tabitha," Eryk said.

Elle wished for everything to go perfectly for her. But by the look of Eryk's face she remembered they still had the Quest to complete. The final phase. The last clue.

"Now where's that tree?" Eryk asked tenaciously.

The Mystics walked over to where Levi stood. He looked up at Eryk in fascination.

"Levi, this is Eryk. Eryk, this is Levi," Elle introduced.

Eryk nodded his head and Levi stared. The combination of Eryk and Elle was stupefying. They looked like two wild panthers from the rainforest. They looked otherworldly. Elle was used to being stared at, but never like this.

"Levi, I need you to do two things for me," Elle said.

"Yeah?" Levi followed.

"I need you to touch this tree until a door, or something opens up," Elle instructed. "And then once you've done that, I need you to walk to that massive tree over there," Elle pointed to the Tree of Remedium, "and do the same thing. Only this time, when a door opens up, go in it."

"Go in it?" Levi questioned, perplexed.

"Yes," Elle answered. "Just step right on in."

"Why?"

"That's where your friend Catherine went, and she's waiting for you."

"What is it? Like some sort of treehouse?" Levi scratched his head where his Charmer pulsed inside like a beating heart.

"You could say that, yeah," Elle clarified.

"But why would she—"

"Just do it," Eryk said. "Trust us."

Levi jumped at Eryk's clear voice. It sounded like deep bells ringing. He nodded his head and rubbed his hand up and down the obsidian covered tree.

"Ouch!" Levi hollered in pain as his hand began to bleed. The sticky red blood puddled and mixed with the dense brown sand.

Eryk and Elle's eyes widened at the sight.

"What just happened?" Elle squealed.

"Something just..." Levi paused. "A lever? It's a lever it looks like, it stabbed my hand."

"Lever?" Eryk queried with squinted eyes.

"Do you think it does the same thing as the triangle on the Remedium Tree?" Elle asked Eryk.

Eryk slumped his shoulders. He wished he could see what the boy was talking about.

"Go for it, pull it," Elle said to Levi.

Levi's forehead wrinkled. "Are you sure?"

"Yes, just do it." Eryk said.

Levi pulled down on the lever, his hand slippery with blood.

Nothing happened.

Elle and Eryk looked at one another and back at Levi.

And then they were falling.

Chapter 26

It was a black void. Darkness consumed all. It felt as if the black was melting on their skin—a heat-filled vacuum that sucked away the chills left over from the coast. It seemed as if they were in some sort of elevator—dropping at a vicious speed.

The tunnel was so dark Elle could not tell if her eyes were open or closed.

Robbed of their eyesight, their other senses took over.

Smoke wafted in the air. The scent of something burning.

But then something caught Elle's attention.

A sound. Growing louder and louder as the elevator fell deeper and deeper. A vociferous chasm in the distance. It had to be the waterfall.

"Eryk," Elle said loudly over the descending elevator.

Eryk struggled to find his balance. "Yeah? Elle? You there?" His hands groped the darkness in front of him.

"I'm here, I'm here."

The lift came to a jerking stop, making Elle and Eryk fall to their knees. Elle bumped her head on the wall, which sent a burst of pain throughout her body.

"Are you okay?" Eryk reached towards her.

Elle rubbed the side of her head as she saw white stars flash in front of her. "Yeah, let's get out of here."

Eryk stood up, but his feet wavered. He rubbed his hands against the walls of the elevator to find the door. He touched what felt like some sort of latch and pulled on it. The door was heavy, but it eventually opened.

Outside the lift everything remained black—crystal black and shiny smooth. The only source of light was hanging torches of bright fire on the walls and massive fire pits protruding from the floor.

Elle and Eryk fumbled out of the lift and rounded the corner behind a protruding wall.

"We need to follow the sound of the waterfall," Elle said.

"I can't even tell where it's coming from." Eryk kept his voice down. "It sounds like it's coming from everywhere."

"Maybe it's in the center," Elle suggested. She hadn't actually thought of the idea, it just came out, but it made sense.

"You think the castle is built around the waterfall?" Eryk queried.

"Perhaps." Elle shrugged her shoulders. The pain on the side of her head throbbed.

Eryk paused. He listened to the sound of the water falling. "Actually," he said, with one finger pointed in the air, "I think you're right."

"Let's go." Elle began to walk hastily away from the cornered wall.

"No, Elle. Wait." Eryk caught her arm and tugged her back. Her head burst with pain. She looked at him fiercely, fiercer than she meant to. "We can NOT get caught."

Elle looked directly in his eyes and they spoke the exact thing she was thinking. The unsaid topic.

She nodded her head, and they tiptoed out of the corner.

The ceiling was miles away, a black pallet of watercolors stretching amongst the sky, cascading down to the ground. It was endless and sparkling. If you stared at the color too long, it began to trick your eyesight, like not knowing if your eyelids were open or closed. Elle imagined that a castle made of obsidian would be dank and chilling, like a cave hidden by the ocean; but with all the surrounding fire, the castle was warm. Uncomfortably warm. She didn't know if she was sweating and out of breath from the stress, or just from the mere lack of oxygen in the air. The fire sucked up all the cold, fresh air like a mosquito sucking blood. Elle could see the sweat building on the side of Eryk's head. His hair stuck to his temples, indicating that he could feel the heat, too.

Eryk walked with urgency. Elle kept pace, something she wasn't able to do before. Training and the Quest had not only transformed her mentally, but also physically.

Eryk looked deep in thought, as he always did when he was determined to get something done. But this time, it was a different, sort of intent look. As if he was remembering something.

But something else itched at the back of Elle's mind, distracting her from Eryk. Something bothersome and uncomfortable. Maybe it was just being in Hostium, Elle thought. Hostium was a place no Mystic had ever travelled to, none that she had heard of anyway.

They continued to keep their heads down as they sped through the halls of the Obsidian Castle. They were fearful of being noticed. Not only for their eyes, but for their overall appearance. Mystics were lively, their eyes vibrant and intriguing; they harnessed color throughout their skin and hair. Charmers were dead, with pale grey skin, and drab, lifeless hair. Black voids for eyes that if you looked too closely, you'd fall in.

Elle and Eryk's fast movements echoed on the obsidian floor. They knew they were loud, but it was something they didn't have time to worry over. They needed to get the water and get out. In and out. Quick, quick.

But that itch. It was distracting.

The majestic castle was a blur as the Mystics walked quickly through the hallways, the ebony colored tiles stretching beyond view. The sparkling wisps of fire that entangled the air were like woven hands and fingers in love. Hostium was something exotic and enchanting. But not like the way Remedium was. No— Remedium was flawlessly beautiful, whimsical. A cast of peace and security. This place, however, was cryptic. Haunting. But lovely and deathly gorgeous. If sirens from Greek mythology were to take form as a building, it would the Obsidian Castle. Hostium was a gargantuan castle, a gargantuan kingdom. A castle that stretched far beyond the imagination. It carried on longer than the Great Wall of China. This place was a never-ending maze of charm and fear. And that odd prickle in the back of Elle's mind...

She dared a glance at Eryk. His eyebrows were furrowed in ambitious thought. His determination rung throughout his firm body. Elle thought that maybe Eryk was thinking about how the enchanted water was going to be mixed with the leaves and the heart; chemically and perfectly combined into a wonderful concoction they had been killing themselves for. And how that wonderful concoction was going to cure Elle's mother, her Charmer. The magical water flowing down her throat to her veins and bloodstream, her lungs and her heart and all the other organs. How she could be saved, and by doing so would save Elle; give her that peace she has always deserved in her long life of torture and heartache. They just needed that water. They could hear it and feel it the closer they got with every step.

Eryk looked up at Elle.

But she was gone.

Chapter 27

Something pulled at Elle like strings on a marionette doll.

Some unknown force willed her away from Eryk.

Her mind spun.

She didn't hear the shoes on obsidian. Or the whispers surrounding her.

She didn't feel the eyes watching her.

She couldn't feel her body moving.

It felt like heaving through thick water. The current was undeniably powerful.

Her mind was focused on one thing.

Crystal-like memories intriguing her mind.

She stopped.

She was standing before her father.

Chapter 28

Suddenly she was in the middle of a vivid flashback, real as life itself.

"Where's momma?" the little girl asked, her brown eyes the size of the moon.

He looked at her. No, he didn't just look at her. He gave her a look of disgust mixed with something she had never before seen on her father's face. An expression she didn't know existed in her father's mind: Guilt. Sad and utter guilt, and hurt.

Pure hurt.

"Not here anymore," he said.

He wouldn't look at her eyes.

"But where?" the small girl questioned.

"I said, NOT HERE." His voice shook the walls and tears burst from the little girl's eyes.

She started crying loudly. Her little hands held each other and her tiny lips quivered. He looked at his little girl, this tiny baby. A sweet, sad face. Desperate and confused, she didn't know what was happening.

He pushed his baby to the ground. He pushed her down, so she could stay down. Because she wasn't there anymore. And she was never going to be there.

Her cries were terrible, worse than any sound on earth.

She tried to stand back up but she was pushed down. His fingers wrapped around her arm, bruising her precious skin. Delicate skin.

Through her own tears, she could see his.

"It's my birthday today," the little girl said.

Her daddy took swig of his drink. The smell was thick, but she was used to it.

"Did you hear me?" she asked again, her little voice high and musical.

He took another swig of his drink.

"Daddy?"

He suddenly stood up and threw the bottle at the wall. Glass fell around them and the noise was frightening.

She was looking at herself in the mirror. The glass was broken and dirty because Daddy threw it at them once. He was drunk and missed, so it was okay.

One, two, three, four, five, six, seven. Only seven bruises. It wasn't too bad. They were only a bluish color too this time, the yellow and green ones were the most painful.

"WHAT DID I SAY ABOUT THE DAMN MIRROR YOU USELESS..." he took a brown blanket and covered the mirror. He looked at the little girl and spit on her. "Never. Touch this again. Do you hear me?"

Chapter 29

Elle was jolted out of her flashback.

Now, her father didn't look like she remembered him. He was not as tall as she remembered and he was not as wide as she remembered. Being a Charmer, he was lifeless and still—cold and gray. His eyes were hallowing black, cryptic to stare into, because she could not physically see him looking at her, but she could feel him. She could feel other eyes looking on her, too.

Although the air was hot, it was suddenly cold. Frozen. She stepped closer to him. Closer—each step ricocheting off the ground and walls. He didn't move, he only stared. She didn't blink, her heartrate was surprisingly steady. She stopped in front of him.

Her eyes searched his pale features.

Remembrance.

Flashbacks.

Her mouth opened, her lips formed his name.

That's when cold sharp fingers clawed at her skin, tearing her away.

This was the second time that had happened to her—being pulled away from her father, only this time she was not crying, she was completely and absolutely still. Frozen with shock and fear.

The sharp fingers punctured skin, blood dripped to the ground.

She did not take her eyes away from his, and he remained immobile. They were like two statues facing each other at a museum.

Her blood trailed with her as she was dragged away, her feet smearing the dark red like a paintbrush. She didn't dare glance behind her to see who tightly gripped her arms. She got the impression the person was female and strong and merciless.

Suddenly, bright orange, hot flames were being thrown in her direction. Elle watched as a huge fireball smashed into a Charmer on her left.

"Elle. Ellisia!" Eryk's voice echoed off of the dense walls, snapping Elle out of her reverie. She couldn't tell where he was coming from. Then, she couldn't see anything at all. Only darkness.

Elle's heartrate spiked. She kicked her legs and wiggled from side to side in an attempt to release herself from the sharp grip. She screamed and twisted and kicked, but she saw nothing. Her vision was nonexistent.

"Eryk, Eryk!" she wailed back. The claws holding her squeezed tighter and more blood gushed out.

Before Elle knew it, she was being thrown at a wall. She heard a metal gate close in front of her.

Elle screamed horrifically. Not having her vision was pure frustration and heightened her fear and adrenaline. She screamed, making her throat raw. Tears ran down her face and she could feel the blood from her arms puddle around her. Her hands were sticky and wet from touching her arms. She could feel the ground was cold and wet—probably wet with blood.

"Elle, Elle!"

Eryk.

He was with her, somewhere, not in her cell, but there.

"Eryk," Elle replied desperately. "Where are you? I can't see anything."

"Neither can I," Eryk answered, his voice not as shaky as Elle's.

"Why? Why can't we see anything?"

"They must have taken our sight," Eryk said.

"They can do that?" Elle asked, terrified.

"Charmer's have access to dark powers that Mystics don't even know about."

"What do we do, Eryk? How are we going to get out of here in time to get what we need and leave?" Elle could feel the reality of the situation setting in. She felt completely useless without her sight.

"Shhh." Eryk hushed. "Don't say too much, we don't know who could be listening."

Elle couldn't help it, but she started crying again. She should have listened to Eryk. She should have stayed focused. They could have the water by now if it weren't for her. They could be on their way back to Remedium, if she had only kept her stupid curious eyes ahead.

"Elle, don't start freaking out, this isn't over," Eryk reassured. "We didn't come this far just to be trapped wherever we are now. We need to figure something out."

Elle couldn't forget what just happened though. She couldn't. She couldn't let it go so quickly.

"Eryk. That was my father. That was my dad, Eryk." And if that wasn't enough for him to understand, she didn't know what else to say.

Eryk went silent. Or at least Elle hoped he did, she didn't want to have lost her hearing, too.

"I haven't seen him since he killed himself right in front of me. I haven't seen him since I was eleven. I never, *ever*, imagined I would see him again."

"I can't imagine what that must feel like," Eryk said in barely a whisper.

"It's a physical form of my thoughts."

"What do you mean?" he asked.

"Seeing him. The person who abused me, emotionally scarred me. Mentally drained me from my life like squeezing all the water out of a sponge. For anyone who has ever been abused, seeing your abuser is like seeing every nightmare you ever had into one physical form, but instead of running from it, you want to understand it. Looking at him—it was like seeing my depression and anxiety walk in front of me."

Her last few words echoed off the walls. It was completely silent, except for the faint sound of the waterfall in the background. Elle could also hear Eryk breathing heavily. He sounded as if he was to her left, probably in his own cell.

He didn't say anything for a long time, but then he said, "When I walked in on Ashlee being raped, I didn't know what was happening. I was too young to understand. All I knew was that there was blood and that she was in pain and the boy on top of her was hurting her. I wanted to help her, I wanted to get the guy off of her and carry her away. It didn't matter to me anymore that she was abusive towards me, it didn't matter that she was the source to all my pain. It's not even that she was physically abusive—most the time—but she was emotionally abusive. You know, absent, neglectful. She was basically my mother, the only mother-like figure in my life, and she didn't care about me at all. I remember people in school complaining how their older siblings were too hard on them, but it wasn't that they were too hard, it was just that they were protective. I've never known what that felt like—being protected. I felt like I had to protect her, if anything. But when I saw her being raped, it no longer mattered how much hatred and mixed emotions I had for her at the time. All that mattered was she was my sister and I wanted—needed—to save her from what was happening, even though I didn't know *what* was happening." He paused. "The people you love, the people you care so much about, have that effect on you. No matter how crazy, psychotic, or messed up they are, all you see is a person who needs help. A person who is desperate for help. No matter how much they have hurt you, they're only as hurt as you are."

There was nothing to say back, because Elle and Eryk knew they both understood. And Elle had never heard truer words spoken. *The people who have hurt you, are only as hurt as you are.* Or else they would not have hurt you.

"Eryk, we need to get out of here," Elle finally said, with urgency behind every whispered word.

"I know."

"We need to get the water, and go," Elle persisted.

"I know," Eryk repeated.

"What do you say we do?"

Elle could hear Eryk get up and walk around his cell. Judging from the sound of it, the cell couldn't be very big. She got up to do the same. She could touch each side of the wall with her arms extended. She couldn't touch the ceiling even when she jumped.

"*Ahhhg!*"

Elle jumped. "What? What's wrong?"

"Careful, don't touch the bars of the cell, they're scorching hot," Eryk said.

"Okay, okay," Elle replied. "What's our plan then? How are we going to get out?"

A loud screeching noise interrupted Elle. Her vision became blurry with colors of black and grey. Her eyes focused like the lens of a camera.

But the sight made her wish she hadn't looked.

Chapter 30

A Charmer stood before them. She was tall and grotesquely thin with white, almost blue skin. Her hair reached her ribcage and was jet black on one side and crystal white on the other. Her eyes were black voids, soulless and ghastly like anthracite. On each of her shoulders sat black and silver colored bats with eyes that resembled her own. Her lips were severely cracked and her nose pointed right at the tip. She wore an extravagant dress made of shimmering black glass that could cut even the toughest of materials. The Charmer was undeniably uncanny.

"I am the Glass Queen, the Queen of Hostium," she spoke, her voice raspy and loud. "You will answer every question I ask, young Mystics. Do you understand?"

Elle was at a loss for words. The Glass Queen was spine-chilling, yet exquisitely beautiful. More beautiful than any Mystic she had ever seen.

"I said, DO YOU UNDERSTAND?" Her voice echoed off every wall. The bats on her shoulders screeched.

Both Elle and Eryk muttered yes. Eryk's voice sounded as unsteady as Elle's. Neither Mystic could muster up the energy to use their Myst on the Glass Queen. It wouldn't do them any good at this point. The Glass Queen was more powerful than either of them knew. *Besides*, Elle thought, *if Eryk was going to use his Myst on her, he would have done it by now. And if he thought it was a bad idea, it was a very bad idea.*

"How did you find Hostium and how did you enter without the blood of a Charmer?" the Glass Queen asked. She wore the slightest smile, as if she was enjoying seeing their fear.

Eryk spoke before Elle could answer. "We found a boy, a Hosted boy to let us in."

"And where is the boy?" the Glass Queen questioned.

"We sent him away after he opened the door for us," Eryk answered.

The Glass Queen chuckled, each laugh echoing from wall to wall. "You just used the boy for your own good." She spat the words like they were venom. "Mystics—such pathetic little hypocrites, aren't you?"

Elle and Eryk didn't reply. They couldn't take their eyes off of her.

"And why would some little juvenile Mystics as yourselves be interested in my Kingdom?" the Glass Queen interrogated.

"We're here because—" Eryk started.

"No," the Glass Queen interrupted. "I want her to speak." She pointed at Elle. Her finger nails were long, pointed and made of shimmering black glass like her dress. As Elle looked closely, she could see blood on the tips of them. Her blood. The Glass Queen was the one who dragged her away from her father and threw her in this pit.

Elle sat frozen, speechless. The Glass Queen must have known that Eryk knew what to say, not her. She must have guessed Elle was going along with Eryk's plan.

"I haven't heard you speak yet, my darling." The Glass Queen smiled an ugly smile. Her thin chapped lips stretched across her face. They gleamed white and her teeth were molded and broken. The sight was petrifying.

When Elle didn't say anything, the Glass Queen took a step forward. Her sharp fingernails caressed Elle's face, over her cheek bone and down her jawline. Elle didn't dare move.

"Don't!" Eryk yelled, even though he couldn't see what was going on. They were in separate cells beside each other, a massive thick wall of obsidian between them. "Don't touch her!"

The Glass Queen turned from Elle and walked to Eryk. Elle sat there, frozen with fear. It was like she was a little girl again. Back in that shack of a house, waiting for her next beating.

"Aww," the Glass Queen said. "You care for this girl. She is not what you think, Eryk."

"How do know my name—"

"You silly, naïve Mystics, you think Hostium does not keep a close eye on Remedium? You think we do not know what events take place in your village." When she laughed her bats screeched along with her. "Atropa, Belladonna do you hear this? They don't believe we follow the Mystics." She talked to her bats and they screeched at the sound of her words as if they were laughing along with her.

"What are you talking about?" Elle finally said.

The Glass Queen's expression lifted at the sound of Elle's voice. She tiptoed over to Elle's cell. "Ellisia. You are not even a Mystic yet. You do not know the lies Remedium tells you yet. You have much to learn, my darling. And so you shall. Your father was quite the pupil in Hostium, perhaps you'll be the same one day. Perhaps you'll be one of us one day."

The mention of her father put Elle back into shock.

"I would never..." Elle's voice trailed off.

The Glass Queen cackled into the air. "Never say never my darling." She paused. "Now, answer me this. Why are you here?"

"Don't answer her Elle! Don't say anything!"

Fiercely, the Glass Queen turned on her heel and scurried over to Eryk. Elle did not know what was happening, but suddenly her cell door closed, and Eryk's screams echoed throughout the chamber.

"Fine. If you do not wish to answer me, you shall lose your sight and your hearing and starve in this chamber until you die."

Chapter 31

Everything went blank—completely and utterly empty. The buzz of the waterfall silenced, the hum of voices stopped and Eryk's shallow breathing cut off. Elle could still feel how cold her skin was and the pool of blood around her. She hadn't even had the chance to get a good look around.

This is it, Elle thought. *This is the end.* She hated herself for being pessimistic and giving up so quickly, when she knew Eryk was already thinking of the next strategy. But what was there to do? They couldn't communicate any longer, they couldn't see a single thing. All they had was their hands and their brains. Shouldn't that be enough?

Elle exhaled as loudly as she could. What did it matter? Eryk couldn't hear her anyway. She screamed again and again and again until suddenly she could feel how hot her skin was. She could feel flames tickle her face and caress her skin. She threw fire in every direction, every which way, aimlessly and carelessly because at this point it didn't matter. She felt the walls around her to check if anything broke or melted, but like she assumed, they were perfectly intact. Fireproof. Charmers were smart. She scorched her skin on the metal bars while feeling if they were still there. They were. And she felt so immensely angry. She was never going to be able to save her mother. She was never going to be able to give Emmie the life she deserved. She was never going to be reunited with her mother and Emmie. Never.

It felt as if days passed by. The silence was the most aggravating silence she had ever experienced. Worse than the silence that comes after a beating. Worse than the silence of the Everson's house at two in the morning. Worse than the silence at group therapy when nobody wants to go first. Worse than the silence of her mother's funeral. Worse than the silence of social workers who took her from place to place without an explanation. Worse than the silence of Mrs. Everson looking at her when she had done something wrong. Worse than the silence of Emmie when she didn't want to talk to her. Worse than the silence of her brain when she was stuck in an empty room with a new foster kid over and over and over and over.

It is so odd, Elle thought, *that by losing your sight and hearing the world continues to go on, but time seems to have stopped for you.* She couldn't imagine how many hours passed them by. Every sweet second slipped through their fingers.

Both her and Eryk were running on peanut butter crackers and trail mix. Hunger began to set in, followed by fatigue. But all she could think, was if Eryk was okay. Then a terrifying thought hit her.

What if he was dead?

What if he was dead in his cell? She wouldn't know. She would have no way of knowing. The last thing she heard from him was his horrible, painful screams.

Elle's screams pierced the air and bright orange flames danced amongst the walls. She was in a mad, panicked state. She moved in a possessed motion and screamed into the air.

Her screams traveled throughout Hostium like a snake following its prey.

She was shaking back and forth, back and forth, back and forth. Wait, no. *Someone* was shaking her back and forth. Her hand—engulfed in raising flames—caught the arms shaking her. They were thin but muscular—a girl's arms. Not the Glass Queen's arms though, hers would have been unusually thin. The girl yanked out of Elle's grasp. The girl was close to her, Elle could feel her breaths on her face. It smelled like coffee and spearmint gum.

Alaina.

Elle stopped. The flames cut out immediately and she stood, looking aimlessly into the air.

Elle felt Alaina's sweaty hands grab her's and guide her out of the cell. Hope fled into her system like a crashing wave. Elle didn't know how in the world Alaina was in Hostium, but she prayed she had a plan to escape the Glass Queen and get enough water for both her mother and Mason.

Suddenly Elle was bumping into Alaina. Alaina had stopped abruptly, and Elle could feel Alaina's body tense up.

Something was wrong.

Elle looked desperately around but everything remained eerily dark.

It felt as if someone was walking their way. An unknown figure moving closer and closer.

Elle reached for Alaina's hand out of fear.

But it wasn't Alaina's hand she grabbed.

It was a long cold hand with sharp glass-like fingernails.

The Glass Queen.

Chapter 32

Fear erupted inside Elle. She pulled her hand away and froze. Her heartbeat thudded throughout her body. She did not know what was happening. There was no movement around, as if time stood still.

Like melting candle wax, Elle slowly regained her sight and hearing.

Her fire caressed the walls and ceiling, making it bright in the dim chamber. Alaina's facial expression was frightening. Her eyes were so widely pulled open as she stared back at Elle. Elle had never seen her so terrified.

Elle glanced at Eryk, who was behind Alaina. The sight of Eryk was petrifying. Blood oozed from his neck and spilled down his shirt like an overflowing cup. He was motionless, frozen in place, except for his eyes. His fierce blue-green eyes screamed for help in desperation. They frantically moved at the sight of Elle and something behind her.

Wait.

Something didn't feel right.

Something was not right.

Something gave her a nervous tick and something in the air felt like static electricity.

Elle kept her frightened eyes on Eryk's. Slowly he began to feel his fingers and limbs again but as soon as he regained control of his body he pointed behind her.

Then it felt like spiders with long, skinny legs were crawling up her spine to her face and through her mouth, hijacking her brain as they spun their cobwebs and made their homes, or their traps.

That was when Elle turned around and looked at her father.

She stood before him. She didn't know what went through her mind.

Then he turned and walked away.

Chapter 33

Elle thought her body would collapse—that her bones would turn to water like waves crashing on the shore. She thought she could hear her mind and heart and organs wilt like flowers with too little water.

At the same time, she felt stronger than she'd ever felt. She felt like her skin was made of gold and her mind was made of power. She felt like power. Because this time—*this time*—she was not the one to walk away.

Eryk and Alaina stared at her. Waiting for her to say something, do something, react. But the only way she reacted was by raising her bloody shoulders and regaining fierceness in her eyes. She could feel the pressure of the Quest weigh on her, she could feel the last hour tick away. There was no time to dwell, think, strategize. It was time to act.

"Let's go," Elle said.

Alaina morphed her eyes into black studs like the rest of the Charmers and changed her hair to be lifeless and white. She even managed to make her skin dull. Eryk and Elle kept their heads down and watched Alaina's footsteps to keep track. The pain in Elle's arm throbbed, but she stayed focused. She repeated "water" over and over.

"We only have an hour left to get back to Remedium," Alaina said.

"How long were we in the chamber?" Elle asked.

"Time works slower in Hostium. You were trapped for a while," Alaina explained.

They turned the corner. They knew the waterfall was in the center of the castle and was easily heard throughout, like a constant ticking clock. The volume of the waterfall became more and more prominent as the Mystics walked throughout the pernicious castle. With every step, Elle's nerves and excitement amplified. She watched Alaina's anxious feet fast-walk with persistence. Elle wondered how Alaina was navigating through the maze-like hallways so well. Hostium was like Remedium in that way—inconsistent paths and incalculable directions. The only Mystics who would be able to navigate through Hostium would be Compasses.

Charmers glared at the three Mystics as they walked by, but when they recognized Alaina's eyes they carried on. Alaina's breath would steady every time they looked away and she quickened her step. The waterfall couldn't be too far away.

The Mystics ran through the countless hallways. Their hearts racing, sweat mixing with blood, and their brains tenacious on the task in front of them. They were so close, forty minutes left of the Quest. Forty minutes to get the water and get out of the castle without getting caught, get to Remedium, run through the forest to the Dealer's adobe and turn in all the ingredients at once.

"Alaina," Eryk fiercely whispered. "Elle!"

Alaina didn't stop moving but looked back carefully.

"What?" both Alaina and Elle said at the same time.

"I'm losing blood, I can't," Eryk tried. "I'm losing too much blood."

His Mystic powers and adrenaline had numbed the pain, but it was slowly regaining enervation.

"Just keep walking Eryk," Alaina whispered frantically. "We're almost there."

"How can you tell?" Elle questioned. "It sounds like it's coming from everywhere."

"Shh!" Alaina hushed. "I'll explain later."

"Alaina!" Eryk said. "She sliced my throat with her fingernail, I'm losing blood!"

"And we're almost there," Alaina begged. They couldn't give up now, and they were beginning to get suspicious looks.

Elle looked back at Eryk who was dragging behind. He looked ghostly pale and dizzy.

Then he collapsed to the ground.

Elle caught one of his arms before he hit the cold obsidian floor. Alaina stopped in her tracks and looked around the room. One Charmer was near them. He looked at the three and ran away before Alaina or Elle could do anything.

"Eryk." Tears burst from Elle's eyes. They weren't going to make it, but they had to. "What do we do?"

"The water will heal him, Elle," Alaina explained. "It can heal everything. We need to keep going."

Elle swallowed her tears and her fear. "Get his other arm."

Alaina didn't argue and grabbed Eryk's other arm. Together, the two girls dragged Eryk towards the sound of the violent waterfall. Elle held onto the last shreds of power, hope, and strength she had left from the Quest.

The sound of the waterfall became increasingly ferocious. All other noises were being drowned out by the fiercely falling water that bounced off every wall and every corner. Eryk was heavy and bloody. Elle tried not to think about the sight—or smell—of his blood as she dragged his unconscious body. She tried not to think how scared she was for him. She concentrated on the slow beats of his working heart and the crashing water that would heal him, Mason, her mother, her, and finally wrap up the traumatic, action-packed Quest they embarked upon days ago.

Alaina, Elle and Eryk rounded the corner and there it was.

The waterfall.

The water was vicious, falling with speed. Droplets sprayed the Mystic's skin and Elle immediately felt relief on her wounds. The water was rapid and daunting and mesmerizing. The sight of it was magnetic. Elle wanted to jump into it, bathe in it, cleanse her hair and skin in it—be immersed in the magic water. She let go of Eryk's arm and moved towards it.

"Careful!" Alaina warned. She had to yell over the water to be heard.

Elle glanced back at her in question.

"You're not fully a Mystic. The water, it can still trick you," Alaina explained.

"What do you mean?" Elle asked.

"The waterfall, it charms people into a sort of trance to make them jump in. But instead of healing them, they die, and become Charmers," Alaina further explained.

Like a spider's web, Elle thought.

She stopped instantly and looked down the chasm. It was impossible to see the bottom—a giant cloud of circling mist covered it. It made Elle's bones rattle inside her, giving her goosebumps.

Eryk began coughing, then wheezing. Elle watched him as the wound on his neck stitched itself back together. A sheen of water coated his skin and dampened his hair.

"It works!" Elle said in awe. "The water works!"

Alaina and Elle laughed in bubbling joy.

Eryk got on his feet and looked at what was before them. The last task. The last ingredient stood before them, and there was a lot of it.

Alaina swung her backpack off her shoulders and rummaged through it quickly. She took out the three mason jars she had packed inside previously, and handed one to each of her friends.

"We need to hurry," Alaina said. "We're running out of time."

Both Elle and Eryk grabbed their jars and headed to the rapid waterfall.

Up close, the water almost shimmered and was an alluring shade of blue.

"Stop!" Eryk yelled.

Elle was standing on the very edge of the platform that surrounded the waterfall. She looked at Eryk with question.

"Elle get down!" Eryk shouted. "Get down!"

Elle looked at the waterfall, and then at him, and back at the water.

She wanted to jump.

Chapter 34

Eryk pulled her down from the platform. The jars filled up quickly, becoming heavy with the magic water. It was going to be difficult to carry them all the way back to Remedium.

Elle felt frustrated with herself, but accepted it wasn't her fault. She wanted to get as far away from the waterfall as possible. She helped Eryk and Alaina gently place the jars in the backpack and Eryk offered to carry it. Elle could tell some of his strength was rejuvenated from the water, and the cut on his neck looked much better. Accomplishment and pride coursed through her body. They figured out the last riddle for the last ingredient and now they had it. They did it. They had all three ingredients. Now it was time to get the hell out of Hostium and back in Remedium—where the Dealer awaited them.

As the Mystics jogged through the twisting hallways of the castle, the water sloshed from side to side in each mason jar.

"Are we sure this is enough water?" Eryk asked to no one in particular.

"It has to be," Elle said.

"And you're sure you know how to get out of here, Alaina?" Eryk asked.

"Yes," Alaina said. "I had help from the Compasses, thanks to Angel and Phoenix. I'll explain everything later."

The three Mystics turned corner after corner, trusting Alaina completely. Only a few Charmer's were out walking the halls. Actually, Elle realized, they had only passed maybe two or three.

Her stomach dropped. Something didn't feel right all of a sudden.

"Guys," Elle said. "Something's strange."

"What do you mean?" Eryk asked.

"Wait."

"What is it?" Alaina turned around.

Elle held a single finger in the air to hush them. She could hear something. Something in the distance. It sounded like a swarm of bees buzzing in a quickening crescendo, almost like the waterfall did. Catching on, Eryk and Alaina began to hear it too.

It was a mass of active feet, running through the castle.

"Run," Elle said.

The three Mystics picked up their speed immediately. Elle could feel the adrenaline pumping through her veins and the hours of training with Angel and Phoenix paying off. The Mystics ran side by side, their strides long and fierce and desperate.

A sharp pain tingled the side of Elle's left arm—the arm that *wasn't* hurt earlier. The pain lingered to her shoulder like static electricity traveling within her. The pain made her vomit. Before Elle knew it, Alaina cried into the air and was falling to the ground and Eryk was vomiting, too. Elle looked behind her and everything turned to slow motion.

A ravenous group of Charmers proceeded towards them. Their black eyes blurred into the darkness of the castle and the silhouettes of their bodies conjoined together to make one giant mob. Silver and blue lights flashed from their bodies, flying towards the Mystics. Elle didn't know what kind of powers she thought Charmers had, but she was not expecting this. This was not something they taught her in training.

Alaina got up and continued to run with Elle and Eryk. Eryk threw massive rounds of fire at the mob behind them. Elle copied Eryk, trying to do the same. Eryk had mastered aiming without looking, something Elle was natural at, but hadn't practiced since setting out on the Quest. She threw fire in aimless patterns and hoped she was helping.

"We're almost there," Alaina shouted.

Elle wanted to be done. Almost there, almost there. She could feel flashes of pain, shot from Charmers, hit her back and shoulders. Eryk and Alaina winced beside her as they got hit as well.

Alaina howled in pain as a Charmer hit the back of her neck.

Elle tuned around with raging anger and shot a tidal wave of fire behind her. The fire formed a massive wall that blocked off the Charmers' path to the Mystics.

Elle lifted Alaina up and Eryk looked at her with utter shock.

"Next left." Alaina coughed. The smoke was suffocating her, so she pulled her shirt over her mouth and nose.

They dashed around the left corner and found magnificent doors made of obsidian and gold that stretched to the very top of the castle.

Eryk pulled one of the grand doors and it slid open like an elevator door.

The three Mystics jumped inside the elevator and the door closed behind them.

Chapter 35

Out of breath, the Mystics didn't say a word as the elevator shot upward, jostling them from side to side. When the door slid open, revealing the sandy beach, Elle cried in triumph.

She ran out, never more relieved to see the beach—a run down, litter-filled beach now overcrowded with surfers and boogey boarders.

As they looked around for the Tree of Remedium, all Elle noticed was the amount of people who were Charmed—their heads pregnant with slimy Charmers who fed off their traumatic memories, leaving them with suicidal thoughts and bad dreams. There was even an Indwelled baby toddling around in the brown sand looking for seashells. It made Elle nauseous. It made her want to go back to Hostium and hunt down each and every Charmer. It made her angry. She wanted to take every person who was Charmed with her to Remedium. But she couldn't right now. She hoped these people were assigned to their own Mystics.

"It's over there." Eryk pointed in the distance.

The Tree was a couple of blocks away. Elle guessed that with so many people Indwelled, the Tree made an easy appearance.

The three began to run.

"Why can't we take some of them with us?" Elle shouted as they ran.

Eryk finally said, "We will one day, Elle. We'll come back."

Elle didn't say anything. It was frustrating, but they needed to stay focused. They were almost there. Sand built up in her shoes as she ran, and people turned heads as the three ran by. She couldn't imagine what they looked like right now. Bloody, dirty, tired, crazed. It was bizarre to her that people were going on with their daily lives—having picnics at the beach, going surfing, taking pictures together—while she and her friends just nearly escaped death and hunted down ingredients for a magical potion. It made Elle wonder what she would be doing at this precise moment if she had never followed Eryk to the Tree of Remedium.

Eryk, Elle and Alaina made it to the Tree in no time. Eryk quickly placed his hand in the triangle and it copied his print instantly. Elle was still amazed at the wondrous colors that ran throughout the tree as the pattern of Eryk's hand wrapped around the branches and trunk.

The elevator popped open and grew in size as the three stepped inside. Elle's heart pumped viciously as the yellow-lit room took them to the security of Remedium.

Alaina, out of breath, began telling how she ended up in Hostium.

"Guys, we have eight minutes to get to the Dealer's adobe," Alaina began. "While you were still on the Quest, I was waiting for Mason to heal. I sat there for hours on end waiting for news and couldn't take it anymore."

"Wait, what exactly *is* wrong with Mason?" Eryk interrupted.

"He's going to be okay. I'll get there in a minute," Alaina proceeded. "Instead of waiting around, I still wanted to help you guys any way that I could from Remedium. So, I did some research. I saw Anastasia leaving the café one night. I was in there because I was upset about Mason and couldn't sleep. So I followed her. I morphed myself to be small and changed my appearance completely, so if I *did* get caught, she wouldn't know it was me."

The elevator came to an abrupt stop and the door opened. The Mystics rushed out and headed to the forest. Elle could feel the security and quietness of Remedium. It felt so strange to be back.

"Anastasia entered the Dealer's adobe and I was cut off. There was no way for me to get in or hear anything. So I waited hours for her to come back out. When she came out, she wasn't alone. She was with Leonardo."

The sound of Leonardo's name made Elle gulp.

"They started walking through the forest and I followed," Alaina went on. "They talked about how they were going on the Quest, and I was outraged."

"Wait," Eryk interrupted again. "You're telling me that the Dealer sent them on the Quest with us?"

"But why?" Elle asked.

"I'll get there," Alaina said. "I asked Tabitha for the twin map that was linked to your map so I could warn you, but the sound wasn't working."

"Oh, so that's why it was incredibly loud when Tabitha tried to call us," Eryk put together.

"Sure," Alaina continued. "I wanted to warn you guys, but I couldn't. I think Tabitha did that on purpose, but I don't know."

Making their way to the Dealer's adobe, they ran as fast as they could. Alaina was out of breath as she spoke.

"I don't think Tabitha is the bad guy here though, I think Leonardo and Anastasia used their Myst on her, making her think it was a good idea to disconnect the maps so she couldn't check on you, and they went as replacements."

"But why? Why did they need to come on the Quest with us?" Elle asked impatiently.

Alaina held up a finger. "So, I continued spying on them, trying to find out as much information as I could. Mason always said in order to defeat the enemy you have to be an expert on them—because he's a total videogame nerd. Anyways, this is just my theory, but I put together that you guys would never have needed replacements if Mason hadn't got sick and we had to go back to Remedium."

Elle gasped.

"I knew it," Eryk said, along with several unruly words.

"Just my theory," Alaina said. "So, I continued to spy on them, but someone snitched on me that I was using my Myst when I shouldn't be. My trainer banned me from using my Myst for a week. Whatever. I talked to Phoenix who talked to Tula's instructors who got me my own map of Remedium. It made it even easier to follow the twins. One night, they thought the café was empty, but I was just on the other side of the door. Idiots. I didn't hear much, to be honest, but what I *did* hear is going to freak you guys out."

"What is it?" Elle and Eryk asked in unison.

"They called the Dealer 'Uncle Saberino,'" Alaina said.

Eryk and Elle exchanged glances.

"They're related to the Dealer?" Elle asked.

"I'm assuming so," Alaina said with excitement, like she was spilling the juiciest gossip. "That's not it though, guys, get this. The three ingredients you found, they're not only for your mom, Elle. They're for someone else, someone named Annaliese."

Eryk cursed under his breath and Elle's heart stopped.

"Wait! These ingredients aren't for my mother? He tricked us into getting them for some girl named Annaliese?" Elle cried.

"No, not necessarily," Alaina reassured. "If I thought that, I wouldn't have gotten the water. The Dealer is tricky, but he never breaks his side of the deal. The ingredients—maybe not all—are still for your mom."

This should have reassured Elle, but she did not feel relieved. She did not just go through the hardest and most dangerous ten days of her life, to find ingredients that didn't pertain to her.

"It still doesn't explain why Leonardo and Anastasia had to go on the Quest," Eryk added.

Alaina pursed her lips. "I don't know for sure, but did you guys ever split up from each other?"

"Yes," Elle and Eryk said.

"They must've had their own plans, perhaps their own ingredient to find," Alaina theorized. She looked down at her watch. "Guys, we have thirty seconds left. We're almost there."

Despite aching muscles, the Mystics picked up their speed.

Twenty seconds.

Dodged through trees and leaves and hanging vines.

Ten seconds.

It was all for this.

Five seconds.

The adobe came into view.

Four.

The outlined door was forming at the sight of them.

Three.

The trees were thinning out.

Two.

On the steps.

Elle twisted the knob.

One.

They ducked inside.

Zero.

Chapter 36

The Dealer sat at his grand desk and rose at the sight of the three Mystics entering his quarters. Leonardo and Anastasia stood on either side of him, and their backs straightened as the door closed behind them. Leonardo held a black, shiny pocket watch. Anastasia's bruises were now light purple. Between them was an empty small pool built into the ground. On the desk sat the bags of leaves and the decrepit heart in a tray.

"Ellisia," The Dealer grinned. "So happy to see you."

Elle shuddered. The Dealer seemed like he'd grown in size. He wore all black and his eyes were darker than the obsidian in Hostium.

"Hello," Elle said, her voice stronger than she felt.

"You have the water, my dear?" the Dealer asked.

Elle nodded. Eryk swung the backpack carefully off of his shoulders and unzipped it. Elle aided him in taking out each and every jar. She handed one to Alaina.

"Wonderful." The Dealer grinned a peculiar grin. "Quite exquisite. You were able to figure out every riddle I created for you, correct?"

"Yes," Elle answered.

"And you were able to collect the correct set of leaves, your father's heart, and the water that runs in the center of Hostium, is that correct?" the Dealer questioned.

"Yes."

"Clever little Mystic." The Dealer eyed her carefully. He paused.

He opened the top drawer in his desk and took out a delicately folded piece of paper.

"Perhaps you will be able to figure out one more."

Chapter 37

Everyone's heart dropped. Elle felt her body go numb, although her hands began to shake. Eryk cursed behind her and Alaina's mouth fell open. Leonardo did not look at his uncle, he looked at the ground. Anastasia pursed her lips.

"You have twenty minutes to give me the last ingredient I need," the Dealer spoke.

"You can't do that," Eryk protested.

"And why not?" the Dealer asked.

"It was not part of the deal! The deal was that Elle gets what you need for the potion and you use them to make her mother human again," Eryk argued.

"Awe, correct," the Dealer agreed. "And this is an ingredient I need. I never said how many riddles or ingredients there would be total. Eighteen minutes."

"Let's go Eryk," Elle said. "There's no point arguing, let's go find it."

Eryk looked at Elle and back at the Dealer. He opened his mouth to say something and then closed it tightly. Alaina pulled on his sleeve and the three left the adobe.

As soon as they were outside the adobe, Eryk began shouting.

"He can't do this Elle! He can't do this to you!"

"Well he did," Elle said. "I'm not killing my mother. I'm not losing after all of this."

"Just read the riddle," Alaina said.

Elle took a deep breath and unfolded the delicate paper.

"I am the thing that comes first. I am also the last. I am like the second. I'm not the third. But the fourth. I'm the second's first," Elle read.

"What?" Eryk sounded defeated.

"We need Mason," Alaina said.

"Do we have time to get him?" Elle asked.

Alaina looked at her watch. "Sixteen minutes."

"Go," Eryk said. "Give him as much water as he needs."

Alaina nodded and began to sprint.

As soon as she was out of view, Eryk said, "Elle, you do know that if you turn your mother back to human and choose to go with her, you won't be a Mystic right?"

"What are you suggesting?" Elle knew Eryk couldn't mean that they should resign from the Quest and not save her mother.

"Nothing. We're going to turn her human again. We can talk about that later."

"One step at a time Rylander," Elle said.

She read the riddle again aloud.

"Wait." Eryk thought deeply. He always squinted his eyes just a tiny bit and looked upwards when he was thinking. "Read it again."

"I am the thing that comes first. I am also the last. I am like the second. I'm not the third. But the fourth. I'm the second's first."

"I think," Eryk continued, "that the 'I'm not the third, but the fourth' is just talking about the order of the ingredients. This is the fourth ingredient."

"Okay. What do you think that means?"

"Well, does that pertain to the rest of the riddle as well?"

"I'm the thing that comes first. I am like the second," Elle tried.

"'I am like the second,'" Eryk repeated. "The second ingredient was the heart."

"You think this ingredient is also a heart?" The thought sent chills down Elle's spine.

"Could be."

The sound of rustling leaves interrupted Elle and Eryk's thought process as Mason appeared through teleportation.

Mason. He looked skinnier and paler, but his vivaciousness was back in his face. He looked frantic and ready.

Eryk and Mason hugged at the sight of each other. And Mason awkwardly hugged Elle, too.

"What's the riddle?" Mason jumped right in.

"I am the thing that comes first. I am also the last. I am like the second. I'm not the third. But the fourth. I'm the second's first," Elle said.

Mason grabbed the paper from Elle's hands.

"We think it's another heart," Eryk said. "'I am like the second,' the second ingredient was the heart."

"I think you're right," Mason said. "It's talking about the order of the ingredients. This is the fourth ingredient, right?"

"Right," Elle and Eryk said in unison.

Everyone thought in silence. Elle recited the riddle over and over.

More leaves rustled. Alaina appeared, out of breath and ghastly pale. Mason explained to her what they came up with.

"So, who's heart?" Alaina questioned in a frenzy.

I am the thing that comes first, Elle muttered to herself. *I'm the second's first.*

Elle froze.

She snatched the paper out of Mason's hand.

She read it one more time.

"Mine."

Chapter 38

Eryk, Alaina and Mason looked at Elle the way you look at a child who just found out they had cancer. They looked at her the way you look at your relative's gravestone.

Eryk's expression transformed.

"No," he said. "Not happening."

He refused. This was not going to happen to the girl he took months Seeking. Preparing, learning, sneaking, breaking rules, to get her to Remedium. The girl who had fire and passion and strength and determination. It wasn't ending here.

"Yes," Elle simply said. "My mother lived just as traumatic of a life as the rest of us. She's been through hell and back like I have. She deserves to have a better life. Even if it's at the cost of my own."

"You also deserve a better life, Elle. You do!" Eryk held her shoulders. "You can still become a Mystic; you don't have to do this. You can save all those people on the beach."

"Eryk," Alaina said in a small voice.

"We all deserve a better life, Eryk." Elle said. "We all do. I saved Catherine and Levi. At least I got to save them. Wouldn't you do it for Ashlee? For your mother?"

Eryk went quiet.

"There has to be another way," Eryk said. "A loophole."

Elle shook her head.

"If this is what it comes to, I'm choosing my mother. This was all for her, anyway. She can be with Emmie." Elle began to cry. A silent cry. "Emmie can finally have a mother again." She just wouldn't be able to be with them.

The door to the adobe opened. It was Anastasia.

"Time's up," she said.

Elle looked at her friends—the three people to whom she had become closest. The three people that were completely and utterly selfless for her sake. The people that cheered her on, made her laugh and showed her what life was really like. The people that taught her how amazing life could be. How wonderful the world could be if you take care of yourself and the people around you. At the start of this— when Eryk knocked on her window and fell into her room— she would've never thought this is what it would come to. She never thought about how much life could transform after a week. But here she was, saying goodbye and meeting her end. She thought it wasn't a bad way to end. To give her mother life, to give her sister and mother a new life. It wasn't a bad way to end. It reminded her of a quote she read long ago by a poet called Margaret Atwood. It said, "In the end, we'll all become stories." And it never felt so true and present. Her story would live on in Remedium. And she was happy with her story.

She hugged her three friends in a group, their love radiating off each other.

Eryk pulled her away and hugged her tightly and kissed the top of her head.

"I would," Eryk said, answering her question from before. He would do it for Ashlee. "I would do it for you."

Chapter 39

Elle walked inside the adobe holding the three jars of water, one only half full from Mason.

Anastasia closed the door, leaving Eryk, Mason and Alaina outside.

Leonardo's eyes were—as usual—unreadable, their expression a mix of emotion. Anxious. Tight. Hesitant. Thoughtful. The Dealer stood beside him with a focused and thoughtful smirk. The slight curve of his lip told Elle he knew he got what he wanted.

"I've reached my decision," Elle said. "I will give you my heart, if—"

"Not if," the Dealer cut her off.

"*If*," Elle persisted, "you tell me why. You tell me everything. Not a single detail left out."

The Dealer smiled. "Making a deal with the Dealer, Ellisia? I'm the one who makes the deals around here."

"Tell her," Leonardo spoke for the first time. His voice was clear and strong like it always was.

The Dealer looked at his nephew. "Do you want your mother back or not?"

Mother?

Elle froze, her mouth gaping open.

"Mother?" she questioned.

"Yes," Leonardo answered before his uncle could. "Uncle Saber, tell her."

"Why do you care?" Anastasia questioned him in disgust. "She's here, we have every ingredient now."

"Hush," the Dealer held his hand up to Anastasia before Leonardo could counter her. "Ellisia can know. The secret will remain a secret, as long as Ellisia is dead."

The words set a shudder down Elle's spine.

"Ellisia, you know how important a loved one is, don't you?" the Dealer asked. He was walking around her, as if inspecting her.

"Yes," Elle said. She thought of Emmie. Her mother. Eryk, Mason and Alaina.

"I was in love once," the Dealer said thoughtfully. "With a girl named Annaliese Lyudmila." He paused. "My name is Saberino Castello; my brother was Gabriel Castello. We weren't the best adolescents so to say. Always getting into trouble, vandalizing the school and other buildings. Dealing drugs here and there. Like you Ellisia, we were foster kids. We didn't know if we had the same mom or the same dad, we just knew we were related somehow. Kids at school would tell us our mother was a whore. It affected me more than it did Gabriel. He got an academic scholarship to go to a local college and I was stuck in the old, rundown town where the crime rate was higher than the population. I met Annaliese when I was almost 19. She was already 19 and had just moved here. That girl was life. She was giggly and vivacious, and I had never met anyone like her in this town."

Elle never could have imagined the Dealer would sound this way before. She'd forgotten he was human, that he had a past and feelings and people who influenced him. Villains are never villains for no reason, Elle realized.

"We would go dancing and she showed me museums and concerts and sometimes we would drink too much and it was fun. She played music and created art, she painted and I didn't know if she had a flaw. We all have flaws," the Dealer continued. "My brother came home from school for summer break. He met Annie and started hanging out with us."

Annie.

Elle had heard the name before. A distant memory, before the Quest. When she went to visit her mother one last time in this very adobe.

I need Annie. The Dealer had said. At the time, Elle thought he was speaking of his niece, Anastasia, for that was the nickname Leonardo used.

"I thought my brother was proud of me for once. I wasn't doing hard drugs, I had a job at the local grocery store. I was with the most amazing girl. I thought he was proud. But before I knew it, they were hanging out without me. I talked to Annaliese and she only laughed. It wasn't a hurtful laugh though, she was confused. She didn't know why I was so upset that her and my brother were hanging out. She didn't know that I was in love with her. I thought we were together, but she thought otherwise. She said that she acts the way she does with me, with everyone. But I was in love with her."

As the Dealer talked, Leonardo and Anastasia began dumping the magic water into the pool in the floor. Leonardo refused to look at Elle. They began preparing the leaves and the mutilated heart to be dumped into the water.

"A couple years passed and we still hung out while my brother was in school. Sometimes I thought she really loved me. She would say things and do things that told me so. But other times, it was nothing. Then she told me she was pregnant. With Gabriel's baby. I didn't realize the importance of a child having a parent, because I never had one. My anger came back to me—something I had been in therapy and ISS and OSS and detention for millions of times. This time, I wasn't going to let my perfect brother win. I created a poison, a powerful poison. I was sure it would work. The thing about this poison though, is that it took several months to develop and was intended for a slow death. So, I put it in his drink and waited. I finally felt at ease. My brother and I would be equals at last. Although, something went terribly wrong. Gabriel called me and told me Annie was sick. He thought she was going into early labor, but I knew what was happening. Every symptom he listed, were the ones he was supposed to be experiencing, not Annie. She couldn't move, she had no energy. A doctor came to the house and told us her nervous system was shutting down. I began to panic. If they discovered it was poison, they could have traced it to me. They put her on complex medicines but nothing worked. I watched her die slowly. It wasn't supposed to be her. It was supposed to be Gabriel. A midwife arrived the next day to deliver the baby before she died or was too weak to carry on. The midwife announced she hadn't carried a single baby, but two. Twins. A boy and girl. The babies were born prematurely, but were healthy, and rushed to the hospital. The twins I speak of are the twins that stand before you. Anastasia Levka Marya Castello—her name taking after her mother's Russian heritage. And Leonardo Gabriel Saberino Castello—taking after his father's Italian heritage. Annaliese died within days after giving birth. She never got to hold her twins. When Annaliese died, I gave up. There was no more of me. There was nowhere for me to go. The poison was untraceable. Nobody knew it was my fault she died. Then I came home from work to find Gabriel hanging from the ceiling. Suicide. I remember envying him. I tried overdosing many times. I had no idea where the twins were. It was when my Seeker found me and told me my niece and nephew were in Remedium. I went straight away. They told me I had to go through the Transformation before I could see them, so I did. I thought I would see Annaliese in them. Funny enough, it's Leonardo who resembles her the most, not Anastasia. The Transformation was painful. The most physical and mental pain I ever experienced. When I came out to kill my Charmer only some of it was there. In ashes and bones. It was an anomaly. They made me go through it again, and I agreed so I could be reunited with my love's children. The Transformation was again excruciatingly painful. And it only led to the same result. My Charmer was too strong for the Transformation. Only forty-seven percent of it died."

Elle drank in the words. Leonardo's head was down; she could almost see tears glistening down his cheek.

"You're still a Charmer?" Elle asked.

Anastasia and Leonardo were now strategically placing the leaves in. The water began to boil.

"Part. Nearly half Mystic, half Charmer. That is why I am bound to this adobe. I am not able to leave. Although, being half Charmer I still have ties to Hostium. Ties to dark magic, Mystics have no idea about. I began studying alchemy, potions—anything I could, to create an antidote to the poison Annaliese accidentally consumed. I thought I almost had it. It was working on dead animals and plants. I thought I was ready. All I needed was the heart of the—"

The door of the adobe smashed open with a blast of fire as her father's heart fell into the pool of magic water and leaves.

"Elle's not the newest member!" Eryk shouted.

Elle turned in shock, what was he talking about?

The Dealer's eyes widened and Leonardo looked up from the ground. Anastasia stood with the same expression as the Dealer.

"What do you mean she's not the newest member of Remedium?" Leonardo questioned.

"She's not the last person to have gone through the Transformation! He is!" Alaina said, who stepped aside to reveal Levi.

Levi.

The surfer from the beach who helped Elle and Eryk get inside Hostium. The boy who Elle brought to Remedium. Her first Seek.

"What is going on?" Elle shouted.

"The last ingredient is the heart of the latest member of Remedium. 'I am also the last,'" Alaina explained.

Levi stood there in horror.

"No," Elle said. "No, it's going to be me. Not Levi."

Eryk, Alaina and Mason weren't surprised. They didn't want to go through with it either. They didn't want to hurt Levi any more than Elle did.

"It has to be the newest member. The last person to become a Mystic," Anastasia said fiercely.

"No, you're not taking Levi!" Elle screamed at Anastasia. Elle shielded Levi with her body. "It's going to be me."

The next moments happened in a blink of an eye. A drop of rain. A slam of a door. A shot of a gun.

Leonardo broke Levi's neck.
And threw him into the boiling pool.

Chapter 40

Eryk held Elle back as she screamed into the air. Into the trees. Into Remedium. Into the world. Her legs and arms lashed out. She cursed at Leonardo as loudly as she could. Leonardo ran out of the adobe without looking at her. His face soaked with tears. And she blacked out.

Two days later, Elle woke up. She laid on a stiff white bed. The ceiling was made of wood with leaves peeking through. She was in Remedium.

"Elle," Eryk said. He stood up from the corner as soon as he saw Elle's warm brown eyes.

She focused on Eryk. She almost didn't recognize him. He was clean. Not a trace of blood or dirt or sweat. He smelled like the earth after it rained—like everyone in Remedium. The wound on his neck was invisible. His hair was more brushed than it had been.

Then everything came back to her. Her mother as a decrepit creature of skin and bone. The list of riddles. The jungle's heat. The vicious river. Screaming Eryk's name when she thought she lost him. Mason uncontrollably throwing up. Emmie not recognizing her. Finding her father's grave.

Losing her hearing and sight. Wanting to jump into the waterfall. Levi.

Leonardo.

How could he?

She thought that maybe there was the slightest bit of trust between the two of them. She thought he was better than what Eryk posed him to be. She defended him.

Then a wave of questions took over. Why were Leonardo and Anastasia on the Quest still? Were all the ingredients for Annaliese? What about her mother? Where was her mother? Why was she not dead? Why was she still in Remedium?

Eryk must have read her expression because he dove into an explanation.

"Your mom is okay. She's still here and still a Charmer. When Leonardo left, he actually went to get Tabitha. They made everyone leave the adobe and brought you to the nurses. You were in shock, dehydrated and sleep deprived—like the rest of us. Leonardo and Anastasia came on the Quest to find their mother's body for the potion. Which they did. And that's why they ended up leaving. Only part of the potion was intended for Annaliese, which makes me so aggravated because the Dealer didn't know if it would work on your mom, too. He only assumed it would. Tabitha let the Dealer carry out his procedure on Annaliese. It worked, for three hours. Apparently, Annaliese was really confused, and then really paranoid. Then she went insane and passed out. She hasn't woken up and never will. The rest of the potion is for your mother, and Tabitha has it in her care."

"He's dead," Elle said, not looking at Eryk.

"Who?"

"Levi. Levi, Eryk! What do you mean who? Levi is dead! My first Seek, and he's dead because of me."

Eryk's shoulders dropped and his expression melted.

"He's not dead because of you, Elle."

"He's dead because of Leonardo! He's dead because I brought him here to be safe and then Leonardo broke his neck and threw him into boiling water." Elle couldn't stop rehearing the sound of Levi's neck breaking. "That's not fair for him. He didn't do anything—he barely even said words! All he did was help us get into Hostium."

"Then you could say it was Alaina's fault for putting him through the Transformation. You could say it was the Charmer's fault for Charming him in the first place. You could blame his parents for giving birth to him to begin with. It's not about fault here, Elle. Fault doesn't exist because of one person."

Elle exhaled. What was there to say? She wasn't going to say he was right, because he was.

"But do you want to hear the good news out of all of this?" Eryk asked.

Elle didn't say anything.

"Catherine, the girl you brought to Remedium along with Levi, she went through the Transformation this morning. It took a lot to convince her. But you were the one who convinced her to get in the elevator in the first place. And now she's a Mystic, because of you."

The words made Elle sit up. Again, she was at a loss for words.

"That makes me really happy," Elle said through tears. "I don't know what to say."

"I'm sorry about Levi, Elle, I really am," Eryk said.

"I am, too," Elle said. "Maybe he's in an even better place than Remedium right now."

"I think he is." Eryk smiled. "Now, do you want to go save your mom?" Eryk took out a hand and offered it to Elle.

She shyly smiled and grabbed his hand.

Chapter 41

They had moved Elle's mother into a room by Tabitha's office near the elevator to the outside world.

Tabitha unlocked the door and Elle entered the room. Her mother looked up at her. She was worse than what Elle remembered. A heap of skin and bone. A sickly face with protruded bones. Dead skin and fair hair and broken fingers. Jagged teeth. It was a nauseating sight.

"I have something for you," Elle said.

The Charmer was so weak she couldn't talk or lift her hands.

Eryk held the single mason jar of the potion.

Elle took the jar from Eryk and opened the lid. She crouched down to her mother and prayed with all her heart that this would work. She set the jar on her mother's cracked lips and tilted it for her.

The water rushed down the Charmer's throat and traveled throughout her body. Her skin slowly became tighter and its warm shade of brown. Her hair slowly became thicker and its lovely shade of black. Elle could hear her mother's bones pop back in place and reconnect. Her mother took the jar from Elle's hands and drank rapidly. Elle could only imagine how good it must have felt.

Elle's mother took her last few sips and dropped the jar to the ground. She looked into her baby's eyes and embraced her.

"Mommy."

After spending several jubilant hours talking to her mother about Remedium, the Quest and her new friends, Eryk pulled Elle out of the room.

"Go," Eryk said.

"What?"

"Be with her," Eryk said. "Be with your mother. Be with Emmie. Go live that life we all envy here. Go be happy with them."

"Eryk, I don't understand," Elle stopped him from saying more. "I'm a Mystic. There's no way, is there?"

Eryk's eyes were soft and his smile delicate. "There's a way. The Transformation can reverse the power on you. But there are two rules that go with it. Your memory of Remedium must be erased by a Mystic and you will never be able to go back through the Transformation again."

"But what about you, and Mason and Alaina, I can't leave you—"

Eryk hushed her with a finger to her lips. "Go, Elle. You will never get this opportunity again. Be with your mother, be with Emmie."

Elle didn't know when she started crying, but tears smeared her face. She didn't need to say anything. She embraced him wholeheartedly—her head on his chest, her arms around his neck. She would never admire someone more in her life.

Chapter 42

Elle's last few hours in Remedium were the most emotional hours she'd ever experienced. The sun was large and golden that day and the sky was a lovely shade of deep blue. The dark green trees sang beautifully in unison with the sky and the sun. Elle had packed her things from her and Alaina's treehouse that morning and ate breakfast with her friends one last time.

Going back through the Transformation was nerve-wracking, but much less painful. Her Myst escaped her body and she didn't feel as light, but somehow, she felt better.

Elle and her mother sat together in a room as they waited for Elle's friends to come and say goodbye and a Mystic to come and take away their memories of Remedium. She was sad that she would never get to experience the full beauty of Remedium—the full beauty of Seeking Season and training with Angel and Phoenix. But every time Elle looked at her mother she wanted to cry and hug her as long as she could. She never, ever, believed she would have her mommy back. She wasn't going back to live with the Everson's. She was going back to live with her mom and her sister and have the life she always wished she had.

When Tabitha knocked on the door and entered, Elle's mother insisted she give them some privacy—even though Elle wanted her to stay.

Tabitha looked at Elle with eyes of amazement, pride and hope. She looked at her like a mother looked at a child graduating with a doctorate degree. She looked at her like Elle was strong and incredible. A way Elle never experienced. She looked at her like she was an accomplishment, a goal, a dream, a wish she always hoped to achieve.

"Are you excited my dear?" Tabitha asked.

Elle smiled. "I'm very happy, Tabitha. Thank you for everything you've done for me."

Tabitha smiled. "You are stronger than you believe, Ellisia. You are stronger than some of the Mystics here. I want you to remember that. Even though you will lose your memory of Remedium, the friends you've made here, and why you were here in the first place, you will continue to be strong. You will continue to persevere through everything you will go through as a human. You may no longer be physically a Mystic, but mentally you always will be one. And don't you forget that."

Tabitha embraced Elle and wiped a tear off her cheek.

"Best wishes to you, my darling," Tabitha said.

Chapter 43

Elle was about to sit down when the door opened again. It was Mason.

His skin was warm, instead of the deadly pale it had been. His eyes were vibrant and honey brown beneath his clunky glasses. His bushy eyebrows were raised and the tips of his ears were pink.

"Elle." Mason's voice was high and nearly cracked.

He gave her a hug and Elle embraced him. He smelled of pine and sweat.

"I'm happy you're here," she said, retreating from his arms.

He gave a slim smile. "I never thought it'd be possible."

"What do you mean?"

"I mean I can't believe you're human again. I never imagined that theory."

It was so like Mason to stay awake at night thinking of millions of theories and possibilities. His intellectual mind was amazing, and Elle loved it. Because if it hadn't been for his insights, she would have never gotten through the Quest. But not only that, his intelligence was raw. It was factual and gave realism to every conversation he had and every situation he was in. She admired his honesty even when he didn't recognize he was being honest.

"Well, here I am," Elle said with a smile. She wanted to keep these last encounters positively sweet. Because if she let herself cry...

"No, I mean it's brilliant, you'll go down in history forever. Truly remarkable."

Elle smiled again and just stared at him. Mason always gave off a genuine likability that made Elle want to be with him. Every conversation she had with him pre-Quest and during the Quest made her ask more questions. She would miss these conversations, she realized.

"Mason, I wanted to thank you for everything you did for me on the Quest. Figuring out the riddle, telling us the second ingredient even on your death bed..."

Mason laughed. "I was hoping that was not too vague of a description. If I'm honest, I can't truly remember everything I did on the Quest."

"You did tremendously helpful things," Elle replied. "I wouldn't have made it on time without your brain."

"Despite how sad this departing is, I couldn't be happier for you. You deserve this, you know? Being with a loving family after everything you've gone through."

Elle's expression contorted. Her stomach twirled. This was the one aspect she felt incredibly guilty about—the one topic she was trying to avoid.

"What?" Mason said, seeing her dropping eyes. "What's the matter?"

"It's just," Elle tried. "It's just, I don't feel I deserve this—"

"What? Of course you do!"

"I mean," Elle tried again. "I mean, sure. This journey has been hell, but hasn't it been for every Mystic? You've watched your mom die in front of you, insomnia struggles, Alaina's BPD, Eryk's abuse, bulimia, rape, cancer, kidnapping—all these things have happened to the people here. Why don't they get to live the fantasy I'm being given?"

Mason looked straight into her eyes. "You haven't truly witnessed the miracle of Remedium, Elle. This place is near heaven for us. This place is our home." Although his eyes were firm, his voice was so kind and smooth like honey. "Remedium is magic and love and acceptance. It's a remedy to all of us. We feel safe here. Yes, we don't get to visit our families we left behind, but family isn't always blood. I'm closer with Eryk and Alaina than I ever was to my mother or grandmother. Eryk and Alaina, they are my family. And Remedium is where I'm meant to be. This place, Remedium, is not where you were meant to be, because if it was, we wouldn't even be in this room having this conversation. Your name would be inscribed into a leaf and your mother as your Charmer would be decapitated."

The words sunk into the air like a pebble thrown into a pond.

Elle nodded her head with absolute assurance. Mason had never spoke truer words. And this time it wasn't just intelligent words from learning, it was wise words from living.

Elle hugged him one last time and whispered "thank you" into his ear.

When they broke apart, she kept it light again.

"I'll miss your intellectualism, all your questions, and your honesty," Elle said. "Tell me how it goes with Alaina."

Mason jerked up at that. "What do you mean, how it goes with Alaina?"

Elle grinned. "Oh, you know—how you're going to ask her out and confess your love to her."

Mason's face went bright pink. "I will let you know, Elle, I will let you know."

And with that, he smiled, gave an awkward wave and left the room.

Chapter 44

Alaina was already crying when she entered the room. Normally Alaina was fierce and confident, like a lion.

Elle saw depth in Alaina from the very beginning. Alaina wasn't just this bold attractive girl, she was compassionate and helpful and empathetic. Alaina was the first person to truly slow things down and help her.

Alaina embraced Elle, her tears soaking Elle's hair.

"Elle, I have so many things that I could say."

Elle's heart quenched. She wasn't one for drama and weeping, but hearing Alaina sob made her want to squeeze her best friend and listen to all her final sappy words.

"I'm happy for you, Elle, I am. I'm happy you get to have a great mom and sweet sister and don't have to have any sort of unnatural disorder. I'm really happy."

Alaina sounded like she was going to say more, but her tears cut her off. Elle rubbed her back. She was never good at coddling, but with Alaina it was easy because she didn't want to be coddled necessarily, she just wanted to be heard, probably because she never was before—except with Mason. Mason would listen to her all day.

"I never got to have a life. I never got to live. I never got to have friends and sleepovers, or play sports and all those things. And now you do."

Elle paused.

"Alaina, do you not think you're living here?"

Alaina looked up. Through her glassy eyes she said, "Well yes? Of course? I love Remedium, but—"

"But nothing. You may not have gotten the opportunity to have this 'typical dream life' you imagine, but you're saving people every day. Every single day. You're bringing people to this beautiful, safe place. I've never felt safer or more secure here."

Alaina looked through Elle's eyes—searching for a response, trying to comprehend what she was saying.

"I'm amazingly lucky to be a Mystic, and I would never change it. Not even to have a regular life. I love Remedium and Mason and Eryk and everyone here. If I were to be human again, I would have no place to go. My parents didn't accept me. I spent my life in hospitals and therapy offices. You have a life—with a sister that wants you, and a mom that wants another chance, just like you. And I'm happy for you. I'm so happy that you have that. I'm just going to miss you forever and ever. But I do want you to remember one thing."

Elle's breath caught. "What is it?"

"I want you to know that just because you won't be a Mystic anymore, doesn't mean you have to stop saving people. Humans can change and influence other humans, as much as Mystics can. So don't stop helping people like Catherine and Levi, because you are still very capable of it."

"I'll never stop," Elle said, soaking in Alaina's advice.

They hugged one last time and Alaina left the room.

Chapter 45

When he stepped into the office, Elle's stomach sank. Her lips froze. Her mind silenced. The air was still and warm and not a sound was to be heard.

Elle looked at him. His hair was tousled like usual, his muscles were tense and unwavering. Although he was frozen, his heart hammered—nearly audible amongst the quiet treehouse. His stance was solid, as if thinking a deep thought. He always seemed so tall to her, but right at this moment she felt like they were the same height. His jaw was clenched, teeth pulled tightly together, as if he didn't want the words behind them to come out. Because this was the last time he would see her.

Eryk looked at her. Just looked. He soaked in her presence and grasped every detail. Her long dark hair that slightly waved at the end. The callus on her middle right finger from her continuous writing. The way her eyelids slightly folded, and the sparkling brown eyes that lived beneath. Her collarbones that delicately protruded from her shirt. And the way she held herself. Determined and thoughtful. He breathed her in. The scent of pine and lavender, maybe vanilla. She smelled of passion and longing and freedom. Her lips gaped open as she looked at him. Her soft nude lips with that Cupid's bow that was a tad big for her mouth.

"Elle."

"I'm sorry, Eryk," she said. Her tone was like candle wax, something trying to be molded but only melting away.

He held up a single finger to hush her from an apology. "You don't need to apologize."

She moved to him. Every nerve in her body pushed her towards him.

Then he held her.

His arms caressed her spine and her long hair. Her head rested on his chest. She could hear his heart beating loudly like a swarm of wasps. Her teeth clenched down on her bottom lip to keep herself from crying. She told herself that she would not cry.

"Listen to me Elle," Eryk said, tugging her back from his grasp. His eyes were serious and wide, staring down at her. His hands were on her shoulders. "Never say sorry. Do not apologize to anyone ever again. Because none of this has been your fault. You have always deserved better. Far better than whatever your beautiful mind can muster. You deserve to live, Ellisia. You deserve to simply live your life. Do you understand me?"

Her welling eyes closed tightly and tears dripped down her face.

"I want you to live with a mother—a mother I never got a chance to have. I want you to live with your sister—a sister I never got a chance to keep. You have the chance and you are choosing correctly. And I will always love you."

Elle embraced him again, her face on his chest. Tears like smeared paint. Water colors.

"Eryk I—"

"Even if we no longer live in the same world, I will never stop Seeking you, Ellisia. There will never be a day that goes by where I'm not thinking of how amazing you are doing."

His eyes looked at hers. It felt like physical contact.

"Eryk. I want you to know, that I am forever thankful for meeting you. I am forever thankful that you were a part of my life. If you had never broken the rules and took me from the Everson's, I would be dead. I was withering away, my mind was already dead, and you were the only person to believe that I would survive. You never looked at me as a weak doll. You looked at me like I was a crafted sculpture. Strong and bold and capable. You believed I could stay alive. You believed I could bring back my mother, and I will never stop loving who you are. The thought of you. Even when I don't have it. And I want you to know that when I am human and my memories are gone, I want you to know that you will still be a part of me. An art to me. And that I will never stop loving you."

His lips found hers before she could say anything else.

They were passionate and lovely and strong. Caring and thoughtful. Purposeful and wonderful. And there was no reassurance needed. No insecurities wavering. No desperation or questioning. It was only two people who knew.

He looked at her one last time.

"Let me tell you one more thing," he said. "Find joy. Ellisia. Don't just look for it, be it. You are a wonderful, beautiful thing. Not only happiness, but pure and raw joy. Create, love, think, explore, dance, jump, talk, travel, paint, sing, write, draw, connect, help—do things you love, to find joy in this new life of yours."

She smiled. "You too, Eryk James. You too."

Chapter 46

The next person to enter the room, was not someone Elle ever expected to see again.

Anastasia.

The bruises on her eyes seemed to have faded almost completely. Her eyes were large and clear, and resembled Leonardo's—but Elle did not want to think of Leonardo.

"You're here to take away my memories, aren't you?"

The corner of Anastasia's lips raised slightly.

"No," she answered. "No Ellisia. I'm here to say thank you."

Elle was taken aback.

"Thank you for understanding and trusting me on the train, even when you shouldn't have. I helped the Dealer send you to your death and you still wanted to help me," Anastasia said.

"But I didn't know I was supposed to die at that point," Elle said.

"And I did," Anastasia snapped. "So I also wanted to say I'm sorry, even though no apology would ever make what I did better. I wanted you to die, in hopes that some potion would bring back my mother—a mother I never even met."

"It's okay."

"It's not okay! I was so caught up in Uncle Saber's plans that I threw everything else away. I was so caught up in having a mother that I didn't recognize my own uncle using me as a tool. Leonardo, my own brother, is never going to speak to me again for as long as I live because of it. Leonardo is the only constant thing in my life, and now he's gone because I wanted to kill the girl he loved."

"What?"

"Love's a silly thing." Anastasia shook her head. "So in this new life, find the right kind of love, Ellisia."

And she walked out the door without another word.

Chapter 47

Elle knew who was going to enter the room next. The last person. The person who was going to take away her memories—or *replace* her memories. And she *knew* who it was going to be.

When he walked in, Elle read sadness, regret, sleeplessness, and desperation in his eyes. His blonde hair was not brushed and his shirt was wrinkled. He came in shaking his head in disgust with himself.

"Are you here to give me an apology?" Elle asked.

Leonardo shook his head.

"No," he said. "No Ellisia, I'm not. I came here to replace your memories. And give you a confession."

Elle slightly rolled her eyes. "Let's hear it."

"I never wanted you to go on that Quest. You must remember that I am your assigned Seeker."

"And why was that, do you think?" Elle interrupted. "So you could find me and bring me to your uncle?"

"My uncle's dead," Leonardo refuted.

The words stung Elle.

"Found him hung to the ceiling last night. Funeral is today, but I guess you won't be able to make it," the sourness in his words were hurtful. He took a breath, reclining his anger.

"I'm sorry," Elle said.

"You're not, but it's okay," Leonardo said. "He was abusive to me and Anastasia. He had Annie wrapped around his finger." Elle remembered the Dealer calling Annaliese Annie. "Tricked us into believing he could really get our mother back. Then I would be in your position now, wouldn't I? I was your Seeker, Ellisia—that is true. Anyways, I never wanted the Quest to happen. I told Uncle Saber a million times that Annie and I and others could go for him. It just so happened that Eryk brought you here before you were supposed to come and you were in a similar predicament. You see, if Eryk hadn't Seeked you, maybe I would be with my mom again."

"The potion didn't work on your mom, Leonardo. Then what? We both don't get what we want?"

Leonardo shook his head again. "You have the wrong idea, Ellisia. I didn't want you to go on that Quest because I knew you had to die by the end of it and I love you!"

"You don't know me!"

"You don't always have to know a person one hundred percent, to know you are in love with them." He didn't say it with anger. He said it quietly. "I doubted my uncle from the beginning. I never believed my mother would come back. She died because of him. Because he was stupid and selfish and infatuated. A psychopath. Why would I trust the man who killed my mother? Anastasia was the one who trusted him and believed every word he said. Because all she wanted was a mother! She never had a mother. She had a foster care father who molested her. And probably an uncle, too."

Elle held her breath as he continued to speak.

"Ellisia, I didn't come here to apologize or yell at you. I came here to tell you that I'm happy for you. I am so happy that the girl I was given to Seek is healthy and thriving and going to live a good life now. I wanted to tell you that it was always for you. I may have been wrapped up in Anastasia's plans, but I couldn't have her thinking that I was weak. I wanted to be strong for her. Maybe give her a mother, even though I didn't think it was going to work. She finally had hope again. I didn't want to tear that from her. The night before you left for the Quest, was genuine. Nobody told me I had to gain your trust. Nobody. I just wanted to."

Now Elle was the one shaking her head.

"Listen to me Ellisia. I don't care what you think of me at this point. I don't. I am only happy for you, and I don't regret what I needed to do to Levi. I feel terrible, yes. But at the same time, I am overjoyed you are in this position. Do you understand what I'm trying to tell you?"

Elle nodded her head. She did understand. And it was reassuring to hear that her trust in Leonardo wasn't a scam. But she could never forgive him for Levi, even if it got her to where she is now.

"Before I replace your memories of Remedium, I want you to take this."

He handed her a little notebook with a firefly on the cover. Inside were notes from Eryk, Alaina and Mason.

"You'll remember these names as counselors from a camp you visited when you were fourteen. But I hope they stick with you, nonetheless."

Elle began crying.

"Thank you, Leonardo. Thank you for this."

He sighed, then took her hands and looked into her eyes. Her deep brown eyes that held so much strength and wisdom and hope. Her deep brown eyes that would be able to experience a better life.

Her memories began draining out of her like water.

Mason Montgomery.

Alaina Black.

Eryk Rylander.

Mystics and Charmers.

The Villages of Remedium.

Fire and passion and jumping and running and screaming and laughing and talking and smiling and hugging and humming and holding and wishing and loving.

Forgotten, but never truly gone.

Epilogue

Ellisia Carroway lived with her mother and younger sister, Emmaline, in an average, small house in Oregon. Ellisia rather liked growing up in Oregon because there were always things to do. She gardened with her mother in the backyard, rode her bike up and down hills with her Emmaline all day and she especially enjoyed climbing trees.

Ellisia wasn't the biggest fan of school, but enjoyed the couple of friends she had. Life was good. She was excited to attend Oregon University next fall to major in social work. It was unexplainable, but she had a passion for foster care and abused kids.

She would miss this little cottage she called home. Every birthday and homemade cake her mom would bake. Every sleepover. Every Christmas and Thanksgiving. Costumes her mother would attempt to sew for her and Emmaline every Halloween. Staying up late and watching movies with her sister. Uncontrollable giggling. Getting ready for school every morning. Doing her hair for the prom that her mother forced her to attend. Taking walks around the neighborhood. Life was average and life was good.

She didn't have a father—he died in a car crash when she was young. She didn't remember him well, but his absence was still noticed. It was just her, her mom, and her baby sister. Living life and loving each other every day, even when they argued and slammed doors.

One night she sat in her room writing in the journal that she got from church camp a couple of years ago. It had a firefly on the front and Ellisia would always doodle it on her papers at school.

It was getting late into the night, but she wasn't tired. The last couple of days of senior year were coming to an end. She wanted to soak up these last few moments as best as she could. She would miss her house and her room and her mom and her sister, but she was ready for a fresh start. To meet new people and live in a new place. To see where life would take her next.

Her pen was running out of ink so she got out of bed to get a new one.

Although, something caught her eye.

Something in the window.

She stopped and glared closely.

"Eryk."

ABOUT THE AUTHOR

Cambria Tognaci has loved reading and writing since she was able to hold a pencil. Going into her Freshman year of high school, she grew a passion for the foster care system and those dealing with mental illness. She is majoring in Social Work and minoring in Creative Writing. Cambria has performed and won multiple poetry slams and has a YouTube channel where she reviews and talks about books and writing advice. You can follow her first novel, Imaginary Friends on Instagram and Facebook @imaginaryfriendsbook.